CAROUSEL GRIFT

A NOVEL

David Lane Williams

Black Rose Writing | Texas

This is a work of fiction. Names, characters, businesses, places, events, and incidents are either the products of the author's imagination or used in a fictitious manner. Any resemblance to actual persons, living or dead, or actual events is purely coincidental.

ISBN: 978-1-68513-666-6
LIBRARY OF CONGRESS CONTROL NUMBER: 2025936745
PUBLISHED BY BLACK ROSE WRITING
www.blackrosewriting.com

Printed in the United States of America
Suggested Retail Price (SRP) $23.95

Carousel Grift is printed in Sabon Lt Std

*As a planet-friendly publisher, Black Rose Writing does its best to eliminate unnecessary waste to reduce paper usage and energy costs, while never compromising the reading experience. As a result, the final word count vs. page count may not meet common expectations.

PRAISE FOR
CAROUSEL GRIFT

"I can only say that I want more…The story exudes the many forms of 'Texas hot.' In my humble opinion, David Lane Williams' work is excellent in all of the elements of writing. A Pleasure!"
–James River Writers

"Holy hell!!!! I LOVED THIS!! Seriously, so, so glad I sat down to read this afternoon. Pure gold!"
–Laura Kaste Broullire, The Women's Fiction Writers Association

"I nearly peed myself from laughing out loud."
–Karen Tkacik Cimms, Bestselling Author of contemporary romantic comedy

"The sense of humor is great, making a seemingly simple trope refreshing and engaging."
–Writer's League of Texas

"One of the most beautiful stories I've ever read."
–Sharon Shaw-Eastin, Librarian, Albuquerque Public Schools

"This experience was an emotional roller coaster for me, no pun intended."
–Lynn Dix, Sisters-in-Crime

"An entirely entertaining story in the most unexpected of ways!"
–Lucille Guarino, Award-Winning author of *Elizabeth's Mountain*

For Melissa...
and all the others who escaped cruel cocoons
to spread their lovely wings.

CAROUSEL
GRIFT

CHAPTER ONE

The Reverend Gershom Sadler had been dead more than half Callie's life, though they still argued from time to time. There was a certain ugly allure to it, like staring at a splattered armadillo receding in the rearview mirror. Thus, Callie visited him out in the barn now and then, never to pick the fight, but always willing to stand her ground. Most days she brought a snack.

Callie picnicked on a faded red and tan pickup bench seat she'd dragged to their dusty corner years earlier. Even back then she'd thought ahead, knowing she'd want a place to sit if a quarrel happened to break out.

Between bites Callie leafed through a water-stained Sears & Roebucks catalog, its spine cracked and the page edges charred.

"Ticket sales are down," she said to the reverend as she flicked a seed off her fork. "Oh hush...wasn't blaming you. Just saying it's too humid for this early in the season."

Callie took the last melon piece and closed the catalog, her eyes landing on the publication date: Fall, 1969. She paused mid-chew as she realized she'd been perusing this same magazine and having this same conversation for three decades.

"Swell."

• • •

Callie ventured from the barn to stroll about her amusement park after lunch. She'd worn a ponytail when out of doors for all her nearing-fifty years, which bobbed in time to her nimble gait and friendly waves to park employees and guests. Her hair was now more gray than chestnut, she'd earned a few extra curvy places and folds she referred to as "life lumps," and her wardrobe could be described as rural-dowdy. Nonetheless, she remained as she had always been—traffic-stopping, heart-aching, art-inspiring gorgeous.

Callie was soon joined on the path by Toribio Lasoya, a rugged fellow sporting a magnificent mustache over a 9:00 a.m. five o'clock shadow. His every move was fluid and rhythmic, as if he alone heard an Argentine tango. Callie slowed upon his arrival, and the two ambled at their accustomed pace with head nods to point out something of interest or a shared smile.

Toribio pined for Callie and had from the first moment he saw her. Deep down she knew and appreciated this, though for reasons only Toribio understood, she had never gotten his name right once in twenty-nine years.

Callie stopped at a vendor's booth to buy them a snow cone. She held it for him to take the first bite and took her own as they continued their stroll. Toribio crunched the flavored ice slowly as if he were enjoying a rare delicacy. Callie paused by a funhouse mirror to wipe snow cone syrup off his mustache. His Adam's apple bobbed up and down in response. The distorted mirror made it look like a gopher was trying to escape his neck. He did his best to groan in silence.

CHAPTER TWO

Commissioner Richard Pastal hadn't seen Callie's daughter, Sophie, since she'd roared out of Elixir Springs eleven years earlier. She hadn't been THE Sophie Wind back then, and he appeared nervous with flushed cheeks and a glisten on his forehead.

He'd brought his nicest felt western hat, the one reserved for election seasons. He rubbed the brim as if giving it a good waxing while he waited outside her dressing room for their meeting.

"Commissioner Pastal," Sophie called to him from a makeup chair as her assistant opened the door. Pastal donned the hat but snatched it back off his head as he entered.

"Hello, Sophie—Ms. Wind, or…"

"Sophie is fine, Commissioner," she replied.

"Fine, fine. Thank you for seeing me."

Commissioner Pastal stared at the woman in slack-jawed testimony that Sophie had grown more charismatic since he last saw her. If one looked too hard, one might see a beaky nose, a pencil-point chin, or a rear-end flat as a legal pad. Few people noticed, though, because she had her mother's eyes, lagoon-blue with lavender flecks that danced like flakes in a snow globe when she smiled. Actors, politicians, athletes, and just plain folk adored her, dreamed of her, invested in her, and it all started with those eyes.

"I only have a few minutes," she told Commissioner Pastal as the man squirmed in an overstuffed loveseat. "I'm preparing for a Wind Gathering."

"I heard," he said. "I've looked forward to seeing you work your magic."

He chuckled; she didn't. He glanced at the door as she glanced at her assistant. When he looked back at her, those eyes were staring at him from the reflection in her makeup mirror, demanding he get to the damn point.

Sophie was already in her famous periwinkle dress and matching satin pumps. All that was left was a little touch-up of her makeup and she'd be out with her audience. Her assistant had allowed Commissioner Pastal eight minutes.

"Well, it's like I was mentioning on the phone—"

"I seriously doubt I can help you." Sophie's voice still held a Texas twang, just enough to delight a listener's ear, infused with a sense of authority and sophistication she'd learned and refined along her path. "I have a real issue with going back to that place."

"It's your home, and your home needs you." Pastal took full note when the assistant squinted at her watch, and he changed his tack when Sophie didn't answer.

"Sophie, it's so great to see you. I know you had no intention of ever coming back to Elixir Springs, but I think you'll agree this is important. We've lost out on so much, but this time I think it's our turn."

"That town had its opportunity forty years ago when it could have told Reverend Sadler to go to hell."

"Cleft is still there, Sophie. I'm sure he'd like to see—"

"Commissioner, I really have to..."

"It's big, Sophie. It's the biggest thing that's ever come along to Elixir Springs. Hell, it could be the biggest thing to ever happen in Texas."

Sophie swiveled in her chair and gave him two more minutes with a simple arch of an exquisite brow.

"They want to put a telescope up. But not just any telescope. It's three hundred ten inches."

"Long or wide?" she asked with a hint of amusement at his enthusiasm.

"I...I don't know, but they say it's one of the biggest of its kind."

"Who are 'they?'"

"NASA, University of Texas, the government; Walmart's even kicking in!"

"What is it? What are you talking about?"

He punched his own thigh and mumbled, "Slow down, Richard," before taking a deep breath and trying again.

"Some people came to meet with us, the county commissioners, before the last regular public meeting. They call it...hold on," and here he had to refer to a stack of documents he pulled from a brand-new tan briefcase.

"They call it the Super Nuclear Activated Kinesis Extruder and it's administered out of the Office of Internal Logistics. It will do more than look at space. The whole thing will be hooked up to a huge magnet; a semi-conductor, they call it. They'll build an oval tube in the ground around all of Elixir Springs, and the magnet in the tube will be so powerful it'll be able to collect beams of light from space, into the telescope, and send the light particles crashing into each other at the speed of light. They're going to make a huge crash, Sophie."

"So, it's a weapon?"

"No! It's not a weapon. I assure you...they assured me."

"And what happens when all these things crash going so fast?"

"Everything! They'll be able to say what caused the universe to start, be able to make computers work better, speed up travel, look backward in time, maybe even forward, and solve problems like...um, diseases and such. For goodness' sake, if this thing works, they say there isn't much they won't be able to do with it. It's amazing, and Elixir Springs could be where it all happens."

Sophie's assistant moved forward to remind her of the waiting audience, but she raised one finger to hold.

"What do they want?" Sophie asked.

"Access to Elixir Springs County if we win," he replied.

"Win? What are you supposed to win?"

"Elixir Springs is one of a few locations in the United States that fit all their needs in terms of terrain, low smog levels, property values, and small population."

"Will the residents have to leave?" she asked as the assistant picked up her briefcase.

"Most of them, at least everyone in the trailer park. The telescope itself will go up right where Callie's restaurant sits, and—"

Sophie laughed out loud. "Ah, so I guess she wasn't at that particular county commissioner's meeting?"

"She was absent."

"Do you think you can get my mother to move?"

"Not so far," he conceded.

"Which is why you want me? Commissioner, I don't own the land. My mother does, and a presidential decree wouldn't make her budge without a fight."

"A fight is the one thing we have to avoid. I want your help to sweet-talk your mother into putting Elixir Springs on the map. The folks from the Office of Internal Logistics will be coming back in a week to check progress, gauge support of the township, take soil samples and measurements. If anybody can get this done, it's you."

Sophie dabbed lipstick onto a napkin and stared past Commissioner Pastal all the way back to Elixir Springs. She considered the irony that it had to be the one place on Earth she'd planned to never revisit.

Commissioner Pastal took her silence to mean no, and he reminded himself not to wilt in the face of failure.

"I'd best get going. My seat is in the mezzanine, so I've got some stairs to climb before the show."

He paused, waiting for one of them to offer a better seating arrangement. Hearing no such offer, he plopped his hat back on and swiveled. Sophie's assistant had her out of the chair and hustling down a corridor toward Stage Right before he was out of sight.

. . .

Sixty-two hundred wide-eyed people waited for Sophie to come onstage inside the Wind Inspiration Center of America. Another two hundred thousand had turned their television stations to watch her Friday evening service. In just over a decade since she'd yelled her goodbye to Elixir Springs, Sophie Wind had become a star.

The Wind Center was dome-shaped and as large as a university basketball arena. Sophie and her designers had created a space to include all faiths, so images such as a crucifix or Star of David were absent. In their place were spectacular pictures of ocean scenes behind the stage, galaxies on the ceilings, and people of all colors and faiths hugging, breaking bread, and getting along. Light melodies played in between performances, and the splash from a sixteen-foot waterfall in the foyer added a pleasant background ambience.

Television cameras and boom microphones hung from ceiling rails, and a glass-enclosed booth behind the audience housed a state-of-the-art production facility. The lighting system rivaled any Broadway theater, and the rows of burgundy pews and stained-glass windows offset any sense of artlessness caused by the equipment.

A warm-up concert of Taiko drummers had pumped the crowd into a rhythmic frenzy, aching for the star. The show included a display of laser and lightning effects, and music played to energize and inspire. Multi-screen video presentations surrounded the audience, and Sophie Wind, the woman they were all there to see and hear, would be right in the center.

"Ladies and gentlemen, good evening and welcome," announced a tuxedo-clad master-of-ceremonies. He bounced onto the theater-in-the-round stage as the Japanese musicians vaulted from the arena.

"It is time!"

The cheer from the crowd was so solid, the veteran announcer took a step back.

"You're ready." He chuckled and was rewarded with a laugh from the audience.

"Please help me welcome your spiritual guide this evening, best-selling author of *Bread-Bowl Soul: Filling Your Heart with The Soup of Life, God Is My CPA: Financial Advice from HIM,* and *Spiritual Colonic For Prosperity: A Six Week Soul Scrubbing to Inner Smiles and Financial Success*; Goodwill ambassador to countries around the globe, friend and advisor to CEOs and world leaders, an inspiration to millions who have read her rags-to-riches tale, and an all-around wonderful human being. Ladies and gentlemen, your hostess for the evening and your inspiration for life: Sophie Wind!"

Sophie entered the auditorium from a platform beneath the stage, rising like a gladiator entering the Coliseum on Roman elevators. Lightning bolts flashed across the ceiling and giant waves crashed on the huge screens. Music thumped and the crowd roared. Sophie stood there, as regal as a beloved princess, as poised as a Hollywood legend, and as flattered as a gal from west Texas who still woke up grateful every morning.

The chanting and clapping subsided so the attendees could hear their leader speak, but Sophie paused and made them wait. Years of practice had made her a showman with the timing of a seasoned stand-up comedian, the acumen of a career politician, and the vitality of a head cheerleader.

"If you think your job or your parents or your spouse or your children are going to fulfill you, lift you to prosperity, give you a purpose in life, I want you to understand right at this moment that they are holding you back."

The auditorium grew quiet. A guy in Section EE, Row Nine, who'd taken out a ballpoint to write a girl's phone number fumbled the pen. People two sections away heard it drop.

"If you think something or someone else can make you happy or rich or beautiful, you're wasting your time."

Couples who'd been holding hands let their grasps fall away. Handmade cardboard signs held aloft started to sink below the waistlines of the crowd. For just a moment Sophie Wind brought her crowd to the brink of despair, for she had learned hope and inspiration are best nurtured from seedlings that sprout after a wildfire.

"Don't misunderstand me," she said after a purposeful pause. "Your loved ones want you to succeed. But the habit of sitting around waiting for good things to happen is like having an old tire strapped to your soul while you're trudging uphill on a dirt road. My friends, I hope you're here to break out of that rut, because that is exactly what I aim to help you accomplish!"

The crowd began to rustle with spirit again. Sophie felt their energy building from an ember into the inferno it would become; a blaze she always controlled.

"You want a business? Why not today? You want a more fulfilling family life? Why not now? You want true freedom—financially, spiritually, intellectually? What are you waiting for? Because if you're waiting for tomorrow, or friends, or a special break, or the lottery, well then, you're just sitting in a boat with no paddle, no rudder, no direction. The river of life is going to take you where it's going to take you, whether you like the destination or not. Don't you want to have a paddle? Well, don't you?"

They roared back they did, indeed, want a paddle and, oh how they wanted her to hand it to them.

Over the next forty minutes she stoked the flame and sheltered it from the storms of doubt, lethargy and rudderless-ness. They chanted when she cheered, raised their hands as one when it was time for them to "stretch toward success," and yelled a wall of yeses when she asked if they were willing to be part of something grand.

Of course they were. They were tired of waiting for someone to give them a life, especially when Sophie Wind was standing right there ready to do just that. Their mission was clear: sell jewelry, shampoo, make-up, inspirational DVDs, books, vitamins, and fashionwear from the Sophie Wind collection to their friends, family members and co-workers. Nothing on Earth rivals the passion of a disciple set upon a quest.

•   •   •

Sophie's evenings never ended right after a Wind Gathering. There were calls to make, notes to pen for top sellers and VIPs, invoices to scrutinize. Two actresses from a comedy described by her assistant as a "big hit about a goofy British Spy" were escorted back to her dressing room after the show. She spent eight minutes with the pair, thanking them for attending the evening's event, trading autographs, and giving both a gift basket filled with products from her line. One actress produced a disposable camera, and the three of them posed for smiling photos until the exposures ran out.

Sophie's assistant brought her a pimiento cheese sandwich cut into triangles, with the crust removed after the actors left. Sophie thanked her for a great evening and sent her home for the night. The conversation with Commissioner Pastal both irritated and intrigued her, and she needed time alone to think.

After the sandwich, she grabbed her purse and ventured out to the auditorium, now bathed in an amber glow from nighttime security lighting. She drifted between the pews before taking a seat on the carpeted steps leading to her stage. Sophie gazed about at the murals and up to the ceiling cameras placed to showcase all she'd accomplished. She blinked as if her eyes had grown irritated from being open too long, and she closed them against the strain.

Sophie Wind was no fool. She had little faith in anyone or any agency being able to solve as many challenges as Commissioner Pastal had described. She was intrigued, however. Pastal was a prolific businessman, but she'd never considered him a big dreamer. If he was this excited, perhaps all the agencies he'd mentioned were interested in this project. If that were true, it really was huge.

"Elixir Springs…of all places." Her whisper echoed in the empty hall.

A telescope to solve so many of life's riddles. To look backwards so far as to see the beginning of it all; to solve problems of energy and resources; to enable travel toward unreachable destinations. Perhaps, in a way, to glimpse the face of God.

"But why on Earth does it have to be on Mother's property?"

The sound of the waterfall from the foyer was so pervasive it generally went unnoticed, so her ears perked when the splashing stopped. The silence felt ominous in the amber glow. She rose from the steps and padded toward the entrance, her heart racing and her fingers trembling.

"May I help you?" Sophie called to a woman standing in the water pooled beneath the fountain cliff.

The woman's back was to Sophie, and a mane of dark curls fell to her waist. She shook her head and replied with a singsong, "No thank you. Shouldn't take long to fix."

Sophie took a step closer, but she clutched her purse to her abdomen and kept half her body hidden behind the archway leading from the auditorium, as if at any moment she might bolt for the phone in her office.

"I wasn't aware anything was broken."

"Well then, what am I doing here?" The woman turned and waded two steps forward in the pool. This put her under one of the security lights, casting an incandescent glow around her head and shoulders. She reminded Sophie of a matriarch who had once taught her the magic of spreading *masa preparada* on corn husks to make tamales during a guided Oaxachan cooking tour.

The older woman smiled and held up a plastic box as if it explained everything.

"I don't have any idea what that is," Sophie said, grimacing when her voice cracked.

"Your pump filter...all gummed up."

"My pump filter?"

"For the waterfall. All gummed up. Nothing flows right when your filter's clogged."

"But who called—"

"I'll have it cleaned out pretty quick."

Sophie shook her head against the nerves and stepped out from the archway to the edge of the pool. She could see the woman wore navy-blue coveralls and a plastic name badge worn by all her facilities personnel, easing her qualms. Perhaps her assistant had arranged the after-hours maintenance.

Sophie squinted at the nametag but looked away when the woman glanced up and caught her.

"Luz," said the woman, as she tugged the nametag so Sophie could better see. "Heating and A/C, a little plumbing...tonight, waterfall pumps."

"I'm sorry. I didn't recognize..."

Luz waved off Sophie's apology with a chuckle.

Sophie felt comforted by this gentle woman standing ankle-deep in an artificial pond.

"Clogged filter?"

"Yes, ma'am. Can't get anything moving when your system's blocked. Best to start at the beginning and work your way along until you find the clog."

Sophie smiled. She looked back over her shoulder at the auditorium as if considering going back in, but she raised an eyebrow and headed to the front doors instead.

"Goodnight, then. Thank you for all you do."

"You're quite welcome, dear."

Sophie stepped outside and walked to the middle of the parking lot before craning her neck to stare up at the galaxy.

·   ·   ·

Luz waited until the door closed behind Sophie before placing the pump motor back in the water behind a faux stone. She reached around an artificial tree to flip a hidden switch, and the pump burbled and surged as water flowed once more. It splashed down upon her, but she stood in the shower with her eyes closed and a cherubic smile across weathered cheeks.

After several minutes she stepped out of the pond, unzipped the sopping coverall and draped it on the side of the little pool. Water puddled about her bare feet, but she seemed to take no notice. She spread her arms as if about to take flight and leaped to frolic through the rows and rows of wine-colored pews.

CHAPTER THREE

Most employees at Pioneer Days Amusement Park wore some type of themed costume bearing ties to the American frontier. Some wore buckskins and leather hats. Others wore cowboy outfits or settler skirts; a few wore Native American dress with mismatched and under-researched collages of as many as half a dozen different cultural tribes.

Not Cleft Hawley. Cleft wore brown Levi's and a blue mechanic's shirt with his name stenciled above the left pocket, the sleeves rolled up to show off arms still blessed with the girth of an anaconda. His hair had remained thick and light, and furrows in his face earned with time and sun added a rugged quality. Once upon a time he'd been a champion under high school football stadium lights; once upon another time he'd been a lawman, committed and heroic. Now he was Head Maintenance Technician at the Pioneer Days Amusement Park.

The walkie-talkie dangling from his tool belt squelched, and the sultry-adjacent voice of Malga, currently manning the ticket booth, called out, "Got a report of a paint job over by the Spike."

Cleft responded by shoving his head under the spigot of a nearby water fountain, clinching his eyes shut as the water drained off the tip of his nose. He wasn't sure he could stand another "painting" today. It meant some kid had eaten a Cheesy Frontier

Dog before riding a roller coaster and was now bawling as a parent dabbed a messy little mouth and prodded the entire family toward the exit. It meant somewhere over by the Golden Spike Miniature Railroad there was a steaming puddle he was duty-bound to clean.

Cleft had picked up an evening shift for overtime, something he now regretted as he meandered toward the Wigwam, a brown shed where he stored tools and cleanup supplies. He wondered for the ten-thousandth time why anyone would torture their loved ones by bringing them to this hellhole lava pit to eat pig food, take rides monitored by dropouts on meth, and make paint spills for him to clean.

Cleft dragged the tool shed door open and plowed the furrow under the door's edge a bit deeper. Inside he filled a coffee can with cat litter and slung a flat-blade shovel and push broom over one shoulder. He hooked a bottle of antibacterial spray onto a belt loop and headed toward the Golden Spike.

Cleft refused to acknowledge Malga, knowing she was smirking as he passed the ticket booth. He noticed Frontier Keith, the park mascot statue, was missing his index finger again. It had likely been broken off by one of the soldiers from nearby Ft. Klinston, many of whom were disappointed upon arriving on their first day of base liberty to learn Pioneer Days was not, as they'd been told by base veterans, a brothel. Thus, Frontier Keith routinely required a new coon-skin cap tail and/or index finger— sometimes an ear or a nose. Cleft had gotten good at repairing the statue with a combination of duct tape, wood putty and Magic Marker.

All amusement parks have a smell, some mix of popcorn and cooking meats, caramelized sugar, fried anything, body odor, chlorine, and wet mops. Pioneer Days had all those, and added wafts of wet poultry, manure from grain-fed cattle, and brackish ponds from nearby Elixir Springs.

It was more carnival than amusement park, alley cat as to puma when compared to Six Flags. The rides creaked but worked most days, and though the park was shabby and weedy to some, it offered a certain romantic charm when the lights came on at night.

Cleft arrived at The Golden Spike to find the "paint" spreading across the path. Families were busy avoiding the mess, pretending not to notice so their children wouldn't call attention to it. One man barked at an eight-year-old who was about to skip into it, and two adolescent girls were laughing and pointing. The perpetrator was long gone.

Cleft eyed the puddle. He could smell it from ten feet away. He always gagged at paint jobs, and mentholated rub shoved up his nostrils or clothes pins pinching his nose never helped. It was all he could do to smother it with the cat litter, scoop, disinfect, and retreat. He took three deep breaths and let the shovel slip off his shoulder, too concentrated on not retching to reflect about glorious life plans changing in about the time it takes to create a paint job.

·   ·   ·

Callie had never been to a spa, had a pedicure, or gone on a clothing spree; instead, she often rewarded herself with an auction after finishing the day's chores. She enjoyed estate sales, bidding for pieces of turquoise and coral jewelry or some work of art that caught her eye.

Sometimes she attended livestock sales, and something about going to a sale barn felt just right after a long day. She parked her two-seater Jeep Wrangler amidst rows of dually pickup trucks and sauntered into the barn. She took a seat with no real aspiration to buy, but she grew excited in the clamor and competition over a bull by the name of Beefo. He'd run into the auction floor from his chute, spraying snot and pawing the ground in search of someone to stomp.

"Twenty-eight hundred, do I hear twenty-eight for this magnificent king of college mascots?" sang out an auctioneer from the auction pit of the San Antonio Livestock and Rodeo. The bespectacled auctioneer moved his auctions fast, often running dozens of horses and cows through the seller's chutes and into the buyer's trucks in an evening. His rhythmic voice lulled crowds, and this evening's audience was enthralled.

The bull was a massive gray Brahma with a neck hump the size of a truck tire and horns pointed straight out toward whatever he targeted. He wowed the crowd as he rammed his head against the chute gate and scanned the audience members as if each was a rival bull to be conquered. He was elegance in brawn, and even the quick-tongued auctioneer paused in his pitch to watch.

"Well, folks," said the auctioneer, "you can see this animal has excellent lines. Just don't ever be alone with him in a round-pen."

The cowboys and breeders laughed, and the auction recommenced.

Callie had no intention of breeding the bull, nor was she planning to butcher him for steaks. She just wanted him, and though she knew how impulsive she was being, she was determined to beat any competitive bidder. The only serious competition turned out to be Commissioner Pastal, sitting on the other side of the arena pit. Callie and Commissioner Pastal raised bids back and forth in rapid fashion. Everyone in the sale barn paused to watch the match.

"The bid is three thousand to you, ma'am," called the auctioneer.

Beefo caught Callie in his sights. His angry eyes grew softer. He blinked. It seemed as if Callie was the only person in the room he had no intention of smashing.

Callie smiled and raised her finger to beat Commissioner Pastal's last bid without taking her eyes off the beast.

"Come now, sir," said the auctioneer, turning back to Commissioner Pastal. "You know this animal's history. Are you gonna let this little lady beat you out today?"

Indeed, everyone in the arena knew Beefo's story. He'd been a Texas legend who fell from grace one fall evening during a Southwesterly Texas State vs. Coastal Plains College game midway through the season.

Beefo was at the sidelines as always, his team winning by a significant margin. The final cannon sounded, and Southwesterly Texas was the victor. Shoving matches and stolen kisses broke out as fans from both teams stormed the field. A group of fraternity fellows wearing Southwesterly Texas State colors ran onto the field and mooned the Coastal Plains College fan side. All hell broke loose, and soon a mob of four thousand or more was on the field rending the turf and tearing the goal posts out of the ground.

Beefo's keepers, the Southwesterly Texas State Rustlers dressed in game-day western hats and tasseled chaps, saw the danger and hustled to remove Beefo from the threat. Too late, because the north end goal post upended, and one of the uprights landed on the left flank of the young stud. The beast's pelvis was fractured, and one of his kidneys destroyed. Struck down in his prime, Beefo's college football days were over.

Callie won the bid and, just like that, Beefo became the newest addition to Pioneer Days Amusement Park. She was so giddy she tipped two cowboys to deliver him to his new home that very night.

• • •

Sophie had a date after the evening's Wind Gathering, and she chastised herself for having stayed at the auditorium so long. This was her third date with the new guy, early in the relationship to show up late. She sped from the parking lot above the Lower

Colorado in west Austin to the downtown restaurant overlooking Town Lake.

The view of the city lights reflected in the water below was spectacular, yet the other diners and wait-staff all craned to see this power couple enter the room. Sophie smiled with grace. The suitor walked with a grim coolness as if wading through crowds to enter a boxing ring.

Dinner was delicious, and the chef fawned at their table. Sophie and the date laughed and discussed current events and vacation destinations. She marveled at the shape of his chin and the contour of his arms through his jacket. They shared interests in hobbies and activities. He was quite a guy, or he could have been, had he not been such an ass to everyone else.

"Can I get some service over here?" he called to a waiter who'd been nothing but attentive since their arrival. The date shook the ice cubes in his nearly full water to get attention, demanded a new fork twice, and sent everything back to the kitchen to be prepared "like the chef was trained beyond using a can opener."

Sophie answered no to the question of dessert. By then she was looking forward to the evening being over. An old memory popped into her mind as her date harangued the maître d over the check.

It was an irksome memory, yet it caused her to smile. The recollection prompted a question which demanded an answer. It was a question she posed as he walked through the front door of the restaurant in front of her.

"What would you say if I called you to come kill a scorpion for me?"

"A scorpion? Easy. I'd kill a lion for you!"

He held out his hand to her in a most dashing manner, and she took it as they crossed the street. They'd made it halfway across when a car ran a red light and came straight toward them. He responded to the danger by throwing Sophie's hand from his own as he jumped back out of the way. Sophie, caught off guard, missed being struck by inches when the car saw her and veered.

Careening cars, lions prowling downtown Austin, scorpions a lifetime ago, a toothless champion…there would not be a fourth date.

. . .

Toribio couldn't sleep, disappointed because Callie had jaunted off to an auction and hadn't invited him. He tossed and turned for hours before giving up and going outside to stroll around. Toribio had never played a round of real golf in his life, but he enjoyed the miniature golf course on the eastern side of the amusement park. Perhaps a round or two would help him unwind.

The miniature golf course was a wild animal theme. A buffalo stood guard at Hole Number One. An eagle appeared to be flying over a gopher mound for Hole Six. An alligator menaced the golfers with a gaping mouth full of teeth at the midway mark, and a cougar scowled at players from atop Hole Fourteen. Frontier Keith himself stood with hands on hips and feet spread apart as if inviting a hole-in-one for the last putt.

By the time Toribio addressed the water obstacle complete with frolicking otters and leaping trout at Hole Eleven, he was feeling better. He'd just decided to head back to his bed when his ears perked up at the sound of whispers coming from over by the carousel. He held the putter at mid-shaft and skulked over toward the sounds. He was surprised at how nervous he felt, and he considered backing away to call the sheriff.

Probably soldiers from Ft. Klinston sneaking in on a dare.

Toribio decided to scare the daylights out of them. He reasoned they'd take the story back to the barracks of some crazy man who'd chased them with a golf club. Perhaps that would dissuade others in the future.

The whispers continued. Toribio scurried through shadows.

"You need to back up a bit," he heard a male voice say.

"I'm in the correct position," seethed a female voice. "Just pull it out further."

"I am!"

"It's too short."

"It's long enough if you'll just move over to—"

"Hiyaaaah!" bellowed Toribio as he leaped from cover behind a cotton candy cart. He held the putter like a samurai sword.

"Mommy!" screamed the man.

"Run!" yelled the woman.

Toribio stared as a man dressed in a gray suit and a severe-looking woman in a gray suitcoat and slacks beat a retreat toward the exit. Their retractable measuring tape skittered to a stop at Toribio's feet.

. . .

Sophie and Commissioner Pastal met at the Magnolia Café on South Congress the morning after her failed date. The Commissioner had suggested Denny's. Sophie chose Magnolia because the staff and clientele there didn't give two feathers about her celebrity.

"The lights won't work," said Pastal after they ordered. "The people with the project say they'll have to go."

"What lights?" asked Sophie as she swirled sweetener into oolong tea.

Pastal poured half a bottle of syrup on his gingerbread pancakes. "From the amusement park. There'll be no point putting a telescope there if we can't eliminate ambient light. They said all those lights at your park—"

"My mother's park."

"—are a deal breaker if they remain."

"I wasn't aware we were close to a deal."

"We don't have a deal, per se. What we have is a contest that has been going on for the last thirty months, with small towns being eliminated as potential sites one by one. Now they are down to two."

"Where is the other one?"

"I don't know, at least not yet."

"Answer me this." Sophie took a sip of tea to hide a smile. "Why should we care if they build this magnetic telescope in Elixir Springs?"

Commissioner Pastal twisted his coffee mug back and forth as he answered.

"For a long time, I've wanted to see Elixir Springs on the map, to have my name attached to something significant. Now there is an opportunity for our hometown to answer questions such as how we all came to be here and what will happen next."

"Ah, but that's what I do for a living. Every weekend, forty-eight weeks out of the year, people sit in my seminars where we work to answer those questions. 'Why are we here, and what can we be doing with our lives?'"

"From what I understand, they leave the auditorium filled with enough enthusiasm to market your products. Not a bad ticket price for enlightenment, I suppose."

"I suppose."

Pastal slathered more butter onto his pancake stack but paused with his knife and fork dipped in the syrup slurry. His voice grew grave as he stared at his plate and said, "It's about a legacy, Sophie. I guess you could argue I built one with all my businesses and such, but this…this is the one of a lifetime."

Sophie revealed her smile. "I'll let you in on a fun secret."

The commissioner had just taken a large bite of pancake, which poked out his cheek like pecans in a squirrel's mouth.

"I had some of my staff check into your project. It's real. This telescope is going to happen. I also happen to know Elixir Springs is by far the superior site. It's like you said: conducive weather, low pollen and smog, removable light pollution; bonus, no large oil companies competing for the site."

"No kidding!?"

"I also found out the region has a foundation of metamorphic rock, which is best for the collider tube and the telescope foundation. They want us. Hell, they need us!"

Commissioner Pastal sat back in his booth. "Well, that…that is gratifying."

She took a sip and smiled. "I'm in."

Pastal cleared his throat. "I don't know if this will be profitable right off the bat."

"If all I was interested in was a bottom line, I would send you and this project team on your way. You spoke of building a legacy. I suppose some would say, like you, I've already done that with my enterprises. Frankly, I don't think I've even started. I believe this project holds my destiny, and everything up to this point has been leading me here."

Pastal spilled his coffee. Sophie continued as he used his napkin, and hers, and every single one in the napkin dispenser to mop the spill.

She continued almost as a sigh, as if Commissioner Pastal, and his flooded pancakes, and his spilled coffee were long gone.

"I want to play a part in something historical, something monumental. And this one…this one is a whopper."

•   •   •

Callie, Toribio, and Cleft sat in the dance hall section of her Wagon Wheel Restaurant the morning after Toribio startled the two trespassers. The dance hall smelled of fresh sawdust and old beer spills. Their voices echoed in the emptiness of a room which would be filled with boot-scooting dancers and jukebox tunes in a few hours.

Callie reviewed invoices while Toribio cut checks for payroll. Cleft held a short rope with a small wooden ball tied at one end. Every few seconds he'd pop the ball off the ground, twist it in a loop, and allow the ball to fall into a midair knot. All three sipped coffee. The morning was no different than most, except for concerns regarding the mysterious events the night before.

"Had you ever seen them before?" Callie asked. Toribio shrugged and jotted a ledger note.

Cleft threw a loop. His old police instincts were aflame, and he very much wanted to solve this case.

"Would you recognize them if you saw them again?" he asked.

"Yes," Toribio replied.

"What the hell were they doing?" wondered Cleft as he untied the knot.

None of them had an answer, and all three took a sip of coffee while imagining possibilities.

"And they were both in business suits?" asked Cleft.

"Yep."

"Should we tell the sheriff?" Callie asked.

Toribio and Cleft looked at one another and back at Callie.

"You want to tell Errol?" asked Cleft.

Toribio poured a bit more sugar into his coffee and stirred.

"Maybe we should let that idea simmer a bit," acknowledged Callie.

"Let's just keep an eye out for them and see what happens." Cleft reached for the coffee pitcher and poured himself another cup. "So now you will please explain why you bought a bull last night?"

• • •

It was a rare county commissioner's meeting when all five commissioners were in attendance. Commissioner Pastal presided over the mundane proceedings, all the while worried about what he knew was upcoming in New Business.

Seven men and three women sat in the audience section. Most were waiting their turn to address the council, though a few were regular attendees who somehow found the proceedings entertaining. Three of the men were concentrated on the state of their fingernails, and the other four compared and contrasted I-Formation versus Wishbone. The women whispered rumors of a tryst between the manager of the Safeway and a nurse's aide working at his mother's nursing home.

The meeting hall had been refurnished a quarter-century earlier when the old wooden railings, bench seating, and Boston-Solid oak chairs were ruined after a roof collapse during a torrential rain. The mid-seventies replacements, citrus hues of lime, lemon, and tangerine in molded plastic, had faded in the intervening years. The commissioners sat in a row of creaky chairs behind a collapsible picnic table. Commissioner Pastal always placed a brass nameplate in the center of the table bearing the inscription:

Commissioner Richard Pastal
Local Proprietor & Chief Justice

Pastal's stomach was churning, and the other council members could hear it. Callie, Mr. Leroy Henley, Mrs. Leroy Henley, and Bandy Banders all pretended to ignore the gurgle. Pastal unwrapped a packet of crackers while one citizen was addressing the panel. Callie and the others declined his offer to share.

The board was confounded by the deplorable state of a one-lane bridge spanning Spinner's Creek. The bridge, all twelve feet of it, was crumbling. Old Man Spinner was at the podium insisting the county do something about it.

"But you're the only one who uses it anymore," said Commissioner Pastal to Old Man Spinner.

Spinner rapped his fist on the lectern. "I pay my taxes, and I demand you fix that bridge."

Callie rubbed her forehead. "I can't believe Commissioner Pastal and I are agreeing on something but using that old bridge must take you at least fifteen extra minutes to get to town now that Pastal Bridge has been erected. It's a straighter shot for you, and—"

"But it ain't named after me and mine," said Spinner with a smug grin, believing he'd just won the argument.

"The estimate to fix it is fifty-seven-thousand dollars," said Commissioner Pastal. "Which would necessitate a tax increase."

"Maybe if we place some nice planters, it could be used more as a walking bridge," suggested Mrs. Henley.

"It ain't no gosh dang walking bridge!" said Old Man Spinner.

"I move we table this discussion for the next meeting to allow for contemplation of the issue," said Bandy Banders, who was always proud of his suggestions to table issues to allow contemplation. He adjusted his ball cap and looked to his fellow commissioners for a second.

"I second," said Mr. Henley and Mrs. Henley simultaneously.

"All in favor of tabling the issue," asked Commissioner Pastal, and the motion carried.

"Contemplate the issue my rear-hole," muttered Old Man Spinner as he shuffled out of the meeting room.

"Which brings us to New Business," said Commissioner Pastal.

"New business?" asked Mrs. Henley, who acted as the de facto secretary for the group.

"Eminent Domain," announced Commissioner Pastal.

Callie groaned.

Pastal cleared his throat and commenced. "My friends, we come to a crossroads, and questions must be posed of this august body which will determine the fate of our lovely county for generations to come."

"Get on with it." Callie was tired and bored and ready for a game of cards with Toribio.

"Well, Callie, it's interesting you are the one to ask—"

"I didn't ask anything—"

"—as you were absent from the last meeting during which representatives from the federal government approached with a proposal—"

"Is this about that ridiculous telescope-time-machine nonsense?"

"It sounded interesting to me," piped in Mr. Henley.

"It's not nonsense, Callie," said Commissioner Pastal. "It's science."

"Science is real important to consider," said Bandy Banders.

Callie snorted. "Eminent domain?"

"Railroads of old, modern highways, bridges, and military installations have all required a certain amount of personal sacrifice for the greater good. Our nation has come to us with a simple request, but conceivably this invitation could turn into a demand supported by eminent domain."

"They're not taking our land," said Callie.

"Exactly," said Commissioner Pastal. "I suggest we initiate negotiations which we control that would harvest the best possible outcome, instead of waiting to see what happens."

"Are you talking about negotiating to give up our land?"

"To reap a profit. And to negotiate certain advantageous positions—"

"Stop, stop, stop! You sound like a politician trying to convince us cow patties smell like lavender."

"I make a motion we table this discussion to allow for contemplation," said Bandy Banders, who foresaw this debate dragging on well past dinner and his favorite television shows.

"No," said Commissioner Pastal. "We're not going to—"

"I second the motion," said Callie with a thin-lipped smile as she reached forward and slid Commissioner Pastal's nameplate askew.

"Dammit, Callie," Pastal murmured as he straightened the plaque. He had no choice but to call a vote. "All in favor of tabling this discussion until the next meeting say aye."

"Aye," said Callie and Bandy Banders.

"Nay," said Commissioner Pastal and Mr. Henley.

All eyes looked to Mrs. Henley who had never voted counter to her husband. Mrs. Henley, however, didn't know what the term "Eminent Domain" meant, and she wasn't about to say so in public. She wanted an opportunity to check out the meaning in her World Book Encyclopedia, and for this reason she wanted time to contemplate the issue at hand.

"Aye," she said.

Mr. Henley choked a bit on his own saliva.

•   •   •

Sophie Wind had learned to drive in a 1964 Chrysler. It was a porpoise-gray boat of a car with a clutch ground down like a third grader's pencil and every radio button tuned to WKIK—"KIK'N Country."

From day one upon receiving her driver's license she drove like she'd robbed a Piggly Wiggly, whether she was heading to the store for her mother or meeting with friends in the Dairy Queen parking lot Friday nights after Cleft's games. At sixteen, Sophie was teeth-gritted, damn the brakes, headed for glory and by-gawd going somewhere!

Life now afforded her a driver in long, glamorous cars. There were people to clean her home which was decidedly not mobile. A plump, married couple took care of her lawn, pool, and horses. A staff of accountants and attorneys worked for no one but her.

But today was going home day. It was a day she'd dreaded, but one she'd decided to wrestle to the ground and conquer like every other challenge in life. For that, she would need to drive herself, arrive home at the helm, just as she'd left. Instead of the old Chrysler, Sophie had chosen her Cadillac El Dorado convertible—Spartacus Blue—buffed to the point one could read small print in its reflection. AM, FM and satellite all tuned to "KIK'N Country."

Sophie reined in the car at her mother's tiny lawn like Annie Oakley on her horse screaming into Bill Cody's arena. She surveyed the façade with a raised eyebrow, noting the cracking picket fence and faded-pink plastic pots holding faded-yellow plastic flowers she'd always fantasized about hacking down with a scythe. The front porch was drooping at one end. Her old bicycle, hot-pink with tassels, leaned against the south side of the house by the spigot, right where she'd left it the day she'd gotten her driver's license.

Sophie wore her hair up with one wispy strand falling past her cheek. She sported a pale-blue blouse, yellow pumps, earrings set with amethyst and a matching necklace. She checked her makeup and dabbed the corners of her eyes. Every step from the Cadillac to the house was drudgery.

The front door was unlocked, but Sophie knocked three times. She looked about the porch at dead potted plants and a rain-stained cardboard box labeled "charity." An extension cord led from the porch to the curbside mailbox where it was connected to three Christmas bulbs.

"Momma," Sophie called out as she poked her head in. She could hear someone rustling around, but no one answered her call. "It's me, Sophie. I...I have returned."

Still no answer, so Sophie opened the door a bit more. She realized it would not open past eighteen inches without butting up against something on the other side, and she craned her neck around the edge to peek. What she saw didn't connect with the image she'd always had of her mother or the home where she grew up.

There were filled ashtrays on every surface, and a stale aroma of cigarette smoke clung to the walls. A king-sized bed placed inextricably on a diagonal to the living room was the object blocking the door, and Sophie realized entering the house meant stepping up onto the mattress.

A collection of charcoal sketches decorated every wall, and one piece of art-de-velvet featuring Elvis dressed as a matador with a bull charging past his cape was taped above the hallway sill. An old Montgomery Ward X-ray machine the retail chain had used to "scientifically fit" customers for shoes in the 1950s was positioned at the foot of the bed, now used as a drying rack for laundry. A picture of Sophie speaking at a Wind Gathering hung frameless and thumbtacked above Callie's headboard.

Sophie heard what sounded like a whole shelf of pans clanging to the ground, and she imagined her mother had fallen and broken a hip. Sophie scrambled up and over the bed in pumps and short skirt. She avoided a cat litter box at the foot of the mattress, sidestepped a nude store mannequin, and vaulted into the kitchen.

There stood her mother holding a sledgehammer above her head. Mangled and dented hubcaps were splayed across the linoleum floor. The two women froze, Sophie in mid-heroic leap, Callie in mid pummel.

Callie was wearing a turquoise hat with a daisy-yellow ribbon and bow, the brim wider than her shoulders. Her wardrobe was completed with a black George Strait T-shirt, yellow sweatpants stuffed into oxblood red western boots, and a silver-beaded necklace bearing a chrome-plated happy face dangling to her navel.

Their eyes locked, communicating in seconds all they'd missed in the last eleven years. Sophie's eyes misted; her mother took a drag from the cigarette dangling from her lips. Sophie's hands went to her face, and Callie's hammer hit the floor.

"There's eggs if you're hungry," said Callie as she sauntered outside, letting the screen door slam back in her daughter's face.

Callie stomped out to the pasture near her barn and sat on the edge of Beefo's water trough. She wriggled a nail protruding from one of her boot heels until it came loose while listening for sounds Sophie had given up and left. She grabbed a curry brush and began to groom Beefo, murmuring all the while about ungrateful daughters and why someone thinks they can just meander back into someone's life.

Her brushing strokes slowed, and her head tilted like a dog learning a new verb. Her gaze drifted past the bull's massive hump, beyond the barn and tree line, all the way back to a memory powerful enough to plop her back into another place and time as if she'd never really left it. Callie sighed in resignation as her eyes blurred and her mind went back to school days…

CHAPTER FOUR

Teenage Callie had always been one to raise her hand, volunteer to feed the class bunny over winter break, and share what needed sharing, whether that be a pencil, half her sandwich, or a pair of dry socks. Her favorite teacher, Mrs. Temple, taught tenth grade typing and shorthand. Mrs. Temple was the sort to lay an embroidered pillowcase over the hands of any girl glancing at her keyboard or to apply a strip of tape over the lips of those caught chatting during dictation exercises. She was a geyser of business-skills wisdom, which she often dispensed over the clacking of two-dozen IBM Selectrics during speed drills.

"White gloves should be worn for job interviews, but they must be doffed for the practical assessment phase."

"Home row is more than a starting place for one's fingertips; home row is a metaphor for life!"

"Hold a thought for germs in the workplace, ladies. The most dangerous peril has always been germs—drunken train conductors and atomic bombs notwithstanding."

It was that last piece of advice which was decidedly on Callie's mind not three weeks after her final class with Mrs. Temple, as she stared at a half-eaten funnel cake abandoned on a picnic table.

"Maybe I could just tear off the parts that touched their mouth," she whispered to four decorated ponies tethered and waiting to be led into the ride pavilion for their evening trudge with sticky, mane-yanking children.

Callie stood in shadows created by the tents of a carnival, rubbing pony muzzles, eyeing the pastry, deciding. She was too thin, brand new to life on the road, and dithering over whether to heed Mrs. Temple's guidance or to shove a contagion-glazed pastry down her gullet.

"Y'all's costumes are so pretty," she murmured as one of the ponies stomped a pixie-sized hoof painted Shamrock green. "One time on Valentine's Day I won the 'prettiest decorated cash register' prize over at the Five-and-Dime."

Another pony tried to remove the red top hat strapped between its ears by rubbing against a tent post. "Won a jumbo-size chocolate bar," Callie added as she ventured two tentative steps toward the picnic table.

Callie reached for the funnel cake as an elderly woman with a gray-haired bun the size of an eight-quart stew pot hissed, "Stop that, wicked child." Callie jerked her hand back in shame and turned toward the ponies as if she had somewhere to go. The crone scowled and followed Callie into the shadows, raising a finger as if she had more to say until another voice stopped her advance.

"Evangeline, leave that poor young lady be," said an aged man who walked up beside the woman. The man peered down kindly at Callie who shivered despite the late afternoon swelter. He looked at the discarded funnel cake, then heavenward, then back at Callie. Her linen dress of pastel pink called attention to the bones of her sternum, in stark contrast to the old woman's dress covering from her chin all the way down to the caliche dust at her feet. Callie wished she was wearing something, anything to cover at least her shoulders and knees.

The man was dressed in a black knee-length coat—an odd choice for the heat—a flat-brimmed straw hat, a white collar yellowing along the neckline, and scuffed tan boots.

"Who provideth the raven for his food?" he asked, and when Callie gave a bewildered shrug, he answered his own question. "The Lord Almighty provides when we are hungry."

"Job 38:41," said Evangeline, who was rewarded with a gentle nod from the man before he turned toward a crowd of carnival-goers. Callie was shocked he'd left her alone with the old woman, who was staring at her in a most vulturine manner.

"Read your Bible," snarled Evangeline.

"Do unto others...stuff like that?" replied Callie. The crone grimaced and seemed about to respond when the man called back over his shoulder.

"A plague of sinners awaits!"

Callie thought he sounded delighted at this prospect as she watched him wade into the throng. He stabbed a pious finger skyward, blustering his way through arm-in-arm couples and roving bands of teens as if parting a sea. Soon the finger was all she could see of him. Evangeline huffed at Callie and turned to follow.

Callie felt momentary appreciation for the old man. He'd uttered the first kind words she'd heard in a while, and he'd stepped in to defend her when no one expected him to do so. A blend of gratitude, curiosity, and desperation produced enough hope in the man's faith and gumption for her to forgo the humiliating pastry and follow as well.

The reverend strode to the center of the carnival and overturned a wooden crate as his pulpit, rising to speak amid the dissonance of diesel generators and carousel medleys. A nearby corndog vendor turned down his transistor radio and propped one foot on a pickle barrel to listen.

"Ye, who are slaves of Satan," the pastor called out to those few who formed about his dais.

"Is this a sideshow?" whispered a woman. Callie slipped through toward the front, nibbling her nails to nubs as she watched the prophetic man challenge the small crowd.

"You're damned to an eternity of hellfire burning your flesh to bone, of horned beasts ravaging your loins—"

"Tell them, Reverend!" yelled Evangeline. "Give them The Word!"

"Say there, pastor," protested a strapping man in overalls still dusty from the fields. "Mind the children and ladyfolk." He moved to shield his wife, a buxom woman wearing a neck-less t-shirt emblazoned with the glittery words, "Feeling Groovy."

"And you, you craven mule, who calls himself a man but allows his woman to show her cleavage in public like a harlot!"

Callie pulled the neck of her dress up.

The man in overalls took a step forward. "Now hold on a minute, reverend—"

"—and then change to demure attire on Sunday morning as if she can somehow avoid the mighty smiting that is God's wrath—"

"Now, I told you that was enough, you son of a bitch!"

"He is offering you salvation!" screeched Evangeline. She bumped past Callie who was tugging the dress hem down below her knees. "Your soul demands attention."

The field hand's face flushed, and his throat quivered. "You'd best tell that old man to shut his damn mouth in front of my wife, or—"

The reverend pointed at the man, so there would be no mistaking who he was condemning. "Damn, you, lying sinner of Beelzebub, for sending your trollop—"

The field hand boxed the reverend's ear and punched his mouth.

"Don't hurt him!" blurted Callie.

"Jeremiah twenty-two, verse nineteen!" the preacher yelled out through bloody gums before a third blow, one index finger raised to the heavens. "He shall be buried with the burial of an ass!"

The field hand spun his wife and left in a huff. The crowd drifted away. The minister dabbed a knuckle at his split lip and stared after their shrugging backs with a look of triumph.

"Shirk God's word, but it is his mercy you have forsaken."

"Why must you taunt them so?' asked Evangeline as she tended a swelling knot above his left eye.

"Because they'll now spend the afternoon less entranced by the blasphemous entertainment and more mindful of the wrath of God. Carnival-mongering on a Sunday…a SIN!"

Evangeline popped his lips with two gnarled fingers. "Gershom Sadler, now that is enough!"

He stared at her in disbelief, and the old woman looked as stricken as if she'd smacked the Holy Spirit. When he next spoke, it was as a snarl.

"And you'd do well to reserve your reproof for Satan himself, for Eve brought sin unto man. I'll not have a sister of my flock pretending any judgment for Adam!"

"I'm sorry, Reverend. Shall I get you some ice?"

He ran a hand through hair slicked back with Brylcreem before standing up and dusting off his trousers.

"Reverend?" said Callie, holding out a wad of napkins she'd pilfered from a soda stand.

"What is it?" he growled as he took the napkins and cleaned his mouth.

"I…I was pulled by your holy words, and…"

"Hey, girl," called a drunken ranch hand standing near a peanut vendor a few yards away. "Get done with that old fart and come give me a diddle. I got a week's pay burning a hole in my pocket."

Lights from the rides reflected in Gershom Sadler's grackle eyes making them appear aflame. Callie's own eyes flooded.

"I'm not a…I…."

"Be gone, willful piglet," cried the minister. "Or I shall call upon The Almighty to strike you down!"

"Yes, sir," whimpered Callie, who turned in shame even as the reverend stepped past her and smote the cowboy's shoulder with his cane. The brawny youth stumbled away, and once more Callie felt a sense of gratitude in having been defended.

"Not you, child," the reverend said, speaking to her as if she were an injured fawn. In that moment it was as if he were seeing her for the first time, and what began as a paternal smile morphed into an enchantment so mesmerizing he didn't seem to notice when a bearded albino lady and dwarfed lizard man sauntered by arm-in-arm. The minister's eyes paused on her Goldilocks' lips and then her tapered ears which seemed to move in the direction of a diving roller coaster off in the distance. He sighed.

Evangeline cleared her throat as if to break his reverie. "Reverend…we must be going."

"But be ye doers of the word, and not just hearers," he responded.

Callie caught a whiff of grilling hamburgers and hoped this righteous man and the sullen Evangeline would buy one for her.

"James 1:22," Evangeline acknowledged.

"Indeed, sister. Let us return to the church with our guest."

Callie looked over her shoulder at the hamburger vendor, and the reverend followed her gaze.

"Pigswill made by faithless sinners is not for you. Fresh bread and stew await."

He strode from the rabble toward a single-cab pickup parked across the field. Evangeline glowered and followed.

Callie followed as well. She'd known as they hopped over furrows and corn roots that Mrs. Temple would not have approved her decision to go with this strange pair. But she also knew her life no longer had anything to do with chocolate prizes or white gloves, and it sure as hell couldn't involve half-eaten funnel cake dipped in germs.

• • •

On the same day Callie met the Reverend and Evangeline, Toribio was on his second afternoon walking north from the border checkpoint in Laredo. The morning had been cool when he started his trek, but now he was sweat soaked as he panted broiling air and stared at a man who'd just tried to crush him with a pickup truck. The truck driver lay crumpled under a large agave with a cactus thorn spiked through one cheek, bleeding here and there and floundering like an overturned tortoise.

"Oh gawdang," moaned the dazed driver, all but incomprehensible due to his impaled mouth and bloody nostrils. "That didn't just…oh sombitch."

Heat shimmered to the horizon, and Toribio reckoned they were miles from civilization. He wanted to head north toward the bus arranged to take him to a cook job in San Antonio, but leaving meant the man would die.

In other parts of the world soldiers were fighting in an Asian jungle, the Beatles were disbanding, and the U.S. was still high from winning the moon race. Here, though, in this sweltering Texas canyon, the world consisted of two rivals and a sun that could destroy them both.

The wounded man had been gaining on Toribio, despite the quarry's jackrabbit-like scurrying. Toribio could hear Lynyrd Skynyrd blaring from an eight-track, and he was terrified the maniac would run him down at any moment.

The driver stood up in the roofless truck, whooping and ramping rabbit holes while yelling, "Get back across that river you wetback sombitch!"

A locust crashed into the fanatic's eyeball, resulting in a catastrophic loss of control. A frantic Toribio glanced back to see the man fly over his windshield as the truck vaulted off a red ant mound.

The driver's head was bleeding, and his left leg was backward from the knee down. The truck's radiator was leaking, and the chassis was shaped like a Z. "Pioneer Days Carnival & Sideshows" was stenciled on the driver's door, the logo creased like a folded paper fan.

Toribio sighed as he tore strips from the truck's grimy cloth seats to make bandages. The fractured leg was a problem because there was no way he could carry the injured man for miles in the heat. The desert didn't provide straight branches which would act as a splint, but Toribio spied a shotgun mounted in the truck.

"No!" said the man as Toribio retrieved the gun. Toribio ejected all the shells, and the injured man realized the gun barrel and stock were being fashioned as a splint.

"Ready?" Toribio asked. The man nodded as if signaling a cowboy to open the gate on a bull ride, and Toribio yanked the mangled leg straight.

The man grunted as Toribio aligned his leg with the gun stock and tightened the cloth strips. The driver's grit turned to a profane run-on, however, when Toribio yanked the cactus spike out of his face and shoved in a grimy sock to plug the hole.

"Sorry about my swearin'," muttered the man once Toribio helped him to a wobbly stand. "Been working on not cursin' so much, but that hurt worse than a catfish snappin' my pecker."

Toribio shrugged as if it were no matter. He put a shoulder under the grunting man's arm and commenced to all but drag him through miles of dust devils, knowing with each tortured step that his bus had not waited.

•　　•　　•

The radio in Reverend Gershom Sadler's truck had been tuned to a sermon transmitted from Tulsa on the night Callie first met his acquaintance at the carnival. The sun had set, and Callie found the glow of the radio dial a source of comfort. She spent the ride wedged in the cab between the reverend and the dour Evangeline, wanting to reach forward and turn up the volume to fill the awkwardness. She'd made a decision to travel toward whereabouts unknown, and her knees were touching the legs of two people she'd just met. She was, to say the least, having doubts.

Reverend Sadler shifted gears, and Evangeline sat as far to the right as the truck door allowed. Telephone poles leaned askew beyond the moonlit horizon.

"Where's your kin?" asked the reverend.

Callie's eyes teared up as she watched the passing fields. She remembered "soybeans," had always been her father's answer to her question, "What are they growing?" in the plowed rows they passed crisscrossing Texas on his sales trips. It became their private joke. It didn't matter if the field was producing corn, cotton, or sorghum; her father answered "soybeans," and Callie would giggle before turning back to the mesmerizing miles of crops, oil pumps and windmills.

"My dad's funeral was eight months ago."

"God rest his soul," said the reverend.

"God rest him," agreed Evangeline, though she kept her gaze out the window.

Callie stared at the radio dial as she continued the story. "His wife took up with my manager from the Winn's Five & Dime right before Easter."

Evangeline harrumphed.

"He gave me a safety razor wrapped in a shoebox for my birthday. Told me it was 'for shaving those sexy legs of mine.'"

"Lustful pagan," murmured the reverend.

"And ever since my stepmom was mad at me every minute of the day."

Reverend Sadler shook his head and used his thumb to rub at a crack in the dashboard as if he could buff it right out. Evangeline turned to give Callie a second look and then swung her attention back to the passing landscape.

"Last month my manager told me he had to let me go at the store because of 'a conflict of interest.' And last week my stepmom told me 'crazies aren't welcome', and that it was 'time to hit the road.'"

Callie noticed a sign for Elixir Springs County, and a few minutes later they turned onto a dirt road. Evangeline lumbered out to open a cattle gate as their journey came to an end.

"Ma'am, I'd be happy to open that for you," offered Callie. Evangeline ignored her and slipped in a mud puddle trying to pull the rusty gate latch.

"Sir, I can open the gate for your wife," said Callie.

"Evangeline is not my bride," he responded. "She is of my flock. And you are our guest, so she'll manage the gate."

Evangeline tried to scrape mud off her boots before climbing back into the cab, all the while refusing to look at Callie or the reverend. Callie could not recall having ever felt so claustrophobic, and she considered springing from the truck and running out to a highway to thumb a ride if they stopped at another cattle gate. Some of her anxiety ebbed, however, as she spotted the destination.

A church and large wooden cross hubbed a wagon-wheel layout of cabins. She could make out a pond beyond the church through the darkness, and she could see a large garden. Callie's mouth tingled as she smelled baking bread.

"Welcome, child," said Reverend Sadler.

"What are your plans?" demanded Evangeline.

The radio signal turned static.

• • •

Toribio hauled the injured man to a small medical clinic tucked between a Safeway and a Dairy Queen and eased him into a wheelchair inside the door. He made sure to catch the eye of a receptionist before giving the wheelchair a little shove in her direction. The man called a dry-throated thank you over his shoulder as his wheelchair rolled toward the reception desk, his splinted leg leading the charge. Toribio remembered the same man had tried to squash him earlier in the day, and he said nothing in response.

Toribio stood at the edge of the parking lot, wondering if he could survive another march through the sand and brush. He had no desire to see how the crazy driver would fare, but he didn't have anywhere else to go until things cooled off. The waiting room was as good a place as any to wait until the sun went down. At least there was air conditioning.

"May I help you?" asked the receptionist as he ventured back inside.

"May I wait in here for my friend?"

"He's in X-Ray, but I'll let you in to visit as soon as the doctor allows."

"Yes, ma'am."

Two hours passed. Toribio drank so often from the fountain the receptionist offered him a paper cup. He read a *Sports Illustrated* and did his best on a Reader's Digest crossword. He wished he had a little money so he could wander down to the Dairy Queen.

Finally, the receptionist said, "You can go back and see him now."

Toribio felt the receptionist would be hurt if she knew he'd lied about being the patient's friend. He also harbored concern she'd call the law if she got suspicious. It seemed both polite and prudent to go in the direction she'd pointed.

Toribio found the injured man moaning with casts on one arm and one leg, and his face sunburned a strawberry ice cream hue. His head and ribs were wrapped in gauze, and a doctor sat on a rolling stool suturing the hole in his cheek.

"Tell me again how this all happened," said the doctor, a stout woman sporting a pageboy.

"Was like I told you," said the injured man, although because of the anesthetic and swelling it came out sounding like, "Duzz ike I dold ooh."

The doctor looped the next stitch.

"Was chasing some Mexican who'd…um…attacked some women…trying to ravage 'em I'd guess. Was doin' my best to bring him to justice when the bastard jumped out in front of me and made me wreck."

The doctor looked over her shoulder at Toribio. The injured man followed her gaze.

"That's him!" blurted the man.

"Him? I thought he was the one who saved your life."

"Well..."

The room went silent. The man looked away from Toribio and stared at the cast on his leg. Toribio inexplicably pulled a tongue depressor from a glass canister, realized he should not have, and handed it over to the physician. Her gaze went back and forth between the men like a detective waiting for one to fess up.

"Doesn't add up," she said. "Errol, I've warned you about this border guard nonsense before."

"Piss on a pinecone, Doc. He was invadin' American soil. It's my duty."

"It isn't your duty, and this is the fourth time I've put a cast on you or stitches in you in the last three months."

"But—"

"How bad was your truck wrecked?"

Errol looked down and shrugged, so the doctor turned to Toribio.

"Sir, how badly was his truck wrecked?"

"Well, back-flippin'-dog, doc!" blurted Errol. "Whatcha askin' him for?"

"You need to find a new hobby. You've got liability in your blood," she said as she left the room.

"Don't leave like that," he yelled after her. "Ain't neither got whatcha-call-it liabil-ny in my blood."

Toribio felt flat-footed. He wondered if he could leave without raising suspicions. He cracked the door wide enough to look down the hallway, but the man on the hospital bed kept talking all the while.

"I ain't never done no liba-linny in my life!"

Toribio shut the door and turned back to the injured man.

"She ain't comin' back in here, is she? Just up and done with me, after all the business I've brought her way. If that ain't just an outhouse in the kitchen."

Toribio nodded, if only to be agreeable. An awkward silence followed, during which Errol stared at the X-rays of his fractures illuminated on a wall-mounted viewer.

"She makes a good point, I guess."

Toribio looked confused.

"That girl doctor. If I'm bein' honest, gotta admit she makes a good point."

Toribio reached for the door handle.

"I mean, truth be told, you might have saved my life."

Toribio shoved one hand in a pocket and scratched his neck with the other.

"Prob'ly did," Errol acknowledged. "Prob'ly did."

Errol motioned toward the wheelchair. Toribio moved it closer to the bed.

"I called me a ride after I got out of the X-ray machine," said Errol, indicating a phone on a bedside table. "I best get out there. She sure as hell won't wait on me long."

The man tried to get up, but he grimaced and groaned while slumping back down onto the bed. Toribio stepped forward to help, and the two grunted until they had him back into the wheelchair.

Toribio pushed the wheelchair toward the door, but he paused upon spying the man's rifle propped in a corner. Dusty strips of the truck seat cover still hung about the barrel and stock.

"Your gun," Toribio said.

"Leave it. Some folks can't handle the combination of firearms and fire water. Guess I'm one of them...and I sure as hell ain't givin' up liquor."

Toribio wheeled the man outside where a red and white VW van bearing the Pioneer Days Carnival & Sideshows logo sat idling. A Rubenesque woman with a bored expression sat in the driver's seat filing the longest fingernails Toribio had ever seen. She glanced with dramatic disdain at the injured man before returning to her filing.

"Can we give you a lift?"

Toribio considered that this gringo was loco, but he looked out at the distance and realized he was still too exhausted to resume his journey on foot.

"I owe you one, mister," the injured man conceded. "Truth is, I owe you big, and I'm real sorry for—for the way I treated you." He extended his one good hand.

A ride to anywhere sounded reasonable to Toribio, and he shook hands.

"This is Malga," said the man as Toribio crawled into the side of the van. "And I'm Errol."

Toribio nodded greetings to the severe-looking woman as she drove them away, and then he fell asleep, too tired to much care if they drove him to jail or back to the border. Thus, he was surprised to see he had arrived at a carnival when he awoke later. The smells from the food vendors made his salivary glands hurt, and the colored lights reminded him of stars reflecting off the lake back home.

Errol handed him a five-dollar bill as he reached to shake Toribio's hand again.

"I thank you for savin' my life, not that I deserved it, I suppose. I shouldn't have done what I did. I get to bein' stupid sometimes, mostly when I'm drinking alone. I'm real sorry."

Toribio shrugged acceptance of the apology.

"You workin'?" asked Errol. His question was punctuated by a chirping bell announcing a prize-winner on the midway somewhere behind him.

Toribio looked out at the horizon.

"Well, I know what a kick in the peanuts that can be. You're welcome to jump on board here if you like. The pay's not great, but the food's free and we travel all across the country."

Malga limped Errol toward an entrance marked "Employees Only," and Errol waved over his shoulder as the door shut behind them. A plaster statue of a mountain man propped next to the ticket booth seemed to beckon Toribio to enter.

He pulled a worn leather wallet shoved into his boot and tucked the five-dollar bill. His eyes landed on a green-tinged card slid into one of the wallet sleeves. It bore his name and a photograph in which he appeared sleepy. Resident Alien heralded the card which had been stamped and dated three days prior. He looked up from the card back toward the quintessentially American statue.

"*La ironía*," Toribio muttered as he finger-combed his hair and walked in through the Employees Only door.

He celebrated his arrival at the carnival with two hot dogs and a root beer. His appetite tamed, he went in search of the man who'd first tried to kill him and then offered him a job. He found Errol sitting in a red clown car with the casted leg hanging from the passenger window and his head poking out the driver's side. A short job interview commenced:

"Can you cook?" slurred Errol as he took a long pull from a bottle of brown liquor.

Toribio murmured a yes.

"I gotta do somethin' with Malga. She's got no willpower. Eatin' two hamburgers out of every three she cooks."

Errol glanced around as if worried Malga might overhear his plans. "Maybe put her in the Buckskin Fine Apparel Outlet. They could use some liftin' help over there."

Toribio raised an eyebrow. Malga would, indeed, be an asset to any team needing help lifting things.

"Anyway, you're hired," said Errol as he took another slug of whiskey. "Come on, I'll show you around."

Errol took off in the little car without looking to see if Toribio followed. Toribio broke into a fast walk-skip-walk to keep up as Errol drove and drank merrily along.

"I used to be a sideshow attraction before I ventured into business," he yelled out to Toribio over the whine of the un-baffled clown-car engine. Carnival employees stepped off the path as he careened along. Customers were also forced to move, but most seemed to think it was all carnival flair.

"I was the World's Thinnest Man, Husband to the World's Fattest Woman."

His eyes glazed as he remembered, and he hiccupped twice before continuing.

"Married up real good." He smirked and used the fingers on his bottle-holding hand to make air quotes as he told the story. "At least until my wife had what she called a 'stomach-stapler-thingy' during a 'vacation' to Florida."

Toribio was distracted by a man on stilts blowing fire from his mouth, but Errol didn't seem to notice.

"She shrank to a size fourteen in six months."

Toribio dodged a cotton candy cart. Malga was sweeping the entryway of a tent boasting pictures of an all-seeing eye and a crystal ball.

"Carousel Grift," Errol yelled, cheerful again. He turned the car sharply and circled a manure pile plopped in the middle of the path while using the bottom of his bottle to point it out to Malga. Toribio thought she might assault him with her broom.

"I started eatin' her extra helpings because it's sinful to waste food," Errol continued. "Pretty soon me and the little woman was standing there being not real skinny and not real fat. This kid points at my belly and yells to his mother, 'Look mommy, his wife made him pregnant like daddy made you pregnant.'"

Errol stopped the car to stare out over the hood as if reliving that nightmarish moment.

"Heard she was in nursin'-assistant school in Tulsa."

Errol still had the belly, though his arms were as thin as kitchen chair legs. He was balding on top, but his hair fell past his shoulder blades, tied back with a brown bandana.

"Left me all this in the divorce, though," Errol said brightening once again. Toribio understood "all this" meant the carnival.

The two had halted next to the King Ranch Lariat Game in which contestants were given three small hoops of thin rope in exchange for fifty cents. A few customers tossed the "lariats" toward rows of fake cattle horns, trying to win an assortment of prizes.

Dusk had descended, and multi-colored lights came on.

"I love to look at the carousel at night," said Errol, who seemed to brighten with the lights.

Toribio was reminded of a fiesta back home.

• • •

"I despise going into that town," Evangeline said the morning after Callie arrived in their little community. The old woman seemed furious at Reverend Sadler's suggestion that she take Callie to buy new clothes. Callie stood on a wooden porch as Evangeline and the minister discussed who would take her into nearby Elixir Springs, neither seeming to notice or care she was standing within earshot.

"I will take her," Reverend Sadler said as if volunteering for a dangerous mission behind enemy lines.

Evangeline scowled. "Oh, for heaven's sake, Gershom. She'll need lady items."

That settled it, and Callie soon found herself back in the old pickup truck with the taciturn Evangeline. Callie suspected the woman was planning to abandon her in some distant place.

Daylight allowed Callie to better see the little community. The cabins were identical brown squares topped with rust-spotted tin and set upon cinder blocks with crawl spaces beneath. Callie spotted a decrepit horse carriage parked next to two faded pickup trucks. The church was whitewashed, a stark contrast to the charcoal-black cross standing taller than the building.

She could now see the garden was quite large, acres she guessed, though she wasn't quite sure the actual size of an acre. Each cabin had its own clothesline, but several members of the community waited in single file for a water pump beneath a magnificent willow tree. The pond beyond the willow was lovely, bordered by idyllic reeds and stout logs for sitting.

Once they entered Elixir Springs, Evangeline purchased Callie two dresses, both tan and ankle length, toiletries, and a pocket Bible.

"You will carry this at all times," said Evangeline as she shoved the little Bible into a pocket of Callie's skirt.

"What if I take a shower?"

Evangeline paused as she considered the problem. "I'll loan you an empty coffee can to keep it dry."

At mid-morning they visited a diner. They entered to find a waitress around Callie's age talking to a wizened man scraping a grill. Callie and Evangeline took a booth, but the older woman declined the waitress's offer of menus. "One runny egg, toast, no butter."

"And for you?" asked the waitress turning to Callie.

Evangeline interjected. "She'll share mine, so bring an extra plate. We will each have our own glass of water."

Following the silent meal Callie and Evangeline climbed back in the truck to head home, but they were blocked from leaving the parking lot by a column of colorful trailers from the Pioneer Days Carnival & Sideshows. The line extended past the edge of town.

Evangeline gripped the steering wheel as if she might yank it from the dashboard. "You'd think one of these heathens would have the manners to let us out."

Callie's eyes widened with amazement at each passing vehicle. One of the trucks slowed to allow them through as if Evangeline's words had made it happen

It was Toribio, of all people, who motioned them through from the driver's seat of a truck hauling four ride cars and a gearbox for the Tilt-A-Whirl. Callie had no way of knowing Toribio's name, but she discerned the man's jaw-dropped awe of her. Callie gasped at the compliment.

"Womanizing hobo," muttered Evangeline as she worked against a sticky clutch to drive through the gap Toribio had created.

· · ·

Reverend Sadler assembled his congregation for a special service a week after Callie's arrival. Evangeline stood with arms folded and lips pursed as she listened to his fiery oratory. It had rained a few minutes earlier, and the resultant mud and humidity seemed to add to her irritation.

"…and as we've read, God will strike down and condemn to the fires of hell all infidels, journalists—"

Evangeline whispered to a bewildered Callie. "Reverend Sadler wants you to go stand on that step below him."

"—actors, except, of course, for Nativity scene and Civil War re-enactors, and anyone unduly afflicted with any of the seven deadly sins."

Callie hesitated.

"—particularly lust and sloth."

"Get on up there," insisted Evangeline.

Sadler raised his voice. "They are doomed to an eternity bereft of salvation, their flesh boiling away, only to re-grow and burn again."

Callie scratched her nape and imagined flesh boiling.

"Demons will ravage them with cat wicks the girth of a tree branch, and other condemned will scratch out their eyes and bite their flesh."

"Oh my," whispered Callie.

"Satan will eat delicacies in front of the condemned. He'll drink of the coldest streams as their screams scrape against their scorched throats. He shall mock them for having neglected to accept the Lord as their Savior."

"Amen," answered many.

"We must save them, my children, those who had once been left out of the kingdom of heaven through no fault of their own. We must bring them into the flock and save them from eternal torture."

"Amen!"

"Callie-child, step forward," Reverend Sadler said. He held out his hand to her. She looked up at him and out into the crowd, mortified she was the center of attention.

"Come," he said again, and she was compelled to ascend the two porch steps to be at his side.

"This heathen child of God—we'll not turn her away as did her family."

"Oh gracious!" said Evangeline.

Reverend Sadler lay hands upon Callie's head. "Let it be known to all men and be heard by the Heavenly Ghost—"

"This is not right." Evangeline said under her breath.

"—that henceforth this sinful waif is to be known as my daughter and heir—"

"No, no, no," whispered Evangeline.

"—for Callie is to be saved from the hell pit for which she was otherwise doomed!"

"What?" asked Callie. "I mean...what?"

"There is His sign that what we do this evening is glorious!" screeched Reverend Sadler. His flock followed his finger pointed toward the sky behind them. Murmurs and gasps rose from the crowd as all beheld a rainbow arcing over the horizon.

"God's promise is a blessing on this deed," the old minister croaked as he looked into the face of his new daughter.

Callie flashed to a memory when she asked her real father what God's face looked like. He'd smiled while pointing at a sunset. "I imagine he looks something like that," he'd said so lovingly Callie reached up and kissed his cheek.

She gazed upon the applause and halleluiahs from the little crowd. Evangeline's expression was terse, but the reverend was elated. His maniacal eyebrows arched like the rainbow, and his smile highlighted teeth the palette of river pebbles. Callie turned toward the exquisite hues formed from the setting sun, hoping like hell her father had been right.

CHAPTER FIVE

Richard Pastal had been content with running businesses and as a county commissioner for most of his adult life. Visions of greater heights, both for himself and for his community, might never have entered his mind had it not been for what he referred to in stump speeches as the "moment of most momentous-ness" in his life.

That moment occurred the year an Olympic torch runner jogged through Elixir Springs. On that fateful day Commissioner Pastal had just won re-election, and the torch runner sat in an air-conditioned bus somewhere west of Alpine. The honored runner was scheduled to carry the torch five miles, culminating with his triumphant arrival at one of the most beautiful towns in Texas.

The runner was a high school football coach from Odessa, where football is played in honor of Christ and the Constitution. The Odessa city council had nominated Coach for the torch runner position after a winning season and a banner year in home-game ticket sales. The booster club paid his entry fee.

Five miles west of what was supposed to be Alpine, Coach stepped off the bus and allowed his torch to be lit by two Boy Scouts. He turned east and stared down the long stretch of road, finding himself misty-eyed at the honor of carrying this great symbol of athleticism and unity.

"Thank you, Lord," he whispered, for he'd been nominated for this honor four years earlier but had lost out to a social studies teacher "from Marfa of all places." Now he would finally carry the torch.

"I best get to it, boys," he said in a grave tone to the admiring Boy Scouts, and he took off at a respectable trot.

Unfortunately, the bus driver had erred, and Coach was heading not toward Alpine whose inhabitants were at that moment stringing bunting and closing shops in anticipation of his grand arrival; where his wife and children stood in their Sunday best ready to encourage him through to his finish line; where the Mayor was walking from his office to the Square so he would bestow upon the runner a scroll proclaiming him an honorary member of his city; but instead toward Elixir Springs, where it was possible no one had ever heard of an Olympic torch.

Fifty minutes later Coach picked up his pace and bounded into town only to find himself confused by deserted streets. Coach ran on, passing a herd of cattle on his right and a gas station to the left. Just one person took note of his arrival. Commissioner Richard Pastal, in brown tweed and brown derby, had been gone from Elixir Springs for two weeks. He'd been on a tour to learn more about starting a brewery, his latest business idea.

Commissioner Pastal's eyes widened as if he'd realized the ominous responsibility this torch runner carried. He dropped his suitcase onto the gravel and applauded with heartfelt gusto before saluting the runner.

Coach returned the gesture by raising the torch a bit higher as he passed. He kept it raised through the length of Elixir Springs, his facial expressions twisting in growing frustration with every step.

"Is that it?" he huffed as the outskirts of town loomed. On he jogged another quarter mile until he passed a field of round hay bales and lost his footing in a drainage ditch.

"Flag on the play!" he exclaimed.

He cursed the torch, calling it a "dumbass thing" as he extinguished it in the muddy ditch before returning in a huff to the bus.

"I know where I got off track," said the bus driver as he pointed to a place on a map. "Want we should give her another go?"

Coach did not want to give her another go.

It was the last year the Olympic committee allowed commercial bus drivers to navigate the route. For insurance purposes, it was also the final year the committee allowed Boy Scouts to light the torch.

What was anticlimactic for Coach was life-shaping for Commissioner Pastal. For some people a song lyric inspires them to reach a higher level than they'd envisioned. For others it could be a movie or a spiritual awakening motivating them out of mediocrity toward greatness.

In years to come Commissioner Pastal would often describe the moment of salute he'd shared with that Olympic messenger, and how he'd felt an awesome gift of responsibility which comes when one is called to prominence. Theretofore he had imagined simple dreams of expanding his business, maybe settling down with a wife, children. Perhaps someday he'd build a little wood shop in his garage.

On that day, however, Commissioner Pastal began to dream bigger, and it was this grander sense of responsibility he recycled in campaign speeches year after year:

"I looked about at Elixir Springs as that man saluted me back with his Olympian torch. Where once I'd seen limitations, I now saw opportunity; where once I'd felt complacence, I now felt duty."

With true Olympian spirit, Commissioner Pastal shouldered the golden opportunity of a true calling that day and made a decision to do everything he could to put little Elixir Springs on the map.

"Shoot," he'd tell anyone who'd listen. "I knew we were halfway there if an Olympic torch runner honored us by coming through."

. . .

Life was good for Toribio during the traveling carnival days. Errol taught him how to do maintenance on the rides, and Toribio also learned how to work the midway contests. Errol seemed appreciative that Toribio was charming and funny around customers, and Toribio was grateful for the opportunities he was afforded.

Over an eighteen-month period the carnival took Toribio to small towns throughout Texas, Missouri, Arkansas, Kansas, Oklahoma, and New Mexico. He loved watching the terrain transform from one region to the next, unexplored paths along a lifestyle of travel he'd lived since his late teens.

Toribio had not left Mexico for the sole purpose of finding work in America. He dreamed the dreams of a wanderer, wanting to see all the Americas, Europe, Africa, and Asia. He'd once stowed away on a cruise ship for nine months, affording him travel through Greece, Turkey, and southern Italy by waiting tables. He was never on the ship's payroll, but he made a bounty in tips, and no one ever caught on.

He'd made friends with a long-haul trucker who took him straight north from Brownsville up through Oklahoma, Kansas, and Nebraska. He'd hiked California and worked as a bike messenger in San Francisco, posed as a Navajo to sell turquoise in the Four Corners, pumped gas and changed tires in New Orleans, and hauled nets on a shrimp boat in Corpus Christi.

His Portuguese was passable during a fall trail-riding excursion through Brazil, and he was eager for a return to Venezuela where he'd worked a season as a forest firefighter. The only place he considered off limits was Chile. It was there he'd possibly fathered a child before being chased away at shotgun point by the woman's brothers who had arranged a more promising marriage for her. That was fine with Toribio who would have stayed to be a father but had only an *añejo*-vague memory of the woman. For four years he'd been satisfied with traveling, meeting new people, and painting what he saw.

Toribio's art was extraordinary and hung in various places of honor including a multi-million-dollar house in Miami and a Manhattan art dealership where his identity was a source of bewilderment. One of his earlier pieces hung in the home of a Major in the Mexican army who had taken a strong fancy to both Toribio and his art. Toribio was able to beg off any more pressing advances by making a gift of the portrait he'd done of the Major in full uniform. He'd deserted the army the same night, seven weeks shy of his twentieth birthday.

Such memories passed through Toribio's mind as the caravan moved toward each next town on the route. Most days he'd drive, and Errol would sit beside him, chattering away for hundreds of miles without seemingly taking a breath. One afternoon the crew drove into a valley deep in the Ozark Mountains. The narrow highway meandered under trees on both sides with branches forming a lush tunnel all about them. Free food, free travel, and amusing people abounded, and he was enjoying the adventure.

He often thought about the beautiful woman sitting in the passenger seat of a pickup truck in some little Texas town, and how she'd held his gaze as a glaring older lady drove them through the gap he'd created for them. Toribio imagined he would never forget the young woman, though he always sighed at the memory, believing he'd never see her again.

• • •

"You have failed me as a daughter," Reverend Sadler decreed one sweltering afternoon as Callie rubbed his feet under the willow tree. He'd caught her casting longing glances toward the coolness of the pond, and his irritation spewed out as her kneading slowed and her energy sapped. It had been a hard year-and-a-half since the adoption, and Callie had no desire to make the day any more difficult.

"I'm sorry, Father," she replied, forcing her attention back to his bunions and pressing his heels with every muscle in her grip.

"What must I do to rid you of your wicked and lustful thoughts?" he demanded.

"No, sir, I wasn't thinking sinfully. I was admiring the water, and—"

"How dare you correct your father? Do you think I don't see your aching desires? Do you think God can't see your yearning to return to your sinful ways?"

"No, sir. I know you see my soul, but please don't thrash me."

"Heathen! Bend your hip so as to purge your heathen-ness."

A thrashing came, this time from a frayed riding crop applied to her right buttock. Each whack stung so badly she wondered if fabric from her skirt was burning into her skin. She sobbed and begged forgiveness and accepted this was her life. Were there struggles and indignities? Of course, but most days she was able to find some peace in the hardship of this mortal life, having learned she was earning an eternal life of bliss. The reverend was a holy man, after all, so what he said must be true.

Thus, it was with puzzlement when Callie began noticing certain un-pious behavior in her adoptive father. They were small issues at first: catching a lustful smile when another man's wife bent from the waist; purchasing a gold-plated crucifix to replace his handmade wooden one; taking the Lord's name in vain when one of the milk cows kicked his hip.

Most concerning, however, was the fact that her whippings seemed to come more frequently and for unjust reasons. This was confusing because she was the only "child" in the community who ever seemed to incur his wrath or warrant his patriarchal attention.

One day it all became clear:

"Sinful," Reverend Sadler would later call her act of walking into his bedroom carrying his folded laundry. But there she saw him, his pants at mid-calf. He was gazing at a Polaroid of her wading in the pond with her skirt hiked to her thighs. Reverend Sadler didn't see her come into the room at first, his lids half closed as he whispered, "God be praised" over and over.

The reverend startled at Callie's tiny sob.

Her hands went to her face, and the laundry tumbled at her feet.

He toppled his chair and spilled his seed all at once which, at least in Callie's memory, hissed and steamed as it burned a hole through the dusty floorboards straight down to hell.

Callie had expected to be chastised, but neither spoke as she walked back out of the room and went to cry in the vegetable garden.

· · ·

Reverend Sadler retreated to his barn for three hours the following morning. He took a pitcher of water and half a loaf of bread in with him and slammed the barn door closed. The congregants milled about and cast curious glances during their chores. Even Callie wondered what the old man was up to in there. They could hear him banging and sawing, but no one could guess.

Reverend Sadler toiled, sawing, measuring, and hammering as his shirt and pants soaked through with sweat. He fell prostrate and gasping on the hay-covered floor. Two cows chewed their cud non-judgmentally, though several hens clucked in reproval of the man's grovel.

He rolled onto his back and looked toward the ceiling when his breath returned. "I cannot look upon her face without feeling at once alive and woeful."

He rubbed handfuls of dirt over his face and chest. "Please, I beg You, allow this toil—this toiling mindfulness of You—to rid me of my cursed covet."

He emerged wearing a shabby woolen robe and shouldering the fruit of his effort, a crucifix well over twice his body length. He paused in the doorway to make sure all the eyes of his congregants were facing him. Many stared in bewilderment, but what mattered was they were watching. Callie was watching. Reverend Sadler snarled.

The cross was so wide he was forced to stand on his toes to keep the lower edge out of the dust. This was unfortunate because when he took his first, triumphant step, the lower edge of the cross dipped back down into the dirt causing him to lurch forward. Everyone stood in awed silence.

Reverend Sadler pivoted the cross back into the barn, and there he took up his handsaw to lop off six inches from one side. He hoisted the crux over his shoulder once more, choosing to overlook the imbalance he'd created.

"What are you doing, Pastor?" asked one of the braver congregants.

"I am a sinner! And as such, I must cleanse my soul. This march will commence from the center of my sin and will finish when I've arrived at the bend in the river where we undertake summer baptisms. Once there, I shall ritually cleanse myself of my own lustful thoughts by immersing once more into those holy waters."

"That part of the river's over a mile away."

"I shall succeed in this pilgrimage, for God gives me the strength of ten men."

Reverend Sadler resumed his trek to the river. His beginning strides conveyed an image of strong, heroic leader for his flock.

Within fifty feet, however, his breath was coming in gulps. Ten yards further, he stumbled.

Reverend Sadler panted and stared off in the direction of the river as all eyes watched. Callie smirked behind a gardening glove.

"We are all sinners...you, me, all of us."

"I know my sins," he said, growing more confident. "Have you acknowledged your own?"

He stared at them one by one, demanding with his glare they confront their sins.

"The river beckons. We shall each shoulder this cross as did our Savior, handing it off in turn to the next sinner until we reach our destination and once again wash the sin from our souls."

Murmurs and glances indicated no one understood what he was asking of them.

He grimaced. "We're all going to take turns carrying this down to the river. Everybody is going to get baptized again once we get there."

No one appeared keen on the idea.

"It's over a hundred degrees," called out one parishioner.

"It's not even a Sunday," said another.

"Everyone participates!" declared Reverend Sadler. "I've already taken my turn, so who is next? Callie-girl; you carry the burden of many sins. Let us start with you."

•   •   •

Reverend Sadler and Callie tried to avoid each other in a community with a population of eighty-seven. Callie often found herself looking out past the limits of the little community, beyond the road which had brought her to this place, horizon-wishing with every passing moment.

The little enclave of Reverend Sadler's founding was intended to be an "oasis of propriety and decency in a desert of sin and debauchery." Contact with the adjacent town of Elixir Springs was limited, though he'd made an exception when Callie had first arrived. Normally, trade for mercantile goods from other Elixir Springs County residents occurred once a month. The bartering occurred from pickup trucks backed tail-bed to tail-bed at a gravel parking lot off Ranch Road 9. Beyond those brief exchanges, Reverend Sadler and his followers lived on their own harvests, ignored all media, and traveled nowhere.

Though it could be said the women of the congregation were somewhat lacking in grace, independence, and life skills, it could as easily be said the menfolk were homely, feeble, and stupid. Sundays and Wednesdays were devoted to worship. The other five days of the week were spent working around the house and garden, tending to the brood of children from the congregation, and praying at every opportunity.

Which all served to bore Callie. She wanted to be "good." Good as defined by Evangeline, which meant nothing colorful or entertaining was allowed; good as defined by Reverend Sadler, which meant even her thoughts were a source of sin needing to be crushed. Part of her felt she owed these people too much to stray from their beliefs, but the other part felt like a lassoed mustang.

Doing Reverend Sadler's laundry was the daily chore she most loathed. There were no electric washing machines in the village, so dirty clothes were loaded into a fifty-gallon oak barrel. Callie spent hours turning a hand crank which gyrated the garments in the sudsy water. This, however, she minded less than putting his dried and folded clothing away. Every evening he stared judgmentally from a rocking chair on the far side of his bedroom. He never seemed to turn pages of his Bible as she hung his shirts and trousers or tucked his undergarments into drawers.

Callie found herself doing things she hadn't thought about in a long time. She perused the pages of a Sears & Roebucks catalog in the waiting room of a doctor's office when one of the children from the congregation had his tonsils removed. She often lapsed into thoughts of pretty hats and high heels...or worse. One night she had a dream in which a former beau from high school ravished her, a fantasy so contrary to all she'd been taught over the last year-and-a-half, she sat up startled in bed and rose to shower.

Callie's mind became a meandering brook of sin despite her earnest efforts toward goodness. At first, she worried she'd never be able to control her imagination. As the months wore on, however, she worried less and less. Her thoughts of pretty things, and of color, music and, yes, men became her respite from the daily churn of drudgery. Callie realized Reverend Sadler was right in that they were all sinners, so she decided to accept the inevitability and keep her transgressions secret.

. . .

Callie first met Luz while taking children from the community to play by the pond. The day was warm, and the bluebonnets were in bloom. Children played and Callie beamed because such times were her opportunity to get away from the stifling community and let her mind wander.

"Hello," said Luz, a mid-fifties woman with flirtatious doe-brown eyes and dark, wavy hair falling past her shoulder blades. She had appeared sitting on a tree stump in the middle of the field bloom, wearing a pastel tie-dye skirt which didn't cover her knees. Daisies and an indigo feather adorned her head, and hoop earrings dangled halfway down her neck. Luz skipped everywhere and laughed at everything. She always showed up from whereabouts unknown within minutes of Callie's arrival with the children.

Callie had yet to speak to the other women in the community on any subject other than fall canning, God's grace, or proper colors for linen dyes. Loneliness was part of her daily routine. Luz became her first real friend since her days at the Winn's Five & Dime.

One afternoon Luz and Callie giggled at the children spinning to get dizzy-drunk in a patch of clover. "I brought you something," said Luz.

Callie turned to see Luz had produced a Sears & Roebucks catalog. The catalog was dated from the fall and had blue-ink scribbles on some of the pages.

"I was reading one in a doctor's office just the other day," Callie said in amazement. "It even had blue scribbles in it, just like this one."

Time with Luz became the most hopeful part of Callie's life. She daydreamed of visits with her while hanging laundry or weeding. Callie became flushed on days when she could take the herd of children on a walk around the pond. She often pushed the limits of acceptable time away from the congregation to eke out a few more minutes with her friend. One magnificent day she kicked off her hiking boots to mimic Luz, and they ran and flapped their arms like seagulls while the children paused agape.

Callie's other source of joy became the Sears & Roebucks. Wednesdays and Sundays were the nights Reverend Sadler went to bed early, as sermons tended to exhaust him. She couldn't bring herself to look at the catalog on Sundays because that seemed all too wicked. On Wednesdays, however, she would sneak out to the barn and peruse the gowns and perfumes. Her pulse quickened and her breath came in puffs as if meeting an illicit lover out in the barn.

One night, Evangeline told Reverend Sadler about Callie's Wednesday nights. "She must be meeting a man, because she always returns with flushed cheeks and a hint of glisten on her forehead." Based on this information, Reverend Sadler snuck into the barn to spy from shadows.

Callie's lips were parted as she turned each page of the catalog with unvarnished glee. "Don't you just love this one?" she asked of Luz who peered at the pages over her shoulder.

"It would be beautiful on you," Luz replied, but her gaze drifted to a dark corner of the barn. She took steps backwards until she was withdrawn in shadow.

Reverend Sadler tiptoed into the light. His breath quickened, and the veins in his temples appeared like fishing worms. Callie stroked her own cheek, oblivious to his presence.

"Harlot!" Sadler bellowed as he jumped from behind the compost bin. He ripped the magazine from her grasp and shoved her into a pile of hay.

"What are you doing?" Callie cried as Reverend Sadler used her candle to ignite the catalog.

Callie saw it then, that look she'd seen in her stepmother's boyfriend. Reverend Sadler's eyes were locked onto her, and his lip curled. His neck reddened, and his breathing intensified. His hands gripped and released, and he grunted like a rutting stag.

Callie glanced around for something heavy she'd use to strike when he advanced. Luz was nowhere to be seen.

"Gershom, you'll stop this now," Evangeline said from the barn door. Reverend Sadler jerked as if startled from hypnosis. He looked over his shoulder at Evangeline and back to Callie.

"Stay there on the ground with the animals, because you're acting like a sow in heat!" he roared.

"What gives you the right?" screamed Callie.

"How dare you ask that!? God gives me the right in all things! I am your father, and His commandment is that you honor me."

"Come with me now," Evangeline hissed.

He left her there in enveloping darkness as Evangeline marched him back to the house. Callie pulled handfuls of straw to hide her face. She remembered hiding under a blanket as a little girl, while her father searched her closet and under the bed to make sure there were no monsters.

• • •

Callie stayed in the barn the entire night. Her feelings of terror subsided, but she could not sleep. She wondered where Luz had gone, but it was just her friend's way to come and go in a twinkling. Callie sensed she would not be back that night.

She dared not light a lantern, but there was enough moon shining through spaces between the wallboards and the still-open barn door that she was able to look around. The stacked hay bales and tack dangling on one wall were comforting. Her gaze came to rest on an old wooden Dunlop tennis racquet hanging from a rafter nail. The racket had been stored in a wooden frame to keep it from warping, and she'd often wondered at the strangeness of such an object in this agrarian setting. Pondering this mystery allowed her to drift into slumber.

At sunrise she ventured out, peering around the barn door to make sure there was no danger. To her delight she saw Luz was waiting outside, swaying with her eyes closed in a patch of spilled straw, as if listening to music Callie could not hear.

"Good morning," said Luz in a tone so cheerful Callie wondered if the terror from the night before had merely been a bad dream. They meandered to the pond out of earshot of others in the community. Luz waded into the water to feed fistfuls of canned corn to a paddling of ducks, her skirt hem floating behind her. Callie paced the bank.

"He wants me," Callie whispered.

"He does," Luz acknowledged as she admired the ducks gliding away.

Callie tried to stifle a sob, but the tears came.

"You just abandoned me there."

"I would never abandon you."

"But you could've said something. He was so...awful."

Luz reached to pet one of the ducks. "I'm not here for Gershom Sadler. I'm here for you."

Callie wiped her face and took a deep breath. She held the air in her lungs as if it were a precious thing she didn't want to let go. When she spoke her voice was clearer, stronger.

"I have to leave."

"You do," Luz replied, sprinkling more corn on the surface of the pond.

Callie had a way of looking sideways from her dark-blue eyes. It was a look of too many unsure days.

"It was so scary before, when I didn't have a place to live...didn't have enough food."

"I brought you something!" Luz said so sprightly that Callie tittered.

Luz spent a moment rummaging through the pockets of her blouse and jeans before remembering a small bag on the ground behind her.

"Here it is!" she announced as she handed the bag to Callie.

"Money?" said Callie as she peeked in the bag.

"Ninety-four dollars; enough for a bus ticket and a motel for a night or two."

"Oh, Luz, I—"

"There's a little makeup kit in there, too. We'll need to get you fixed up a bit before you go."

"But, maybe I can't."

"Oh goodness, sweetie, you can and you must. I also got you this."

Luz produced the singed Sears and Roebucks catalog. "Saved it from burning all the way to ash. I know how much you like it."

Callie gave her friend a hug so tight she worried she might poof and disappear. When they separated, Luz wiped away Callie's remaining tears, and the two laughed out loud.

"Now, let's see how pretty we can make you today."

Luz gave Callie a little makeover right there on the log bench next to the pond. She wove daisies into Callie's ponytail, explaining this was what one did on May Day. All the while she told stories about dancing around May Poles in Europe and of her great loves and her life's joys.

Callie peeked in the compact mirror after Luz finished. She saw for the first time since her father died that she was lovely. She had no means or real skill in this world, but she would find a way without selling herself or giving in to a hypocrite.

Luz gave her a hug and whispered, "You're ready."

Callie squared her shoulders and headed for noon service to pick a fight.

•   •   •

Things took a scary turn for Toribio as the troupe was setting up for a three-day peach festival near Fredericksburg, Texas. Toribio was enjoying the cool weather and looking forward to the jubilee. The day was perfect for the labor of setting up the cables, tents, and rides.

A wiry fellow by the nickname of "So-So," who sported a mullet haircut and a lopsided rebel flag tattoo on one shoulder, was the cause of the drama to come. Toribio hadn't trusted So-So, but Errol hired him based on the man's experience.

"He's like a bonerfried electrician," said Errol in defense of his new hire. "Says on his application he's installed drive-up malt shop menu and a neon sign for a Stuckey's!"

"But—"

"You can't get top-of-the-line electrical savvy just anywhere, amigo, but here he is working for us now."

Toribio held his opinion, confident So-So would show his true colors. It took less than a week.

"Picked her up in town last night," said a hung-over So-So to Errol and Toribio on his first Saturday morning as part of the carnival crew. The three of them stared at a cherry-red Ford Maverick So-So had driven onto the lot a few minutes earlier.

"Where were you last night?" demanded Errol. "We had work to do after closin'."

"Told you. Walked into town and had me a time. Whoodog what a time! Hotties, tequila, and got me this here little present for myself."

"Well, I hope you ain't too hung over, 'cause you've got around thirty burned out bulbs to replace all over the show. Best get on it."

"Yes, sir, boss-man, sir," said So-So with a mock salute.

"Get on those bulbs or get out," said Errol.

So-So bristled but turned to his duties. Toribio squinted inside the Ford and saw the keyhole ignition looked damaged.

Two sheriff deputies arrived before lunch, and it took them all of thirty seconds to spot the car in the gravel parking lot.

"Who drives this red Ford?" asked one of the deputies of Toribio, who was using every ounce of discipline to refrain from fleeing. His hand drifted toward his wallet as if he needed to assure himself he had his green card handy, but even this did little to calm his anxiety. He'd known lawmen on both sides of the river that didn't seem to much care if he was there legally or not, and the urge to bolt was strong.

Instead, he gave a head-nod in the direction of So-So who was ratcheting a cable line taut over by the kiddie rides. The two officers thanked him and made their ominous way toward their suspect.

So-So saw them thirty feet out, and they gained another five steps as he jumped from the line and stumbled in a mad dash to get away. He was in handcuffs in less time than it took Malga to finish a hot dog.

So-So did not go peacefully. He kicked, dragged his knees, and said awful things about the lawmen's mothers.

"Sir, you're under arrest for stealing that Ford Maverick," said one of the deputies.

"I just borrowed it!" So-So screamed. "Why don't you go arrest some real criminals instead of picking on the working man?"

The deputies remained professional and knew nothing but trouble would come from answering.

"There's one right there!" So-So yelled and pointed with his nose and toes in Toribio's direction. "He's as illegal as they come. No papers or nothing."

The deputies paused and looked back at Toribio, who once more had to fight the urge to flee. He wanted to reach for his wallet to show them his green card, but he was afraid to move. One of the deputies took a step toward him, and Toribio's mouth went dry.

"This fellow belongs right here, deputies," said Errol who ambled between the deputies and Toribio. "Don't you let that catfish-hemorrhoid fool you."

Errol's kind gesture might still not have saved Toribio from deportation. It was evident the two deputies were considering their next move, but So-So made up their minds when he kicked the shin of the officer on his left.

The full attention of the two lawmen was re-directed back on the man they'd come to find in the first place. It took a good five minutes to wrestle So-So into the police car, and all thoughts of running an identity check on Toribio were long forgotten by the time they slammed the door shut. Errol and Toribio could hear So-So screaming profanities as the police car drove away in a trail of white dust.

"*Gracias*," said Toribio.

"Ain't no gracias about it. Just what friends do."

• • •

"May Day," said Reverend Gershom Sadler with a sneer. "Right now in the world, there are those celebrating spring with music…merry-making…dancing of all things."

Evangeline shuddered.

"But not here! In this community we strive for reverence…grave, grave reverence."

Reverend Sadler frowned at his flock as he gripped his pulpit and launched into his sermon. "We read in Hebrews 11:30 Joshua planned to assault the Canaanites with sword and fire, but God told him to trust in a different tactic. Amen!"

"Amen!" answered Evangeline. Others in the congregation answered as well, though Evangeline was by far the most fervent.

Reverend Sadler raised a hand scythe used for cutting corn stalks at the word "sword." The congregants stood motionless, as if mired in spiritual spackle.

"God told Joshua the walls of Jericho would come tumbling down and lay open the land He had promised. But only if they were to march around the solid walls whilst blowing upon their mighty ram horns. God be praised!"

"Hallelujah!" shouted Evangeline. Her voice warbled from the passion of a Holy Spirit passing through her bony frame.

"Today we use our horns to tumble the walls of Satan," continued the reverend. "This is a blessed thing we do. For Satan is here! Make no mistake. He is here to tempt us from Salvation and directly into his sin-infested heart."

The reverend handed the scythe to Evangeline so he could descend from his pulpit to stand amongst his followers.

"So, we take up the horn and march against the leftist circle of Satan, against the hedonism of pagan rituals. We move as the hands of the clock, as did Joshua and his mighty army moved. Every step of every circuit of every day brings us closer to the right hand of God. Amen!"

He blew a kazoo-like note on a hollowed-out deer antler to begin the march, which was about the same moment Callie arrived.

"Be brave," encouraged Luz.

Reverend Sadler stepped out of the vanguard as if to meet the challenge. The others turned to stare.

"Keep marching," admonished Evangeline to the trudging congregants who had slowed to watch the show. The pace picked back up, though all eyes shifted hard to the right. Gershom and Callie glared at one another inside a circling, gawking herd.

A few strands of Callie's daisy-laced ponytail had slipped out of the rubber band to fall across one of her eyes. The rage left Reverend Sadler's face, and for a moment he seemed to soften as if he might forgive her.

But he didn't.

"Harlot!" he cried.

For several seconds, Callie almost allowed herself to be cowed. She could still wipe off the makeup and pull out the daisies, still apologize for her behavior, still smile.

But she didn't.

It wasn't Gershom Sadler's bullying and hypocrisy which bolstered her resolve, but his thumb-length nose punctuated with a burgundy mole just left of the tip. She hated that mole. She'd fantasized many times about snipping it off with garden shears, and within the darkened bubble of that thought, she committed.

"Pornographer!"

One of the women snickered and was shushed.

Evangeline shrieked with rage. "Vex your tongue, you misbehaving ingrate!"

"Shut up, you old biddy," Callie shouted back.

For several moments the only sound was Reverend Sadler's heavy breathing and the shuffling of the congregants' feet around the cross. Callie began marching around the cross as well— counterclockwise—to a chorus of gasps.

Sadler howled, "You were a sinful harlot when I found you, and you will always be a harlot."

"You pleasure yourself with pictures of your own daughter!"

"His adopted daughter!" screeched Evangeline.

Reverend Sadler stomped the ground until the heel popped off one of his boots. He charged Callie, jabbing his index finger so close to her face it made her blink. "Go cut me a switch, harlot!

Cut it as a whip and make bare your hip so all can see how trollops are to be treated!"

"Fine!" Callie answered, and she turned to the old willow tree near the cross. There were plenty of skinny branches which would serve nicely, and Luz stepped forward to hand her pruning shears. Callie cut Sadler's switch, and then she cut one for herself.

"The sermon is over and the lesson hath begun," Sadler announced.

"You don't have to do this," Luz whispered. "You could just leave."

"He deserves a whipping."

"Don't take him a switch. Swat him and run."

Callie paused as if considering Luz's suggestion. "No, he was decent enough to feed me when I was hungry, and now I'm disgracing him. He gets his own switch."

"Mend her wicked ways once and for all, Reverend!" shouted Evangeline from the circle.

"I shall, Sister. I shall."

Reverend Sadler had taken off his jacket and was rolling up his sleeves as Callie returned. He tilted his head and knitted his brow when he spied the two switches, and his face turned ginger as she offered him one and kept the other. He hesitated for a moment, seeing she had pulled her whip back behind her shoulder.

Reverend Sadler snarled as he came down with the switch, catching Callie on the left hip. She retaliated by lashing him across the neck. A general moan rippled through the congregation.

"You ungrateful…" started Evangeline, who was so appalled she couldn't finish the sentence. Callie adopted a fencer's stance for the next attack.

Reverend Sadler's face turned Passover-blood-red, and he delivered a series of lashes to her buttocks, torso, and shoulders. She matched him stroke for stroke. The two fought a vicious duel across the front lawn, down into the pond, through the hanging linen, around a water hand-pump, and back up onto the grassy mound where the old wooden cross was planted.

Both grew weary, and the action paused. For several seconds the combatants panted and stared at one another. Sadler threw down his switch at the foot of the cross and pointed a gnarled finger at Callie's face.

"I am God's messenger. What you have done to me this day, you have done unto Him."

"You've damned yourself, you hussy," Evangeline screeched.

"Indeed," said the reverend. "I condemn thee straight to hell!"

Callie replied by whacking him once more across the face.

"Cut two switches and be ready when I get there."

"Leave, you ungrateful temptress," Evangeline howled. "You are damned to an eternity of hellfire!"

"Don't turn around," said Luz as she put a comforting arm over Callie's shoulder.

Sadler regained his footing and called out as well. "Enjoy the pit as your flesh burns to bone, as beasts ravage you!"

"You can't avoid God's wrath!" Evangeline shrieked, her voice fading with distance.

Callie's eyes flooded, but she heeded Luz's advice and didn't look back.

"What have I done?"

Luz, still smiling, still chipper, smoothed Callie's mussed hair. "Birth is always painful, sugar…especially the rebirth kind."

Callie stopped short and wiped her eyes with the back of her hand. She smiled at her best friend despite the acidic taunts from those behind her as she collected her Sears and Roebucks catalog and walked out of her old life forever.

CHAPTER SIX

Sophie had been startled to see her mother tromping into a field and approaching a huge bull in the paddock after their brief encounter in the kitchen. She was about to call out a warning when Callie grabbed a brush to groom the beast.

Sophie considered walking out to the fence and trying again to start a conversation, but she decided the best course would be to let her mother have a few minutes. She sat on a back porch rocking chair to wait.

Sophie could just make out snippets of what sounded like a scolding. Callie gesticulated with the brush to punctuate assertions, and the bull snorted as if agreeing with each point.

"Destiny!?" Callie barked. "What does destiny have to do with it?"

Sophie's breath caught, and her eyes widened. *Surely, she's not talking to...*

"She's just here to make me crazy."

My mother is talking to a bull.

"Just like Gershom Sadler has made me crazy for years."

Beefo turned his head toward the porch, and it seemed to Sophie as if he were staring straight at her. His demeanor seemed somehow judgmental, but Sophie squinted her eyes at the silliness of that notion.

Callie brushed Beefo so vigorously a dust cloud rose off his back. The bull moaned and took a sidestep closer to her as she kept talking.

"…figure out what she's doing here…a lot of nerve…of course she looks nice…no, she can't come to dinner… called six times in eleven years! Six!"

Sophie watched as her mother's brush strokes stalled and her gaze drifted toward the horizon. Callie stayed quite still for a time, only her lips quivering now and then. Beefo's eyes drifted closed, and Sophie thumbed through a dog-eared paperback romance novel she found tucked beneath the rocking chair cushion.

She was two chapters into the novel when Callie flung the brush back onto the picnic table and headed her way. Sophie smoothed her skirt and marked the page in preparation for more conversation, but her mother strode right past without a word.

Callie walked back inside and picked up three of the battered hubcaps from her kitchen floor, which she carried back down the porch steps and across her lawn to a large willow tree. There she used bent coat hangers to hang the dimpled caps on various branches of the tree, adding to a mobile of metallic discs already there. A gentle clanking as the hubcaps ruffled in the wind was melodic, and Sophie's lips parted in wonder.

A thousand times Sophie had thought about what she'd say, believing small talk or, "I missed you," or, "How have you been," would earn her nothing but scorn.

Callie finished hanging the latest addition to the tree sculpture. She pulled some almonds from a sweatpants pocket and stared at her daughter.

"Were you talking to that bull?" Sophie asked.

"He's a confidante."

Sophie stared out at Beefo but decided to leave the matter for another time. She approached the topic she'd come to discuss as a businesswoman, something she knew Callie would understand.

Business was their common language, no interpreter needed, and enterprise, not sentiment, would drive their first conversation.

"Momma, I want to establish a branch of the Sophie Wind Corporation in Elixir Springs. Here, on our property."

Her mother continued munching. She watched her daughter as a security guard would watch a shoplifter about to stuff a CD down his pants. Sophie flushed with an excitement she hadn't felt in a boardroom for years.

"I want to bring a division of my business here, where the dream started—where I started. It will be good for Elixir Springs. It'll create a lot of jobs and garner media attention. It would breathe life and hope into this place."

"So, you're going to swoop in and save us," said Callie in a voice low and sinister.

"Oh, here we go!"

"You need to get your butt back in that pretty car of yours and go back to Austin."

"All these years, and you're still trying to tell me what to do."

"Sell the world your divine raindrops-to-oceans philosophy—"

"Why won't you just—"

"Tell your worshippers you can change their lives if they sell your crap."

"It's not as simple as all that, and you'd know it if—"

"But leave this place alone. We don't need you."

Sophie's neck flushed, and she shrugged in an, "I tried," fashion. She pivoted and strode around the corner of her mother's house, nearly tripping on a pink-tasseled bicycle in her haste to get away.

•   •   •

The following morning broke with an unusual coolness. Cleft shared a breakfast of peanut butter sandwiches and coffee with Errol as the two rode to Pioneer Days in the sheriff's patrol truck.

The park would open in two hours, and there were rides to inspect, parts to grease. Cleft wanted to get the heavy work done before the heat slammed into the day, and Errol rode along for company before he started his patrol shift.

Cleft heard a strange sound as they trudged into the park, and it took a moment before he placed the hum and creak of the carousel.

Errol cleared his throat. "Why's the carousel on so early?"

Somehow the clacking and whirring made Cleft feel as if the entire world was tilted like a camera angle in a noir film. He noticed the crunch of the gravel on the walkway, two crows arguing over remnants of a hotdog, the morning's heat vapors writhing like a choreographed dance of ribbons.

Miniature covered wagons, plow horses, bobbing pinto ponies, and a pair of oxen turned a slow merry-go-round circle as Cleft and Errol came into view of the ride. Next came the four figurines which to Cleft had always seemed out of place with the frontier decor. Four horses, all angry and gnashing, rearing instead of plodding, heading to hell instead of hope followed the pastoral figures. The beasts were always the last figures chosen by families, and the ones on which children tended most to bawl.

The ride's calliope music was not turned on, and somehow this made the four horses seem even more sinister. Cleft and Errol stared as a man who appeared dead, frost-bitten, and duct-taped to the fiercest of the four horses bobbed by.

The mystery deepened as they spotted Callie holding onto the same horse's mane. She was lighting one cigarette off another and smiling out at a clearly uncomfortable Commissioner Pastal standing beside the revolving platform.

Commissioner Pastal clicked a mechanical counter each time the frozen preacher made the circuit. Pastal grimaced upon seeing Errol and Cleft and cast a worried look at Callie. The newcomers stood motionless and, for once, Errol seemed at a loss for words.

"That's seven," announced Commissioner Pastal, putting the counter clicker into his pants pocket to jot into a notebook. He pulled a bottle of pink antacid from his coat pocket and swigged until half was gone.

"He seems to be having more fun than usual this year," called Callie from the carousel platform. "Give us a few more turns."

"Absolutely not," said Pastal. "I officially acknowledge you have abided by the terms."

Callie sighed at his stern expression before calling out to Cleft and Errol.

"Happy May Day, boys. Errol, would you turn it off? I'm gonna need help lifting him down this year." She hopped off the carousel platform and gave Commissioner Pastal an indignant glance.

"I'm sorry, but as I told you, my ulcer is flared up and, besides, I'm not obligated to assist you in this...this...farce."

Cleft didn't take his eyes off the man strapped to the horse figurine. "I don't understand."

"This 'farce' has been pretty profitable for you," Callie countered Pastal.

"Where did your cook go?" Pastal asked in a clumsy maneuver to change the subject. "He was just here."

"He went back to the restaurant. We're getting a delivery of produce."

"Who is that?" asked Cleft pointing toward the reverend. "Why is a frozen dead man riding the carousel?"

Callie took a long drag off her cigarette.

"He asked for it."

Errol's eyes were as wide as they'd go. "Must be a law against—"

"There's not," said Callie. "I could use your help getting him down."

Cleft jumped up on the platform and pulled his pocketknife to cut the tape. All the while he grumbled about working conditions, and respecting the dead, and crazy old women.

"I'll leave it to you," announced Commissioner Pastal in his best county commissioner's voice as he wiped pink liquid off his lips and stomped away.

"Let's do this again next year," Callie called out. Cleft thought he saw Pastal's shoulders sag.

"Can I turn on the music while we work?" called Errol as he wound his way through the carousel poles toward the control panel. No one answered him. He shrugged while opening the little door in the hub of the ride to access the control buttons. As he did, he noted the remnant of an old cross which had once stood beside Gershom Sadler's long-gone church. The cross was charred, a mere stub within the hollow of the hub, still planted in the ground after all these years.

"I remember how hard it was to build the carousel around this cross," Errol called out, though neither Callie nor Cleft seemed to pay him any mind.

"Still think we should've ripped it out of the ground," Errol mumbled.

"Why do you do this?" Cleft asked Callie. She waited so long to answer Cleft thought she might not have heard.

"Callie, why do you—"

"You ever pick a fight you knew you couldn't win?"

She struck the lighter flint for a new cigarette as Errol flipped the music on and the first notes from the calliope hit her ears. She stared trance-like at the carousel, oblivious to the flame flickering in her hand or the unlit cigarette dangling from her lower lip.

"You say a fight?" Cleft asked as he swiveled the reverend on his heels toward the edge of the platform.

But Callie wasn't there to explain further, her thoughts having already dissolved back to her days of wandering…

CHAPTER SEVEN

Young Callie meandered for months after leaving Reverend Sadler's congregation. She picked up tip money waiting tables, and she occasionally financed a meal by redeeming soda bottles.

She used her thumb to travel, and she had little care where she went. During a leg out of Amarillo she caught a ride with one Private First-Class Dakota Wind. He was driving his matador-red Camaro one last time on Route 66 before he was to ship out for Vietnam, and he'd nearly rolled the car in his haste to pull over upon seeing her on the side of the road in cutoff jean shorts.

"Where you headed?" asked Private Wind.

"Anywhere."

"I happen to be going anywhere."

They were in love by Flagstaff.

•   •   •

"That's the prettiest sight I've ever seen," Callie said as she and Private Wind stared at the Pacific Ocean from a Santa Barbara hillside.

"You're the prettiest sight I've ever seen," he replied. He kissed her head, and she squeezed his butt. The sunset made him cry.

They roamed before returning to his home in east Texas. By Fresno she'd promised to wait for his return from deployment. She became Mrs. Callie Wind in Las Vegas, made a giggly call to his parents from a phone booth in Durango and was pregnant by Dodge City.

Callie sobbed at the airport during their last kiss, but she dried her tears and swelled with pride when he turned before boarding the plane and saluted his nation's flag flapping in a heavy breeze. He waved once more to her, and she knew with her whole soul he would never return.

The marriage afforded her housing on base at Ft. Hood. She lived in a tan apartment with chocolate-brown carpeting and fawn walls, sand-colored wallpaper printed with mahogany-toned clovers in the kitchen and bath, and matching coffee-colored refrigerator, oven and coffee maker. A previous tenant had left four olive-green placemats in a kitchen drawer, perhaps for a splash of color during mealtimes.

Callie received three letters from her husband over the next ninety days. She sent him one hundred and seven in the same time frame. He told her he was eating well and gaining muscle, firing rifles was cool, one of his sergeants said he was good at map reading, he missed her eyes, her boobs, her smile.

She wrote that she really missed him terribly, she felt guilty for spending their meager funds on two record albums, she really missed him a lot, her scrambled eggs had improved, she couldn't wait to feel the baby kick for the first time, and she really, really, really missed him so much.

In her second trimester Callie received a visit from the base chaplain who told her what a hero Private First-Class Dakota Wind had been. She'd always known the moment would come. She had expected her heart to break, but she'd not foreseen the wracking agony in her ribs, her throat, and her eyes, the ache in every joint with the slightest movement, or the monumental effort it took to brush her teeth or tinkle. Every breath came as if through wet burlap; every waking moment was a sledgehammer punch to the pelvis.

Callie grieved for three months, rarely leaving the apartment. She picked at food other military wives brought her, and she slept through entire days.

"Was Reverend Sadler right?" she asked Luz one morning. "Am I condemned to hell?"

It was a morning in which she'd not had the strength to move off the floor. It had been two days since she'd last eaten, and she feared she was cursed.

Luz smiled and sat on the edge of the bed to stroke Callie's hair. "No, sweetie. You're not condemned. Grief is hell, but you're not destined to stay here."

"He said I insulted God," moaned Callie.

"God wasn't insulted in the least," said Luz. "Magnificent day, as I recall."

Callie sighed. "Maybe all this is a retribution."

"Or maybe all this is a blessing."

The baby kicked hard. Luz beamed, and Callie sat upright. She realized she could no more stay in this place of monochrome sorrow than her baby could stay tucked and safe within her belly. Two months shy of her due date she raised her hitchhiking thumb again.

She picked up a job cleaning motel rooms in Killeen. The job came with a room and breakfast every day. The owners, a tiny couple from Pakistan, were eager to help her. Callie would perhaps never again meet two more kind, polite people. Life at the little motel was pleasant enough, and she made friends with the other staff members. The place was small, but it was painted in pastels and smelled like jasmine. She'd about decided she could live there indefinitely when, once again, that baby grabbed her attention and wouldn't let go.

• • •

"Will you forgive me if I come to you of my own hand?" Reverend Sadler had asked while standing on a sheer cliff edge overlooking the Nueces River. His boot toes were already out over the edge.

"I know. I know you can't forgive me that sin. But could you please deliver a mighty wind to my back, Lord? I cannot tolerate this agony of that, that…harlot's creation."

It had been a year since the willow switch duel with Callie, and Reverend Sadler had not fared well since. He didn't eat without severe gastric consequences, his back hurt between his shoulder blades, and his tongue tasted metallic. His sermons became nothing more than hate-filled rants about the sins of Eve, Delilah, and women in general. In the last several months, however, he'd taken to avoiding church altogether.

He knew the pains in his head and intestines to be wrath from Satan for losing control over the woman who had become the most important person in his life. There were nights he cried into his barley pillow so hard his ribs felt like they were being squeezed by a giant anaconda. The misery of his broken heart had reached a point of crisis.

So, there he stood, dusty pebbles from under his feet tumbling down the cliff face as if showing him the way. He closed his eyes, waiting for the divine nudge. He was ready, and a sense of peace blossomed in his chest. His face relaxed and warmth spread across his shoulders.

"I'm coming, Lord! I'm coming to see your face!"

It was then that Reverend Sadler heard a crunching of grass and leaves in the wooded area behind him. This caused strain on his curiosity, enough to make him lean back not a moment too soon. He reasoned God could send the requested deadly breeze after HE revealed what was causing the sound.

The reverend turned from the precipice as an emaciated raccoon came walking out of the scrub brush. The animal listed as if drunk. Its eyes appeared milky and unfocused as she sniffed her way toward him. Sadler stood transfixed. He knew seeing a nocturnal animal out at this time of day was unnatural and, therefore, directed by God.

All thoughts of flying off the cliff were forgotten as the old girl sniffed his pants. The raccoon rose up on her hind legs and used her front paws to embrace him around the calf. She hugged him—he could think of no other way to explain it—and then she died right there at his feet.

Reverend Sadler sank to his knees beside the little animal. His wild eyebrows crested and dipped. He sobbed and cackled while he stroked the little dead animal and picked burrs from her coat.

At one point he engaged in a long conversation with his Maker. The talk was less like a prayer and more like the two of them were discussing their latest book club selection. Life and faith evolved for Reverend Sadler at the edge of that cliff in ways he could not have imagined prior to Callie. He considered the epiphany to be the most important of his life. He arose a new man, believing himself enlightened for the first time and stronger than he'd ever been.

For people were offensive, whereas God's creatures, bright and beautiful, great and small, were glorious. "I've been doing it all wrong...trying to save wretched, undeserving souls. God gave his son to atone for man's sin, and man has proved unworthy."

Sadler cackled as he rose in a burst of energy. He hugged the dead raccoon to his breast and whispered in her ear as if he were calming a colicky baby. He held her at arm's length and stared into her cloudy eyes, speaking as if he were addressing the Divine.

"You created living creatures produced by the land, and it was so on the sixth day, Genesis 24, amen. And You created them before man. You created them before us, as you created the heavens and the stars and the oceans before us because they were to be more precious. You blessed them more, and it was good. I have been blind but now I see. How sweet the sound."

Tears ran from his cracked and smiling face to plop into the rocky soil mere inches from the cliff edge. Yet, he had no further intention of allowing a wind to send him into paradise. A message of destiny had been delivered unto him from a rabid creature whose last moments on Earth were spent providing comfort to his soul. Sadler would, by God, live on.

Reverend Sadler held the raccoon like a swaddled infant. "I have heard you, Almighty, and I am reborn once more."

.   .   .

Callie picked up a temp job serving beer at a Grateful Dead concert held in the middle of a Quarter Horse racetrack. By then she could prop a tray of drinks on her belly to the great amusement of the stoned crowds, and she raked in tips while people float-danced in front of her little drink stand. She ended up earning more than she would have in three weeks at the motel, while she spent most of the evening chuckling at the concertgoers who danced and swayed in ways Callie had never imagined.

"Hey, dollface. When are you due?" asked a drunk fraternity kid.

"Due?" she replied with a wink to his friends. "What makes you think I'm pregnant?"

"I'm...oh...uh...I thought..."

The man's friends laughed at his discomfort. Callie bent as best she could to pat him on the cheek.

"I mean...you are...right?" he asked.

"Sweetie, I'm so far along, it may happen on my break."

The evening continued in the same light tone, and Callie realized she was feeling happy for the first time in months. She looked forward to telling Luz the next time she saw her.

Part of her pay was for cleanup after the concert. She and several dozen others were charged with restoring the venue to near pristine conditions. They were to have the cleanup done before horse racing began the next day, and she was set for a long night.

She'd first been told to remove folding chairs from behind the huge concert speakers and stack them onto a trailer in the back area. She did her best, but her calves and feet swelled, and she grunted each time she bent to collapse one of the folding chairs. Her waddle worried the event supervisor, who handed her a broom and relieved her of chair duty.

All was going well as she swept the stage. Some of the musicians' instruments were still awaiting removal by roadies. Callie plucked one of the guitar strings. Empty bottles of Jack Daniels and marijuana roaches piled up in her sweep, as did a few bras and panties. A picture of Richard Nixon with doodles of an arrow through his head had been folded into a paper airplane.

Callie paused for a moment as she stood next to the microphone stand center-stage. She looked out at the acres of property where people had been dancing and singing a few hours earlier, and she wondered what it would be like to perform for such a crowd.

The lights from a nearby carnival were blinking off for the night, and she also wondered about all the people working there. Where did the carnival workers come from? Did they have families? What dreams might they have?

Callie leaned on her broom handle to take some pressure off her lower back, but she felt more alive and hopeful than she had in a long time. Something about the festivity and message of unity through lyrics and melody reminded her there was purpose in her life. She found herself believing Luz that great things were in store.

And then her water broke.

. . .

Commissioner Richard Pastal was a beefy man with veins in his cheeks, a friendly fellow who carried a lifelong obsession with business and a penchant for politics. His next election was drawing nigh, and he intended to keep his seat. That meant buying barbeque for anyone who would sit down long enough to hear his stump speech. Commissioner Pastal had never been welcome at Reverend Sadler's community, but the Commissioner had heard rumors the old minister was distracted, if not senile. He'd taken this as an opportunity to meet and greet a whole new voter pond.

The old minister wasn't around when Commissioner Pastal drove his orange-over-white Chevy Suburban into the yard near the church. In minutes he'd invited everyone in the community to join him in "breaking bread and cracking bones," a joke he repeated often on campaign trails.

"Can't see no harm," said one of the congregants. In no time they were seated and enjoying a meal. Commissioner Pastal worked the crowd. He fawned over children, offered to spoon more coleslaw onto paper plates, and mixed in platform points with conversation. He was doing well until Reverend Sadler arrived back home carrying a dead raccoon.

"What is this wickedness?" he yelled as he limped into the midst of the church picnic. "Gluttony! Gluttony and sloth!"

The reverend scowled at the members of his church. His gaze rested on a startled-looking Evangeline as a drop of barbecue sauce slid off her chin. "I see we're long overdue for a sermon. Make no mistake, you brought this on yourselves."

He tromped to the barn where he stored his old wooden pulpit. The congregation chewed as he dragged it to the picnic tables.

"They are all God's creatures," he began while holding aloft the raccoon corpse. For the first time his voice cracked in frantic tones instead of his traditional voice of authority and passion.

"We can't eat them anymore. It would be like eating part of God's soul."

"What are you saying, friend?" asked Commissioner Pastal.

"Who are you?" demanded the minister.

"I'm Commissioner Richard Pastal, Reverend. We've known each other for years. I'm your elected official."

Reverend Sadler's gaze was blank, so Commissioner Pastal tried again.

"You gave me a cattle grazing lease on ten acres three months ago."

Reverend Sadler scowled. "What I'm saying is…I'm saying, we can no longer eat of the flesh. It is a sin! Stop eating!"

"Everyone stop eating!" screeched Evangeline as she reached across her table to swat ribs out of hands.

"Reverend," said Commissioner Pastal. "God put animals here so we have food to eat and so we could use their hides and bones to make shelter and tools."

"Sacrilege!" roared Reverend Sadler, setting off confused discussion. "We must revere God's creatures, not slaughter them." His larynx cracked with the strain of his passion.

"You suggest we worship false idols?" parried Commissioner Pastal. He seemed quite proud he'd been able to use a biblical reference in his argument.

"Not false idols, you heathen; vessels of souls blessed by God Almighty! They are more worthy of praise and devotion than any of you, you sinners, you minions of Satan. Follow God's commands, or you will surely burn in hellfire!"

"God has directed us to hug beef cattle and open our homes to mice and rats?" Pastal replied.

Evangeline rose to defend her church leader. "Why you arrogant—"

"Would you strike down Christ should he appear to you at this moment?"

Members of the church would not meet Sadler's demanding glare.

"What if He came to us in the form of a deer or a ferret? Would you strike him down in that body so you could savor his flesh? I demand an answer. HE demands an answer!"

"Man was created in God's image," Pastal replied. People around him were starting to nod at his comments and pat his back.

"God created the animals on the sixth day," Reverend Sadler responded, though it was clear his energy was fading. "He made animals first, so they're more important. It's in the book of Genesis. It's all right there…in the…the Book."

He held his bible as high as the raccoon, but his arm muscles trembled as if under terrible strain. His voice weakened to little more than a whisper. All held their breath as if watching something valuable about to fall and break.

"And Jesus went into the temple of God," he muttered.

His gaze moved up toward the heavens.

"And cast out all of them that bought and sold in the temple, and overthrew the tables of the moneychangers, and the seats of them that sold doves."

"Matthew 21:12," said Evangeline.

"Matthew 21:12!" Reverend Sadler screamed, and he upended their tables with the fury of an angry god. Sauce spattered, coleslaw flew, and gnashed bones pelted about the lawn. Most of the eaters sat slack jawed. Sadler's diatribe withered, and a befuddled silence descended over the splintering congregation like a morning fog at Gettysburg.

·   ·   ·

Reverend Sadler stood amidst the broken plates and strewn food long after the congregants drifted away. Dusk came, and crickets wooed mates. Bluegrass music played from a phonograph in one of the cabins, and the smell of baked ham wafted through the village.

Sadler trudged to the wooden cross imbedded beside the church and sank to his knees. "I have failed you, Lord," he whispered. "I have failed."

Evangeline called out to him. "Gershom, come inside so I can get this mess cleaned up."

"It'll wait until morning," he replied.

"I'll not have a bunch of possums and raccoons coming up here to steal scraps in the middle of the night. Once they're here they'll be back every night."

"Raccoons?" whispered Sadler. "The Mother Raccoon. Dear Lord, what did I almost do? I almost failed you once more!"

He was animated for the first time in hours. Evangeline looked pleased until he told her why he was so inspired.

"We must bury Her! She is the mother of all that is holy and wise, I tell you!"

"Reverend, please come ins—"

He was sobbing, laughing hysterically, and stroking the furry body with an obsessive reverence.

"Oh, Gershom," she said under her breath.

"A ceremony," he said more to his wooden cross than to Evangeline. "She must have a ceremony, for we must not fail Her now."

His eyebrows arched as if seeing Evangeline standing there was a surprise. "Summon the congregation. We shall dig Her grave at the foot of our cross."

Evangeline continued staring at him. Her hands wrung a dishtowel, and a single tear slid down her cheek.

"You wretched female; why are you not moving? I shall damn you to hellfire if you don't do as I say. Move!"

Evangeline turned and went back inside. Sadler stomped off toward the barn to retrieve a shovel and pickaxe.

"We must perform the ceremony You deserve," he remarked toward the raccoon carcass upon his return. He raised the pick high and slammed it down as if pounding a railroad spike. The first strike bounced off rock.

There may be no harder soil than the crusts of southwest Texas. Yet, Reverend Sadler seemed desperate to finish the task of digging the raccoon's grave. Occasionally he'd pause to take a swig from a water bucket Evangeline provided. Each water break coincided with him stroking the dead animal.

No one came to help or to participate in the funeral, though he hardly noticed. Hours passed, stars twinkled, and cabin lanterns were doused. None of it registered in his obsessed mind, and his digging continued as he muttered the One-Hundred-Fourth Psalm.

Reverend Sadler filled in the grave as dawn broke. He was too exhausted to say even a few words to send the animal's soul on its spiritual journey. Sadler slumped against his beloved cross, and the moment passed as if the raccoon was a dead varmint being dropped down a hole.

The lightning bolt which came from a cloudless sky to strike at the apex of the cross was as miraculous and ominous as anything ever printed in the Bible. Some would say the jolt killed Gershom Sadler, although his body continued to exist for several more days. In truth, the lightning, coming as if from a divine finger, merely punctuated the story of his life. For something else entirely had already broken his heart.

CHAPTER EIGHT

"Callie, your lighter!" bellowed Cleft from the carousel platform. He was currently holding Reverend Sadler under the shoulders as he passed the dead man's unbending legs down to Errol, but they'd paused upon realizing Callie was mesmerized and oblivious to the still-lit flame in her hand.

Callie blinked, seemingly surprised to see Cleft and Errol holding the frozen mummy aloft. The lighter blistered her finger, and she dropped it beside her lawn chair as the cigarette she'd meant to light fell from her lips and bounced off her chest.

Cleft sprang off the carousel to check Callie's hand.

"Are you burned?"

She shooed him back and squinted as if to regain emotional balance.

"I thought I'd been punished when He took my husband," she murmured to no one in particular. "I let myself believe I was forgiven when Sophie was born. But then she left, too, so what do I know?"

Callie paused to pull another cigarette out of a pack, changed her mind, and pushed it back in with her fingertip.

"She's back."

"Sophie's here!?" said Cleft, his voice an octave higher than he would've preferred.

"But she'll leave again and take a chunk of my heart when she goes."

Her eyes settled on the blue-tinged corpse. "He never lets it end."

Errol was still holding the Reverend at the knees, with the embalmed head and shoulders propped on the platform. Callie realized he was waiting for some direction.

"Reverend Sadler lives in the barn," she said. "You'll need to get him back inside the freezer before he thaws."

Cleft kept looking back and forth between Callie, Reverend Sadler, and the casket lying open atop a flatbed pushcart, trying to understand Callie's cryptic message.

"Can't have him thawin' out, I reckon," offered Errol in his most official lawman's voice.

•   •   •

That afternoon Toribio plated a slab of meatloaf ordered by Commissioner Pastal and stared over the counter at booth number four. A taciturn couple sat in the booth with Commissioner Pastal, and everything about their presence worried Toribio. He spooned green beans onto the plate and dinged the bell to send it out.

"That's them?" asked Callie. Toribio wiped his counter and nodded.

The two strangers wore dark-gray business suits. They sat on the same side of the booth opposite the commissioner, so close together their shoulders appeared attached. Neither looked like they appreciated anything offered on the menu, and the man kept flipping his over as if new choices might appear on the back.

"The Commissioner keeps looking at me," said Callie.

"I saw," said Toribio in a burst of dialogue.

"It's not good, I think."

Toribio clicked his tongue in agreement.

Sheriff Errol Clanton walked in. He tipped his hat to the employees and customers, and a waitress sauntered off to get his sweet tea and put in his regular order: chicken-fried Frontier Keith steak, toast with double butter, iceberg lettuce salad—no tomatoes—with Thousand Island, extra toast.

The Sheriff pulled up a chair to Commissioner Pastal's booth table and gave a friendly hello to the two sitting to his left. Neither returned his greeting.

"Sheriff, thank you for meeting us," said Pastal.

"What can I do you for you, Your Honor?"

"Let me first introduce Ms. Jones and Mr. Smith with the Office of Internal Logistics," said Commissioner Pastal.

The sheriff moved to shake hands, realized neither of the newcomers offered theirs, and put his hand back down. "Nice to meet you."

"Thank you," said Ms. Jones.

"Excuse me, but do you have a vegetarian menu?" Mr. Smith called out to Callie as she walked by. Callie snorted and kept going.

"Sheriff," said Commissioner Pastal, "Elixir Springs is being considered for a high-level government project. I'm under instructions to maintain a level of secrecy about this, so I'll have to ask you to keep this under your hat."

"All rightee," replied Errol.

"Basically, we're going to need your assistance in streamlining the process so the project can move forward."

"I don't follow," said Errol, who, to be fair, could not possibly have followed.

"There's a chance Elixir Springs could land on the map," said Pastal. "We can make a big splash in this state, maybe worldwide."

"What kind of splash?"

"Not sure what I'll find appealing on this menu," whispered Mr. Smith to Ms. Jones.

"That's what I'm saying," said Commissioner Pastal. "I'm obliged not to say much just yet."

"Sir," said Errol. "You keep saying 'we.' Who is with you for all the splashin'?"

"That's one of those things I'm not allowed to say," said Commissioner Pastal. "But we need to know if you're on board."

"They have a chef salad," suggested Ms. Jones. "You can just have them leave off the ham and turkey."

"On board with what?" asked Errol.

"With the project!" replied an increasingly agitated Commissioner Pastal.

"Well, gawdang, of course I'm on board with the project," replied Errol. He was at least savvy enough to know when he was being a burr under the saddle, even if he didn't know why.

"Excellent," said Commissioner Pastal. "So, what we need to know is how long does a person have after you serve an eviction notice before they are required to vacate a domicile?"

The mystery deepened for Errol, but he wasn't about to stop the conversation with another question.

"Thirty days unless there's an emergency clause."

"What is an emergency clause?"

"I hope they get my order right," whispered Mr. Smith.

"Say, for instance, you've got your folks ruinin' a piece of property due to operating a moonshine still or a meth lab, or say you've got your folks partyin' so much they tear up a place. Well, you'd have reason to operate under an emergency eviction clause. Who is it getting evicted and I can tell you better what your options are?"

"We're considering eviction notices going out to the trailer park," replied Pastal in a conspiratorial whisper. It was the whisper that made Toribio perk up and listen as he bussed the table behind them.

"Who are you looking at evicting from the trailer park?" asked Errol.

At this, Mr. Smith and Ms. Jones ceased all concerns with his salad and paid rapt attention.

"Everybody," said Commissioner Pastal.

"Everybody? You mean everybody livin' there right now has to move?"

"Everyone must leave," confirmed Ms. Jones.

"Why?" asked Toribio who had paused while wiping chili off a menu.

An "oh crap" silence settled over the table. Errol had been wondering the same thing, but he was glad he didn't have to ask. Commissioner Pastal tried to glare Toribio into looking away, but Toribio stood there as a drip from his wipe rag slid down his hand and slopped onto the linoleum.

"Look," said Commissioner Pastal, "Elixir Springs has a chance to move into a fast track of business opportunity and technological advancement. We're not talking about making you or anybody else homeless. I assure you I'll find you a place to live. You have my word."

Toribio leaned over and rested his knuckles on their table.

"We have to be thinking about the future," continued Pastal, whose voice cracked like a teenager at his first dance. "And to accomplish that, certain sacrifices are in order. That property where the trailers are parked could become very enticing to the powers that be in the next few weeks. Those powers will need room for their own folks."

Callie drifted over with Errol's lunch on a tray and stood behind Toribio.

Pastal tore bits off his napkin, and everyone around the table could see his fingers trembling. "People with a certain skill set, you understand; levels of experience and training beyond what waitresses and carnival workers can manage. You understand? This is for the greater good."

Toribio looked over his shoulder at Callie.

"I heard," said Callie in a voice which conveyed her business acumen, her world-weariness, and her medieval ferocity. "What I haven't heard is why and how."

Pastal cleared his throat. "There had been a number of issues…concerns about squatter's rights—"

"Workplace safety breaches," said Ms. Jones.

Mr. Smith tossed his menu on the table with a grimace. "Health code violations, I'd assume."

Pastal groaned but tried to stay on topic. "And we mustn't forget what a grand opportunity—"

"Health code violations?" interrupted Callie. "Hmm. I guess if there's health code violations, I can't serve this." Callie tipped the tray holding Errol's dinner, allowing his favorite meal to smash on the floor.

Errol pouted out his bottom lip, for he'd been salivating all during the conversation. Everyone stared at the shattered plates, the splattered gravy, and the mélange of lettuce and fried meat, knowing full well war had just been declared.

• • •

Commissioner Pastal was a front porch guitar player, sitting in with bands during election seasons. In accounting school he'd formed a folk duo called *Two Late for Coffee*, and there'd been a time when he hoped to tour. This dream involved a van, a different guitar for every song, horny groupies—he thought he might try that marijuana while out on the road. Of course, he'd chosen a different path, but during times of stress he often grabbed a six-string to take the edge off.

Tension was about to bore a hole in his gut. He'd talked Sophie Wind into a project which could explode in his face. Pastal knew she was already in Elixir Springs, but she hadn't called him yet.

Making matters worse, more people were finding out about Gershom Sadler's "preserved" condition. Pastal's neck hurt, and he felt thirsty every minute of the day. He had already sweated through four shirts since the fiasco at Callie's restaurant. The man was frazzled.

Thanks to a deal Pastal had made with Callie years earlier, he'd been able to grow his original little butcher shop into thriving businesses across the county. Entrepreneurship was as comfortable to him as playing his guitar. Now, though, he'd come to a project leagues outside his comfort zone. He knew nothing of science, and it had occurred to him too many times that he'd trusted the word of Mr. Smith and Ms. Jones regarding the huge telescope and super-collider project. He'd brought in Sophie Wind as a partner because the challenge was colossal, and he needed powerhouse help. The thought of failure and a mysterious flutter in his chest made him fear a stroke was imminent.

Pastal was sitting on the lid of his commode because he liked the acoustics in his bathroom. Plus, he didn't want any of his constituents to come knocking on his door with gripes about this bridge or that traffic light. He wanted to be alone, play his guitar, and drink. A pearl-white Gibson Les Paul with gold tuners was perched on his lap, and a pitcher of Everclear margarita was on the sink within straw's reach of his lips. He'd placed a small footstool under his ankles to keep his knees higher so his legs wouldn't fall asleep.

He'd been playing in that position for two hours, glancing out the window above his vanity at the green and blue neon sign for Pastal's Fur City off in the distance. The guitar strumming and grain alcohol worked their magic. Any responsibility he felt to raise Elixir Springs from a scrubby piece of nowhere marked with a town limit sign into a place known around the world had ebbed, replaced by a sleepy calm.

Pastal drooled, and a lustrous string of saliva leaked down his cheek and slid across the fret board as he crooned, "I-gotna peemull, neesy fffeeling..." He burped and snorted, convinced

Glenn Frey's classic had never sounded so good. His eyelids drooped.

Pastal paused his song long enough to sip the drink, but his hands remained on his guitar ready to strum the next F#m. His lips stretched like two octopus arms seeking out the straw, latching on like a commercial milking machine. He emptied the pitcher with three last gulps.

Pastal smiled goofily at the illuminated beaver mascot above his Fur City sign and slurred out the next line. "I know-ooh mon't et-me..."

Pastal sobbed, dropped the guitar, and melted off the commode. A discordant bong from the guitar bridge striking bathtub porcelain was the last thing he heard before his brain switched to insensible.

·   ·   ·

Callie couldn't sleep after the incident at the Wagon Wheel, so she grabbed milk and a cookie jar and drifted out to the barn. She sat on the old pickup bench seat and stared at the door leading to where Cleft and Errol had stored her adoptive father.

"Sophie wants to bring her circus here, and now Pastal plans to kick everybody out."

She dunked a pecan shortbread cookie in her milk, but she waited to take a bite as she considered the equation. "Are they in this together?"

Milk dripped off the cookie onto her knee, so she nibbled an edge. "Sophie will never let off; never has when she wants something."

She scowled at the closed door as she took a bite. "What have you gone and done, Reverend?"

It was dawn when she stretched out on the bench seat and slept, waking several hours later to the sounds of the park already open for the day. She popped up and yanked open the storage door.

"Time you show me what they're up to," she said to the casket. "Up for a little ride?"

It took great effort to hoist and slide the casket onto the pushcart without assistance, but she was eventually able to roll Sadler out of the barn. She wheeled him through the back entrance of the amusement park and pushed him onto a pathway populated by a light morning crowd, all the while speaking through the casket lid. "Are you interested in going on some rides or just seeing the sights?"

Guests noticed her pushing the coffin. Most thought it was a quirky sideshow, though one woman squeaked when she realized what she was seeing. Two teenage boys asked if they could ride on the lid.

"Momma, what are you doing?" said a wide-eyed Sophie. She'd walked into Callie's path with a hung-over Commissioner Pastal.

"Speak of the devil!" Callie said, addressing the casket.

"Callie, what are you trying to pull now?" asked Commissioner Pastal, who winced from the effort.

Callie ignored him and continued speaking, all the while staring at her daughter.

"You tore us apart," she said, her voice raspy and her eyes glistening.

Sophie held out her hands as if trying to talk a jumper off a bridge. "Momma, maybe you should sit down."

"You turned her against me!" Callie shouted at the coffin. She toppled the pushcart, causing the casket to slide off. The lid struck the ground and burst open, and a frozen Gershom Sadler rolled out onto the walkway. Guests screamed. Commissioner Pastal groaned. The irreverent teenagers were awestruck.

Callie leaped on Reverend Sadler and punched him blow after blow about his ears and mouth.

"Momma, stop!"

Callie howled and sobbed so hard she couldn't catch her breath.

Toribio rushed through the crowd and hugged her around the shoulders.

"It's okay," he soothed. "Callie, you're okay. Just look at me."

One man who'd stepped off the Grand Teton Roller Coaster shouted, "She's a feisty little nut!" which drew a laugh from the gathering crowd.

"That'll do," said Toribio, and the rude man disappeared into the hubbub.

"We've got to get this cleaned up," said Commissioner Pastal.

Sophie took slow backward steps until she butted against a sidewalk railing. She stared open-mouthed, seeing in her mother a side she'd never witnessed before. Here on the ground before her was a woman who appeared delusional and irrational. Sophie's face went grim with resolve. She had discovered the plan which would allow her to gain control of the property.

It was too bad her mother would hate it so much.

CHAPTER NINE

On the night Callie went into labor with Sophie, Toribio and a few carnies picked up extra work helping to clean up after the Grateful Dead concert. Toribio had battened the carnival rides at closing time and walked across the racetrack to get his assignment. He arrived at the job as Callie's amniotic puddle spread across the stage.

"Sir, can you...?" she grunted as Toribio came into view. She was bent at the waist and holding onto a concert speaker for support.

Toribio looked around to see who she was talking to, and he realized he was the only person around. He leaped onto the stage and grabbed a stool from behind the drummer's kit. Her clumsiness and his nervousness made her sitting onto the swiveling chair an acrobatic feat. She laughed despite the pain, and he grinned at their plight.

Errol came driving around the corner. His pickup truck bed was brimming with trash bags full of plastic cups, wrappers and beer cans from the concert. Toribio and Callie looked up at Errol with wild eyes.

"Well, gawdang!" Errol managed.

Callie had a contraction, causing her to shove back against the pain with her right heel. This had the effect of rotating her on the drummer's swivel seat. Toribio ran in a tiny orbit to keep her from falling off before he was able to stop her spin.

"Is that a baby comin'?" asked Errol with his head leaning out of the truck window. "Want I should go call an ambulance or somethin'?"

"Can't afford that. Maybe a ride?"

"Well sure, sure," said Errol. "You betcha."

Callie moaned like a calving elk.

Errol's eyes darted toward Toribio. "Or maybe you should take her. You can borrow my truck."

Errol fumbled for his keys as he bolted from his truck cab. Toribio helped Callie off the stage.

"Don't you worry about nothin'," Errol said, while standing ten feet back.

Toribio guided Callie up into the truck cab, wondering if it was acceptable to support her by the arm.

"Buckle up for safety and all," said Errol.

Toribio vaulted to the driver's seat, waved to Errol, and yanked the column shifter into first. The back tires of the truck furrowed the horse racetrack as he sped from the venue.

Callie glanced over at the man who'd volunteered to drive her to the hospital. She felt no fear of him, but she did feel guilty he was going so far out of his way for her. "I really appreciate this."

Toribio gripped the wheel tighter.

"I'm Callie," she said right before a contraction and groan.

Toribio found himself afflicted in the presence of this beautiful woman with an overwhelming shyness about his English competency. Thus, at the moment she most needed him to be precise and clear, he lapsed into Spanish.

"Toribio," he replied, though this was drowned out as she groaned and he changed gears. "*Soy un cocinero*," to further explain he was a cook by trade.

"Nice to meet you, Cocinero. I hope they don't—dear Lord, that does not feel good!—dock your pay."

"Oh, *cocinero* isn't my—" but Callie let out a roar of pain.

Toribio's thigh cramped from shoving the accelerator. He further flattened a dead armadillo while sliding around a curve and stared at the corpse from his rearview mirror. The tachometer bounced just under the red, and the truck axles squealed like they were about ready to give up the fight. He harbored concern the wheels would disengage at any moment, and concert trash flew off the tail bed like it was snowing. Toribio asked for every horse under the hood of Errol's pickup, reaching over to offer a comforting pat on Callie's shoulder from time to time.

Callie's labor pains were coming closer together, and Toribio was trying to decide if he should pull over. He worked to remember anything about delivering a baby. Callie groaned through contractions and tried to keep up a conversation after each one.

"Do you sing?" she asked. "Maybe if we sing something it will take my mind off...arrrgh!"

Callie's heels were propped on Errol's dashboard. The plastic heater vent snapped from the pressure, and Toribio was worried she might crack the windshield.

"That is...that is not fun," she mumbled.

It had been less than a minute since her last arrrgh, and Toribio knew he'd run out of time. He spotted a parking lot ahead and made the decision.

"*Tenemos que parar*," he muttered, forgetting to tell Callie in English they needed to stop.

"Is that a song?" she panted.

Toribio pulled into the parking lot of a closed gas station and leaped out of the driver's side.

"What are we doing?" she asked. This was followed by another arrrgh.

"*Esperas ahí!*" he called over his shoulder, but remembering to translate, "You wait there," as he dashed to a newspaper machine by the front door.

"I'll wait right…oh my loooord!"

Toribio had remembered from military training long ago that newspaper was clean enough to use as a makeshift wound dressing; something about the heat and chemicals involved in printing.

"What are you doing?" demanded Callie from the truck cab.

"I need cloths for to catch the baby!"

He searched his pocket for a dime to buy the previous day's paper from the vending machine.

"He needs cloths," Callie groaned to her stomach.

Toribio dashed back across the dark parking lot with his newspaper prize in hand. He found Callie grimacing and holding her breath, staring down at a baby's head crowning between her thighs.

Toribio jerked the passenger door open, twisted her toward him, and stuffed the paper beneath her bottom.

"Breathe, *chica*," Toribio coached. "You have to breathe, and—*como se dice*?—push…push when I tell you to push."

Callie braced her left heel on the windshield above the dashboard and her right on the inside frame of the truck door.

"You can do this."

"I can do…oh my God, I can't do this!

"*Ahora*." said Toribio. "Now. Push now!"

Callie pushed like hell. "Ahhgahh, puma-nah-booh!"

Toribio stayed focused through her howls. He wiped the baby's nostrils with his shirtsleeve as he cradled its head and supported the little shoulders during the next push.

"Foofamah duh!"

Toribio caught the baby with the paper and rubbed her tiny body with a shop towel from the truck floorboard. Moments later, the infant took her first breath.

"I did that!" Callie blurted, followed by a prolonged laugh of relief and sobs of joy.

Toribio sacrificed a shoelace to tie off the umbilical cord before cutting the baby free with his pocketknife. He handed Callie her baby, still wrapped with newspaper. He took a step back, marveling at the quiet loveliness which so replaced the chaos mere seconds ago.

"We may go," he suggested after a few minutes.

Callie looked up from the baby long enough to nod. Toribio wiped his hands on his jeans as he climbed back in the driver's side to carry on. He almost worked up the nerve to sing an old Mexican folk song as he drove the fawning mother and cooing baby to the nearest hospital.

. . .

Toribio shocked the triage nurse when he carried Callie in from the truck as she held the newspaper-swaddled baby. Toribio followed directions to which room and laid the new mother and child onto a bed.

He edged toward the door once she was settled, unsure of his role but mesmerized. Medical staff moved all around him, and he did his best to keep his back to a wall and out of their way. He felt he'd overstayed, and he waved around the medical staff to tell Callie goodbye.

"Don't go," she said. "I mean, if you need to leave, I understand, but I'd like it if you'd stay."

Toribio took a chair across the room. He'd stay as long as she wanted.

. . .

Hours later Toribio awoke in the chair to see Callie supporting her baby in a little bedside bassinet filled with warm water. The child was paddling perfect baby legs and arms, frog-like, and

Callie splashed warm water over her belly. The baby smiled, and Callie looked over her shoulder at Toribio who wiped his eyes.

A nurse came in to check on mother and baby. She turned on the transistor radio in the room and Callie hummed to David Partridge and his family singing, "I Think I Love You."

"*Una princesa*," murmured Toribio when the nurse offered for him to hold the swaddled infant. "She is a princess."

"I named her Sophie," said Callie. "It means wisdom."

He put his face closer to the sleeping child and whispered, "The wise *Princesa* Sophie."

Toribio handed Sophie back to her mother. He felt like it was appropriate he go, but he could barely stand the thought of never seeing this woman or her child again. He looked around the room until he spied a notepad. The pad advertised a stool softener, but it was all he had to write an address where she could find him later. His hand trembled as he handed the page to Callie.

"If you need..." Toribio paused, mortified he'd thought she might want to contact him.

"Thank you, Cocinero."

Toribio thought once again about correcting her on his name, but Callie was snuggling Sophie too tenderly for him to bring up something so selfish.

•   •   •

"Did she have it?" Errol asked as soon as Toribio arrived back at the carnival. Toribio nodded an exhausted yes, hoping Errol wouldn't want more details.

"So, give me the details," said Errol, whose energy was bolstered by having gotten paid for his part of the cleanup duties and the fact he'd half-finished a bottle of blueberry wine.

"I pulled over to catch it," said Toribio.

"You delivered the baby!?" exclaimed Errol in undisguised admiration. Toribio chuckled in answer.

"Well, gawdang! I mean, that's like some real hero-ness!"

Toribio sat with an un-heroic oomph on the stage and thought it might be nice to lay back and go to sleep.

"Got us a bottle to celebrate," said Errol, who handed Toribio the blueberry wine.

Toribio eyed the bottle for a moment, and he thought back to the woman and child with whom he'd shared his life's most intimate moment.

"*Que dimonios*," he murmured as he took the bottle in a "what the hell, I'm a hero" manner and tilted it back like a leather *bota*.

• • •

Commissioner Pastal was startled one evening upon leaving his butcher shop to see Evangeline waiting outside for him. It was about to rain, and her entire person blended like camouflage with the overcast gloom.

"The reverend has need of your services." She left before the Commissioner said a word in reply, her message delivered.

Reverend Sadler was dying, that much Commissioner Pastal knew as Evangeline showed him into the bedroom later. The entry wound in Sadler's left forearm where the lightning had speared his body was gangrenous. The smell mixed with the ammonia of his incontinence and the stench of his quivering bowels was almost enough to send the Commissioner skittering away.

Reverend Sadler lay naked, his soiled sheets bunched. Pastal's first reaction was to feign intense interest in a ceiling corner of the room. A rash was developing between Sadler's thighs, his eyes were rheumy, and his hair was matted. Here before Commissioner Pastal lay a pre-corpse, magnificent in that it held onto life when it should have long since gone into general organ failure.

Evangeline scowled from the bedroom door at the dying man. Her pupils were the size of nickels, her brow was furrowed, and her hands were balled into trembling fists.

"Pastal? That you?" Reverend Sadler murmured from the mattress.

"Yes, sir, it's me."

Evangeline turned in a huff and strode across the hall to another bedroom.

"Welcome…Your Honor," said Reverend Sadler with a smirk Pastal didn't notice.

"Thank you, Reverend. I'm honored to be your public servant. How may I help you?"

"I imagine there's not a damn thing you can do for me. I'll be in heaven by the time you're home and eating your dinner."

Pastal opened his mouth as if to debate this point, but he said nothing. The reverend smiled at Pastal's good grace and continued.

"I'd like to dictate my last will and testament to you."

Evangeline groaned from the room across the hall, and Pastal glanced over his shoulder to see her throwing clothing into a tan leather suitcase on the floor.

"Sir, I'm not an attorney. I'd be happy—"

"You'll do. That woman who was here earlier—can't recall her name just now…"

Evangeline shrieked. "Good lord, Gershom! You can't even remember my name?"

"…laid out quill, ink and parchment for you. Won't take long, and I'd like someone in an official capacity to take this down and bear witness."

Pastal glanced at a little bedside table where there was, in fact, a real feather quill and a bottle of ink. A rough square of parchment awaited dictation.

Pastal took a seat next to the bed. He dipped the tip of the feather and took a position of readiness.

"Pretty simple," croaked Reverend Sadler. "Here before Lord God Almighty…" He paused, because Pastal wasn't writing.

"This is it. This is the part I want you to write down."

"Oh, sorry," said Pastal who obligingly transcribed the preamble. The reverend went on about his lifetime service to God and his unending quest to vanquish heathen-ness and devil worship in this world "rife with sinners, whores, heretics, tax-men, federal agents, women who wear makeup, people who manufacture makeup, men who lay with farm animals—and sinners."

Pastal saw a dresser drawer fly past the door frame across the hall and smash on the bedroom wall. He concentrated despite the tumult, splotching here, smearing there. Reverend Sadler dictated in a manner which made Pastal believe the man had gone over this in his mind dozens of times.

To Evangeline, Gershom Sadler left a decent sum of cash to be extracted from a metal box hidden in the barn. To the wayward adopted Callie went the property…sort of. Reverend Sadler finished and settled back into his grimy pillow with a sigh reserved for the last day of one's life.

"Stole ninety-four dollars from my jar the day she left," he declared.

Commissioner Pastal paused in his scribing, and it became evident the old man was growing sleepy as his lids drifted downward and his speech slurred to little more than a mutter. Just when Pastal thought Reverend Sadler had fallen asleep the old man pointed a trembling finger across the room. The commissioner followed the direction until he spotted a small wooden box on top of a dresser drawer.

"The box? You want the box?"

Commissioner Pastal jumped up to fetch it. He tried to hand it to the minister, but it was apparent the old man didn't have the strength. Gingerly, Pastal opened the carved lid and held it low enough for Sadler to see the contents.

Reverend Sadler rifled his index finger through the items: two flint arrowheads, a Goldwater for President button, a name badge from Cashway Discount Lumber bearing Gershom Sadler's name over a blue ribbon declaring him Employee of the Month. His finger came to rest on a pewter pocket watch etched with a boot in a stirrup. Pastal helped him lift the watch from the box and opened the latch when Sadler indicated he needed help.

The slamming and banging in the next bedroom ended with Evangeline re-entering Reverend Sadler's room. She stood with the suitcase in one hand, the fury on her face now replaced with sorrow as she whispered, "Then Athaliah tore her clothes and cried, 'Treason! Treason!'"

Sadler's voice cracked as he answered, "Second Kings, 11:14."

Reverend Sadler pulled his milky gaze from Evangeline to stare at a yellowed photo attached within the case lid of the watch. Pastal craned his head to see the image, a college-aged woman with a pleasant face and a faraway look.

Commissioner Pastal looked over his shoulder at Evangeline. "Is this you?"

Evangeline's eyes clouded dark once more and her upper lip snarled as she replied, "My sister...the dentist." She turned and clomped out the front door, slamming it in a way Pastal surmised she meant never to return.

Reverend Sadler seemed not to have noticed her departure. After more than a minute of silent contemplation, Sadler grunted and clapped the watch shut. He fixed his stare back on Pastal. "That Jezebel...she'll circle that cross with me. By God, she will. You make sure of it."

CHAPTER TEN

Gershom Sadler had spilled out of his casket onto the footpath right about where Commissioner Pastal had once taken the deathbed dictation for Sadler's last will and testament. This sent a shudder along his spine and a stifled yelp to the back of his throat.

Callie stared at Pastal and laughed through her tears at his obvious anxiety. She looked over at Sophie with a smirk and abandoned Reverend Sadler and the others right in the middle of the footpath. She sauntered away on Toribio's arm as if nothing unusual had occurred.

Errol and Cleft came running to help, and Cleft almost tripped over the body upon seeing Sophie. He tipped an imaginary hat with the feigned cool air of a man who'd almost tripped over a corpse. Sophie was deadpan as she turned to wade away through the gathering crowd.

Cleft and Errol bent and picked Reverend Sadler off the ground to set him back on the pushcart.

"How many times you think a fellow can thaw out before he starts to go bad?" asked Errol as they wheeled the pastor back to his freezer unit.

·   ·   ·

Callie ambled into her restaurant and drifted past the counter into the dance hall area.

"Callie?" Toribio said, but she didn't answer. Instead, she moved over to the jukebox and dug in her pockets for coins. She placed a quarter in the machine, enough for five song choices, but she chose just one: "Crazy," by Patsy Cline.

The piano solo began, and Callie swayed in time to the music. Toribio moved around her as if in a narrow aisle of porcelain figurines, worried anything he did to break her reverie might break her as well.

Callie placed her hand on the back of his neck and pulled his arm around her waist, rocking gently until his rhythm matched her own.

•   •   •

Sophie formulated an idea for removing her mother from the property, but she hadn't trusted the competence or discretion of either of the two attorneys in Elixir Springs County. She never held important meetings over the phone, preferring instead to see people's eyes when she discussed critical topics. Thus, she'd flown to Austin to meet with her corporate attorneys on the same day she witnessed her mother attack the late Reverend Sadler.

She and her staff met at Sophie's primary residence, as she preferred this to meeting in the corporate offices downtown. Sophie's home sat atop a tall hill on the west side of Austin. It had been constructed from the natural white rock provided by the area, and it boasted large, covered patio areas, lush gardens, and seven fireplaces. Sophie's favorite feature, and the reason she'd bought the property in the first place, was the view from her back patio. Austin lay before her in full glory. She loved to sit in her hot tub or pool and stare out at the lights of the state capital, the University of Texas tower, and the reflections from a thousand buildings off the river running through the city.

This afternoon she was all business, though, and her team of attorneys and advisers could feel her determination as they sat around a ten-chair conference table in a room she'd added to the house for such meetings. That driving obsession when she had an idea was something they'd all seen in her before. It was their job to make her vision become reality, and her agenda for the day's conference had become clear within the first three minutes.

"So, do you all think this is a workable plan?" she asked of them.

"The statute is clear, and you make a good case," answered one attorney.

"It would pave the way for the improvements you've suggested," said another.

Sophie felt gratified until her eyes turned toward her oldest adviser, a man she'd met in the early days of her career. A retired minister, he was the only person in the room besides herself who was not an attorney. She trusted him because he had an irritating habit of telling her when he thought she was wrong.

"I think you're wrong," the wizened man said.

Sophie sighed and resigned herself to listen to his counsel.

"This is the stuff of souls," the old minister cautioned. "You can't un-say or un-do this once you've started, and I'm afraid your mother may never forgive you."

·   ·   ·

Commissioner Pastal picked Sophie up at the Pastal International Airport, which was a quarter mile stretch of gravel road fenced off with barbed wire. The strip was marked with a wind flag bent forty degrees following a hay mower mishap three summers earlier. Pastal watched the private jet landing, marveling at the pilot's skill to put the thing down in so tiny an area bordered by hay fields and livestock.

A flock of emus in a round pen near the runway went into a wing-flapping frenzy when the jet descended, as if the great god of all birds had come to collect their souls. Giant birds tried to climb aboard each other like drowning men vying for the last life ring, and the whole herd ran in frantic circles.

"My mother has lost her mind," Sophie told Pastal as they drove from the small airfield into town.

"She's always been a bit odd."

"No, I mean now she's actually ill. I'm convinced her mind is fragmenting, and we have to take action before it is too late."

"Action like...?"

"Decisive action. She's become a danger to herself. We can't let her get worse."

Pastal rode in quiet understanding as he stared straight ahead through the windshield. He noted the mile upon mile of arid cattle pastures and the distinctive odor of sludge being toiled from the ground by mechanical armies of rust-streaked oil wells. He drove past a one-pump gas station and the Dairy Queen missing the D and y on the front sign. An old dog food processing plant was falling down on its foundation, and a defunct gravel quarry had long ago flooded with bracken spring water. Despite all his efforts, Elixir Springs was dying.

"I wonder sometimes," he muttered. Sophie looked over at him but waited for him to finish his thought. "I wonder about going too far, if I've done things..."

"Commissioner, listen, really listen to me...the idea of transforming this patch of desolation into a commercial and scientific mecca is compelling. The fact Elixir Springs is so dilapidated makes the potential for transition to something alive and vibrant more alluring."

He was emboldened by her enthusiasm and determination. "You're right. I know you are. I just worry."

"There's nothing to worry about. We'll get momma the help she needs, and then we'll set about—how did you phrase it—putting Elixir Springs on the map."

. . .

Callie couldn't remember ever feeling so embarrassed after her tantrum on the footpath earlier in the day. Her head ached, and she was so exhausted she hadn't found the energy to help in the restaurant.

Toribio came to check on her after he finished with the dinner crowd. Surmising the situation, he went into action. Callie sat on her porch swing as Toribio fed her spoonful's of chicken tortilla soup.

Neither spoke, though they both smiled when she slurped. She chuckled as he wiped her mouth with a napkin and offered another spoonful.

"Things are about to start moving fast around here," she said in something of a sigh. Toribio stirred the bowl to collect a chunk of chicken into the spoon.

"Sophie is going to make things happen," Callie continued. "She always has. You know that."

A possum rooted for grubs in brush a few yards away. Both paused to see if they could spot him.

"What if she makes me leave?"

Toribio set the bowl down and fluffed a couch cushion he'd brought outside for her. "You'll come back."

"I'll...come back." A worry line between her eyebrows relaxed as she leaned forward for another spoonful of soup.

. . .

Errol glanced about in awe of the federal courtroom from where he sat in the third row. Thirty-seven immigrants stood shoulder-to-shoulder at the front of the room, and many of them looked out at the friends and family members sitting in the audience.

Toribio was among those standing, a man whose ancestor of the same name had fought and died at the Alamo; a man who'd snuck into this country if only to pursue his dream of travel and adventure; a man who'd been thrust into the role of Samaritan and who chose kindness over self; a man who loved a woman so passionately he'd foresworn all else to be near her; and a man who would on this day take an oath of allegiance to the United States of America.

There had been a number of false starts over the years, resulting in patchwork visas and extensions. It helped that Elixir Springs County wasn't on any federal agent's radar, and Toribio did nothing to attract attention. There'd been hundreds of late-night study sessions for the citizenship test, annual off-season sojourns back to Mexico, and grammatically pockmarked, albeit passionate, letters from Errol on sheriff's department letterhead. The time had arrived.

"Please raise your right hand and repeat after me," instructed the administrator swearing in the new citizens. "I hereby declare, on oath…"

The group repeated the words which had come to mean so much.

"…so help me God," they all confirmed one minute and one new life later.

Errol was the first to stand and applaud, tears streaming down his face. Toribio grinned out at him, and Errol kept clapping long after everyone else had stopped. All the way home Toribio thought about telling Callie what he'd accomplished, but he decided it might seem too much like bragging.

•   •   •

Errol dropped Toribio off at the Wagon Wheel and surprised him with a congratulatory hug before dashing off to go meet Cleft.

"What is it you wanted to talk to me about?" asked Cleft when Errol picked him up in front of the ticket booth.

"It's a matter I'd like to discuss in private."

"We are in private."

"I mean, not around the park. Prying eyes, and all."

Cleft looked around to see if there were any prying eyes directed at the police truck, but he said nothing as Errol drove to the mesa overlooking Elixir Springs. Errol's mood was somber, and the radio station was playing Loretta Lynn.

"Saw something real inspirin' today," he told Cleft.

"Oh yeah?"

"Real, real inspirin'. It's made me want to…I don't know…be better, I guess."

"I'm not following you."

"It's just…"

Cleft could see his throat muscles writhing, as if Errol was working up the strength to say his thoughts.

"I don't want nothin' to do with those evictions, but I know they're gonna make me serve them."

The old truck smelled of Corn Nuts and Big Red, and it hadn't been dusted in years. Errol fiddled with loose bullets and a pair of handcuffs in the console tray between them. He looked like his heart was breaking.

"Everybody has to leave if they get their way. And now that Sophie's back, they're gonna get their way for sure. Ain't right."

"You're in a position where you can make them stop."

"No, I'm not," said Errol in a voice more sage and tired than Cleft had ever heard from him. "I'm not the man to do it. You know I'm right. I'm tired. I just want a simple life like I had workin' for Callie. She already told me I can have my job back."

Cleft knew Errol had thrown in the towel, and part of him knew it was the right thing to do. Powerful players had descended onto their little town, and Errol wasn't up to the challenge. Cleft realized this quirky, awkward man had become his friend over the years, and he spoke to him in a voice grown husky with the weight of it all.

"Remember that time you arrested those fellows making crystal meth in the projection booth at the movie theater, and everybody was so mad because you shut the place down for three weeks? You did the right thing, Errol. You did."

Errol's eyes were shiny and his nose sniffling. "It was a cruddy movie."

Cleft chuckled. "You did a lot of good. That's what matters. A lot of good."

Errol stared at the Sheriff badge in his hand. "Here. It should always have been yours anyway. I was just fillin' in until you were ready again."

Cleft's face screwed in bewilderment. "Errol, I don't think…"

Errol smiled and pinned it on his friend's chest. Cleft looked down at it, and it took several seconds before it all registered in his mind. He sat a little taller when it did.

Errol smiled through a sniffle. "Somethin' right just happened."

Cleft looked up at Errol and nodded grim agreement. Just like that, he was a lawman again.

CHAPTER ELEVEN

Commissioner Pastal had remained sitting beside Reverend Sadler for half an hour after the old man's last breath, now so many years ago. Pastal had not wanted to move, as if the reverend might awaken and sit up. The commissioner replaced the quill beside the last will and testament and gave Reverend Sadler a light pat on his shoulder.

"Rest now. I'll make sure it gets done."

Pastal made the appropriate arrangements with the coroner and funeral home and set about the duty of locating Callie. This wasn't an easy task, as Pastal had no way of knowing she'd married a soldier and taken his last name. For that matter, he didn't know Callie had been pregnant or traveled half the country since leaving Elixir Springs.

What Pastal did know was he paid employees at Pastal's Meats and Taxidermy, and each one had to file income tax returns. Pastal also knew the county clerk, Carol Ann Hathaway, and that Carol Ann had a penchant for center-cut tenderloin and an affable personality. It took Carol Ann one phone call placed to her cousin, Lorene Anne Glover, who worked for the Internal Revenue Service, to discover the identity of one Callie Wind, whose last known address was a pay-by-the-week motel in Texarkana.

Lorene Anne was able to provide a phone number in exchange for two racks of ribs shipped in dry ice to her office in Dallas.

The original conversation with Callie had been difficult. The phone line was scratchy, plus Callie had no intention of returning to Elixir Springs. She was breast feeding Sophie at the time, supporting the baby in her left arm and balancing the phone on her shoulder.

"Why?" she asked when Pastal suggested she return to Elixir Springs.

"Because you need to make proper arrangements for your father and lay him to rest."

"I'm pretty busy. I just had a baby. I don't mean to sound cold-hearted, but you know Gershom Sadler wasn't my real father. He and I weren't on the best of terms."

"I'm sorry—the phone—I couldn't hear that last part."

"I said I'm not coming. You handle it."

"There is a will. The law requires that it be read. Maybe this is a way for you to say goodbye. As I said before, the county will pay all expenses."

She paused long enough that he added:

"He left something for you. Be worth your while to come on over."

Callie paused, thinking about how once again Reverend Sadler was hell bent on controlling her. At the same time, she wondered if he'd left anything which would allow her to better raise and support Sophie. The baby had fallen asleep at the breast.

Callie looked out the phone booth toward the efficiency apartment she was renting. It was tidy but tiny, and as flat in color as had been her room on the military base. She lived within walls of gray accented by ash-toned appliances and charcoal furniture framed in hues of slate.

The neighbors frightened her. One fellow always wore military fatigues and shot an air pistol at a picture of Ho Chi Minh while blotto on Wild Turkey every night after his shift at the wheel factory. An elderly man who claimed to be blind knocked on her door every morning. He stared dead on at her milk-enhanced bosom as she read his mail.

College kids were selling dope in the apartment above hers, and their criminal enterprise was festering out of control. Two tough looking men had pounded on their door the night before, and the angry men flattened the tires on the college kid's cars when they failed to answer. Profanities shouted from the parking lot went unanswered by those cowering in the apartment above. A promise to come back and "finish this" was made.

No, Callie decided. This was not where she wanted to raise her precious little girl.

The next morning Callie was on a bus home feeling a mix of frustration, mild nostalgia, and anticipation. She sat in the front seat, causing the driver consternation each time she fed Sophie.

Callie read and caught catnaps while the baby slept. She considered the possibility this was all a colossal joke, something her adoptive father would love to pull on her as one last jab from hell.

Sophie was all that mattered. Callie looked down at the sleeping infant's perfect feathery eyelashes and her perfect rosebud mouth, wondering how she was going to care for her.

"Lunch," called the driver as he yanked the Greyhound into a gravel lot next to a roadside diner. "Thirty minutes," he called out to the four passengers. He helped Callie off the bus and hurried off to order first.

Callie ordered coffee in a booth right by the door, though she declined a menu when the waitress greeted her.

"Sweetie, you've got to eat so you can keep feeding little precious there," said the waitress a few minutes later as she set a turkey sandwich and a tall glass of milk in front of Callie. The woman was mid-forties with dark and a Jane Russell figure. The nametag pinned to her powder-blue uniform read, "Sunny."

Without invitation Sunny slipped in the booth across from Callie and sipped her own cup of coffee. Callie liked the sandwich, and this made Sunny smile.

"Where you heading?" Sunny asked as she added more cream to her coffee.

"Elixir Springs," replied Callie with a hint of embarrassment.

"What are your plans once you get there? You have family?"

"I don't know what I'm going to do, except I'm going to take care of my baby."

"I'd say that's about the best plan I ever heard."

The two fell silent, Sunny stirring her coffee and Callie staring at Sophie.

"I was in a movie once," said Sunny. "A real movie called *Paris Blues*. Paul Newman was in it. I played a waitress," she said with a laugh, and Callie joined her. Sophie gurgled, and Callie dabbed her little mouth.

"You should watch it sometime. It comes on TV now and again."

"I'll watch for it. So, what happened after the movie?"

"I fell in love, had three children, and we moved here. He's the supervisor on an okra farm. You know those frozen okra you can buy in a bag? They might come from his farm." Sunny said this with such pride Callie reached out and touched her hand.

Sunny looked around, spying a man at the counter who was signaling for a coffee refill. "It's a good life, and it's the only one I'll need from now on. Once you find peace with that, life is as grand as you want it to be."

Sunny hustled off to refill beverages and slice pies. The bus driver dropped his wadded napkin on his plate and ambled to the cash register. Callie headed to the restroom to change Sophie, so dazed by the conversation with Sunny she didn't recall getting back on the bus.

Had she looked back through the bus window as they rolled away, Callie might have noticed Sunny weaving daisies into her hair, raising her arms as if to take flight, and scampering barefoot into the green meadow beyond.

• • •

Commissioner Pastal met Callie at the bus stop in Elixir Springs. He helped her with a stroller, a diaper bag, and her own small case. For the mother of a small child Callie packed light, though it was also every possession she had in the world. She didn't know if anything would come of this meeting, but she had no plans to return to the efficiency apartment.

The Commissioner made small talk on the way to the courthouse where the will would be read. He complimented the baby, asked Callie if she was all right, and updated her on recent weather activity.

"How have you been since you left our little town?" asked Commissioner Pastal.

"Married, pregnant, widowed, and maternal since I saw you last. So, I'm dandy."

"Can I offer you coffee? I might have muffins."

Callie stared in a "get on with it" manner.

"No? Of course, let's get down to business."

Commissioner Pastal took a moment to pull Reverend Sadler's Last Will and Testament from an accordion folder. He scrutinized the parchment as if seeing it for the first time before commencing.

"Essentially, your adoptive father has done an unusual thing. Um. Let me read it in its entirety."

It took ten minutes. Most of the time was taken up by what constituted Reverend Gershom Sadler's last sermon. The emphasis was on the Fifth Commandment: Honor thy father. Callie nursed Sophie as Commissioner Pastal read. She got some amusement in how unsettling this was for him. Pastal stammered to a finish and looked up with a politician's practiced look of sincere concern.

"The property is yours, but only until the moment of your father's burial. At that point ownership is transferred to the county to be used as is seen fit by the county commissioners."

"Aren't you a county commissioner?" she asked.

"Your father told me that he wished for the property to be used by all citizens of this area. He evidently wanted the honor of title-ship to be yours upon his demise, though the actual property would be more, um…shared."

"No, he just wanted to screw me. I think he always did."

"Oh my!"

"So," Callie continued, "The rules are I own it, all—"

"Seven hundred twelve acres—'

"—and I can do with it as I see fit until the moment he is in his grave, and then I lose the back fifty acres including access to the only water source within ten miles."

"Correct."

"And even though he's dead, he still wants me to make sure he circles that damned cross—"

"Which must remain in the ground and never moved," Pastal added.

"—seven times every May 1st 'in perpetuity.'"

"Yes. That means forever."

"Got it. And I'm required to participate in this, this fiasco—how does he put it?"

She peered across the desk at the will. "'Witnessed with mine own heathen eyes and borne by my own pagan hands'— every single year?'"

"You're required to walk around the cross with him each year. Reverend Sadler stipulated—"

"He loved a good stipulation."

"—that the remaining portion of the property would be transferred from your hands if either of you were ever to miss this celebration. He uses the word 'banishment,' but I'm sure he meant eviction."

"Banishment is precisely what he meant."

"The portion of property he specified allows for the only access from the roadway. Without said access you would either have to arrange for an easement or fly in and out each day. I'm sorry, but your father was specific on this point."

"Of course he was. Have you made any funeral arrangements?"

"Oh, no," Commissioner Pastal replied. "Reverend Sadler has been embalmed so as to slow decay while these matters are settled. We felt those arrangements were most appropriately suited to family; to you in this case."

"Where's Evangeline?"

"She went to live with family in Mississippi the day Reverend Sadler died."

"Hmm."

The room was silent for a time, save for a suckling babe, an occasional grinding of Pastal's jaws, and the creak of his chair each time he checked his watch. Callie looked down at Sophie and grinned like she had on the day the girl was born.

"Commissioner?"

"Yes, ma'am?"

"Can you recommend a good taxidermist?"

• • •

"It's a crazy idea!" Commissioner Pastal had said to Callie's proposal. "A crazy idea from a crazy woman!"

He stood and left his office with not so much as a "good day" to her.

She followed. He kept striding to his butcher shop four blocks away.

"Listen to me," she called out.

"No!" he called over his shoulder as he quickened his pace. She kept up despite the baby on her hip, chattering all the way.

Pastal headed to the back of the shop and into the frigid walk-in cooler area where he began carving a hanging cow carcass.

"I won't do it!" he declared. He sliced a cleaver into shoulder sinew to make his point.

Callie used a blanket from her diaper bag to bundle Sophie against the cold. Pastal didn't offer her a coat, and she did her best to keep from shivering in front of him.

"It's a win-win proposal," she said.

"It's ridiculous."

"Mr. Pastal, I barely have enough motel money for a week, but what I do have now is property. I know you once had a deal with   Gershom   Sadler—"

"Who destroyed that deal with his insane ideas and ridiculous pride," said Commissioner Pastal. He was trying hard not to wheeze in front of her.

"Sir, I'm not Reverend Sadler. I want to do business, and what I propose works for both of us."

"You're desperate."

She shrugged. "I'm down to three cloth diapers that are starting to fall apart from too many washings. I have half a jar of peanut butter and some crackers I took from a diner during my bus ride here. You're right. I am desperate, but I never figured you for a man to take advantage of a woman in this predicament."

"I'm a businessman," waving his huge knife in a universal circle to point out all he'd built.

"And I intend to be a businesswoman, starting with a deal to allow you lifetime leases on my property. If Gershom Sadler destroyed your deal, let me make you a new one."

"In exchange for what?"

"In exchange for wholesale prices on any meat I buy from you in the future, and for stuffing my father before the sheriff forces me to bury him."

"Are you insane!?"

"There's nothing in the will that says he can't be stuffed. It only says I lose the property if he's buried."

"That's a loophole he surely never intended."

"Not my fault."

"How about I throw in a kitchen sink and a magic lamp while I'm at it?"

"I'm freezing, and I'm tired of you sneaking glances at my boobs. This is win-win. Do we have a deal or not?"

"We don't. What you're asking can't be done."

"How do you know if you haven't tried?"

For the first time, Richard Pastal looked glum. "I've tried."

•   •   •

Pastal's previous attempt at "stuffing" a human body had occurred back in Tennessee. At the time he was the proprietor of Pastal's Mortuary and Taxidermy, and the townspeople solicited his services upon the death of their eleven-term mayor. Many had realized the value in hiring a man such as Pastal who was skilled both in the funerary arts and taxidermy, and all agreed such an undertaking was most fitting for the beloved mayor.

Pastal turned them down, informing them he wasn't certain stuffing a man would work. He explained that human skin is quite elastic and, thus, ill-suited for taxidermy. They all but pleaded, but he assured them such efforts would end in dismal failure.

That was what he told the town's committee. The real reason he didn't want the job was the fact Pastal despised the deceased mayor. This was due in part to the fact Pastal had previously wooed a woman who would eventually leave him to marry said mayor. Also, the mayor had once borrowed four dollars from Pastal when the mayor discovered he'd left his wallet at home and could not pay for a club sandwich, soda, and a slice of carrot cake. Pastal's generosity turned to loathing as months went by and the mayor never paid him back.

Pastal was dumbfounded, therefore, when his former heartthrob pounded on his door and reiterated the townsfolk's request. She pleaded with Pastal to make her husband "look like an action-y movie star," for the funeral, courting him with compliments such as, "You're the only man in the world who could do this," and, "Won't you consider it for me, you know, for old times' sake?"

The flirting was nice, but Pastal was more compelled by the knowledge that she and her deceased spouse had trucks of money. She offered a lot of it to Pastal if he'd stuff her husband, and he felt willing to try. He announced he would be honored to make her dream a reality.

Pastal got drunk that night as he stared at the corpse of this man who had been so disrespectful over the years. He contemplated the lump of human clay he would make art, considering and discarding ideas as quickly as he consumed the liquor. At moments he obsessed over ideas to ridicule and lessen the man. At others he envisioned a masterpiece which would thrust him into fame and fortune, making him the envy of all in mortuary and taxidermy enterprises.

He settled on the concept of mummifying the man in a standing position like a stuffed bear displayed in an attack stance. He worked all night to sculpt his masterpiece. Occasionally he'd stand back to scrutinize his work and take another swig. By morning he'd produced an upright specimen dressed in a Sunday suit with hands raised in a ferocious clawing motion. Pastal posed the man with teeth bared. He judged this "action-y."

Due to the skin elasticity issue, however, the dead man was in an advanced state of settling by the time the wife took her first look that afternoon. Pastal's deceased adversary was bent at the waist as if scooping down to pick gum off his shoe. His legs had filled to elephantine proportions with bathroom tile caulk Pastal had used in a moment of panic around 3:00 AM. The man's face had drooped and looked more like that of a stroke victim than a growling alpha predator.

The fact the dead mayor had also been a renowned war veteran and outgoing president of the local Rotary had not helped matters at all. Pastal was directed to leave Tennessee by the same townspeople who'd begged him to take the job. He left, recognizing in them a significant level of menace.

Several weeks later he stopped in a faraway place called Elixir Springs, Texas for a burger and Coke. He was tired of traveling, and the town seemed pleasant. It was far enough away from Tennessee he could start fresh, and a sign in the window next to the cafe indicated the local butcher shop was for sale. Pastal had found his next home, and he'd been fine with that decision until the day Callie returned. He'd stored memories of his past life away, but she'd brought all that agony and humiliation right back.

Callie had paused in her pitch when she realized Pastal's attention was elsewhere. The cleaver in his hand rested on the cutting table, and his gaze was on something far away or long ago. He looked up and seemed to remember her standing there.

"Won't work; skin's too stretchy."

•   •   •

Callie harbored no qualms about her idea to mummify Reverend Sadler. As she pointed out many times to Commissioner Pastal, it was Sadler who had stated in his will that he be trotted around in a circle on a special day every year.

"It's what he wanted!"

It took Callie two days to talk Pastal into a modified version of her plan.

"I know you want my property," said Callie during the final discussion.

She sensed she'd worn him down.

"I'm offering an immediate investment opportunity, and I'm going to find someone else to do this for me if you won't."

It was this threat that someone else might get access to the property which was so jarring for Pastal. He'd come to realize during Callie's siege that she would deny him the lease property if he didn't go her way. What he had not shared with her was he needed her leases if his businesses were to grow. He had dreams: Pastal's Mobile Homes and RV's, Pastal's Fine Furniture Outlet, and maybe even Pastal's Beer. The idea someone else would get what he coveted was unacceptable, and Commissioner Pastal eventually agreed to her "insane proposition." The next day the two of them stood in his workroom and admired the outcome.

"I think it's my finest work," he said.

Callie stood with one finger tapping her lips as if scrutinizing an abstract work in a museum.

"You did amazing."

Reverend Sadler looked twenty years younger than he'd been in life. Their compromise had been that the reverend be placed within one of Pastal's "Economy" caskets, which would be frozen, thus avoiding the process of burial altogether.

The true worth of her offer to Pastal dawned on Callie when he installed one of his own meat freezer units within the barn. He assured her keeping the well-embalmed Reverend Sadler in the walk-in cooler would forestall decomposition. Sadler wasn't stuffed, per se, but he was going to be around to circle his cross for a long time to come.

"We'll consider this his mausoleum," said Pastal. He said it in a manner which implied he still wasn't quite sure this was the right thing to do.

He and Callie maneuvered the casket into the freezer using a large pushcart he'd modified with a flat wooden platform. Callie reasoned the cart would make pulling him out of the freezer easier each May 1st.

Pastal looked worried to the point of being unwell. He tugged on his eyebrows as if this would relieve the stress.

Callie smirked. "Mausoleum...sure." She was happy they'd reached some agreement, now fully aware how far Pastal would go to keep it.

Pastal had second thoughts right before he closed the walk-in door.

"I mean, maybe we could just bury him and say we..."

"The man said he didn't want to be buried," interrupted Callie. "You and I both know this was his way of mocking me, but he was specific about how much he wanted to stick around. I assume that was so he could irritate me if I figured out a way to grant his wish. Either way, we'll do it as he instructed."

"Okay, but it's important we keep this our secret."

Callie looked at him with a "no kidding" grin. The property remained hers for now. She'd work out the details later.

· · ·

As Callie was completing her first business negotiation in a walk-in-cooler, Toribio and Errol were making gloomy decisions having to do with the carnival circuit.

"Well, crack a teacup!" said Errol two months shy of Toribio's second anniversary with the carnival. "I've gone and done it again."

Toribio was busy mixing the spices for a new hamburger recipe in his food truck. He listened as he sifted and stirred.

Errol waved legal documents as if they were stuck to his hand with tar.

"I'm such a sorry monkey rectum. I've ruined us!"

The paperwork in hand was a lawsuit filed against Pioneer Days Carnival & Sideshow. The document detailed Errol's most recent misadventure.

"Carnivals have been gettin' run outta towns for a hundred years, and I have to go and get us kicked out over a gawdang slice of cake."

Errol had gotten intoxicated one afternoon while the carnival had been set up in the lovely town of Marble Falls, Texas. At some point he wandered into the Marble Falls Public Library, hiding his pint within the waistband of his blue-jean shorts and smiling as he entered the quiet foyer. Over the next hour he perused the shelves, mulled book covers, nodded in a friendly manner to all, and snuck nips from the bottle.

Errol was thrilled to be inside a library. He felt more intelligent just being among the stacks, and this made him feel confident, handsome even. He opted to show his charming side by poking the rear end of one of the librarians.

Errol instantly recognized his error. He ran from the building with librarians protesting, patrons staring, and the library custodian chasing him with a push-broom. Errol's inebriation did nothing for his already pitiful physical condition. He was puffing by the time he ran down the front steps and past the flagpole. An on-the-ball police force captured him before he made it four blocks. He was wearing a shirt and baseball cap emblazoned with the Pioneer Days Carnival & Sideshows logo at the time of capture.

Errol's possessions upon arrest included a folding knife and four library books on tape: *I'm Okay, You're Okay, Hondo, The Feminine Mystique*, and *The Very Hungry Caterpillar*. He also had the remaining Georgia Moon Corn Whiskey, and a list labeled "Girl Dog Names for a Girl Dog" scrawled on the back of the liquor receipt. The name "Mabel" merited two check marks.

The police search of Errol's pockets led to the discovery of two mashed pieces of cake wrapped in napkins. Smudged but decipherable were the words, "_OOD LUC_" and "_OUISE" in yellow icing. This appalled the already incensed librarians.

"Poor Louise," said one of the librarians. "She deserved a quiet retirement party, and now this."

"He must have snuck into the breakroom!" another realized.

"I'm real sorry, ma'am," Errol said over his shoulder by twisting around in the handcuffs.

"That's an employee's-only break room!" the librarian replied.

"Yes, ma'am. I'm just a real sorry catfish. I sure am."

Charges were filed, lawsuits were submitted, editorials were written and heads would roll. Errol realized it would be his own head. The Pioneer Days Carnival & Sideshows had worn out its welcome in Marble Falls. Errol had been around long enough to know other towns would follow.

"Crap on a cracker. I don't know what we're gonna do."

Toribio sniffed his hamburger meat and decided on another quarter teaspoon of cumin.

"*Es un rompecabeza.*"

"What's that?" Errol asked while staring at his front-page picture, the carnival logo on his t-shirt taking up most of the space above the fold.

Toribio paused to recall how to say his comment in English.

"How do you say...a puzzler."

· · ·

"*Come visit us any time*," said the letter from Callie. Toribio had read and re-read the letter at least eight times, and each time he felt a surge of energy. Callie had included a Polaroid photo of her holding little Sophie.

Toribio had thought about Callie and her baby every day since leaving them in the hospital, and Callie's letter made him miss them even more. She'd moved back to her old home, and she hinted she could use some help. Toribio wanted nothing more than to help her, and he worked up the nerve to show the letter to Errol.

Errol had stopped the carnival troupe outside Belton, deciding he needed to figure out a next move before wasting a lot of gasoline driving around aimlessly. He and Toribio were washing the miniature railroad cars. Neither of them knew why they were scrubbing rides when there was little hope the carnival would ever re-open, but it seemed a proper thing to do.

Errol murmured, "Hmm," and "Well I'll..." as he read the letter. "Says you are welcome. It doesn't say nothin' about a whole carnival troupe."

"She's nice."

Errol surveyed his little crew, a motley lot prone to untreated mental illness, substance abuse, and run-ins with the law.

"Sure would be agreeable not to have to set up in a new town every week for a while."

Toribio was surprised at how much he wanted Errol and the other carnies to go with him, but he stood by, allowing Errol to decide on his own.

"Well, salt on a pickle. I suppose it wouldn't hurt to ask."

Toribio was thrilled, celebrating with a paradiddle tapped with two fingers on his knee.

CHAPTER TWELVE

Commissioner Pastal parked at the county courthouse and watched as Sophie gathered her purse and briefcase. She was all business in a tailored pinstripe blazer and pencil skirt. His shirt was untucked, and a runny egg had splotched his trousers at breakfast.

"Are you sure you don't want to come inside?" she asked. "It's so hot out here."

"I'm fine."

"I'm doing what's best for Momma."

Pastal picked at a frayed thread in the fabric of his driver's seat and didn't look up as he answered, "Sure, I understand. Gotta do what's best for...for your mother."

Sophie pursed her lips. "Okay, then, I'll be back out in a few minutes." Pastal waited until she was gone before reaching into the glove box for a bottle of antacids.

Sophie made her way into the courthouse and asked directions to the clerk's office. She waited in line for two other customers, and then she pulled a ream of writs from her briefcase and handed them across a linoleum counter to the clerk. County Clerk Carol Ann Hathaway soon realized what legal papers Sophie needed file-marked, and she clucked judgmentally as she stamped each page.

She was on the phone with Cousin Lorene Ann up in Dallas before Sophie was back out in the parking lot.

"You will not believe what just happened!"

·   ·   ·

Two hours later Sophie and Commissioner Pastal stood behind the curtain of a small stage inside the Elixir Springs Public School Gymnasium/Auditorium/Drama Theater/Lunchroom. She wore her periwinkle gown as if it were any other "Wind Gathering." Commissioner Pastal was in blue jeans and red flannel shirt, and Sophie was considering whether to tell him to take off the paisley tie he'd added to "fancy up" for the occasion.

"Do you foresee Elixir Springs opening up a new revenue stream?" Commissioner Pastal asked in a clumsy attempt to talk business.

"Tonight isn't about revenue, Commissioner."

Two hundred-plus folks from as far away as Balmorhea and Del Rio had arrived for a hastily arranged Sophie Wind Gathering to be held in the auditorium. Sophie had flown in a small staff from Austin to produce the event.

Beneath one of the basketball backboards were several long tables which held an assortment of pastries, fruits, and cheeses. An ice sculpture in the middle of the banquet depicted an idyllic pond, and an oscillating blue light set beneath the ice made it look like the pond was rippling.

All about the room, blue banners accented the poster-sized photos of Sophie Wind. In one picture she was receiving a plaque naming her Businesswoman of the Year. In another she was helping to cut the ribbon leading to the front doors of the lavish new corporate headquarters in Austin. In still another, Sophie was arm-in-arm with the First Lady of the United States. Each was an instant which could have been considered the most extraordinary moment in an ordinary person's life, but which seemed expected of Sophie Wind's charmed and charged existence.

"It's a small group compared to what you're used to, I suppose," said Commissioner Pastal seconds before Sophie was about to walk out in front of the audience.

"It wouldn't matter if there were just two people out there. I'd still hold the Gathering. We're growing a garden here, and you can't do that without planting a seed."

She paraded out to the middle of the basketball court and stood upon the nose of the Elixir Springs School mascot, Frontier Keith. Sophie didn't speak right away, and she embraced the silence which followed her own. She admired her audience as a maestro would appreciate her orchestra before the concert. She seemed to be thanking them for choosing to be here with her this night, letting them know it had been the right choice before her first word was ever uttered.

Every breath in the room was held, every ear waited for the words of wisdom and hope they knew were coming. Errol was in attendance, and he leaned forward in his seat with the look of a child watching a magic show.

"Do you have a vision?" Sophie Wind asked her audience. Errol shook his head no until he realized everyone else was nodding yes, at which point he switched directions.

"Because God wants you to have a vision. Tonight I'm going to tell you about my vision, but more importantly, I want to hear about yours. I want to hear them, because until you say them, until you acknowledge them and make them real, until you desire them more than anything in this world and commit to making them a reality..."

And here she trailed off, waiting as they came to realize nothing at all would happen if they didn't take action to make their dreams come true.

"I think you know what happens to dreams which aren't allowed to blossom. We've all had dreams that never had a hope of coming true because they never had anyone breathe life into them, to make them real and alive and valuable."

"Nobody ever breathed on my dreams," whispered Errol.

"This is a night of unlimited potential…adventures…hopes. Don't ignore them or let them fester with regret. Bring them into the light and let them shine!"

Errol and the rest sat literally on the edges of their seats.

"Now let me ask you one more time. Do you have a vision?"

"Yes!" yelled Errol in chorus with the others.

"Are you willing to do what it takes to make that vision a reality?"

"Yes!"

"Are you ready to kick in doors leading to success and launch your journey toward triumph?"

"Yes! Yes! Yes!"

Some of the attendees cried or laughed, acknowledging their epiphany with unabashed joy. Others mind-traveled through the challenges they'd encounter and the rewards they would receive for the effort. Errol got a little choked up and used his shirt sleeve to smear tears away.

•　•　•

"That traitor," Callie muttered to Toribio for the tenth time that evening. They were sitting on her porch swing, and for the last half hour he'd listened as she ranted about Commissioner Pastal. Callie was trying a new hobby, origami, copying each step on how to fashion a paper swan from sketches in a library book perched on her lap.

"You're certain he's thrown in with Sophie?"

Toribio said nothing, which Callie knew was his way of giving a long-winded explanation about how he was certain Sophie and Pastal were plotting something.

"Sophie being Sophie, I get that. But Commissioner Pastal, that son of a…we've been in business for years. And now he wants my property to put his name on yet another enterprise, like he doesn't have enough of those already."

Toribio pulled his pocketknife and carved off a splinter from the porch swing.

She folded a wing, realized it was backwards, folded it again. "And what the hell kind of business is it? What kind of fiasco would my daughter and Commissioner Pastal venture into?"

Toribio flicked the splinter and checked the knife blade sharpness with his thumb.

"Well, it's wrong. Plain wrong, and I aim to do something about it."

Toribio turned to look at her in a "what are you about to do?" fashion.

Callie held up her creation, which looked more like a crumpled cube with a television antenna than a swan, as she replied with a wicked grin.

"Something rash."

•   •   •

"Are there any questions?" Sophie asked as she finished the opening portion of The Gathering. "Please. There's nothing in the world I enjoy talking about more than this company I've asked you to join, and there's no one I'd rather talk to about it than you."

She needn't have prodded, as more than two-dozen hands went up at the first opportunity. Sophie called first on Errol who was waving as if trying to flag down a roadside assistance tow truck.

Errol stood, chuckling and rubbing his neck as all the others in the room turned to him. His voice quivered unintelligibly.

"Sorry. I'm just so nervous."

Sophie smiled at him like a doting mother watching a child learning to play the recorder.

"I was just wonderin' if you'd...see I was wantin' to know more about them circles in the water you was talkin' about."

Sophie smiled again. "Of course. By the way, it's Errol, isn't it?"

"Yes, ma'am," he replied, puffing out his chest because she'd remembered him after so many years.

"Errol has worked with our family for as long as I can remember. I'm so pleased to see you here."

He was so flabbergasted he wobbled on the bleachers.

"Errol, that is an important question, and one I want to make sure every single person in this room understands before they leave here. It is the cornerstone of my philosophy, and it is the key for each of you to fulfill all the dreams you've ever imagined."

Sophie swept her hand like a princess in a magical carriage, and a moving picture appeared on the wall behind the basketball backboard. She positioned herself so the images leaped about her, creating a sense she was a part of the film.

"Here is a magnificent scene of ocean waves crashing against dark crag, sea foam leaping to heaven before rolling back to sea. It is a God-created scene at once romantic and mysterious, ferocious and peaceful. It is from here that we all came. This is life! This is opportunity!"

Sophie lifted her arms to heaven, as would a sorceress casting a spell. A wave crashed behind her, the force of the water seeming to engulf the Earth. Sophie brought her arms down. The image behind her transformed from a dynamic coastline to a stagnant, swampy area, thick with rotting vegetation and brown clumps of goo.

"I like to think of this picture as a place where dreams failed because of inaction or poor judgment. Maybe for you that represents living paycheck to paycheck or driving a car that is older than your parents."

"Or havin' a flatbed trailer you can't get unhooked from your truck," murmured Errol.

"Maybe this image is about not having enough quality time to spend with your children or spouses. Ladies, maybe it's about having to spend too much time with your husbands."

Her audience tittered. Errol guffawed and slapped his thigh.

"In this place, there is life, but is it the kind of life you want? If it isn't, maybe it's time to start doing something about it."

Drops of rain began to fall on the stagnant pond on the screen behind Sophie. Each created a ripple as it hit the surface, and the mucky water turned lively.

"Each ripple is intriguing, but together, all the thousands of ripples, add strength to one another, push each other to become a pulsating energy!"

The scene changed from dreary to exciting as the ripples grew into vibrant waves once more. "This is it! This is the Ripple Effect, an energy surge unlike anything before. People relying on each other, assisting one another to conquer fears, overcome obstacles, and create something magnificent."

The image faded on the gym wall, and eyes in the room returned to Sophie. She was pleased at the shared rhythm their breathing had adopted. Errol's hand shot up again.

"Yes, Errol?"

"Miss Wind, I'm real sorry to bother you and all, but I'm just wonderin' about one more thing. I've been hearin' about them pyramid plans, and I was wonderin' how this is better. I'm askin' in the most respectful way you understand."

"No, Errol. I'm quite pleased you asked. In a pyramid scheme, and that's what it is, a scheme, there are always a few people at the top who make money and see their dreams come true, but that same plan also calls for some people to be on the bottom, holding the entire weight of the successful on their backs, never receiving a reward for their effort. To me, that isn't fair."

"Ain't fair at all."

"In the Ripple Effect, what you have is a wonderful process of symbiosis. I succeed when you succeed. See the difference? A pyramid is a place to bury dead nobility, whereas a rippling body of water is full of life and dreams."

Errol belly laughed. "A place to bury…"

"Put another way, put in a way which makes good business sense, in a pyramid scheme, and in many multi-level marketing plans, you, the distributor, buy product from the corporation, and sell product to others at a profit. But there's a catch."

"Always gotta be a catch."

"If you're one of the first ones to begin selling the product, you stand to make a substantial gain because you will be allowed to share in the profits of all those holding up the pyramid below you. In a Ripple Effect, your profit is my profit, and my profit is yours. The more Ripples we can bring into the pond, the more energy we create. I can see you beginning to understand how vital this is."

"It's real, real vital."

"The Sophie Wind Corporation has hundreds of beauty aids, cosmetics, perfumes, vitamins, colonic solutions and herbal tea varieties to distribute. If you join us, you will never pay an up-front fee for the product you move. Indeed, even if you were to never sell one bar of soap, but were able to bring in other Ripples who could do the selling for you, you would have created a Pond Ripple which could be the beginning of a Lake Ripple and someday even an Ocean Ripple. And unlike a pyramid scheme, the initial franchise fee is substantially lower."

"Subanshully…a bunch lower," muttered Errol to a woman sitting next to him. "That's real good business sense, right there."

"What we look for in a Regional Ripple Manager is a one-time outlay of two-hundred-twelve dollars and a commitment to bring in three other distributors within a month. That's just one person every ten days, and we have found that if each interested person does a serious assessment of family members and friends, bringing in three people in a month's time is just a token of your commitment to your new family."

"Just a little gawdang token."

Errol and the other two hundred members of his new family couldn't wait to get their checkbooks out and start their new lives together. Soon they moved to the snack-filled tables to further discuss the boundless possibilities offered in the Wind Ripple System. Sophie made her graceful exit to ovations and thunderous applause, leaving her staff to take orders and answer further questions.

. . .

Toribio agreed to accompany Callie on her mission to do something rash, but he shook his head when she started to hop into one of the Pioneer Days delivery trucks. She was about to protest but instead murmured, "Ah," as he pointed to the company logo on the side of the truck.

"That's good thinking, but I don't own any cars without that logo," she said. He left and returned a few minutes later in a dusty Datsun B210 sedan.

"Where did you get that?"

"It's mine."

"You own a car? I've never seen you drive anything other than a carnival truck or one of our delivery vehicles." The passenger door screeched when he opened it for her, and the shock absorbers groaned against their weight, but it started right up.

They soon found themselves skulking behind a barn on Commissioner Pastal's property. It reminded him of military exercises and clandestine border crossings. Callie sent a thrill through his spine when she touched the back of his shoulder. She'd chosen rubber galoshes, which squeaked over the soft clucking of chickens and an occasional snort from a cow inside the barn.

Toribio was silent in a pair of brown orthopedic sneakers he wore for lunch and dinner rushes.

Ten feet from the barn door Callie grabbed him by the belt. She'd stopped him from rounding the corner of the barn a moment before he would have stepped into view of Commissioner Pastal. The Commissioner was standing fifty yards away on the front porch of his house, and a faint scent of pipe smoke wafted to them as they watched his pipe glow. Pastal picked up a guitar and began to pluck.

Toribio made motions as if to retreat to the car. Callie's face was firm, however, and she put both hands on her hips.

Half an hour passed. Callie peed near the foundation of the building; a coyote howled for a date; eggs were laid inside the barn, and the commissioner's pipe was re-lit twice; Toribio was distracted by the fact Callie had tinkled in front of him.

Eventually, Pastal stopped strumming and went inside his house. Toribio thought it wise to wait a few minutes before they acted. Callie wouldn't have it, and she prodded him forward.

Toribio moved around the corner of the barn. He thought he could hear the tone of the chicken clucks change. It was as if they knew something was amiss, and tension rippled through the flock.

The barn door was made of corrugated tin latched with a broken stick. The stick was worn smooth from being pulled and inserted hundreds of times, but the door itself was a sound machine. They tried to enter silently, but it was useless. The tin scraped, the hinges screeched, and the clucking rose.

Both Toribio and Callie knew they'd blown it. Everything was loud and jagged, but they'd come too far. Toribio grabbed one door, Callie the other, and they swung them open with such force both doors banged into the wall. They fled back to the shadows to watch the results.

Nothing happened. The chickens and herd of four milk cows stayed where they were. Why should they leave a lovely barn to go outside into the night where there might be wolves, coyotes, or chickens from other barns? There was no scattering of feathers in the rush to freedom, no hooves bolting for safer pastures. The chickens went back to clucking and laying, and the cows chewed hay.

"Who the hell is out there?" demanded Pastal who'd stepped out onto his porch with a line of toothpaste foam running off his chin. "Trespassers!"

Toribio and Callie couldn't comprehend the huge explosion emitted from Pastal's gun had only fired bird shot. It meant little to them that the energy from the small projectiles was all but spent by the time they reached them. All Toribio and Callie knew was an angry man with a loud gun was shooting at them. They did what any practical person would do in a similar situation; they ran the other way.

Toribio and Callie briefly lost sight of one another, and he was terrified Callie had gotten hurt. Seconds later they collided on a deer path. Their relief at seeing each other was short lived as another blast from the shotgun rang out across the meadow. Seconds later they heard little BBs pelting the branches around them like fat raindrops plopping on elephant ear fronds.

This motivated a sprint back to Toribio's car. They were relieved to see the Datsun was still parked off the road. They roared away as Pastal leveled one more shot over the roof.

Toribio pulled over onto a narrow shoulder two miles down the road. He and Callie were still catching their breath and laughing at the sheer exhilaration of surviving an adventure. A birdshot pellet rolled off his hair and dribbled off his shoulder. They stared as it landed in the ashtray and vibrated a bit before coming to rest.

And then came the look lovers have shared throughout the history of the world. He stroked her hair, she lay a palm on his chest. Their kiss made him dizzy. There was a clumsy, giggly rush to de-clothe. He fumbled with her blouse buttons; she yanked on his belt. His leg got caught under the steering wheel; she knocked the car into neutral, then back into park. All the while they kissed like two people who had finally dropped a dreadful diet plan in favor of an all-you-can-eat kissing buffet.

CHAPTER THIRTEEN

Reverend Sadler's church building had been in a state of deterioration on the day Callie and her newborn had taken ownership of his property. The floorboards were rotting, and most of the pews were warped due to roof leaks. His old cross out front was so charred from the lightning strike that keeping it up posed a danger.

Luz arrived a few minutes after Callie started taking stock. They hugged and spent time fawning over Sophie before venturing out for a stroll. Luz's attention seemed diverted, whether from breezes rustling tree leaves, the far-off call of a hawk, or a bee greeting a flower. Everything caught her eye, and it all made her smile.

"Do you have any plans?" Luz asked as they passed the old pond where she and Callie first met.

"I think I'd like to open a restaurant."

"That would be nice. Something family oriented."

"And maybe a dance floor. My father used to take me to dances when I was a girl."

"Love it!"

Callie stopped to feed Sophie by the barn. Luz took off her shoes and waltzed on the grass.

"I just love the smell of sawdust on a dance floor," said Luz.

Callie looked up from Sophie. "And the sparkle of a crystal ball hanging from the ceiling."

She realized Luz had stopped dancing and was looking far off down the road. Callie saw nothing but caliche gravel and trees to the horizon, but Luz kept staring with a faint smile.

"I'll be going now," said Luz as she collected her shoes and bent to kiss Sophie's forehead.

"Already?"

"I'm proud of you," Luz said before ambling back down to the pond. "Keep going, Callie," she called over her shoulder. Callie's last sight of Luz was as she picked bluebonnets and tucked them into her hair.

Callie sighed and turned to look back down the road. She could finally see it, a caravan of odd trucks and vans weaving around potholes. A few minutes later a downtrodden group rolled up to the barn. Callie was burping Sophie as trucks hauling roller coaster cars, midway booths, and sections of a Ferris wheel raised a cloud of white dust coming to a halt.

"Cocinero?" Callie called out to Toribio driving the lead truck.

"I came," he said with a sheepish grin as he raised the letter she'd sent him.

"I see. And you brought friends."

"Howdy, ma'am," said Errol, who plunged his hand out with the zeal of a salesman about to close the deal on a used tractor.

"What's going on?" asked Callie as she scooted Sophie a little higher on her shoulder. Toribio thrust his hands in his pockets and stared down at a clod of dirt. He looked as if he wanted to explain their presence, but something kept him mute. Errol jumped right in.

"You see, ma'am, we're just a bunch of carnies, but we was wonderin'…well, we heard you might be hiring. A bunch of us have farmed before, and we've all got strong backs."

"Mister, I don't have anything to pay you."

"Well, that's a real thump in the shins, ma'am. We've come a long way."

"Truth is, I don't know what I'm supposed to do with all this property. It was left to me by a—by the man who adopted me."

"I used to know the pastor who preached in that church over there. Fellow by the name of Reverend Sadler."

"That's him."

"Well, cow patties and moon pies! He used to come preach at our venues. Sorry to hear of his passin'."

"You knew Gershom Sadler?"

"He was a fiery old bird; said carnival workers was Satan's taffy pullers."

"So, you want room for your whole group to stay?"

"Well, ma'am, that's kinda what we was hopin'. At least if we could lay up here for the winter and get our bearings for next season."

"I own this place now. You'd answer to me."

"That's fine, ma'am. We won't be no bother. We can all work for you to get this place fixed up nice, and we can still attend your services."

"Not holding services. You can find God on your own. I'd like to know about that carousel, though. Does it work?"

"Why, yes ma'am. It works fine—music and a brass ring and everything."

"Fine. You can stay as long as no one in your group does anything to hurt my daughter or give her a bad upbringing."

"Oh, no ma'am. Never. I've been working real hard on my cursin', and I've all but given up chew."

"And the carousel stays through May Day every year. You can head out on your tour after that if you like, but the ride stays here until then."

"Well, Miss..."

"Callie."

"Miss Callie...by gumby, you've got yourself a deal!"

. . .

Errol and Toribio set about helping Callie fix up the property and erect the carnival as a stationary amusement park. The carnies set up a mobile home community on the western section of the land, and they helped build a little restaurant for Callie's dream. Every new hire received the same speech from Errol: "No gawdang cursin', and no cheatin' with another fella's wife."

As promised, the carousel was erected. It was an oddity to the work crew that Callie insisted the charred and decaying cross remain where it was and that the ride be set up around it. None of them, however, looked at the gift of having a place to call home, rent-free no less, with anything but gratitude. The idea of going back on the road after May Day frittered away and was never mentioned again.

Crowds came, tickets sold, and life, for once, looked pretty gawdang good.

. . .

No mother and daughter were ever closer than Callie and Sophie in the early years. They cooked, danced, laughed, painted nails, photographed, hiked, and did any manner of joyous things together. Callie loved every moment, and the little girl thrived under the watchful eyes and vibrant pageantry of her carnie family.

One evening when Sophie was four, Callie read "Where the Wild Things Are" as they lay on a bed Toribio had made for them, atop soft linens and oversized pillows Callie had sewn during a short-lived needle-work period. The room was eggshell white with gauzy fabrics draped about the four posts of the bed. Lilac-scented candles glowed, and fresh flowers in three vases were placed about the room. It was a haven, their place in the end room of their little trailer house.

Sophie's eyes drifted shut as she snuggled up against her mother, her head on Callie's chest, her little feet hugging her mother's thighs.

"I love you, Momma," whispered Sophie.

"I love you, too, baby," Callie replied. She stroked her daughter's hair and read in a deepening, singsong voice.

"Momma," Sophie whispered.

"Yes, sugar."

"You're my best friend."

Sophie's breathing grew rhythmic and shallow, and Callie bent to kiss the precious girl on the top of her head. She sobbed, and she prayed God had forgiven her sin of having challenged his messenger with a willow switch. For a while, at least, she thought He might have.

· · ·

"What flavor, sugar?" Callie had asked of young Sophie one afternoon. Pioneer Days Amusement Park had been open for six years.

Callie and Sophie had taken a walk with Toribio, and he'd offered to make them snow cones as they passed one of the vendor carts in the park. Sophie was sporting pigtails in pink bows and three tooth gaps in her smile.

"Rainbow," replied Sophie.

Toribio smiled as he poured stripes of blue, red, yellow, and purple over ice.

"A rainbow for a *princesa*," he said as he handed her the treat. She giggled and thanked him.

They sat at a picnic table near the Squanto Canoe Ride and watched the youngest of the park attendees. The children went on a slow circular ride in little dugouts painted primary colors, floating in a slow-moving circle of water. Their parents beamed and collected Kodak moments.

"Someday this will all be yours," Callie told Sophie with a sigh.

Even at six, Sophie knew her mother had lost all hope of ever reclaiming a life of adventure or aspirations. Her mother's biggest dream was to see Sophie take over her business, but Sophie already knew she had no desire or intention of doing so. Dreams of a Barbie-doll-like life full of travel, glamour, and choices were her destiny.

In those days, Sophie was kind enough to keep it to herself. She reached over to give her mother a hug, knowing somehow her mother needed it more than all the snow cones in the world. The hug caused Sophie to lose her grip on the snow cone, and her colorful treat smacked onto the gravel walkway.

"It's okay, *princesa*," said Toribio.

"My rainbow spilled," said Sophie. Her lower lip trembled as she tried not to cry.

"We'll get you another one," said Callie, smiling.

"We can put all the colors back," said Toribio. He hopped into the vendor cart and poured another beautiful rainbow over ice.

CHAPTER FOURTEEN

Callie and Toribio lay panting and laughing in the backseat of the Datsun after their romp at Commissioner Pastal's property. Toribio's pants were in the floorboard, and her bra was dangling from the front seat headrest. She'd thrown his belt out the window in the rush, and her own panties were down around her left ankle.

"I don't think I've ever seen you smile this long," she said, which made Toribio grin wider.

They'd been so passionate in their haste to disrobe that Toribio had left the car lights on. A mist had descended, and a glow from the headlights created an aurora. Callie smoothed her hair as Toribio pulled on his boots and stepped out to pee. She giggled at Toribio as he stood off the road shoulder, but she returned her attention to the kaleidoscopic halo.

"Do you remember that time Sophie dropped her snow cone at the park? She must've been around six or seven."

Toribio's stream started, and he grunted as he remembered.

"She dropped it on the ground, and you made her another one. She wanted rainbow flavors."

Toribio chuckled at the memory and leaned back to look at the stars while he finished.

"I feel like a rainbow right now," she whispered.

• • •

"There's been a stampede!" was what Commissioner Pastal screamed into the phone to the Sheriff's department after Callie and Toribio fled the scene. Pastal described a mad flight of his stock and reported a "mob of hooligans" had attacked his property and driven his cattle to panic.

"I want all their miscreant butts in jail! I want them locked up, and no bread and no water. Miscreants! Do you hear me!?"

Joyce, the dispatcher, heard him, and a sheriff's deputy was sent to the farm.

"I'm in the area," announced Cleft over his car radio. "Go ahead and log me handling the complaint."

"Ten-four, Sheriff," Joyce replied through a bite of her Reuben sandwich.

Within minutes Cleft located the herd of four cows, all munching on grass from a field they'd not been allowed to visit in months. The moon was full, and a single coyote call was so far off the cows swished their tails in accompaniment.

It had been Pastal's shotgun blasts which prodded the cattle out of their comfortable stalls and into the night air. It hadn't been so much a stampede as an exodus just above the speed of plod. The cattle trotted five or six steps out of the barn, slowed to a head-bobbing walk, and decelerated to a leisurely step, step, eat grass, step, step, chew cud, step, step.

Beefo called out to the cows from his paddock several acres away, but they paid him no mind and sashayed along at their leisurely pace. They were far into the pasture when Pastal returned a few minutes after trying to locate the bandits in his pickup, and the "stampede" tale was born.

Cleft spent a few minutes herding the cows back to their barn, earning splatters of mud on his uniform and a scratch on his palm while opening the paddock gate. All four of the cattle, however, seemed content to be back inside. Commissioner Pastal harangued Cleft about crime rates and "hoodlum-ism" the entire time.

"I want them arrested, convicted, sentenced to hard labor. The hardest labor you can find."

"I understand," said Cleft as he closed the last stall door and made his way back out to the police truck.

"Parole is too good for scoundrels such as this! They need to be breaking rocks, and then breaking those rocks into smaller rocks until there's only dust left. And then they get another pile of rocks."

"Goodnight, Commissioner," sighed Cleft. "I'll let you know when we find them."

Cleft climbed into his truck and drove away. He wiped a bit of mud spatter off his badge and scrutinized his scraped palm to make sure it didn't need attention. His boots were caked, and his brand-new uniform would have to go to the cleaners. It was good to be back.

●　　●　　●

A short time later Cleft spied a little Datsun matching the description of the one given by Pastal. The car was sitting a few feet off a two-lane highway, and Cleft could see someone moving around in the back seat. There was also a man a few yards from the car urinating and looking up at the moon.

"Joyce, I think I have the suspect vehicle out here on FM Twenty-Two. I'm gonna check the occupants."

"Ten-four, Sheriff," responded Joyce, who swallowed her Cherry Coke down the wrong pipe and set off a half-minute of spasmodic coughing.

It had already been a busy evening for Cleft. He and the deputies under his charge had arrested two drunk drivers, intervened in a parking lot fight at a bar, and investigated the fact someone had broken the tail off the beaver logo at Pastal's Fur

City. He pulled in behind the Datsun, called in the license plate, and flipped on the rotating lights atop his truck.

"Cops!" announced Callie. "Get in!"

Toribio looked over his shoulder at the approaching squad car and hightailed it into the woods, naked from his waist to his boots.

"There's a male running from the car into the woods," Cleft said into the police radio.

"Oh crap, crap, crap!" yelled Callie as she vaulted into the front seat and took off so fast gravel from her squealing tires pinged Cleft's squad truck.

"Are you in foot pursuit?" asked Joyce, who was still wiping soda off her chin and blouse.

"Negative. He's got a hundred yards on me, and a lot of forest to hide in. I'm going after the car."

"Ten-four," said Joyce, who was so excited she took another bite of sandwich with a Cherry Coke chaser.

Callie saw the police lights coming up fast, and she slowed down to pull over. "You can't outrun him, you idiot." She stopped the car and rummaged for her bra.

Cleft crept up on the little car, pistol in hand. He moved to the passenger side in a tactical stance ready to engage any threat. Callie looked out the window and saw Cleft staring down at her. She clamped her legs together, wrapped her breasts with Toribio's jacket, and turned off the car engine with all the dignity she could muster.

Cleft looked away when he realized she was all but nude. "Callie, what the hell are you doing out here? And who ran off into the woods?"

"I don't like the tone you're taking, young man."

A deputy from a neighboring county who'd heard Cleft announce his pursuit over the radio crossed over the county line to back his fellow officer.

"Evening, Sheriff," hailed the deputy as he stepped out of his squad car and sauntered over to stand by Cleft.

"Evening."

"These the folks who caused the ruckus over at that farm?"

"One of them," said Cleft, all the while wishing the deputy would leave so he could handle this with some level of flexibility. The deputy was bored, however, and there was no polite way to ask him to leave after he'd made such a supportive gesture from one peace officer to another. Cleft could see he was intrigued and that he would not be leaving any time soon, so he turned back to Callie.

"Someone caused a stampede earlier tonight!"

"A stampede?"

"I need to know who was in the car with you."

"Well, you can keep on asking, but I'm not going to tell you." Callie crossed her arms and pushed out her bottom lip.

"The car is registered to a Toribio Lasoya. Who is he?"

"I have no idea." Her brow furrowed in confusion, because Cocinero had said he owned the car, and she didn't have any idea who Toribio Lasoya might be.

"Callie, you have to tell me. Don't make me arrest you."

"You're being mean."

"No, I'm not. Who was in the car?"

"Not telling."

Cleft could feel the deputy inching up on the car as if he wanted to dive in after this disrespectful woman. With a heavy heart Cleft realized he had no other choice.

"Fine, you're under arrest." Cleft yanked open the passenger side door and waited for Callie to exit. She thought about sitting in icy silence. Something in his demeanor made her realize she'd pushed too far and put him in an awkward position.

Had the other deputy not been there Cleft might have had other options, but it dawned on Callie he was an officer of the law once more. She knew he'd missed it terribly, and she realized he could not be seen showing favoritism. Callie climbed out to present herself for handcuffing.

"Watch your head, ma'am," said the visiting deputy as he placed Callie in Cleft's car. "Have a good evening, Sheriff," he called as Cleft drove away.

Cleft looked into his rearview mirror and wondered if he'd made the right decision in accepting his badge back. The ride into town was silent for the first few minutes. Cleft's jaw muscles worked, and Callie tried to keep her tears at bay.

"Cleft, I'm sorry," she said as his squad car pulled into the parking lot of the Sheriff's office.

"Me, too. You didn't leave me with many choices."

"I planned to set those cows free as a prank on Pastal, that's true, but all the cattle and chickens were still in their barn when we left. I swear they were."

Cleft looked again at Callie's face in his rearview mirror. She was staring at the entrance to the jail, and his heart broke as he saw how frightened she was.

"You're not going to tell me who was in the car, are you?"

"My goodness, no."

Cleft rubbed his face. "I'm taking you home."

Callie wiped away a tear.

"Sheriff," called out a deputy who'd seen his car and walked out to the parking lot. "I have some paperwork that came over from the courthouse a while ago, and..."

The deputy stopped short upon seeing Callie in the back seat of the car.

"What is it?" asked Cleft.

"It's just...some papers, and..."

"Well, what are they?" He took the paperwork from the deputy, who was still staring at Callie.

"Oh, no," said Cleft once he'd read the document.

"Cleft, what is it?" she asked.

"It's a court order for you to appear tomorrow."

"Appear? Appear where?"

"In court. You have to go to court to answer a summons."

"A summons? What the hell kind of summons?"

Cleft paused. "This alleges you're unable to care for yourself. Callie...Commissioner Pastal and your daughter are trying to commit you to a psychiatric hospital."

CHAPTER FIFTEEN

Sophie's life had been relatively lonely as she grew up. For the first five years she and her mother lived in the trailer park surrounded by carnies, and there were rarely other children around to play. There was no school within thirty miles, so Sophie learned reading and the arts from her mother, math and social sciences from Toribio, and poorly formed but always well-intentioned philosophy from Errol.

Sophie's prized possession was a used thrift store Barbie doll she kept on a paint-peeled dresser in her room. Some of the doll's hair was worn away, but she still looked Barbie-pretty.

When Sophie was ten, she briefly befriended the daughter of Malga: Queen of the Lizard People. Sophie's new friend also owned a Barbie doll and treated hers with reverence as well. Though neither said anything, it was obvious the other girl's doll was the more glamorous. It had all its original hair, and it sported a gorgeous periwinkle blue sequined dress. Malga had created the dress with her own hand for her daughter's doll, and somehow that one-of-a-kind dress made the already vivacious Barbie all the more radiant.

The dress became the most coveted thing in Sophie's life. She was overcome with a driving passion unlike anything she'd ever experienced before. She knew with all her soul she would have it for her doll.

Malga's daughter also desired something. It took mere minutes for young, driven Sophie to learn her new friend wanted a makeup set with nail polish and eye shadow advertised in the Green Stamps catalog. The two girls lay on the floor in Sophie's room, their feet swaying from the knees, their eyes glued to the page.

Sophie knew what she had to do. Her eyes darted to the column on the side of the page as her mesmerized friend gawked at the makeup set in the catalog. Sophie matched the letter of the item to its corresponding description, and she shouted with joy when she read it would take two-hundred stamps to make it hers.

Sophie didn't have two nickels back then, but what she did have were S&H Green Stamps—hundreds of them. She collected them from Toribio who earned them buying gasoline, and from her mother who received them at the grocery store. Often Toribio would ask, "Do you have enough stamps to buy your castle, little *Princesa?*"

Sophie had never used the stamps for herself, having redeemed them only for gifts. She believed if she could maintain a discipline about the process, she would indeed someday be able to buy her own castle. Sophie took a leap toward that goal the day she learned to negotiate with her young friend.

The precious periwinkle blue dress was hers in the time it took to redeem stamps at the S&H Store and make the trade with her friend. Sophie stared at the dress once she'd slipped it onto her own Barbie, contemplating castles and other boundless possibilities as her friend sat on the kitchen linoleum and spread beauty across her face and nails.

"Look," Sophie later said as she showed off the dress to Toribio. The man gazed at the little girl he'd helped bring into this world. For the first time since he held her as a swaddled newborn he bent and kissed the top of her head.

"You will live in a castle one day, *Princesa*."

Sophie liked the sound of that.

• • •

The friendship lasted four months until Callie fired the girl's mother. Malga had been stealing snow cone syrup (which she used as highball mixers) and stirring up all the other carnie wives by sleeping with their husbands.

Sophie was all set for a poignant goodbye with the girl, so she was shocked when Malga's daughter demanded the Barbie dress back.

"But we traded," said Sophie.

"My mom says I wasn't supposed to trade, so you have to give it back."

Sophie felt her ears getting hot, and for the first time in her life she felt indignant fury. "Does your mother know you already used half the makeup kit? I can't return it to the Green Stamp store now."

"Doesn't matter. She said you have to give me my dress back."

The other girl outweighed Sophie by ten pounds of sinew, but Sophie was fearless as she glared into her eyes. "It's not your dress anymore."

The stare-off lasted an agonizing twenty seconds, but Malga's daughter was the first to blink. "Fine, then. You probably just got me grounded."

Malga and her daughter rolled out of the trailer park the following morning. Sophie waved a stoic goodbye. Malga's daughter shot the finger from the back window. The friendship hadn't endured, but the lessons in free enterprise and standing up for herself would last forever.

• • •

Toribio had been invited to every Christmas with Callie and Sophie from the time he'd moved to the property. Annual traditions resulted, including a gelatin dessert called Orange Fluff Toribio hankered for all year, his purchase of a small bottle of perfume for Callie, and the shared joy of watching "their girl" see what Santa brought. It was also customary he help Callie prepare and wrap the gifts for Sophie every year.

They stayed up all night on Christmas Eve the year Sophie was twelve. He'd had an idea about decorating her new bicycle to look like Rudolph the Reindeer, complete with antlers, a red nose and jingle bells.

Callie and Toribio had gotten tickled around two in the morning as they tried to quietly attach the bells to the pink bike so as not to wake the girl. Their efforts to laugh silently made things only more hilarious. Soon the two were belly-laughing on the floor amidst the tree, wrapping paper, and cardboard boxes.

There was a moment, that moment when two people make a silent agreement to kiss for the first time or not. Callie's eyes met Toribio's, and their lips were mere inches apart. She'd considered it many times before, though she'd always decided against as it would have been awful if a romance ended up not working out.

What would that do to Sophie? Callie wondered. She never dared allow herself the question of what it would do to herself. That night, however, maybe because of candle glow, wine, or the season itself, Callie was more open to the idea, and she leaned in.

Toribio's eyelids were mere slits, and his cheeks blossomed as he moved to meet her. A Merlot-scented breath passed between them. Callie's left palm came to rest on his shoulder as a moment and a lifetime became indistinguishable.

"Momma?" called Sophie from her bedroom.

Callie pulled back and whispered, "I'll be right back."

Toribio finished decorating the bike by attaching a bulbous red nose to the middle of the handlebars, all the while muttering *cobarde*—Spanish for coward—under his breath.

. . .

To Sophie at sixteen, romantic love pertained to posters of teen idols on her bedroom walls, kissing practice on a lavender pillow, and listening to crooners over and over and over on vinyl records. That is, until the morning Cleft Hawley walked into the restaurant to get a toasted egg sandwich. Cleft, a sandy-haired teen with the stride of a natural athlete, scanned the restaurant for a table with the feigned coolness of a guy who didn't care if any of the veteran amusement park workers invited him to sit with them.

Callie watched her daughter, hiding a smile as the girl dropped a tray of sweet tea onto the laps of three customers.

"That boy is all she's gonna talk about for weeks," Callie said to Toribio.

She watched the young man's expression change from casual to dumbstruck as he stared at teenage Sophie wiping tables. The new kid poured salt on his sandwich and failed to notice how high the granules were piling as he gawked.

"I'd also guess he just became our most regular customer."

. . .

Pioneer Days Park would have folded as an amusement park in the first year had it not been for the Wagon Wheel Restaurant Callie designed and Toribio ran. It was the kind of place folks traveled some distance to visit. People in the know told their friends they were craving a "Frontier," short for the Frontier Keith Burger.

Callie's real father had always loved the Daniel Boone television show, so in his honor she decided on the original theme for the restaurant as "Mountain Man," which went well with the Pioneer Days logo on all of Errol's rides. No one had wanted to spring for the paint to obliterate the old name.

Old traps and animal furs were tacked to the wall. Waiters and waitresses dressed in tan with buckskin-like fringe sewn onto the sleeves and hems. Drinks were served in powder horn mugs. Children who cleaned their plate were awarded a coonskin cap or a plastic tomahawk.

Most regular customers cut all condiments on their Frontier Keith, save the occasional slice of cheese. The real draw was the hamburger patty itself. Strained marriages were saved from the sharing of a fresh, hot bite of a Frontier Keith Burger. National conferences held in San Antonio, Austin and Houston often used the Wagon Wheel for catering. One event promoter said Frontier Keith Burgers added a sense of true Texana and worldly refinement, and Texas Monthly Magazine had once referred to Frontier Keith Burgers as "the mating of five-star *joie de vivre* with football tailgate-er savvy."

People might ride the Wampum Slide, the Tipi Twister, or the Lewis and Clark Canoe Plunge, but they came for Toribio's burgers. The entire Pioneer Days village lived on, year after dusty year, because it hosted a tiny, semi-famous restaurant. Over the years Callie and Toribio served two presidents, several hundred birthday parties, the 1976 and 1988 U.S. Olympic dive teams, and one British prince on visit for the state's Sesquicentennial.

It was a good burger.

The other surprising attraction was the dance hall in back. Callie's father had enjoyed few hobbies or diversions in his life, but he'd loved a good country-western dance hall. He passed that passion onto Callie, often taking her to establishments during their road trips together.

Callie had grown up entranced with places such as the Crystal Ballroom in Taylor, Gruene Hall in Gruene, The Albert Dance Hall in Stonewall, and The Broken Spoke in Austin. She and her father had waltzed across Texas, two-stepped under crystal balls, and jitterbugged to hopping bands whenever he had a night off near one of the dance hall towns. He was a Lone Star Beer man; she was a Shirley Temple gal.

Callie erected her dance floor in the back of the restaurant with the assistance of Errol's roustabouts those many years ago. It was a place of hardwood flooring, low rails for propping boots, and high rails to hold cold beers. A little bar served selections of bottled beer, but only Lone Star on tap.

Scents of chewed tobacco, beer foam and sawdust were ingrained in the wood throughout. A sign over the doorway read: No Fighting, No Smoking, No Spitting On the Floor…Violators Will Be Hung, Insulted, and Charged Double.

It had long been a natural hangout for the amusement park staff every night of the week, as well as an attraction for the customers. Even the soldiers from nearby Ft. Klinston found it suitable, though some were irritated Callie enforced the No Fighting policy.

The dance floor was Callie's happiest place. She danced often with anyone who asked, not caring if they were good dancers or bad. She often cajoled a shy newcomer to come onto the floor and give it a try. For her, it was all about the music and the counter-clockwise flow around the floor. Often, she would close her eyes and allow the mirrored neon lights to spill across her face as she twirled.

One evening Sophie watched her mother out on the floor. Perhaps it was her blossoming adolescence or the fact she'd developed her first crush on a boy, but Sophie noticed something in her mother which she'd not recognized before. She realized her mother was smiling in a way which never happened off the floor. Something in her step seemed lighter and more fluid. Sophie washed beer mugs behind the bar and smiled at Callie's happiness.

Sophie also noticed Toribio standing in the doorway leading back into the restaurant. The kitchen had long since closed, and he'd finished cleaning up for the night. Sophie had never seen Toribio in the dance hall portion. She'd always assumed he was too shy to come in. She followed his intent gaze and realized he, too, was watching Callie. Sophie liked this and felt it time to take matters toward action.

"You should ask her to dance."

"I've got some prep work for tomorrow's lunch."

"No, you don't."

He looked like he was about to turn and go.

"I could teach you how," she offered.

"I know how."

"Where'd you learn to dance?"

"My sisters."

"So, go ask mom."

"I really…"

"Show me you know how, and I'll leave you alone."

Toribio gulped and walked out toward Callie. A song had just finished, and dancers were dispersing.

Callie looked surprised to see Toribio heading toward her, and she grinned when he held out his hand. Callie took it, and the two sauntered toward the middle. He prayed he remembered what to do.

A nickel dropped and Bob Wills' fiddle started a romp with his Texas Playboys. Toribio realized with the greatest relief he did, in fact, know what to do: Swing Dance!

Callie gave little squeals of exhilaration when he spun, twirled and tossed her as if they'd been a dancing pair for years. Both were out of breath when the song ended. "I'm sorry that's over," she said. "Wouldn't mind a slower song to catch my breath."

The bartender plunking coins into the jukebox must have felt the same way because the next selected melody was a hope-filled Loretta Lynn love song. Toribio held out his hand, and she took it as they glided about the dance floor. Each slow turn brought them closer. Her head lowered onto his shoulder, and she closed her eyes as they swayed beneath the glittering mirrored ball.

A drunk fellow dancing too boisterously for the song's tempo bumped into Callie's back. Her eyes flew open to see the man giddily clomping away, his dance partner rolling her eyes and mouthing an apology as he yanked her around the floor.

Callie looked up at Toribio who was smiling and looking past her to navigate around the other dancers. She wanted to melt back into his arms, but the reverie was shattered. The ball chandelier no longer reflected neon lights but, instead, images of maniacal eyebrows arching in disdain over stained and crooked teeth leering down at her.

The music morphed from a blissful country western to a howling lament sung out of tune by forlorn women in beige, ankle-length skirts. The bartender's voice calling out, "What can I get you?" to a patron hearkened back to an Army chaplain entering her drab base apartment to describe how her husband had been a hero, explaining in parables how her worst nightmare was somehow a hidden blessing. And Sophie, beaming from across the dance floor, became an anxiety-inducing reminder that her sole mission in life was to protect her baby, regardless of sacrifice.

"I'm sorry," she said as she drifted from Toribio's embrace. She saw his expression change from joy to pain in the space of a chord change, so she offered a conciliatory shoulder pat before wading off the floor and walking home alone.

· · ·

Young Cleft Hawley visited the Wagon Wheel every day for breakfast and lunch, though after five weeks he'd barely worked up the nerve to speak to Sophie beyond ordering food. Sophie eventually gathered the reins herself.

"This just arrived," Sophie told Cleft one breakfast, thrusting a new Green Stamps catalog under his chin as he shoveled a large spoonful of oatmeal into his mouth. He was so startled he gagged a bit, and it was several seconds before he looked at the picture of a blue sequined cocktail dress she was showing him.

"It's real pretty," he said when he was able to swallow.

"I'd like to wear it out."

"Okay."

"Where should we go?"

"We? I mean…sure. I mean. You wanna go out—in that dress—you wanna go out sometime?"

"I don't care where we go as long as I can wear this."

"Okay."

"More sweet tea?"

• • •

Later that week—three hours before the big night—Callie informed Toribio she was "perfectly, absolutely ready" for Sophie's first date. Yet as the time grew closer Callie found herself hyperventilating at the prospect of her baby being alone with a boy. She decided to have a talk with Sophie before Cleft arrived.

Callie talked her daughter into a little crafting. Sophie wasn't keen on the idea, worried she might get glue on the dress, and that she needed to re-fix her hair. Callie assured her the hair was just right, the dress was lovely, those sandals were the correct choice, and there was no lipstick on her teeth. Sophie acknowledged crafting might help with her nervous energy.

The two sat at the kitchen table to design jewelry, a favorite pastime on those rare nights when Callie took off from the restaurant. Sophie's talent in imagining and drawing intriguing designs was remarkable, and her skill at bending wire and light metals to match the concepts was masterful. Callie enjoyed gluing rhinestones onto the rings and bracelets to make her daughter's concepts become real. Together they made things of genuine beauty often given as gifts

"Do you think my nose is too long?" Sophie asked as she twisted wire to shape a butterfly wing.

"Your nose is perfect. Are you excited?"

"Kinda. I hope he takes me to the movies. I don't want to go to the amusement park, so maybe the movies."

"I'm sure he will," said Callie, concentrating on the finishing touch of a blue rhinestone with her glue gun. She knew there was little else for two teenagers to do within thirty miles except go to Pioneer Days Park, drive to the theater over in Alpine, or have some level of sex in a car.

"We need to talk about boys and life," said Callie, placing her glue gun onto its cradle. "It's important."

"I know all about that stuff. You don't have to—"

"No, it's important. I've been thinking a lot about what to say to you, and I've come up with some rules."

"Rules?" Sophie said, her right eyebrow arching.

"Just three," said Callie, struggling to stifle her own growing embarrassment. "First off, no drugs or alcohol."

Sophie responded with a goofy grunt to let her mother know that wouldn't be an issue.

"Second, no grandchildren for me—at least until you're twenty-five."

"But I was planning on having a litter before I graduated high school." Sophie broke into a laugh. Callie chuckled and hoped beyond hope her daughter would strictly adhere to rule number two.

Sophie went back to work on the wire ring. "Okay. What's the last rule? Lay it on me."

Callie put down her glue gun before answering. "No church. At least not with a boy."

"Huh?"

"Boys only take a pretty girl to church for one reason. It's more than trying to get inside your clothes."

Callie paused, her teeth gnawing at her lower lip. "It's not enough for a man to have your body, and Cleft Hawley will want your body, sugar, trust me."

"Momma!"

"A guy will tell you church is for your soul. I guess part of him believes it because men love to wear capes and be a hero when there's no real sacrifice in it. But a man taking a woman to church, especially a young woman, he's trying to take something more precious than her virginity. He's trying to take her heart—not the falling in love part of her heart—the part that makes her real and alive. You can't let anyone take that from you, Sophie. You can't."

Callie's eyes had brimmed over. Sophie stared as a mascara-laden tear slid past her mother's nose, caressed her jaw and fell onto the floor. Callie sniffled and resumed her efforts with the glue gun.

"I think I'll add one more rule."

"What's that?"

"Take care of you," murmured Callie.

Sophie's eyes filled as well, though she maintained her own cheerful façade.

"That pretty much accounts for rules one, two, and three."

Callie bent to kiss Sophie's lovely head. "That's my last rule, sugar. Just take care of you."

•   •   •

At the same moment Callie was giving her dating rules to Sophie, Cleft was greasing a gigantic chain link on the Stampede Stomper. Sludge was smeared in his hair and under his nails, and he was so nervous about the date he kept fumbling the oily links. Errol's incessant chatter only made matters worse, as the older man had taken it upon himself to instruct Cleft in the ways of women.

Errol was practicing sleight-of-hand with a quarter as he rambled.

"Don't you fret, 'cause I'm about to toss a bucket down into my well of wisdom."

Whereupon Errol opined on subjects ranging from taco condiments, his four months in Cub Scouts, why zippers were a mistake, and the superiority of buzzard noses. Around the midway mark he opened his hands with a flourish, but the quarter splashed into Cleft's grease can.

All of which left Cleft to wonder if Errol's well-bucket of wisdom would ever reach the water. Errol settled into the topic at hand as Cleft packed grease and wished the whole conversation would end soon.

Errol fished in the oily can for the coin as he zeroed in on the matter at hand.

"So, how many?"

Cleft pretended to focus on the chain, but Errol waited for his reply. Cleft sighed.

"Three. Three's all."

"Three different girls, or three kisses for one girl?" Errol's eyes brightened as his fingers found the quarter and he pulled it out of the grease.

"Three different girls," replied Cleft in a defensive tone.

"Like how?" Errol's tone implied he was a professional seeking facts so he could give his best advice. He wiped the coin off with the hem of his t-shirt.

"It was at a birthday party last October. There was this game where we made this bottle spin, and—"

"All three was at the same party?"

The chain slipped out of Cleft's hands, and he stared at it lying there on the ground. Errol's tone softened, as if he could tell the boy was shy about his lack of experience.

"But you like this girl?"

"She's about all I think about every minute of the day."

"Well, you'd best listen to me, 'cause your experience is pretty lack-buster. First off, I suggest you take her to church."

"Church? For our first date?"

"Fastest way to tunnel into a girl's heart is by takin' her to church. Especially a church where they go on and on about sin and whatnot. That's the kind of thing they write about in their diaries."

"I don't know," said Cleft. "I mean, I could take her to the movies or bring her here to the park or something."

"Everybody goes to the movies. You want to be the guy who does somethin' different. And you're not takin' her to her mother's own amusement park. How lame would that be?"

"Pretty lame, I guess."

"But if you take her to church, it'll show her you're interested in her spirit. It shows deepness. Women like deepness and stuff."

"Which church?" asked Cleft, both irritated and intrigued.

"I'd take her to First Baptist if I was you. The pastor over there goes on and on about sin. He's the type to wag a finger because he knows."

"He knows what?"

"Sinnin' and Gomorrah and whatnot. That's the kind of preachin' what gets a woman's love chemicals to boilin'."

"Guess I'm about done with the chain. Might oughtta be going so I can get ready if that's okay."

"You bet, you bet," said Errol. "You go on and have a real good time."

"Yes, sir," replied Cleft as he turned to leave.

"One more thing."

"Yes, sir?"

"You be nice to that little girl. She's like a rainbow on a sunny day, and her mom's always done right by me."

"I will." Cleft grinned as if embarrassed by Errol's admonition.

"I'm serious. This ain't some catfish noodle. If you want her to love you, you'd best make sure to put her first. Truth be told, wish I'd learned that lesson a long time ago."

Errol reached forward and pretended to pull the quarter out of Cleft's ear. Cleft smiled politely as Errol pressed the slimy coin into his palm with a wink.

"Buy her a soda on me."

• • •

Cleft came to the door and said all the right things to Callie, whose stern countenance was so unnerving Sophie admonished her while walking out the door. "Oh, Momma, leave him alone. We'll be home by ten."

"Nine would be better," Callie called to the couple as they walked toward Cleft's car.

"You said ten," said Sophie with a laugh and a wave over her shoulder.

"I said a lot of things," said Callie as Cleft opened the passenger side door.

Sophie rolled her eyes, which did nothing to dissuade her mother from calling out once more.

"Young man, I said a lot of things to her."

Cleft stood with the door open as if waiting for someone to tell him what to do next. "Yes, ma'am. I'm sure she listened." He looked at Sophie sitting in his car. "I mean, you did listen?"

Sophie smiled at him as if he were the cutest puppy in the litter.

"Yes, I listened to her."

Cleft looked relieved as he yelled back across the lawn: "Ma'am, she says she listened. I'll have her home before ten."

Callie waited until the teenagers drove away before slamming the door and going in search of her best friend.

• • •

Toribio had been going through a charcoal phase. He'd taken a fancy to drawing carnival rides, and he found it intriguing to use shades of black, gray and white to represent a place where color and light were everywhere.

What he liked most about charcoal was that Callie seemed drawn to watch as he worked. She chastised herself for "lollygagging," yet she always remained fixed and intent on his creations as he sketched.

"It's like all the warmth in my body washes through me when I watch you do that," she'd tell him. "My hair stands up on my head, and…I don't know why I like it, but I do."

Toribio smiled and continued making marks on the canvas as the image of the train cars circling the park or a particular seat on the carousel developed.

During one of those moments the two of them were sitting on a bench near the Bearskin Tilt-A-Whirl, Toribio sketching and Callie fretting about Sophie's date. She was so concerned about what might happen that, for once, she didn't pay attention to what he was drawing. Toribio noticed this and shifted his position so he could start a new drawing without her seeing.

"I mean, what do we know about Cleft Hawley? Cocinero, what if he's some sort of—I don't know—a pervert or something!"

He smiled and shook his head that after all these years Callie still believed his profession was his actual name. For the thousandth time he considered correcting her but, as always, he continued the task at hand and wondered what it would be like to hear her say Toribio.

"He came up to the door and greeted me properly. I'll give him that, but wouldn't you expect a child molester to be polite?"

Toribio chuckled.

"I know, I know. I'm being a little dramatic, but her first date! Are all mothers this crazy on their daughter's first date?"

He made sweeping motions with the charcoal.

"You're right. I need to calm down."

He finished the canvas and turned it for her to see. It was of Callie, and it was stunning.

"Oh my," she whispered.

Callie looked up at Toribio. He tore off the work and gifted it to her before jaunting off to prepare for the dinner crowd. She stared at him as he walked off, smiling as if all worries about Sophie's first date were forgotten.

. . .

Sophie felt guiltier about going to church than she did about making out with Cleft in his car afterwards. He was pleasant and amusing. Church, however, was glorious.

Sophie loved everything about the place: the candles, the stained glass, the choir, and the little glasses of grape juice. She'd listened to the minister extol her many sins and the fact she would be forgiven for each. She adored the friendly people who took such interest in her salvation. Everything was wondrous, and she knew she would go again and again.

The make-out session in the car afterwards was less remarkable, though pleasant enough. Cleft got his fingers caught in her hair, but he kissed like he was drinking from a fountain once he calmed down. She checked him as his hand drifted to her chest, and he was gentlemanly enough to stop.

Sophie's mind kept drifting back to the church. What most fascinated her was the fact there were so many people who wanted to know if she'd been "saved."

"Have you received the salvation of Christ yet, dear?" asked one woman.

"I don't know," replied Sophie, who was shuffled from one person to the next in blurring rapidity.

"You'll be forgiven of all your sins, dear."

"You'll sit by the side of God and Christ in eternal life and bliss, sweet thing."

"All your Earthly desires will be fulfilled in life everlasting."

All of which was quite appealing to Sophie who liked the idea of being forgiven for her mistakes and of meeting and sitting beside important people. She was energized with thoughts of doing something with her life beyond what she'd come to consider ordinary and stifling.

While many visitors to the church might have felt awkward and hard-sold, Sophie felt a surging energy. She likened it to the exhilarating, sand-shifting undertow off the beach at Corpus Christi. Sophie loved that feeling of water beneath the waves rushing to get back to sea, inviting her to come along. She always thrilled to the bigger waves reminding her there were powerful forces in the universe.

Sophie realized these people sincerely wanted her to belong to something with them, something larger than herself. She could feel strength and peace from acceptance. It was all she could do to pry herself away from the chapel and accompany her date back out to his car after the service.

Cleft and Sophie necked for twenty minutes before women from the church came outside to grab potluck trays from car trunks. He had parked his orange Chevy Vega behind the church dumpster at the farthest portion of the parking lot from the church, but Sophie worried the women had seen what they were doing.

"I wanna thank you for bringing me tonight," said Sophie. She smoothed her dress, and Cleft checked his hair in the rearview mirror.

"To church? Sure! Glad you came. I thought about taking you to your mother's park or something, but…"

Sophie giggled. "Lame."

"For sure, for sure."

Cleft nervously flipped his sun visor up and down as he spoke. "And, hey, I'm real sorry I didn't have enough gas to get to the movie theater."

"I understand."

"But I thought church visiting might be a nice first date."

"I wasn't supposed to go," she replied while re-applying lipstick.

"To church? Why's that?"

"Just my mom trying too hard."

A man from the church passed their car and fetched an ice chest from the bed of a pickup. He seemed startled when he saw them sitting in the car, but he turned away as if he'd not noticed. He grumbled something they couldn't make out as he lumbered back inside.

"Well," said Cleft. "I got a whole bunch of deep stuff out of the sermon and all. Deep stuff and whatnot."

"Me too! So, do you think it's true what they were saying in there?"

"Which part?"

"About being forgiven and getting to sit by God."

"Well sure. I mean...what do you think?"

"I think I'm going back in and get baptized at the 8:30 service!"

"What? It's your first time."

"Tonight is a night of first times. I'm going to do it."

"But—I mean—but."

•   •   •

Sophie was right. It was a night of firsts; her first date, her first church service, her first make-out session, and her first baptism. It was also the first night she and her mother began to fracture. In about the amount of time it takes to fill a bathtub, Sophie found herself in front of the congregation. The minister seemed giddy about the impromptu ceremony. The man who'd fetched the ice from the truck outside seemed put out dinner would have to wait, but everyone else was excited by the idea of a baptism before they ate.

The baptismal tub was a Victorian antique set on a wooden cart which four deacons wheeled out from stage right. They filled the tub with warm water, and Sophie was called to the altar.

"Do you accept Jesus Christ as your personal savior?" asked the portly minister.

"I do."

She felt she had returned to the ocean and become one with the universe as the minister plunged her backwards into her baptismal womb. She emerged reborn and full of all the potential life has to offer.

A chorus of halleluiahs battered the inner walls of the church. Cleft applauded and whistled through his teeth. Sophie gasped with joy.

And Callie kicked in the chapel door.

•   •   •

Callie had been oblivious to her daughter's rule violations, and she'd never envisioned Sophie would immolate said rules by doing something unthinkable like getting baptized. She might have stayed unwitting had not Errol thrown a fit in the restaurant that evening.

"Them sorry zebra butts!" yelled Errol upon opening a large cardboard box. The contents of the box were what he'd often referred to as "the merchandise" over the preceding months. The merchandise was still tucked inside as he'd packed and shipped it two weeks earlier.

Toribio was sharpening knives on the back porch next to Callie who was reading a western. He listened sympathetically as Errol lamented. Callie rolled her eyes a lot.

Errol pulled an envelope from atop the stack of eighty pairs of tan leather moccasins he'd assembled, laced, stitched, and beaded over a four-month process. He scanned the letter addressed from Craft-World Assembly, Incorporated: A Family Company.

"Them sorry sons of canker sores! Says here—says right here, 'none of the demonstrated product attained the quality of manufacture required for wholesale purchase from an independent vendor.'"

Toribio's brow furrowed as he scraped along the whetstone. Callie flipped the page of her book. Errol dug into the box to inspect the merchandise.

"I spent two hundred dollars for their kit. Two hundred dollars! And now those sorry sheep kissers won't buy back the finished product."

"Say 'sorry sheep kissers' three times fast," suggested Callie.

"How am I supposed to get rich if companies like this are takin' the little folk for two-hundred-dollars? This was supposed to net me double, and now they won't buy it back."

Callie licked her finger to turn another page. Her mouth opened, but she glanced at Toribio before "I told you so," tumbled out. He shook his head. Callie smiled like a puppy caught nibbling a shoe and kept quiet.

Toribio looked down into the box at all the footwear. For months he'd watched Errol follow the pattern design with determination. Toribio had been supportive each time the man punctured a fingertip with the provided threading needles. He'd helped calm Errol many evenings when he became frustrated with the instructions.

"They look good," Toribio said.

Errol looked up to see if he was being mocked, but he realized Toribio meant it. He picked up a pair on top of the stack and handed it to his friend. "Happy early birthday."

Errol looked at Callie, who still seemed unconcerned for his plight.

"You don't get any."

"Shucks."

"Well, just for that, I ain't gonna tell you about Cleft and Sophie's plans for the evenin'."

Callie looked up from her book with a look so sinister Toribio lowered the knife so it would be out of her line of vision.

"What plans? I thought they were going to a movie."

"It's a spiritual-type decision. Can't really talk about it."

Callie glared. Toribio slid the sharpened knife into its slot in the block and pulled keys from his pocket.

"I'll warm up the truck."

Errol turned back to Callie with a look of panic splashed across his face.

"I ain't allowed to say nothin' about nothin'."

He confessed in less time than it takes to thread a moccasin bead.

•   •   •

"You've got no right!" Callie shrieked from the chapel doors as the minister brought Sophie up from the baptismal water. Callie rushed the altar and kicked the bewildered pastor in the shin. She yanked Sophie from the Victorian tub, and the First Baptist congregation's halleluiahs withered into gasps.

"Momma, what are you doing?" sobbed a drenched Sophie.

Callie wheeled the porcelain bathtub off the dais with the Herculean strength of an enraged mother. She smirked at the smashed tub and the resultant flooding of the nave before turning on the speechless minister. "You had no right!"

The poor man gaped at the calamity of ruined carpet and flooded pews. The choir director sitting in the first row glowered while squishing her soggy stockings. Two deacons ran for mops.

"You...you," the preacher stammered.

Callie yanked a tapered candle from its candelabra and brandished it like a dagger.

"I swear I'll stab you in the eye if you call me a harlot."

"You…sinner!" he sputtered.

Callie snorted at his impotence.

"Sophie, get your purse and get your little butt in the car."

"I can't believe you did this to me!" said Sophie. Her dripping robe created a puddle beneath the offering plates.

"What are the rules, Sophie? You just heard them two hours ago. What are the damn rules?"

"You've got no say over me anymore! I answer to Jesus from here on out!"

Sophie ran from the church with Cleft in tow.

Callie stood there as the congregants built up enough indignation to say something. Life had been wonderful, her relationship with Sophie as blessed as her old friend Luz had predicted. Now Callie felt awkward and estranged, much like she had half a lifetime earlier while standing homeless and hungry outside a pony-ride tent. It occurred to her that HE had begun to lower the celestial boom.

CHAPTER SIXTEEN

Cleft approached Toribio at the restaurant a few days after the dramatic scene at the baptism, seeking advice about Sophie. Toribio held a large metal spatula as he eyed the hamburger patty he'd thrown on the grill for Cleft. A United States history book stood propped open next to the tomatoes and onions, and Toribio glanced long enough to absorb a paragraph between flips of the burger.

The two were alone in the restaurant at a time midway between breakfast and lunch, so the only sounds were the sizzling meat and a Mel Tillis song playing from the jukebox.

"It's Sophie, sir. I can't stop thinking of her. Is she not the most beautiful woman you've ever seen?"

Toribio wiped extra grease off his grill and turned the page in his book.

"I can't sleep. I can't concentrate."

Toribio flipped the burger and lifted an eyebrow.

"But I don't have any money."

The older man chuckled.

"And the other thing is, she's all eaten up with this church stuff. It's all she talks about."

Toribio sprinkled coarse salt on the burger and prepared a plate with tomato and pickle.

"I know, I know," said Cleft. "It's what makes her happy, so I need to let her get it out of her system."

Toribio pulled some French fries onto the plate and grunted a mild reproof.

"I mean…I said it wrong; not so much get it out of her system as let this church business run its course. She's gonna be interested in other stuff someday."

Toribio slid Cleft's plate across the counter and wiped the spatula.

"It's my pride. I have to get past it. I'll do what I can to spend time with her. She'll see how much I care."

Toribio pointed at Cleft with his spatula in approval.

"Thank you, sir. Thank you."

The older man began pulling spices for his chicken salad recipe.

"Have you ever experienced a love like this?" asked Cleft.

Toribio started chopping celery.

• • •

Beefo's days following the auction where he and Callie first met were mostly his own once he arrived at Pioneer Days. Twice daily he was herded into a narrow chute while children gawked and fed him twenty-five-cent handfuls of beer-soaked grain labeled Pastal Pellets they'd purchased from a vending machine hung on his corral fence.

The pellets had been an invention of Commissioner Pastal who'd heard tales of beer-fed cattle in Japan. He'd mixed beer from his own brewing attempts with alfalfa pellets in the hope of generating a new revenue stream among ranchers. He manufactured over a ton of the stuff before he realized no one was buying. Bags of it sat frozen in his butcher shop, and Beefo was the one creature on Earth to reap the benefits.

Beefo endured the insult of little hands touching his rump because he so enjoyed Pastal Pellets. He ignored syrupy fingers pulling his tail and stretching through the bars trying to touch his snout. Twelve to fifteen handfuls later, Beefo ambled back out to his field where he could be admired from afar.

Beefo would spend the next hour or so admiring individual flower petals and standing mesmerized by the long, arduous track made by a single insect. Beefo would have acknowledged life at the park wasn't half bad had he spent time considering his situation. He could eat what he wanted, he had plenty of free time, and he got snot-slinging drunk on Pastal Pellets twice daily. From time to time, however, he'd spy a heifer or hear artillery cannon drills from Ft. Klinston. In those moments his head would go up in the proud posture he'd displayed during his college days.

Callie liked to imagine that in those moments her bull was no longer an invalid on disability. In his imagination he was still Beefo, King of the Mascots!

· · ·

"Can you come over?" Sophie asked Cleft over the phone one night. It was a quarter past two, and Cleft spent most of the call trying to comprehend who had called, why she'd called, and what she wanted of him.

"Um," he replied, his eyes still closed.

"There's a scorpion in my room!"

"A scorpion?" he murmured.

"I got up to tinkle, and it was there on the floor in front of my door. It's staring at me."

"Like...a scorpion?"

"Hold on," she replied.

Cleft heard sounds of items spilling off Sophie's dresser. He was about to call out her name when she came back on.

"I covered it with that bowl you had those Spaghetti-O's in. I kept thinking I should take it to the kitchen, and I was kind of irritated you didn't rinse it out, but now I'm glad you didn't."

"Okay," he said, still not registering what it was she wanted of him.

"So, can you come over and kill it?"

"Oh."

"Please, Cleft. I'm scared. I don't mind spiders, and I touched a snake once when a guy brought one to school for assembly day, and the snake moved, and I squealed a little when that happened, but it wasn't slimy like I thought, so I pet it, and can you come over? Please?"

"Um, sure," he whispered, hanging up the phone.

His breathing became rhythmic. He tried to remember what he was supposed to do as he pulled a pillow up to his chest and settled into a comfortable position. He sighed through his nose and felt sleep pull him into the mattress.

Suddenly he sat straight up in bed with the alarm of someone awaking twelve minutes after class already started. He leaped from the mattress and scrambled for jeans. He searched under dirty laundry and around a messy desk for his car keys before dashing out to save his lady from a monster who'd dared menace her.

Minutes later he clambered up to her window, worried Sophie's mother might shoot him as he climbed in.

Sophie, who'd been unable to get him to answer the phone again, had taken matters into her own hand. She had donned knee-high leather boots in case the scorpion leaped at her shins, and she armed herself with a can of White Rain hairspray. Sophie prayed to Jesus for strength, lifted the edge of the marinara-encrusted bowl with her longest comb, and sprayed the entire contents of the can under the edge.

Cleft was nonplused at finding the insect dead on its back. The two coughed from all the hairspray vapor in the room, which woke Callie. She rushed into Sophie's room to find a shirtless and shoeless teenage boy, her daughter holding a spray can, a fumigated room, and a dead insect beside a dirty dish on the floor. The three of them stood motionless for several seconds. Callie zeroed in on Cleft, then Sophie, then back to the half-naked boy.

She harrumphed a "'night," and turned to go back to her bedroom.

"Goodnight," said Cleft and Sophie in chorus. They listened until her mother closed her bedroom door, whereupon Sophie jumped into Cleft's arms.

"Thank you, thank you, thank you!"

"But it's already dead. I didn't do anything."

"You came," she whispered.

· · ·

Callie tried to understand why Sophie's determination to attend church services caused her anxiety. Part of her had to acknowledge the simple act of disobedience from a young woman was not, in and of itself, a disaster. Had it been any other mother and daughter their fights might have been about drinking liquor, not doing chores, or breaking curfew.

Sophie's sneaking around to attend services was more than a child breaking rules, though. Callie believed her daughter had made a grave mistake in deciding to adopt a faith so spontaneously, that such an act must be the result of teenage foolishness manipulated by church members armed with centuries of proselytizing shrewdness. Reverend Gershom Sadler's religion had never been Callie's problem. His hypocrisy, however, was a source of perpetual anger. She was determined her daughter would not fall prey to such pretense.

For her part, Sophie wanted to be left alone to do as she wished. She told substantial lies to Callie for the first time in her life. Callie usually knew when Sophie had snuck to church against her wishes. Like a parent who knows her child has begun smoking cigarettes, Callie lost sleep and paced a lot. The only night she had any peace was Fridays because she knew Sophie was watching Cleft play football and going out for burgers after. Sundays and Wednesdays were miserable.

Oh, how to fight? Callie spent a lot of time trying to answer that question. Spying on her daughter, confronting her, making her do the most menial of chores at the restaurant, and trying to have heart-to-heart talks with her at home wasn't working. There seemed to be no amount of leverage or pleas which would get the girl to mind. Callie developed constant neck pain thinking about it.

"This has to stop," Callie demanded one afternoon as she challenged her daughter in the barn. She'd caught Sophie changing out of the jeans and t-shirt she'd said she was wearing for a date with Cleft into a cotton dress.

"Callie, it's no big deal," said Luz, who had arrived that evening. Callie hadn't seen her old friend in years, but Luz appeared unchanged and as chipper as ever. Neither said a word about the time which had passed since they'd last talked, and Luz got right to work kneading tension out of Callie's shoulders and neck.

Callie was in a confrontational mood, and Sophie standing there with a feigned look of innocence was pissing her off.

"It is a big deal, and I won't tolerate you lying about where you're going any more, Sophie."

"Well, I wouldn't have to lie if you let me be who I want to be!"

"Stop being so stupid!" yelled Callie.

"Callie, please don't speak to her that way," pleaded Luz.

"I'm stupid because I'm following what's in my heart?" asked Sophie, her voice quivering.

"You're stupid because you're doing it for all the wrong reasons. You like the lights and attention. That's not some divine calling. That's just you being prissy."

"At least I'm not so stupid I wasted my life in this stupid desert and in this stupid amusement park around these stupid people. My life is changing. I'm going places. I wouldn't trade where I'm going for your waste of a life."

"You're not going anywhere!"

"Callie, stop," said Luz.

"I'm going," Sophie yelled back.

Callie spied a little blue case decorated with Barbie stickers Sophie had long used to secrete her most precious items. For no clear reason other than tantrum-rage she jumped at the case and yanked it open.

"Stop, Callie," admonished Luz. "You're ruining everything!"

"Stop, Momma!" screamed Sophie as Callie tore the Green Stamp books into pieces and snapped off one of Barbie's legs.

There could be no thicker silence than the moments following the outburst. The women stared at the tattered items as if hoping they could take it all back if they just didn't move. Sophie crossed to her case and extracted the little blue Barbie dress she'd once negotiated for a makeup kit. Sophie held the dress to her chest as she left the barn without ever looking back at her mother.

Luz turned toward an old closet in a dusty corner of the barn. A stunned Callie followed her gaze.

"He's smiling in there," whispered Luz.

"I don't want to look."

.   .   .

Toribio was heading to buy dry goods for the restaurant, unaware of the fight between Callie and Sophie in the barn. He spotted Sophie striding across a soybean field, and he pulled over to see if she wanted a ride. Sophie, who'd tromped off without water or a destination in mind, took him up on the offer.

"Why so angry, *Princesa*?"

"You know why."

"Ah."

"Why won't she just let me live my life?"

"She loves you, Sophie."

Sophie realized it was the first time he had ever used her real name.

"I know she loves me, but she doesn't seem to like me."

"You've lied to her...a lot."

"Because she won't let me go!"

Toribio shifted gears and said nothing. The two rode past sluggish oil wells and miles of fence line.

"You know I'm going to leave here someday," Sophie said.

"I know."

"Have you ever thought about leaving?"

"Not for a long time. I used to travel. I've been to many places, but..."

"But what?"

"Maybe I will again someday."

"Do you stay for her?"

Toribio laughed goofily and shifted gears.

"You're in love with her!"

He shook his head and turned on the radio.

"You are! Oh my gosh, you've gotta tell her."

"Nothing to tell."

A tumbleweed popped up from the road and bounced off the windshield. Sophie watched it roll and bounce behind them. She tried to get a grasp on what this revelation meant.

"I wish you'd tell her."

"I—she doesn't—maybe someday."

"Like maybe someday you'll travel again?"

"You should explain to her why you want to go to church."

"That was a pretty clumsy subject change," she laughed. He chuckled.

"Why don't you let me off here," she suggested as they pulled in front of the movie theater.

Toribio eyed the box office, clearly wondering if that was her intended destination.

"I'll pick you up in a couple of hours," he told her as he handed her a few dollar bills.

Sophie took a few steps from the truck before turning to say, "I would like it if you were my father someday."

Toribio waited until she was inside the theater and he'd driven around the corner into an empty parking lot before he allowed himself the first happy tears of his life.

•   •   •

"Vegetarians love their children even if they become butchers," said Luz a few days after Callie and teenage-Sophie's row. The strain between mother and daughter had gotten worse, and Luz seemed to want nothing more than for them to make amends. She and Callie were back in the barn applying stain to an old door they'd sanded. Luz wiped her face and smeared stain across her cheek and nose.

"Criminals embrace sons who graduate from the police academy. That is how unconditional love goes, the nature, the burden, and the joy of parenthood."

"I get the burden part," said Callie as she tossed her paint brush into the stain can.

"It's her eighteenth birthday, and it's all she wants."

Callie eventually agreed to attend a church revival. She dreaded the outing, but she felt the need to make up for her tantrum the week before.

Callie applied makeup and dressed in a light skirt and heels, accented with a string of pearls and matching earrings. The finishing touch was a pillbox hat. She retched as she brushed her teeth. Eating breakfast was a fruitless exercise in moving eggs from one side of the plate to the other. It was all Callie could do to keep up a chipper expression to not ruin her daughter's special day. Sophie, conversely, was so giddy she was dancing about the house.

Callie ventured out to the closet in the barn a few minutes before it was time to leave. Sophie had wondered about the locked closet throughout the years, but Callie had always brushed off her queries by telling her the door led to a dark hole she'd have filled in someday.

Callie pulled the old truck seat away from the door and stared at the rusty closet door handle. She wanted to tear the lock off the door frame or kick the damn thing down. She refrained and instead used the key she kept atop a two-by-four joist to unlock the door.

Callie pulled open the freezer door and raised the casket lid. She nodded to Gershom Sadler lying there. Gingerly she picked up her old Sears and Roebucks catalog and leafed through the cracking pages.

"Look what you've done." She spoke to him without looking up from the pages. "I don't know how you do it, but you've recruited another one of us."

There was a long pause during which she flipped the pages back and forth, and the floodgates opened. "It's Sophie! Why Sophie, you bastard?"

Tears spattered onto a page of tablecloth patterns. Callie's shoulders heaved.

"Momma," Sophie called from the barn entrance.

Children, even grown children, have a way of stopping a good cry or a long-delayed kiss. Callie wiped away all evidence of her tears using the corner of an old saddle blanket.

"I'll be right there, sugar," she called back in her cheeriest tone. "I'm just looking for something."

"We need to go pretty soon, or we'll be late."

"I know, hon. Let me check my makeup."

Callie found Sophie sitting in the backseat of Cleft's Chevy. The car was a four-cylinder heap with a serious rain leak in the windshield and a passenger side door which could not be opened from the inside.

Cleft leaped from the driver's side to open Callie's door. He was rewarded with disdain.

"Morning, Miss Callie. Sure is a nice day."

Callie sat and stared straight ahead as Cleft ran back around the car.

"Miss Callie, would you mind putting on your safety belt?" asked Cleft.

Callie's silence was smothering.

"Did you fix your radio yet, baby?" asked Sophie, her voice squeaky.

"I sure did! Wrapped the fuse in foil. Works fine now."

Cleft reached forward to turn it on, but Callie popped his hand away.

"I like the quiet."

They rode in that quiet for three miles before Sophie couldn't stand it any longer.

"Momma, Cleft has a surprise."

"Yes, ma'am," said Cleft. "I've been accepted into the police academy!"

"Is that so?" replied Callie. "And do you think they'll teach you about following a mother's rules if you're dating her daughter at this police academy?"

"Oh, Momma!"

"Miss Callie, I'm real—"

"Cleft, I'd zip that mouth of yours," said Callie. "I told Sophie I'd go, but one more word—one word—and I'll walk the rest of the way."

Cleft looked back at Sophie in the rearview mirror. She shook her head as if to warn him against saying one more word, including, "Yes" or "ma'am."

. . .

Sophie tried to persuade her mother to sit in one of the front pews, but Callie chose the second-to-last. Her anxiety about being in the church was compounded when she noticed the minister nod in what she interpreted as a conspiratorial manner toward Sophie and saw her daughter nod back. Callie saw Cleft squeeze Sophie's hand as if he were in on the secret.

Sophie leaned toward Callie and murmured, "The minister says I'm special."

"Real special," added Cleft whose smile evaporated under Callie's glare.

Luz breezed into the church with her arms wide open as if extending a gigantic embrace to everyone already seated. She wore a teal gossamer skirt and matching ballerina slippers, and she sat in the pew just in front of Callie. She grabbed a hymnal and turned to Callie as if to ask about the first song selection, but Callie wasn't interested.

Callie's eyes were set on her daughter. "Sophie, what the hell is going on?"

As if in response, the minister addressed his congregation. "We'll now hear from Miss Sophie Wind who has asked to witness to us this fine morning." He looked overjoyed when Sophie stood up, but he also glanced at Callie with a look of grave concern. The water stains from the overturned bathtub incident were still evident below his podium.

"Go get 'em, baby," Cleft whispered as his girlfriend smoothed her skirt and stepped into the aisle.

Callie had not known Sophie would be speaking at the ceremony. She was so surprised when the beaming minister beckoned her daughter that she inhaled saliva and experienced a short coughing fit.

"Sometimes it helps to raise your arms above your head," offered Luz, as she patted her old friend on the back.

Callie's coughing fit subsided, and she held up an OK sign so Luz would stop patting.

"You're okay, then?" asked Luz. Callie's eyes were transfixed on Sophie making her way to the front of the church.

Luz held the hymnal close to her chest as she rose and whispered over her shoulder.

"I'm just going to move forward a few rows so I can see better."

Callie watched her friend move up three rows, sit, shake her head, and move once more to the front. Luz slid in a small space on the aisle next to the minister's wife and shook with gleeful anticipation.

Sophie felt a mix of glory and trepidation as she made her way to the altar. She was resolved to say something profound, but she had no idea what that message might be. She decided she would quote some passages she'd memorized from previous services and see where the Spirit led her.

"We read in John 3:16 that God so loved the world that he gave his one and only son, that whoever believes in him shall not perish but have eternal life, and...and..."

Sophie faltered, for her faith was fresh and real but her thoughts were no more organized or fluid than what she'd learned verbatim. Looking out over the congregation, she felt keenly the responsibility of meeting their expectations. She froze like a teenage boy caught sneaking into his girlfriend's window. Sophie couldn't formulate a single additional word past what she'd already said. The longer she stood there trying to think of something, the drier her mouth and thoughts became.

Dozens of people in their Sunday best stared at her, all concerned for her anguish or irritated by her lack of grace.

Cleft called out, "It's okay, baby," but he shrank into the pew when every eye in the building turned on him.

Luz rose to a crouch and skittered across the aisle to better see around the pulpit.

The minister murmured to Sophie that she was doing fine.

But Sophie was not doing fine. She wanted to disappear, to never return, to go back in time as if she'd never come to this church. Her eyes filled, and she stepped back from the altar as if a little more distance would end the nightmare.

And just then Callie saw the Reverend Gershom Sadler enter from the wings. Reverend Sadler was blue-tinged, and his eyes were red-rimmed. He leered at Callie as he propped his rear on the choir railing. He shifted his gaze from Callie to Sophie. Callie's face darkened and her head dipped like a winged raptor about to pounce on a squirrel when she realized the man was smirking at her daughter's plight.

"No, sir," murmured Callie. "No, you will not."

All eyes followed Callie as she marched down the aisle toward her drowning daughter. Luz clasped her hands together in prayer, and Cleft squeezed a hymnal in vicarious agony. A man snored in the fourth pew, and a grandmother with crusty rings and a dragonfly brooch harrumphed at Sophie's panic. A mother dabbed at a grape juice stain on her restless child's jacket.

Callie raised an eyebrow at Reverend Sadler as she passed, and then she moved her gaze back to Sophie. Her meaning was clear, like an old-west gunslinger turning her back on a foe: You are no threat, and you mean nothing to me. Sadler responded with a muffled harrumph.

"Why is this important to you?" Callie whispered to Sophie as the two met center pulpit. Sophie kept glancing over her mother's shoulder at all those people.

"I've told you about Gershom Sadler," Callie continued. "How he sucked the souls of people right in and used them in ways I can't believe God ever intended."

Reverend Sadler cleared his throat in frustration. Luz moved back to her seat beside the minister's wife and gave a supportive smile to Callie.

Sophie furrowed her brow in worried concentration.

"Sophie, look at me. Reverend Sadler was a flawed man who did ugly things, but he did one thing well. He told people every day why this was all so important to him. As much as it pains me to point this out, when you can do that, when you know why it's important that you bare your soul to these people, and convince them it's important they listen to you, that's when all this can mean something."

Sophie had stopped peering at the congregation, now looking at her mother.

"Sugar, it doesn't matter if you can quote that book."

"Does so!" Reverend Sadler called out, though no one paid him any mind.

"It matters more that you know what the words mean to you."

Luz extended her knees and flutter-kicked her feet in clear delight.

"Amen, amen, amen, amen!"

Sophie dabbed a tear, and she giggled. Callie turned and sat down in a velvet-covered chair next to the minister who flushed at this breach of protocol. A single tear rolled down Luz's cheek and lolled around the corner of her beaming mouth. The child with the juice stain stopped squiggling. The snoring man woke up and leaned forward with elbows on knees. The harrumphing woman with the gold jewelry rested a white-gloved hand on her bosom as her lips parted in rapt attention.

Reverend Sadler brushed his upper arms as if they'd sprouted lint and left in the same direction he'd entered. Callie betrayed the slightest smile as she tilted her head to listen to her daughter's wise words.

Sophie cleared her throat and tried again.

"What I wanted to say to y'all was that in the last few months all of you, and this book, this place, my place here, well, it's all gotten so significant to me. I feel like I'm, I don't know, just a little drop in a pond, but when I think about how each one of us is a drop, and together we make up the whole pond—more—a lake that flows into a river that goes out and becomes part of the whole ocean, well, I feel like I'm not so small because I'm part of something that is important."

Sophie gazed out at the congregation which had been so terrifying moments before.

"I have to be part of this. I'm sorry I didn't do this witness as well as I had planned, but that's what's in my heart, and I wanted you to know."

The congregation burst into applause and halleluiahs. The minister's eyes widened when the offering trays came back spilling over, and Sophie ate up the pats on the back and handshakes. Cleft beamed as he gave her a hug and was rewarded with a kiss on his cheek. Callie left out a side door, flanked by Luz.

"That was a wonderful thing you did," said Luz.

"Feels like I just sent her off to war with a love note and a box of bullets."

CHAPTER SEVENTEEN

Callie and Sophie spent a lot of effort avoiding one another after Sophie's big moment at the church. One afternoon Callie stopped to cry in the school-supply aisle of Winn's Five & Dime. Another day she gave herself a kitchen sink perm and cried again when she left the chemical in too long resulting in a brittle nest.

"You're winning," she admitted to Gershom Sadler one evening as she waited in the barn for Sophie to come home. "I'd like to wipe that sneer right off your damn mouth."

She flung the door lock at his chest and felt worse as it thumped off his lifeless belly.

. . .

Forty-seven police cadets sat in rapt attention as the academy commander addressed them on their graduation day four months later. Cleft listened with pride as Sophie, Errol, Toribio and Callie looked on from the audience. Even Callie had to admit the uniform looked good on him.

"Some people will despise you for the profession you've chosen," said the commencement speaker. "They don't know you or what is in your heart. All they see is that badge pinned to your chest and that firearm strapped to your hip. All they can imagine is that you're there to deprive them. But, your mission is to serve them and protect them, and it is to their great loss they fail to see."

Sophie was sniffling, and Callie glanced over to see Errol was as well.

"Cadets, soon you will cross this stage and join our ranks. As you leave here, I challenge you to always remember the honor of this profession comes not in forcing others to obey you but, instead, to live each day in pursuit of the mission."

Toribio also misted up, and Callie patted his arm. The ceremony continued with the graduates receiving their certificates. Cleft was honored with the top marksmanship award for the class. Sophie came forward and fulfilled the honor of pinning on his badge to mark his ascension from cadet to peace officer. She patted the new badge on his chest as rivulets of mascara ran down her cheeks.

Two months later Cleft performed CPR on a woman whose heart had stopped as she sat in her Oldsmobile at a cross walk. He received a dozen burned cookies for his heroics after her release from the hospital. She gleefully watched him eat every single one as they sat on her veranda, and he continued chewing even when he realized she'd confused salt for sugar in the recipe.

In the months to come he joined the county SWAT team and made the most arrests for drunk driving. His uniform was always precise, and his judgment tended to be prudent. He passed his year as a probationary officer as if he was born to the job. His captain told him he had a fine future. He dated the prettiest girl in Texas and had the best job in the world. Cleft Hawley was happier than he'd ever been in his life.

·   ·   ·

Sophie's fame spread through the Bible belt in the months following her first talk at the church. The minister recognized potential, and soon her name was on the tongue of every deacon and pastor across six counties. She loved radio and improved at spreading the Gospel at tent revivals and church services. It was a rare Sunday or Wednesday when she wasn't invited to this church or that gathering. She, too, was living a dream. Something was missing, though, and Cleft believed he had the answer.

"So, what do you think?" he asked. Sophie looked up from the ring he'd offered. She decided to squash the irritation she was feeling because he looked so earnest and hopeful.

What annoyed her was not the size of the ring, which boasted a diamelle the size of a sesame seed. Of course, she dreamed of big jewels and a lavish lifestyle, but she'd never expected Cleft to be able to provide those things. Sophie had grown into a young woman practical enough to know she'd have to provide those things herself.

No, the source of her irritation was not the offered ring, but the setting for the question. Cleft—earnest, giddy Cleft—had decided to pop the question within the confines of his patrol car. Sophie sat in the passenger seat, complete with prisoner partition cage, RADAR gun, handcuffs hanging from the floodlight handle, and police-band radio between them.

Sophie paused for so long Cleft asked, "Have I done something wrong?"

"You know I love you."

"But, what?"

"I've made a decision. It's a whopper, and I've gotta know you're good with it before I can say yes to this."

"Anything!"

"Cleft," she began before pausing once more. "I don't—okay, I don't want to have any kids."

"Children?"

"Children. No children. I have my career to think about. Besides, I realized it would be harder for your job as well."

"How do you mean?"

"I mean, what with all the evildoers out there."

"Plenty of 'em."

"Right, and they'd just love to get their hands on our offspring so you'd be forced to ignore their crimes."

"Sure, sure, but—you don't want kids?"

"Gotta say, no kids."

It was Cleft's turn to pause. The decision was monumental.

"It's not like I feel a big tractor pull to be a father, but I always sort of assumed..."

Sophie's lips were pressed, and she wasn't blinking.

"You're probably right," he answered. "Just you and me. You set up your little jewelry store, and I'll make sergeant in five years. No kids. Make saving for a bass boat go faster."

He slipped the little ring onto her finger, grinning like a porpoise high on smoked tuna.

• • •

Callie and Toribio were returning from running errands one afternoon when she stumbled across a recorded program while searching for a clear radio channel in Toribio's truck. Sophie had a catchphrase by then:

"We're all a ripple in God's pond," and it was this snippet Callie heard as she scrolled across AM 1370.

Toribio heard it as well, and his eyes grew wide as he stared straight ahead and wondered what Callie's response might be. It was silence for the next twenty miles until they reached Pioneer Days Park and she barreled out of the truck cab before he'd pulled to a complete stop.

Toribio had to hustle to catch up. The duo continued until Callie reached her destination, the bumper car ride in the middle of the park.

Callie raised a few protests as she bypassed the line of patrons waiting their turn for a spin in the bumper cars. Yet even those who'd never met her recognized her as full of venom when she selected a car, sat down, and strapped in. The ride operator glanced over at Toribio and flipped the ON switch. Callie and twenty other riders felt the surge of electricity energize their little convertibles, and she mashed her foot down onto the accelerator to let loose.

It was carnage, as far as bumper cars go, with Callie targeting any and all. Neither the youthful nor the elderly were safe from the menace of her plowing into them head on, T-boning them in the side, ramming them from the rear, or slamming into them with her car in full-speed reverse. Pioneer Days had rules against such maliciousness but damn the rules. Callie wanted to bash things, as Toribio looked on with growing concern.

A dozen turns later Callie gave up her jalopy to the ride operator who pulled it out of rotation pending extensive body work. Her left ribs and right knee would turn blue and purple over the next few days, and a trickle of blood oozed from a nostril to congeal with hair mussed along one cheek. She had the air of a woman spent and satisfied, and she pat Toribio's cheek as she passed him.

"Guess it's time we should start prepping for the dinner rush," she said in a husky voice Toribio found alluring.

*   *   *

Sophie's concern something was missing in her life returned within weeks of the engagement to Cleft. The wedding had been scheduled for the following June, but she'd yet to feel any desire to plan the event. Cleft seemed focused on his work, to the point she often thought he'd forgotten about her. It was as if he'd already settled into a more dormant, matrimonial lifestyle. This all came to a head one evening as she tried to get him to take her on a date to a church function.

"I think we'd have a good time. There's gonna be potluck and a live band for dancing after I give my witness."

"I think I shouldn't be going to such affairs anymore, Sophie," Cleft replied as he settled down onto his workbench to measure out gunpowder he'd use to manufacture target-practice bullets.

"Well, why not!?"

"With me being an officer of the law and all…"

"What does that have to do with anything, Cleft?"

"Sophie, I can't be cavorting with—"

"Oh my lord, Cleft. It's a church social in Bandera. Cavorting?"

"I can't be seen cavorting."

"Well, I hope you'll be able to leave all this luxury from time to time after we get married because I sure as hell don't intend to watch you make bullets every night for the rest of my life."

"Sounds good, hon," he answered absentmindedly, too focused on powder grains to realize she'd already left with a lemon Bundt cake and a mind to cavort.

•   •   •

The wedding plans continued, if for no other reason than steamrolling inertia and a compass-heading unfazed by ambivalence. That meant a to-do list which included Cleft following up on his pre-nuptial commitment. He'd promised no kids, and the day had arrived to make a checkmark by that particular bullet item.

Sophie was companionable when she walked into the clinic on Cleft's arm. She smiled and rubbed his shoulder as he signed in. His hand trembled when he handed the clerk his insurance card.

He was handsome and in uniform; she was pretty in her side-pony and a thrift store blouse she'd bought for the occasion. She hunted for hidden objects on the back cover of a Highlights Magazine as they waited. He stared at a scuff on the toe of his boot and picked at a cuticle.

"I decided against wearing boxers," Cleft whispered. "I was getting dressed for my shift earlier, and I thought it might, you know, facilitate the process. If I don't have them on, all I have to do is take my pants off."

"Good idea, I guess," replied Sophie. "Are you planning to leave your shirt on?"

"Thought I would," he replied. "I feel like I should maintain some sense of decorum for the procedure."

"Oh."

"Got a little chafed without the boxers during the shift, though."

"Sure. All part of the plan."

"Love you."

"You, too."

"Cleft Hawley," called a nurse from the door leading back into the surgical suites. Cleft felt his stomach plummet to his pelvis, but he stood and walked toward the nurse after receiving one last kiss on the cheek from Sophie.

"I'll be right here, baby."

He nodded once in the stoic manner worthy of a lawman and strode to the back.

The clinic beyond the waiting room smelled of lemon disinfectant, soap, rubbing alcohol, and essence of terror-sweat from a thousand men before him. Framed photos of bird dogs covered the dark wood paneling in the waiting room, a theme which continued down the hall to the procedure room.

Cleft appeared stoic despite fighting like hell to keep from gagging. He didn't notice much as the skinny nurse led him to the exam room. Cleft nearly bolted when he entered the nine-by-ten box decked with pastel green ceramic tile atop more wood paneling.

A second door on the opposite side was open. Cleft spied his doctor sipping coffee and eating a sandwich in the next room. The nurse shut the door as she gave her instructions.

Cleft hung his pants and cap on a coat stand, his tactical boots on the floor beside the exam table. His shirttails remained in place with elastic suspenders attached to his socks. He'd had plenty of time to change out of uniform after his patrol shift, but how much better to walk into a specialist's office wearing the symbol of your life's mission for all to see. Despite Sophie's offer to bring him sweatpants and a t-shirt, Cleft had walked his gal into the waiting room with the straightest back and proudest chest of any man in the county.

Cleft had never been in examination stirrups before, and he got the impression from his nurse he was doing it all wrong.

"Your feet go in the stirrups and your bottom comes toward me. That's right...scooch your butt more towards me...no, more...more, hon...more towards me now...okay, that's fine...no, a little more...okay. The doctor will be in shortly."

Cleft had never felt so vulnerable with "Ricky and the Bongos" dangling down at the other end, in clear view of doctor, nurse and anyone else who might wander through to the break room. A set of stainless instruments lay on a sterile towel three feet from his right leg.

I am a brave man, he thought. I do nervy things for a living. This is not scary as crap.

Cleft worked up enough saliva to speak. "Is this gonna hurt much, ma'am?"

The nurse smirked. "It'll feel like a little bee sting."

This did nothing to comfort Cleft as he remembered where on his body the bee was going to attack.

Doctor, whose name Cleft could not recall, entered from the break room, and his presence went a long way toward calming Cleft. The physician was dignified, with a graying, conservative haircut and rimless glasses. He moved with the grace of a man who'd done the procedure countless times.

"I'm going to make a sterile field around the area," said Doctor while framing Cleft's giblets in blue towels. "So, have you been to the café out by the amusement park?"

"All the time," said Cleft with a dry throat.

"Best burger I've ever had, including medical school."

"Real good," replied Cleft, which was about as clever a response as he could manage.

Doctor continued the chatter as he shaved his patient and made clippie forceps sounds around the area of Cleft's body he least wanted shaved and clipped.

"Here's the injection," said Doctor in his most somber tone. "You're going to feel a little bee sting and some pressure that will feel like a horse kick."

Cleft mewed like a calf. To cover his embarrassment, he offered a mumbling moment-by-moment report.

"Bee sting…horse kick…yes, yes, doctor…I concur."

Doctor changed angles with the syringe. "So, you're a police officer, I see."

"I'm uh, a deputy sheriff."

"Cop's a cop," said the nurse.

"I give up," chuckled Doctor as he held up his hands in the universal sign of "I give up."

This took on a different meaning as Doctor stood there with forceps in one hand, scalpel in the other. This dignified professional, this skilled surgeon who asked polite questions about one's family without ever once letting slip a snotty tubule, morphed into something different. Doctor became every tank-top wearing, get-me-a-beer-dammit, screw the neighbors if they don't like cars parked on my own damn lawn, tattoo-on-the-calf redneck Cleft had ever had to deal with on a payday Friday night.

There were so many places Cleft couldn't go anymore because of people who took pleasure inflicting the extra little nicks life has to offer: The barber who gave him three consecutive haircuts with large bald spots shaved into the back. It took Cleft that long to realize the barber had a brother he'd arrested for drunk driving. The shoplifting teenager who worked at the Dairy Mart whom Cleft suspected was licking his pickle slices before wrapping up his double with cheese. The punk neighbor kid who was destined for prison, and who always managed to weed-eat chunks of paint off Cleft's police car fender.

And now it was the surgical mask twins in command of his manhood, living the dream, drunk on the power of having a cop firmly by the balls.

•   •   •

Sophie thumbed through a People magazine as she waited for Cleft. Three clearly nervous men sat with their legs crossed in other parts of the waiting room. Two of them were in their mid-thirties, and she figured they would have vasectomies that day as well. One man was in his seventies, and he'd already been to the men's room four times.

Sophie was bored, but she chastised herself for not concentrating on Cleft's plight. She imagined tending him later, acting like a good fiancée should in nursing him back to health. She scrawled a shopping list of suitable menu items for her convalescing sweetheart in the margins of a Reader's Digest crossword: noodle soup, spray cheese, Vienna sausages, Saltines, Jell-O.

A giant of a man entered the clinic carrying a little brown bag. A five-year-old on the first day of kindergarten might have displayed more moxie than did this mighty fellow. He slid the bag across the counter to the receptionist as if handing his parents a poor report card.

"I've got my sample here," he said. His voice carried across the room, despite his attempt at a whisper.

"Did you write your name on it?" the receptionist asked. Sophie wondered if she were being loud on purpose.

"Yes, ma'am."

"Super! I'm sure the doctor explained you may still have live spermatozoa in your ejaculate?"

"Yes, ma'am. He explained—"

"So, you should refrain from unprotected intercourse for at least six weeks?"

"Yes, ma'am, I understand." He was getting frantic now, moving backwards toward the door. He didn't seem to notice a clerk giggling from the file racks, or a smirking nurse as she filed her nails behind the receptionist.

"Did he also explain that frequent masturbation may speed the process of eliminating any live swimmers from your vas deferens?"

"Jesus, ma'am, yes he told me!"

He glanced over his shoulder and made accidental eye contact with Sophie. He had a look of the condemned. Sophie looked away and felt embarrassed for him.

"We'll have your semen sample analyzed and call you if any sperm are found still alive. If so, we'll need another sample from you in two weeks."

"That's fine, ma'am. Thank you. I've got a...I've got to go."

He bolted for his pickup in the parking lot and roared away. Sophie seriously doubted he would ever come back to this place again, and the thought made her despair for Cleft.

Any feelings of sadness evaporated a moment later when Callie shoved in the clinic door.

• • •

Nurse never looked at Cleft's face during the rest of the procedure. She talked to his scrotum, or rather, she told off his scrotum.

"I got pulled by some cop on a motorcycle a few weeks ago, and your buddy—"

"—I'm sure I don't know him."

"—made me spend four hours in district court because they couldn't find his paperwork. But do you think I ever got paid for those four hours, and do you think anyone ever apologized for hammering me for half a day?"

"They should have apolo—"

"—and I was sick, but do you think that jackass prosecuting attorney cared?"

"No, I don't think he cared, and he was wrong. He should have cared so, so much."

Instruments passed between Nurse and Doctor, their efforts rhythmic and well-practiced. Cleft could feel Nurse's loathing, her power as she passed sharpened steel over his glans. He wanted nothing more than for a representative of the Fraternal Order of Police to come running in with a hand-scripted apology and a cashier's check for whatever this woman earned in four hours.

"That's all right," she said. "You can make it up to me by giving me some advice about a no insurance ticket I got last month."

He never felt the incisions, but Cleft heard little electric buzzing like mosquitoes hitting a bug zapper as Doctor cauterized a vas deferens shut for good. A smell like burning bacon scented the room. Aside from an overwhelming urge to kick, scratch, bite, eye gouge and run away from a hot electric prod burning his bongos, Cleft didn't feel a thing.

Until there was a tug; not a little tug like uncontested monofilament reeling home to rod, but more of an un-greased lawn mower pull-rope tug. A piece of sinew Cleft never knew existed stretched from his groin to his collar bone. His eyebrows met his hairline, his rectum puckered, and his diaphragm went on strike.

"Woah! Now hold on now."

"Oh, are you feeling that?" Doctor asked.

Cleft answered with a sad little whistle. He was rewarded with another bee sting and horse kick.

"Let me ask you a question, you bein' an officer of the court, and all," said Doctor. It hit Cleft that Doctor's accent had changed from Yale Cum Laude to paint-huffing crawdad fisherman.

"I've got me this neighbor with this dog, see? And this sombitch takes one humongous crap in my lilies every damn morning, and I was wonderin', you bein' an officer of the court and such, if I could, all legal like, sue the sombitch."

"Your neighbor or the dog?" Cleft asked, which he knew was a mistake when the sinew stretched again.

Do not do that, screamed Cleft inside his head. *Do not twist them like that. You're the sombitch! You're the sombitch!*

"The neighbor," said Doctor with the innocence of a kid caught passing notes in class. "Or maybe, and I was considering, you know, maybe a little anti-freeze in hamburger A- La-King."

Chuckle. Guffaw. Wink. Nurse dabbed and smiled.

"I'm tidying up a bit," said Doctor as he bent to scrutinize his work.

"Tidy...appreciated."

Nurse and Doctor looked up at Cleft. It was eerie how synchronized they were. They stared at him over their surgical masks like he was in "the chair" in some interrogation room and they were waiting for a confession.

"You think you'll be able to help with our little problems?" asked Doctor.

Cleft knew Doctor was asking about a rogue neighbor dog and an insurance ticket. He knew these were more than little problems to them; that they had been the subject of indignant break room discussions; that Doctor and Nurse had spent hours white-knuckle clenching their steering wheels on the drives home, Doctor imagining the perfect comeback to a thoughtless neighbor, Nurse wishing she'd said something wilting to that motorcycle cop; that the "System" not getting the dog to stop pooping on Doctor's lawn or some ticket writing butthole with a radar gun son-of-a-bitch represented the whole of the Law; and for God and gonad's sake, Cleft had best consider modifying that image pronto.

Cleft felt the tug again. This time it was up around his navel, but with an ominous hint the pull could go higher and deeper at any moment. Any sense of duty toward a higher purpose or standing firm in the face of coercion went poof.

"Why, yes, I can. I certainly can help you."

"Well," said Doctor, once again professorial, "let's get to this right side, and you'll be done."

Cleft hadn't realized they were only halfway through, and his heart sank. He hummed one flat note in a good-natured way, and resigned himself to more bee stings, horse kicks and tugs on drawstrings running the length of his body. Doctor made the incision, reached in with forceps, and pulled out a slippery loop of tube. He connected the clamps, wiped a bit of blood away so he could better see his second target, and took the proffered scalpel from Nurse.

This is it, thought Cleft, as the instrument descended, the cut that would seal the deal. Cleft began to panic over the thought of never siring children. He imagined being somehow less a man for not being able to ejaculate his little swimmers, and he almost grabbed Doctor's wrist.

But he didn't.

You're being silly; all part of the plan.

· · ·

Just as the night of Sophie's baptism had been a night of first times, the day of Cleft's attempt to give Sophie a life without children was a day of lasts. It was the last time Cleft and Sophie would see one another for over a decade. It was the day of Callie and Sophie's final fight about her going to church; the curtain call for Cleft's life plan and the finale for Callie's hope her family would stay together; the last time Sophie put her own dreams on a back burner.

Sophie felt all the oxygen had been sucked from the room when her mother entered like she'd ignored the "No Females Allowed" warning sign in an old west saloon.

Sophie expected her mother to curse and break things. Callie had done it before, after all. Sophie knew she was in for a lecture about life choices, responsibility, respect for one's mother, and not being sucked in by the charlatans of this world. She received, instead, silence.

Callie sat in a chair opposite her daughter, nothing but a magazine-strewn coffee table between them. Neither spoke for a whole, awful minute.

Sophie broke first. "Momma, I'm sorry, but we have a plan."

Callie reached into a fringed leather purse she'd made during her traveling days. She extracted a sequined diary and a bejeweled pair of eyeglasses. These she tossed onto the coffee table like an attorney throwing down a bloody glove in front of a jury.

The two women stared at the items, knowing what they symbolized. The diary was Sophie's, a journal she'd redeemed with her green stamp collection when she was eleven. She'd documented her most private thoughts and moments in script so small she'd made it last seven lovely years.

The eyeglasses had been purchased with the journal as a set from the Spy Barbie collection. The pale blue diary had come with a matching pen and four replacement ink cartridges. The cool thing about the set was that the ink in the pen was invisible unless you were wearing the glasses.

The lenses on the glasses were transparent red plastic, which revealed hundreds of thoughts and dreams Sophie had nurtured through her adolescent years. How many times had Callie passed by Sophie's room and chuckled to herself to see her baby girl jotting with bauble-encrusted Barbie Spy Lenses perched on the bridge of her nose?

Sophie was aghast. "You read my…my diary?"

"There's a man on the other side of that wall doing something that will change him forever. You wrote in your journal last night that you want to leave. You said if you stay in Elixir Springs your soul is going to drown"

"I can't believe you read it!"

"Dammit, girl, don't be cruel. Cleft is in there trying to give you a gift he thinks you want, and you're mad I'm making you be honest. Do what's right, Sophie. That's my last rule for you. Do what's right."

Sophie finally understood the irrevocability of Cleft's procedure. The deteriorating relationship with her mother had become a new kind of clarifying glasses. She couldn't live life amidst faux wood paneling and plastic flowers, controlled by her mother, married to an unimaginative deputy sheriff, 'till death would they part.'

She suddenly understood she couldn't allow Cleft to proceed with the vasectomy. It wasn't fair when it was all being done for her. What if he found another girlfriend someday? The thought irked her, but she was mature enough to know it was likely.

So, with equal parts restrained dignity and rising panic she'd waited too long, Sophie strode past the objecting receptionist and into the back of the clinic. She peered in every treatment room until she came to the one in which Cleft lay supine and on display.

"Hello?" she managed to squeak out.

Doctor held Cleft's right vas deferens with forceps, his scalpel poised midway between two clamps squeezing the tube.

"You can't come in here," said Nurse.

"I think I've made a mistake. Cleft, I'm so sorry, but this is a mistake."

"This? Me getting my swimmer tubes cut, this?"

Doctor and Nurse stood back and waited, enjoying real life drama right there in the operating room. Nurse stepped back in long enough to dab him once more, took two paces backwards and cleared the lane.

"I'm doing this for you...for us," said Cleft, in a voice he regretted as too whiny. "You said children weren't part of the plan, and this was the most caring gesture you'd ever heard of."

"I know, I know, but this is too much, especially since I don't know where we're headed, anymore."

Cleft, still in stirrups, was flabbergasted.

"What are you talking about!? We're getting married in five weeks—a sheathe-free wedding night. How can you not know where we're headed?"

"I've been sitting in the waiting room, and I've come to realize our relationship is based on nonsense. All the passion we've ever felt for one another was just that—passion. I love you but I don't know anyone else. I want to travel, and you want to enforce the law in this county for the rest of your life. I want to make a fortune, and you want to retire with enough pension to buy an RV. I'm sorry, but it's not enough."

Cleft jabbed both index fingers toward his groin. "How is this not enough!?"

Sophie closed her eyes in acknowledgement of this monumental sacrifice, but he'd known her long enough to see she'd made up her mind. In the space of time it had taken to have his goodies shaved and poked, the love of his life had changed her mind.

She looked down at the surgical area for the first time. It took her a moment to realize how close Cleft had come to having both superhighways shut down. Her eyes flooded as she looked from the area to Cleft and to the doctor.

"Please don't cut the other one," she whispered while handing Cleft her engagement ring.

Sophie flung out of the operating room and past her mother. She fled the clinic, screeching out of the parking lot with the same intensity as the giant man a few minutes earlier. Half an hour later she left the county with one packed suitcase and a shoebox of cassette tapes.

"And I'm never coming back!" she bellowed out the window as she plugged in a cassette, shoved the accelerator to the floor and headed toward anywhere else.

CHAPTER EIGHTEEN

It had taken Cleft a few moments to register it all before he realized his feet were still aloft in stirrups. The urologist stitched and the nurse dabbed, both as ready for Cleft to leave as he was. The doctor fitted him with what he called a "squirrel sack," and it was hours before dazed Cleft understood the "nut" joke.

Cleft went right back to work, telling the county dispatcher he was available for service as he pulled out of the clinic parking lot. Dispatcher Joyce took him up on it by sending him to a domestic disturbance.

A blotto husband had argued with his hammered wife over control of the television remote. The result was a free-for-all. He smashed one of her Tammy Wynette Limited Edition Collector Plates, so she slugged his concave chest with all the strength in her ham-thick arms. He demanded makeup sex; she bit him on the shoulder, drawing blood from a botched Confederate flag tattoo. He yanked a hank of her hair out of her scalp, whereupon she stabbed him in the ear with the TV antenna.

A neighbor who preferred to remain anonymous summoned the police.

Cleft arrived when the fight was still on. The wife wielded a baseball bat. The husband had chosen to de-root and brandish an Aloe Vera plant.

Cleft would later write in his report he "exited the vehicle and attempted to intervene in the disturbance." He did not report that one loose stitch in his groin had bled through the squirrel sack, and that his tan pants were stained red from his belt buckle to his coccyx. The first to notice was the husband who paused in the violent pursuit of his wife to point and laugh.

"What the hell, dude? You on the rag or something?"

Cleft looked down and saw the spreading blood blot. Seeing blood coming from his own groin made him swimmy headed. To keep from passing out Cleft lowered his head to his knees, at which point the husband slapped him in the back of the head with the jagged cactus branch. Four little crimson cuts appeared on Cleft's neck, and the pain they caused made him forget his stitches.

Cleft knocked the husband out with one mighty blow to the chin. In response, the wife swung her bat like a golf club, right where she knew he'd feel it most. More blood flooded across Cleft's thighs and began leaking to his knees.

The husband came to, and before other officers arrived, he and his wife took turns kicking the fallen deputy. They belly-laughed as they took his gun out and fired it dry into the air. They hosed him with his own pepper spray and assaulted his car with blows from his own baton.

Cleft stayed two days in the hospital after the attack, feeling humiliation the entire time, both over Sophie's leaving him and the fact he'd gotten his butt so thoroughly kicked. He tried to put his mind back to work after his release, but he couldn't muster the passion and vision he'd once held. He was certain the other deputies were laughing behind his back, and truth be told, he was a little scared every time he was dispatched to a violent scene.

"I guess I'm gonna have to leave it," said Cleft to Errol as the two of them had a beer at the Wagon Wheel restaurant a few weeks later.

Errol was upset. Callie had ordered him to stay away from the amusement park, again. This time was because Errol had gotten drunk and ridden the Lewis and Clark Canoe Plunge. It could have been overlooked except for the fact Errol had removed all his clothing during the ride. He stood up to deliver a raucous, "God Bless Texas!" as the canoe took the final plunge off the "Rocky Mountain" summit. Unfortunate timing, because a group of foreign exchange students visiting from Ireland had just arrived in the line for the same ride.

It made the papers.

"If that ain't the scratchiest butt of a gawdang situation. How can she fire me?"

"She didn't fire you," replied Cleft.

"I mean, I own the rides. Ain't right."

"I get all nervous every time I go out on a call," said Cleft.

"I know I shouldn't have taken off my clothes, but..." Cleft stared at the bubbles in his glass.

"I feel like I could get over it if I could get away for a while, but lately I don't see the point."

Errol took the last sip of his beer and murmured, "Maybe a reprimand or something, but to fire me and such...ain't right."

"I mean, if Sophie was still here, maybe I could stick it out. I just don't know anymore."

"I think I'm gonna quit," said Errol.

"Me, too," said Cleft.

"You are?"

Cleft popped his palm on the bar, decided. Errol sat a little straighter and cleared his throat.

"Well, in that case—and I don't want to horn in or nothin'—but maybe you could put in a good word to the sheriff for me?"

"Huh?" said Cleft.

"I mean, they'll be needin' a replacement for you and all, and what with my career options becomin' limited here and..."

"You wanna be a deputy? You?"

"Well, sure. Why not? So, would you mind...puttin' in a word?"

Cleft gritted his teeth as he answered, "Sure."

"That's great! That's real great."

Cleft motioned to the bartender for another beer. Errol's elbow toppled a bowl of pretzels.

"So, how long until I get a pistol?"

•   •   •

Cleft turned in his resignation the next morning and took a job as an appliance repairman. He had no training, but he'd always been handy with tools. The time he'd spent working for Callie as a teenager had given him a fair amount of experience working with machinery. The pay was good, and the clients were nicer to him than in his past profession, but he was bored.

One afternoon he was heading to a service call to replace a motor in a clothes dryer. He found himself stuck on a two-lane highway behind an eighteen-wheeler. A placard on the back offered a telephone number for anyone interested in driving trucks for a living.

Sophie always said I need to travel more.

Instantly, he chastised himself for caring about what Sophie thought. He'd taken to wearing a thick rubber band on his wrist, and he commenced what he'd come to call his "corrective therapy" upon realizing he was experiencing a nice thought about her. This involved pulling the rubber band to maximum stretch and releasing it. The result was a half-dollar-sized welt on the inside of his wrist, but an hour or so of not having to think about Sophie.

•   •   •

Things were not great for Sophie the first two years after leaving Elixir Springs. She ran out of gas on lonely highways twice. She subsisted on a steady diet of canned tuna, wheat crackers, and grape juice. She raced through a series of part-time jobs as she bounced from town to town.

In Dallas she detailed cars for a Chrysler dealership. San Marcos provided a job renting inner tubes to happy people floating down the river. In Tyler she sold postcards and Lady Bird Johnson rose seed packets at Brookshire's World of Wildlife and Country Store. Corpus Christi offered work in a bait shop where she learned how to lure suspicious crabs into a net using chicken necks on a string.

Austin was her favorite. She decided she was home after landing a job at the Fox Theater selling popcorn and tickets. She rented a little apartment within walking distance of the theater. Cheese, bread, a travel iron, and seven apples comprised her shopping list after her first paycheck.

Sophie started attending a different church every week in hopes of finding a place where she could dispense her insights and build her fortune. Problem was, no one in Austin was aware of how precious she'd been in Elixir Springs. Though she was welcomed, given communion, invited to any number of potluck Sunday lunches and introduced to a passel of preacher's sons, she was never allowed to speak in any substantial capacity. She didn't make a dime beyond her theater wages.

Sophie would remember this as the most exciting and frustrating time of her life in her autobiography years later. She knew she had a gift for making people realize their potential, but she had no idea how to generate a following. Eventually she broached her concerns to a kindly Lutheran minister who listened as she spoke of her plans.

They sat on a picnic table bench. Servings of fried chicken, three different King Ranch Chicken recipes, four coleslaw varieties, baked beans and green bean casserole were spread across the table. Children were taking turns at the ice cream crank, and some of the older men were tossing washers. A softball game was starting.

"So, in essence," Reverend Grisham said when Sophie came up for air after forty-five minutes, "You want to preach to a congregation. And you also want to build a cathedral of some type and have it become the most visited, beautiful sanctuary in Texas. Am I understanding you correctly?"

"Oh, yes, Reverend," Sophie gushed. "I want to grow a place where people from all over the world will come to worship. I want people to feel like they belong even as just a tiny drop in an ocean, and when they drop into that ocean, they become part of something bigger than themselves."

Reverend Grisham smiled. He was a kind man who had spent a lifetime being faithful to God, his wife, his children and his values. His sincerity and generosity were as present and clear as the hue of a flower or the joy of a belly laugh. He'd worn his hair, now white, in the same severe part from right to left since grade school. He'd only ever kissed one girl.

It would have been easy for such a versed man to insult the pretentious young lady before him. He was as wise as he was kind, though, and it never would have occurred to him to mock Sophie's dream.

"Sophie, why God?"

"What do you mean?"

"My dear, there are so many ways for you to do what you imagine, and only one of them involves the ministry. You say you want to help people realize their full potential, yet you haven't reached your own. Let me ask you this; have you studied the ministry, perhaps in a seminary?"

She shook her head and looked down at her lap in shame.

"Don't fret. You are so close. We'll get there together. Have you ever read the Bible? I mean from cover to cover?"

Again, she was forced to shake her head.

"Sophie, I believe you when you say you have a gift. I believe you will find a way to create a scaffold for your dreams so they can stop being as wispy as clouds and start becoming real. I believe this is what's missing in your own ministry, if you will."

"What do you mean?"

"We all approach God in different ways. You seem to be intent on spreading a message based on how others have spread it before you. This may have played well in your own small town, but—please forgive me—it comes off as disingenuous and a little childish to a more worldly or cynical population. Sophie, you're special, so the way you speak to others must be special as well. Call it style, call it Divine guidance, whatever you wish, but your calling must be unique to you. Otherwise, it will never grow into your glorious dream."

Sophie spent the next half hour with the minister, laughing and crying, hugging him and giggling as she punched him playfully on the arm. They ate as he told her stories of how he met his wife, and he made a sound, hilarious argument on why homemade peach ice cream was the finest flavor the world had ever known. By the end of the picnic Sophie knew in her heart the reverend was right.

"May I ask about your necklace?" the minister's wife asked Sophie later in the day as a group of women cleaned up after the picnic. The men were loading vans and trucks with picnic tables and sports equipment. "Where did you get it?"

"I made it myself," replied Sophie with a mixture of pride and wariness. She wasn't confident the woman was admiring the piece, a sterling chain with flecks of amethyst and alexandrite.

"It's lovely. Do you have others?"

Sophie realized all the women were looking at her. "I have a few. I like to design them during slow times at the theater. I put them together when I can buy a few stones."

"I'd be interested in looking at your stock."

Some might say the conversation and the subsequent sales of half a dozen necklaces and bracelets was predestined by God. It was, after all, a life-changing event because of a church picnic.

What is certain was that Sophie launched a business that day. Those same women from the church began asking if she'd let them sell her wares in their own shops and homes. Sophie immersed herself in learning how to run an enterprise.

In just over a decade, she steered a small business into one of the most recognized multi-national corporations in North America. It had not come without sacrifice. She worked one-hundred twenty-hour weeks at first. She spoke to as many congregations as would let her in. Nothing came overnight, and there were many times she subsisted on noodles in broth or a single piece of cheese.

Her vision for the future never dimmed, though. The payoff became a legacy she'd been proud of until Commissioner Pastal introduced her to what she'd come to see as her new destiny. She might have wondered how much happiness this new venture would bring, though she'd never slowed down enough to ask herself.

•   •   •

Cleft found truck driving pleasant enough. He saw the country and enjoyed the solitude. Bouts with anxiety and grief over Sophie melted away, though he still wished for a day when he didn't think of her at all.

He dated women he met in truck stop diners or motel clerks, but he compared them all to her. He gained a reputation on the road as a womanizer, which he hated but acknowledged as accurate.

He also took up a new hobby of visiting used bookstores. Despite his anger and pain for her having left, he had to acknowledge she'd been right about him having little knowledge of the world outside crime fighting and fishing. One evening after a dinner of steak and tamales in Fayetteville, Arkansas he'd spotted an establishment called Dickson Street Bookshop. A clerk looked up from a novel, and Cleft was too shy to ask about what kind of book might make him understand the world better. He walked past the clerk and waded toward the back of the store. In moments he was surrounded by stacks as high as the ceiling and a musky scent of leather and old pages.

The store was a catacomb organized in a way only the owners or a true bibliophile could understand. Yet, Cleft was enthralled, first with a large section on military history, and then a subtle transition into works of philosophy and religion. Over there, fiction, beyond that, sheet music, next a section on art, and further in, selections on literature and every imaginable science. Cleft, who'd not read a book since being assigned Gulliver's Travels in high school, found himself not daunted or bored, but instead full of wonder. He selected a biography on Theodore Roosevelt.

He felt like a fraud as he checked out with the clerk, but he left the store excited to get back to his truck cab and start reading. To his astonishment, he finished it cover-to-cover in four days. By Denver he was hankering for a new read, and a few inquiries at a truck stop led him to a treasure trove called The Tattered Cover. It became his routine to find such a store in each town where he stayed for the night, and to buy one or two offerings every time.

One afternoon Cleft was doing a haul from Brownsville to Austin with a load of cantaloupe. Things were fine. Interstate 35 was flowing for once, and he'd located a good station on the radio. He was humming along to the music when he spotted the marquee sign for the Frank Erwin Center, a huge entertainment auditorium off the freeway. The auditorium was designed in the shape of a huge Stetson hat, and there was no missing Sophie's smiling face lit up on the marquee like a fireworks display.

"ONE NIGHT ONLY! SOPHIE WIND...LIVE!!"

Cleft felt like beating the dashboard but didn't feel like repairing it later. He smacked his knee instead. He was passing Pflugerville before he realized he'd missed his exit and had to turn around.

Cleft dropped the load of fruit half an hour later. He grabbed a Dr Pepper and a Frito Pie in the warehouse break room as a crew unloaded the truck, after which he headed back out to his rig with an assignment to go pick up his next load in Waco.

Cleft sat in the depot parking lot and tried to turn right to go north. Waco is north, he reminded himself. Go north. Turn right, damn you.

He turned left.

Cleft had no memory of parking the big truck in the Erwin Center parking lot. He didn't notice purchasing a ticket for the event. It was once he was inside that the bustling crowds and barking vendors called him back to attention. He felt relieved his ticket was in the mezzanine section so there'd be no possibility she'd see him.

Cleft saw Sophie, though, and what he saw was unattainable. The glamour and lights, her poise and capture of the audience, the sheer magnificence of the spectacle was daunting. It all had the effect of making Cleft feel small.

Sophie came out on stage amidst a wall of applause, whistles and shouted adoration. From the cheap seats Cleft could see she was more beautiful than ever. He was unable to listen to what she had to say.

Adrenaline and testosterone coursed through him and unintentional bumps from the people seated next to him caused irritation. Every nerve in his body was as sensitive as a bitten tongue. He knew it was time to leave when he turned to glare at a grandmotherly woman who'd called out, "We love you, Sophie!"

Cleft left the event an hour early. The parking lot was all but deserted of people except for a couple of police officers and a homeless man collecting aluminum cans. He climbed back into the cab of the truck and sat with the engine idling until the enthusiastic crowds came spilling out of the auditorium. Cleft decided he would not be going to Waco for the next load. Instead, he headed to Elixir Springs.

.   .   .

The next day was a rainy one. Cleft had traded out the trucking company's rig for his own pickup, and he was doing his best to keep control over muddy ruts in the dirt road. He could see the top of the Ferris wheel in the distance, and somehow it felt satisfying to be home.

Callie was out in the field plucking mushrooms and plopping each one into a yellow bucket. She was dressed in a long, peach skirt muddied from hem to knee. She wore an old T-shirt from the White Elephant Saloon in Fort Worth, and a yellow fisherman's rain hat.

"Howdy, Cleft."

"Hey, Miss Callie. What are you doing out here in the rain?"

"I got a hankering for mushroom soup." She tilted the bucket so he could see all she'd collected. "I'll have plenty to share, if you like."

"I'm not one for mushrooms."

"Some folks like the flavor but not the texture. Maybe it's the texture you don't like."

"I was wondering if maybe—"

"You here for work? Happy to have you."

"Um, I mean, thank you!"

"You're welcome. And I hope it's okay."

"What's that?"

"We pay in mushrooms now."

Cleft grinned. He looked past Callie to the skyline of Pioneer Days Park, knowing it was likely the one place on Earth where he'd never have to see Sophie again.

CHAPTER NINETEEN

Cleft was so furious about the summons alleging Callie was unfit that he didn't trust himself to speak as he drove her home the night of Commissioner Pastal's not-quite cow stampede. He was cordial and sympathetic when he dropped her off, and she gave him a hug when he walked her to the door.

Once back in the police truck, however, he gripped and twisted the steering wheel so hard he tore pieces off the rubber grip. In minutes he'd crossed town and arrived at Sophie's "Wind Gathering" in the high school gym. He used the entrance reserved for visiting basketball teams and strode to the auditorium stage wing.

Sophie hadn't seen him standing behind the curtain yet. She stepped a few feet closer to her gymnasium audience, and Cleft fixated on the flow of her periwinkle dress and a certain tilt of her chin. Nothing had changed. He glanced around for a rubber band; finding none in the wings, he punched himself in the thigh and prepped his mind for the fight to come.

• • •

Sophie walked off the high school auditorium stage flushed and optimistic. Her Elixir Springs seed had been planted, and she wanted to celebrate. Which was why she was so flummoxed to see Cleft in a sheriff's uniform waiting for her. He stood by the door leading to the girl's locker room, his hands shoved between his belt and the small of his back. She recognized the posture as classic Cleft in a stubborn mood, something he'd done even when they'd first met as teenagers.

He looked dashing in a pressed khaki shirt with the badge pinned to his chest and his sidearm holstered to his hip, one lock of hair falling over his right eyebrow. There were a few smudges of mud on his uniform as if he'd been out fighting crime, which added to the image of dedicated lawman. Sophie's heart fluttered, though she wasn't sure if it was from dormant feelings for the man or a hint of fear he might be there to arrest her.

"Congratulations, I hear you're the new sheriff in—"

"What the hell is wrong with you!?"

Sophie stepped backwards for one moment, but she stepped right back to within inches of Cleft's chin and engaged.

"I could ask the same thing of you!"

"Don't give me that. The prodigal daughter returns to build a monument to her own glory, and who gives a damn if she kills her mother in the process."

"I'm not killing her. She needs help. Professional help."

"And on top of that, you're planning to evict everyone from their homes?"

"It's for their own good. I can make so many improvements around here."

"I'm stopping the evictions."

"Why would you do that?"

"These people deserve better. Your mother deserves better, and what you're trying to do with this court hearing is cruel. I won't stand for it."

"You just don't want anything to change around here."

"Oh, bull crap. This is all about you and what you want again."

"I think you'd better heed what Commissioner Pastal has to say on the matter."

"I don't give two waffles about what he has to say. He may make the laws in this county, but I enforce them, and this is not going to happen."

"So maybe you shouldn't be wearing that badge."

"So maybe you and your people should come and try to take it off."

· · ·

Toribio trudged through the woods and berated himself for having run when the police car pulled up. A hoot owl called out his presence, and three pairs of yellow eyes watched as he passed. He swatted at mosquitoes and felt a savage sting as bull nettle raked his bare thigh.

"I'm a citizen," he reminded himself. "I don't have to run from police lights."

He felt cowardly for leaving Callie. He wondered if she'd ever see him the same way, though he acknowledged she'd driven off before he could get back in the car. He tromped through the woods, thankful he at least had boots on. A full moon lit a game path, which he followed in the general direction of his trailer. He spooked a small herd of sleeping deer at one point and later heard a small coyote pack moving through brush off to his left.

It took three hours to reach home. He detoured away from the trailer park so he could check in on Callie. He was relieved to see her home safe, sitting on her porch swing. Had he not been nude and embarrassed about leaving her he would have stepped right up and sat next to her.

As it was, he was not sure what to do. He was anxious to know if she was angry, but he couldn't stand facing the consequences if she was.

"Sorry I ran off," he said, the lower half of his body shielded by the porch.

"Sorry for nothing," she replied. "I left you out there, and besides it would have been embarrassing if Cleft had found us a minute earlier."

They both laughed.

"It made me think, though," Callie continued. "I've never asked, but are you in this country…legally?"

"Yes."

"Your yearly visits back to Mexico and always reading up on American history…I just wondered."

Toribio shrugged, too exhausted to explain.

"I have a feeling there's a long and fascinating story behind that yes," said Callie. "I look forward to hearing it."

"I…I look forward to telling it."

"I'm glad you're home," said Callie as she rose to go inside. He was just about to ask the whereabouts of his car so he could get his clothes when she came back out on the porch to toss him a faded mint-green terrycloth robe.

"Sweet dreams," she said before smiling once more and bending under the porch railing to kiss him goodnight.

Toribio donned the robe and turned toward his own house. This required sprinting across an open field and crawling under a barbed wire fence. From there it was a matter of dashing from trailer to trailer, avoiding a cobweb of pirated television cable strewn up and over rooftops, under trailer axles, through trees, and around cars up on blocks.

Toribio was aware of every sound and sight. Dogs who might have barked, instead wagged tails for the man who always brought them scraps from the restaurant. Happy, guttural sounds were coming from inside Errol's trailer, and Toribio thought he recognized the raspy voice of Malga-Queen of the Lizard People. Next door the supervisor of the ticket booth had fallen asleep in an old recliner chair while watching re-runs of Adam-12 with the windows open.

Toribio made it to his own back door and slipped inside, safe at last. He stood looking at his body in the bathroom mirror as he waited for the water in the shower to heat. He was chigger-bitten from neck to ankles, smeared with mud, scraped along his ribs and legs, and swollen around one eye where he'd stumbled into a fence post.

He reflected on Callie's crazy scheme to cause mayhem for Commissioner Pastal; about how they'd waited in the dark for hours, been shot at, run for their lives, had to run again when the police showed up. But he also thought about kissing her, of finally feeling her chest against his own. He reflected on the allure of her wanting him to tell his whole story, and of the smile which said tonight's adventure would not be their last. Shower steam filled the room, and Toribio turned from the mirror smiling.

"Worth it."

•   •   •

Callie walked into the courtroom the next morning as if she were entering a department store with a full line of credit, despite the fact she'd had her heart re-broken by her daughter the night before. She curtsied to observers and small groups of attorneys as if she'd known them all her life. On this day she wore yet another hat, a mauve straw number, broad-brimmed with daisies bunched in a pink ribbon encircling the headpiece. She wore her oxblood-red boots under a sleeveless yellow dress with more daisies around the neckline.

Her manner exuded swagger. Except for the fact two sheriff's deputies were following her, Callie looked like a woman coming to court on some breezy civil matter she fully expected to win.

"You'll sit here, ma'am," said Cleft as he motioned her into a chair reserved for defendants. Observers waiting for their moment to have a stamp placed on their uncontested divorces or to get some judgment on a property foreclosure were pulled to this new drama. Callie was the most interesting item on the day's docket, though few knew the nature of her case.

Sophie and Commissioner Pastal walked in moments later. Sophie was stunning in a navy blue dress with pearls, dark red nails, and lipstick to match. She sat in the audience section, though she knew she would be called to testify. Despite her glam, she had gagged twice in the bathroom. She prayed it would not happen while she was on the witness stand. Sophie reminded herself that this was best for her mother, for Elixir Springs, and for her own business plan.

Toribio walked in as well, irritated Callie had not told him of the day's proceedings. He'd heard about it twenty minutes earlier from Cleft who'd stopped by the restaurant for coffee.

"No," said Callie to Toribio as he walked in. She stood with her hand out like a crosswalk guard, stopping the man from approaching. "Please, I don't want you here."

Toribio looked shocked, but he spun and left the courtroom.

"What was that about?" asked Cleft.

"I don't want him to see me like this," she said as she turned toward the front of the courtroom and prepared for battle.

"He was the one with you in the car!"

"Shush."

Everyone rose as the presiding judge entered the courtroom. He was a bitter septuagenarian who had once gambled on George McGovern for president. This had destroyed any shot he might have had at a federal judgeship. He'd been "sentenced" to county court for life, an extraordinary honor for most, but a frustrating daily slap in the face for him.

Witnesses in the Elixir Springs County vs. Callie Wind case were asked to rise and raise their right hands. Sophie, Callie, and another woman Callie didn't recognize rose and took their oaths.

Commissioner Pastal made a show of pulling files from his briefcase and whispering with the prosecuting attorney.

"We are here today," began the judge, "to decide in the matter of Elixir Springs County versus Callie Wind, a Ms. Sophie Wind having filed a petition to commit the respondent to a psychiatric facility, laying claim under oath that Respondent suffers from a mental disease or defect and does, as a result, pose a danger to herself and/or others."

Callie snorted and the judge looked up over his glasses. Cleft put a finger to his lips and gave her a respectful shake of his head. The judge called on the prosecuting attorney to introduce his witnesses. The attorney rose from his chair as if preparing to address a jury in a capital murder trial. Callie had opted to represent herself.

The prosecuting attorney called Sophie to the stand and prompted her to tell the court of her concerns regarding her mother. Sophie sniffled as she testified about a woman who had led a hard life, and who now needed help in coping; a woman who had built up something significant from nothing, and was in jeopardy of losing it all were the court not to step in and allow Sophie to make decisions for her; a woman whose sanity was in question, and who had reached a state of undeniable threat to herself and this community.

"And you say she has an unusual friendship with a Brahma bull?" prodded the attorney.

"Sophie dabbed a corner of her eye. "I'm not suggesting anything salacious, mind you, but I've witnessed her carry on a conversation with Beefo."

"Could be salacious," chimed in Callie. "You don't know."

"The famous Beefo?" asked the attorney in mock surprise.

"Yes, and in my absence, she's taken to beating metal hubcaps with a hammer."

"It's art!" Callie shouted.

The attorney paused as if letting Callie's outburst echo throughout the room. "And, Ms. Wind, am I to understand she's had her father frozen?"

"Adoptive father," screeched Callie.

"She has," said Sophie through a tiny sob. "She froze him and now she hauls him around the park on a pushcart."

Callie snorted. "Well, I'm not gonna carry him under my arm."

Commissioner Pastal listened to the testimony, often glancing over at Callie to see her reaction. He was so involved he'd failed to notice his own finger pointing skyward as if punctuating some point Sophie had made. The gestures became so vivid the judge had to say something.

"Commissioner Pastal, I'll ask you to exercise control over your own actions," the judge said. Pastal's neck turned maroon, but he accepted the admonishment.

Callie appeared to be a cross of southern belle and European royalty. She was at once rustic and refined, wary and gracious. She had seen Commissioner Pastal assessing her. She was still quite angry with him, but she acknowledged he was intelligent and decent. Committing her to a hospital would weigh on him, she thought.

"Sophie should know better," she whispered. Cleft once again put a finger to his lips. She winked at him.

Sophie finished her testimony and stepped down, bearing an intense glare from her mother as she strode back to the pews and took her seat.

"I now call Doctor Hazel Plumber," announced the attorney in so dramatic a fashion the judge rolled his eyes.

Dr. Plumber had had her hair done for the proceeding, but most people noticed her calves were the girth of a bologna roll as she walked in wide, practical heels to the witness stand.

"Doctor, what are your findings relative to the Respondent?" the attorney asked of Dr. Plumber once she sat and adjusted the microphone.

"In my opinion, Ms. Sadler—"

Callie slapped her table. "My name is Wind…Callie Wind, you idiot."

"Forgive me," continued Dr. Plumber, rattled she'd made a mistake right off the bat. "Ms. Wind is suffering from a psychotic episode, not otherwise specified, and to release her to fend for herself would be both cruel and dangerous. The attack on her father—"

"Adoptive father!"

"—was merely a manifestation of her anger toward all men and, to a larger extent, all of society. She suffers at some level from a past traumatic event, and those memories, long suppressed, are now being extruded from her psyche manifesting as violence. This is further supported by the fact Ms. Wind had her own father frozen, and she has spent decades parading him in what has been described to me as a 'gleeful manner' as if enjoying the ability to taunt him."

Callie glared at Commissioner Pastal who looked away.

"Look at me!" Callie demanded of Pastal.

"That will do, Ms. Wind," admonished the judge.

"In this case," continued the psychiatrist, "her adoptive father, has become The Beast, as in evil, sin, and violence perpetrated against her."

"You're a muttonhead," said Callie.

The judge raised an eyebrow for silence.

The attorney paraphrased. "So, doctor, you believe Ms. Wind suffers from a mental disease or defect."

"I do."

"And it's your professional opinion that she is a danger to herself or others because of this."

"Most definitely. I believe a residual, cavernous void of inimical paradigms—"

"You believe she is a danger to herself."

"Most certainly. This woman walks daily with a dangerous beast—"

"A large bull, is it?"

"Yes, a large and violent Brahma bull, and it is my understanding she carries on conversations with the animal."

"He's a hell of a lot more interesting than you," said Callie. Cleft grimaced.

The attorney smirked and continued. "And you believe it is in the best interest of Ms. Wind to be committed to a psychiatric facility for a length of time to be determined based on her response to treatment."

"I do."

"Your witness," said the attorney with a slight bow to Callie.

Callie sat still for so long that the judge asked if she had any questions for this witness. She stared at the doctor as one might stare at a truculent child on a playground waiting for her to perform some brutish act worthy of discipline.

"It's your turn," Cleft whispered.

Callie rose from her chair and strode to the podium to face the witness against her. The full weight and responsibility of due process, of the American system of jurisprudence, the value of a system where truth rises in fair and refereed antagonism permeated the courtroom as she took a stance like a frontier woman atop the Sierra Madre Mountains and adopted a withering stare.

Attorneys who had been whispering in the back of the courtroom stopped to watch; observers in the pews licked their lips and leaned forward; the psychiatrist shifted from one buttock to the other and re-arranged her file folder; the judge took off his glasses and interlaced his fingers; Commissioner Pastal leaned forward and rested his temples on two fingers; Sophie alone did not look at her mother, choosing instead to stare out the courtroom window at a man pruning bushes in the park across the street.

Callie bowed toward the judge, to Commissioner Pastal, the courtroom audience members, and one last courtly motion to the psychiatrist. She cleared her throat, adjusted her hat, and kissed the amulet hanging around her neck before asking her first question:

"Doctor?"

"Yes?"

"How long have you been imbecilic?"

"Objection," blurted the attorney.

"Did your parents raise you to be a big old half-wit, or was that something you learned in school?"

"Ms. Wind," admonished the judge. "I'll thank you to maintain a sense of decorum and dignity toward all witnesses, regardless of your personal feelings."

"I thought it was a reasonable question, your honor. I apologize to this court, although I'm not clear what the answer to my question would have been, except maybe she'd say something like 'I don't know because I'm a big old idiot.' Anyway, that's all the questions I have for this witness—who is a great big—"

"Madam—"

"—dumbass."

The psychiatrist was released, and she huffed from the courtroom. Callie was invited to testify on her own behalf, should she choose. Cleft believed Callie should rest her case, convinced the attorney had not met the burden this court would require to deem her unfit.

But Callie would have her say, and it was with the energy of a foal that she all but pranced up to the witness chair and smiled back at her observers. She took a moment to compose herself, nodding her head in a most regal manner once more at His Honor.

The courtroom was hushed, the anticipation as taut as at the first sentence of an Easter Sunday sermon. The freedom of a woman who was potentially as nutty as a monkey on fermented grapes, albeit as wise as a *curandera* at a breech birth, was at stake.

Callie tapped the microphone twice to measure her volume. She leaned in and stared at Commissioner Pastal with a provocative smile.

"Commissioner Pastal, can you hear me?" she asked into the microphone, her voice now a purr.

Commissioner Pastal looked around the courtroom as if there might be another Commissioner Pastal in the room.

"Richard! I'm talking to you. I want to know if you can hear me."

"Yes, Callie," Commissioner Pastal answered in a seething whisper.

Callie's voice dropped to a whisper. "Do I sound sexy?"

Cleft put up his hands and took two steps toward her. "Callie, No! Now you're just being a pill."

"Madam, please," admonished the presiding judge.

Callie launched into a boisterous rendition of *The Eyes of Texas*. The judge banged his gavel.

"Your honor, please instruct the court reporter to submit a few of his pubic hairs for DNA testing. He's the father of my children, but he won't pay child support."

The court reporter, who had worn a bow tie to this judge's courtroom for thirty years of dependable service quaked, "I swear I'm not, your honor. I've never even dated—"

"Order," yelled the judge.

"Callie, calm down," pleaded Cleft.

Callie pointed an accusatory finger at the poor reporter who, to his credit, was still stenographing every word. "I'll kick him in the shins if he won't acknowledge his children, your honor!"

Commissioner Pastal found his voice. "Callie, you must stop."

Callie responded by jumping into her chair and announcing, "What God has created let no frozen carcass put asunder!" She grabbed the gavel from the stunned judge's hand and began chasing Commissioner Pastal around the courtroom.

"Your honor, please!" begged Pastal as Cleft tried to shield him.

"Momma, stop!" pleaded Sophie who was now weeping in the second row.

"Miss Callie, you have to control yourself," said Cleft.

"Keep going, harlot," said the Reverend Gershom Sadler who entered the courtroom from the door leading to the judge's chamber. Callie froze with the gavel held above her head.

Reverend Sadler kept his eyes on Callie as he took a seat in the jury box. His lip curled in a sneer, and his carbon-black eyes appeared like gun muzzles tracking on crippled game. "I said keep going. It's about time everybody else started to see what a crazy hussy you truly are."

Callie began to shiver, and the gavel dropped as her hands rose to cover her face. She panted and glanced maniacally at the judge, Pastal, Sophie, and Cleft, but it was if she didn't see them.

"Momma!?" Sophie called out.

Callie's shoulders slumped and her spine curled as if she could somehow diminish and disappear.

Cleft took a step towards her. "Miss Callie, you okay?"

She stumbled backwards and landed in an awkward heap beside the lectern, her legs and red boots splayed in caricature. Gasps reverberated through the courtroom.

Callie looked toward the jury box, and most in the room followed her gaze to thirteen empty chairs. Her voice quivered as she called out, "Why are you doing this to me!?"

The courtroom was silent, save for Sophie's sniffles and the creaky leather of Cleft's gun belt as he knelt to help Callie up. Those in the audience who'd been engrossed in the show feigned attention on legal briefs.

"Miss Callie, you're okay," murmured Cleft. "Just hold onto my arm."

The old judge cleared his throat and waited until Cleft had righted Callie. His gruff demeanor was gone, replaced by a genuine sadness for what he'd decided.

"Sheriff, I'm instructing you to take Ms. Callie Wind into custody and deliver her to a treatment facility, forthwith."

Callie pried her eyes off the derisive Reverend Sadler until she located her daughter.

"You're not the only one who had a life, Sophie," Callie said as a whisper. "You're not the only one."

CHAPTER TWENTY

Toribio could not recall having ever felt more upset or embarrassed as he left the courthouse. He didn't understand why his heart's desire had ordered him away when all he wanted was to be in that courtroom defending her and making her feel safe. The joy he'd felt the night before turned to anguish, and he wondered if he'd been wasting his time and emotions.

He kneaded the steering wheel of his little Datsun as he drove from the courthouse, and he passed the turn to go to the amusement park. He was on the highway heading north before he knew it. Toribio had but one thought, and that was to get far away from Elixir Springs County and Callie. The former world traveler was back on an open road with a tank full of gas and a set of retread tires. He'd figure out the rest later.

.   .   .

Callie never faltered when going into a pasture with Beefo. They had mutual respect. Beefo had not always had such a good relationship with his employers because he'd thought too highly of himself in his younger years. Understandable; he'd been sleek as a cover model, fast as heated honey, and as crafty as a lunch-stealing bear.

Beefo was also a biter. He'd bite anyone making demands of him, and like an old zoo zebra, he never let go of what he'd bitten until he was good and ready. He'd scarred eight men during his football years, always a blood red horseshoe shape from the lower teeth ridges. His preferred target was the fleshy triceps region of any Southwesterly State Rustler who happened to piss him off.

Through trial and error, the Rustlers had discovered the way to get Beefo to release his jaws was to smear Vicks mentholated rub into the animal's nostrils. Prior to that they'd been forced to wait until the bull tired or grew bored. Tempting him with carrots didn't work. Whacking his rump with a bent coat hanger didn't do it, and cattle prods just made him bite harder.

So, until the Vicks' rub discovery the Rustlers had taken to straddling the corral fence, taking bets on how long it would be, and spitting out dabs of tobacco juice along with words of encouragement to the victim. One such incident Beefo held one of the wranglers for a quarter of an hour. He'd stopped screaming after seven minutes and stood shoulder to shoulder with Beefo, blood dripping from his arm onto the loam of the round pen.

The Rustlers would have killed him long ago were it not for the fear of the alumni members and the athletic director. They wanted to, often staying awake through the wee hours plotting the perfect murder of a celebrity bull. How to make it look like an accident? How to get rid of the murder weapon? Could they conjure up a fake tear when the news cameras showed up? Beefo was despised by his keepers until Callie made him a home where he was fed beer-soaked grain daily, a home where no one except Callie and children ever touched him.

This history could have been why Beefo resented the two men and a woman entering his pasture with a tripod and camera. He didn't know them, and something about them reminded him of Southwesterly State Rustlers. He watched them set up the tripod on a rise two-hundred yards away, biding his time as he decided how best to let them know his feelings.

"I'd like to at least get some photos of this western edge of the property before the sun goes down," said Ms. Jones of the Office of Internal Logistics. She'd traded her business skirt for brand new hiking boots, a photographer's vest, and a pith helmet.

"And you're sure we have the owner's permission to be here?" asked Mr. Smith. He was still in his suit, having traded his business shoes for running sneakers.

"Sophie Wind has been granted power of attorney while her mother is away," said Commissioner Pastal.

"Excellent," commented Ms. Jones.

"And Ms. Wind said we were welcome to do whatever we need to do to finalize our decisions," continued the commissioner.

"Excellent," said Mr. Smith as he mounted the camera on the tripod and began shooting panoramic shots of the property line.

"I think we've found our site," said Ms. Jones with a satisfied sigh. Commissioner Pastal clenched both fists in triumph behind his back while maintaining a calm façade.

"Agreed," said Mr. Smith, still shooting away.

Beefo, being a bull, could not say why these people were ticking him off. It might have been the way the man was bending over a little metal tree he'd erected, or the way the woman kept pacing and pointing, or the way the other man smelled of dead animals. Regardless, Beefo had had enough, and he started up the rise at an intimidating trot.

• • •

"Cleft, please take me by the park before we go," said Callie as Cleft drove her from the courthouse after her hearing. His jaws were gnashing in frustration, but he thought it was a simple enough request. Soon the two of them were at Pioneer Days Park, heading toward the carousel.

There was no line for the ride, so she and Cleft walked through the turnstile and had their choice of figures. Callie used her hand to dust off seats on the covered wagon figure of the carousel, and the two of them sat.

"You don't need to start it up unless somebody else comes," she said to the ride operator. Cleft thought he'd never seen her look quite so frail.

"Why, Callie? Why did you...?"

"Throw a tantrum?"

"Act all crazy. I mean, it was an act, right?"

Callie shrugged. "I went into that hearing prepared to fight, to show Sophie I'm fine. But something happened to me as I sat there watching her. In all that time she was gone..."

"She had to leave," said Cleft. "My trailer, this town, the plans I had for us—ridiculous—they made her claustrophobic as hell. I don't guess she had much of a choice, looking back."

Callie twirled a blade of windmill grass in her fingers. "I know why she had to leave, and it sure wasn't all because of you. But she left so...completely. I'd see her face on a magazine cover or see her talking her nonsense about God and jewelry and pond ripples while flipping through television channels. There she was for everyone except me."

"And me."

Callie laughed, sobbed, and laughed once more.

"So, I sort of snapped when that clod of a doctor broke down my life and everything I've done into little, logical, damaged parts."

"What does 'snapped' mean?"

"At first I just lost my temper. But then I saw things I couldn't have seen." She shrugged again. "Snapped."

The carousel shifted in the wind, the squeakiness of the old ride more evident when the music was off. Callie swiped their ride seat with the palm of her hand.

"This ride is so creaky and dusty. Things around here have been that way for too long. My life—your life; we're just biding time and gathering dust. There was a time before all this when I made things happen instead of waiting for them to happen to me."

Cleft stared at a chipped ear on one of the carousel oxen figures. He chuckled mirthlessly and rubbed his forehead with a palm.

Callie followed his gaze to the oxen.

"Cleft, I remember those big plans you had. They weren't ridiculous. I don't even have a plan, but today on that stand I knew I had to do something to start shaking off this dust."

Ticketholders arrived, and the ride operator hit the start button. The ride circled, and they rode in silence for a while.

"I'm gonna give it all over to Sophie," said Callie. "She and Pastal can do whatever they want."

"What? Why?"

"Don't you feel how tired I am?"

Cleft ground his jaw in frustration.

"I keep fighting people," she said. "It used to be Reverend Sadler, and I still feel like I'm grappling with him. Then it was Sophie the teenager, and now Sophie the woman. There's Commissioner Pastal, and I even struggled with you for a time. I'm so tired of fighting."

Cleft sighed. "I understand."

"I'll sign it over to her and finally be done."

•   •   •

"Look out!" screamed Ms. Jones.

Beefo's chest landed on Mr. Smith's unsuspecting flanks as he bent to look through the camera lens. Mr. Smith was driven into the soil with no more hope than a pill bug in floodwaters. There was a catastrophic separation of ear from lobe and hair from scalp. One of his new sneakers flew off.

No sooner had the animal made his move than he evidently realized his dreadful mistake. Beefo backed away from Mr. Smith and the mangled tripod and camera. Mr. Smith's body lay in a crumpled lump.

"Beefo!" howled Commissioner Pastal. "What have you done!?"

Beefo snorted and looked in every direction as if he knew it was time to go. Perhaps his mind pictured a Vicks-wielding posse of college cowboys. With a final look at the broken mess beneath him, Beefo emptied his massive bladder and smashed forehead-first through his wooden fence. In less than a minute he found himself inside the amusement park and running along gravel trails he'd only seen from the other side of the railing.

Cleft and Callie heard the screams and jumped from their ride to investigate.

Snot flung from Beefo's heaving nostrils as parents grabbed children and Malga swung a Pioneer Days souvenir umbrella at his rump. Cleft joined in the chase at the Midway. Beefo ran through the Lewis and Clark Canoe Plunge, the Salty Miner's Cave Ride, and Hanky's Sawmill Ice Cream Shoppe.

Cleft caught up near the Volunteer Firemen's Petting Zoo area, perhaps because Beefo smelled something soothing and safe in that direction. Cleft cleared the area of families and set up a perimeter with a few other employees.

"Whoa there. It's okay, big fellow."

"It is NOT okay," said Commissioner Pastal, who arrived on the scene. He and Ms. Jones were helping Mr. Smith who was bleeding from the ear, rubbing an abrasion on his scalp, and sneezing dirt shoved up his nostrils.

"That animal is a menace," yelled Ms. Jones.

Cleft kept his eyes on the bull as he called out, "I'll handle it, Commissioner."

"Where were you when this beast charged us?" demanded Pastal, who spotted Callie standing near the throng. "And why is she not in the hospital?"

"I'll take her as soon as we get this animal back in a paddock."
All the while Cleft stayed on guard in case the bull changed his
mind about calming down. A park employee ran up with a halter,
a lead rope, and handfuls of Pastal Pellets pouched in his shirttail.

"I'll take him," said Callie, who reached forward for the
halter.

"You'll do nothing of the kind," insisted Commissioner Pastal
who moved his body to intervene. Beefo responded with an
intimidating snort, and Pastal relented. Callie took the halter from
the employee, slipped it over the bull's head, and led him away.

"That animal is the first thing to go when transfer of the
property ownership is completed," said Commissioner Pastal.
He'd meant this to be heard by Mr. Smith and Ms. Jones, but
Callie heard him as well. She stopped in her tracks, and Beefo
halted beside her as if he was a well-trained contestant at a dog
show. Callie addressed them in a more menacing tone of voice
than Cleft had ever heard.

"This," she said, pointing at Mr. Smith and Ms. Jones, "is
never going to happen."

CHAPTER TWENTY-ONE

Toribio had driven for fifteen hours straight, stopping only for gasoline or to pee behind trees and cactus. His route meandered below highway speed, his only thought that he'd wasted most of his life on a fruitless dream: the only woman worthy of sheltering in place for thirty years would never return his love.

Toribio roamed onto two-lane highways without a destination in mind. His path took him past the caverns of Sonora, seven circuits of the downtown square in Brady, Lake Waxahachie, Spindletop Hill in Beaumont, and skirted the Gulf of Mexico from Freeport to Harlingen. He didn't remember any of it.

He grew punchy from sleep deprivation, but his focus remained transfixed on Callie. His foggy plan was to keep going. Maybe he'd head west. Oregon? Washington? Perhaps he'd head straight north to the Canadian border and cross the country eastbound toward Maine. A never-before-used credit card with a nine-hundred-dollar limit seemed full of possibilities.

That is until he nodded off while cruising at sixty-five over the Queen Isabella Causeway crossing the Gulf into South Padre Island. It was a mistake which brought him within eight feet of launching off into the choppy water below. He decided South Padre would be a good place to nap. His soul was down on one knee, and it was time to take a breather.

.   .   .

Callie rode in the front passenger seat of Cleft's patrol truck during the silent ride to the hospital. She noticed windmills, the rustic beauty of the Texas Hill Country, and grazing cattle in a way she might not have in other circumstances. An elderly couple waved to her from a roadside fruit stand as she and Cleft drove toward a stunning sunset. Callie put her palm to the glass and stared back at them until the road curved, and then she hid her face between the headrest and doorframe so Cleft wouldn't see her tears.

She and Cleft arrived at the hospital after dark. Their goodbyes were quiet and restrained as he left her with staff and drove away. She watched from the lobby window until his taillights faded.

She'd wanted nothing to do with other patients or staff members, and she asked to be shown to her bed. The escorting staff member had reached to turn on her room light, but Callie asked her to leave it off. Callie didn't even take off her clothes before lying on the assigned bed to stare at the ceiling. She lay awake until dawn.

.   .   .

Cleft was in a poor mood the morning after driving Callie to the psychiatric hospital and his argument with Sophie at the high school auditorium. He decided to shoot a few targets to lift his spirits. He lived in a scrubby area set away from the rest of the trailer park. Years earlier he'd bought a decommissioned railroad car, which he'd stuffed with enough dry goods and canned products to survive on for at least a year. Narrow passageways allowed him to move from one end to the other.

The other sides of the compound included his trailer and a pungent compost area for his vegetable garden. These were framed by an old bass boat, a cedar picnic table and matching Adirondack chairs he'd made from discarded lumber.

Cleft had erected silhouetted targets for a gun range. They were placed at one-hundred-yard increments going out fifteen-hundred yards from the covered platform where he fired his rifles.

Beefo wandered up to an adjacent fence line and stood watching Cleft as he practiced. The bull chewed cud until Cleft fired a round, and then he would turn in the direction of the target as if scrutinizing Cleft's shot placement.

"Feels like I'm living a country song," Cleft called out to Beefo. Cleft fired four rounds and pulled a small screwdriver from his pants to adjust the rear sight of his rifle.

"Boy meets girl, boy proposes to girl, boy gets half a vasectomy for girl, girl leaves boy, girl returns to boy as a rich she-devil."

Cleft sighted the distant target once again and took two more shots.

Beefo dropped a cow patty onto the sod.

"Just like a country song."

•   •   •

Sophie wasn't happy people had to move, but no one could be allowed to keep a trailer on the property if Elixir Springs County was to win the competition for the magnificent telescope technology. Winning the contest had gone from exciting prospect to obsession for her. Yet, a little voice she'd been trying to suppress for over a decade kept nagging this was her home, albeit one she'd always known she would leave.

Commissioner Pastal had cautioned her against serving the eviction notices herself, offering to send professional process servers to get the job done. He warned her telling people they had to leave soon could invoke conflict.

Sophie insisted. She believed she could convince them her company would pay their moving expenses and set them up in better homes in nicer neighborhoods. She considered it her responsibility to break the news, and nothing would dissuade her. So, armed with writs of eviction, she ventured out toward the fifty-unit trailer park.

Sophie wore jeans and riding boots for her task, and she rented a four-wheel-drive Range Rover to save her car from the dirt roads. Sophie drove past eight hundred acres of onions on property owned by one of her mother's neighbors. The field was two weeks past prime harvest time, and the onions were beginning to soften and rot for lack of workers to pick them. Expansion was ever on her mind, and Sophie made a mental note to have Commissioner Pastal contact the owner of the property and make an offer.

A few of the tenants were home, but before knocking on doors something made her turn toward the cream over beige double-wide trailer set on cinder blocks where she and her mother had once lived. The front door was off its hinges, and the wooden stairs leading to the entrance were rotted. Two windows were broken and peering in she could see the place was emptied.

On a whim she pulled herself up through the front door to avoid having to use the crumbling stairs. She tested the foyer with the toe of her boot to make sure the composite-wood floor would support her weight.

She ventured inside and scanned the musty carpeted floor of the living room. She leafed through an old copy of TV Guide lying in one corner, smiling as she recalled watching an episode of *The Waltons* and sharing a bowl of popcorn with her mother.

Sophie floated from the living area toward the two bedrooms in the back, trancelike as memories flooded her mind. Entering her old bedroom was like instant time traveling back to a place she'd dreamed of leaving. A crayon picture of a tree with pink leaves and a smiling sun still hung on the back of her door. Empty wire clothes hangers dangled in her closet.

A bottle of Tickle Pink nail polish had long ago spilled on the burnt-orange shag carpet. The polish was crusty, but she wrapped the dainty bottle in toilet paper from a partial roll still in the bathroom and slipped it into her pants pocket.

A single black track shoe with three white stripes, size four, was on the floor of the closet. She picked up the little shoe and remembered her mother helping her try it on in the store. She recalled how the salesman had asked her to jump up and down and run a short distance to "make sure the shoes were fast."

Something was inside the shoe, something which made Sophie's breath catch when she remembered what she'd placed for safekeeping after a big argument with her mother. She tugged at a bit of periwinkle blue fabric and extracted the sequined Barbie dress. Sophie held the little garment to her lips, and her eyes welled. She stood there in the middle of her old bedroom and swayed back and forth, cherishing the mix of joy and regret only a memory can offer.

•   •   •

Sophie heard distant rifle booms. They were far enough away she wasn't startled, but loud enough to break her reverie. She tucked the little dress into her pants pocket before lowering herself out the front door. The sound came from the direction she knew was Cleft's portion of the property.

She dreaded the encounter as much as anything she'd ever done. This man, her first love, and a living symbol of everything she'd needed to leave behind, was around a wooded bend. Part of her wanted to hand him the legal notices with an air of disdain, saying nothing, turning as soon as the document was in his hands and walking out of his life once more. The other part acknowledged he was still handsome enough to make her lips part and her hands shake.

The reports grew louder, and Sophie grew more apprehensive with each step. The thought occurred to her Cleft might shoot her through the trees. He might believe her to be an intruder or miss his intended target and hit her. She smirked, knowing Cleft had already seen her.

She rounded the bend and saw him shooting a rifle with mounted scope at targets off in the distance. The pile of bullet casings on the ground by his right leg was evidence of how long he'd been practicing.

Cleft took aim, the rifle resting on a wooden ledge beneath a tin roof. Heat shimmers danced off the tin and a dust devil gyrated and fell off to her right. Dry grasses rubbed together to make rattle sounds, and Sophie could smell chili simmering from inside Cleft's trailer.

She could tell from the back of Cleft's neck and shoulders he knew she was there. He didn't turn until his final shot blasted a target six-hundred yards away.

A tapering line of sweat soaked through the back of Cleft's shirt was provocative. His movements to sight the target, squeeze the trigger, and eject the shell were hypnotic. She found herself mesmerized until he spoke with his back still toward her.

"What do you want?"

"I have some…I have papers," she said, hating that she'd stammered, knowing he'd noticed.

"I already told you, those don't mean anything to me."

"It's a court order from a federal judge ordering the sheriff of this county to serve my eviction notices."

"Leave it on the hood of my truck. I'll walk it out to a target in a few minutes."

"You can't shoot it, Cleft! It's a court order."

"From a federal magistrate who has no jurisdiction here! Dammit, Sophie, you can't keep wrecking people's lives. "

"I'm not wrecking their lives. I'm trying to make them better."

"You've never asked any of us what we want. God, could you be any more arrogant?"

"I'm not arrogant because I have vision. I've been able to help a lot of people."

"So, go help them."

"I'm not leaving."

"But leaving is what you do best."

"I knew that's what this was about. You know I had to leave. I'm sorry I hurt you, but I had to go."

"All you're doing is causing pain and getting folks riled up. This isn't for them; this is for you."

Sophie put her hands on her hips and set her jaw in that stubborn way he knew so well. A hot wind blew a wisp of hair across her eyes, and Cleft gnawed on his lower lip. With a primal grunt he dropped the rifle in his hands and crossed to her in three long strides, taking her in his arms and kissing her like he'd never kissed her as a younger man.

Sophie stiffened, then softened into his embrace, but the years intruded, and they both backed away. Eleven years of self-doubt and being stuck in dust-gathering neutral for him; eleven years of empire building for her, knowing she'd hurt this man in order to live her dream. It seemed like an awfully wide river between them.

They stared at one another. Beefo's moo wafted from far across the pasture, and Sophie's thoughts flashed to wind chimes which had swayed in a tree on the patio of a Mexican restaurant the night they became engaged.

Cleft broke the quiet in a voice at once wounded and dignified. "It's best if you leave and never come back."

Sophie's jaw set again. She marched the court order out to a handgun target twenty yards downrange and used a ballpoint pen to stick it over the bullseye.

"Serve the eviction notices and you'll never have to see me again."

"No."

"I'm going to roll over you."

"I know."

"And I'm not going to apologize."

"I know that, too."

258　CAROUSEL GRIFT

"I'm going to roll over you."

"I know."

"And I'm not going to apologize."

"I know that, too."

CHAPTER TWENTY-TWO

Toribio slept near a jetty in South Padre until just before dawn, and he awoke to violet and pink reflections off the water. He was in awe as he watched waves crash on dark rocks, a pod of dolphins heading south, and a beach stretching as far as his eyes could see in both directions.

Here before him was evidence of God and of hope, and he realized his journey was only half completed. No meandering this time; a mile down the road he stopped at a 7-Eleven for coffee, donuts, gas and a map. His path lay northwest, and he was determined to find the fastest route home possible.

• • •

As the sun lit Callie's hospital room, she could see it was sparse with two cream-colored beds and a shared bathroom, but Callie had the room to herself. She sat up, tested the bounce of the mattress and checked to make sure the tap worked. She changed into a robe and brushed her teeth. Therapy would start in the afternoon. She gagged on her toothbrush just thinking about it.

She left her room and ventured to the cafeteria. The idea of eating breakfast sounded awful, but she poured a cup of coffee and made her way to a small arboretum area outside a glassed-in portion of the cafeteria. She sat beside a Koi fishpond and blew on the coffee until it was cool enough to drink. An orderly peeked through the window at her. She was otherwise alone until Dr. Plumber, the psychiatrist who testified at her hearing, came out to talk.

"Good morning, Callie. How did you sleep?"

"Like a baby."

"Wonderful!"

"Like a teething baby with colic."

"I see."

"So, not great."

"Yes, well, Callie, this is a safe place. You're free to tell me what you're feeling and what you need."

"I feel like it would be fun to watch you choke on diapers, and I need you to go away and never come back."

"I'll be back in a few minutes with your pills."

"Okay, but can I ask you something before you go? It has to do with my mental health."

"Of course."

"Is it a bad sign that I hope your rectum falls out of your butt before you return?"

"I see we have a lot to work on," said Dr. Plummer who left in an unmistakable huff.

Callie turned to watch the fish, mesmerized by the flow of water over lily pads. She didn't like her surroundings, but the panicked feeling she'd had as Cleft left the evening before had ebbed. She'd begun to feel like she could survive her time in the hospital.

That is until Reverend Gershom Sadler approached her with a reptilian grin.

"Good morning, Harlot."

Callie gasped and glanced about as if seeking escape.

"What do you want?"

"I'm here to chat." He pulled up a chair so close his knees touched her own.

"Go away. You're not welcome."

"At least let me have the chance to tell you goodbye." He no longer looked frozen. He was animated, his furry brow bobbing up and down, and his smile so wide it appeared as a grimace. Callie couldn't bear to look at him.

"Goodbye. Now go away."

Reverend Sadler picked at dried mud on the heel of one boot.

"Not that simple. Things to get off my chest first."

"So get them off your chest and be done with me."

"What a horrible mother you turned out to be." He looked at her as if viewing something ugly and incomprehensible.

"Don't."

"You spy on your own daughter—"

"Please."

"—deny her dreams until you drive her away."

She sobbed, "Why are you doing this to me?"

"Slothfulness and lust, Callie. Those have always been your sins."

"No. My sin has been pride. I think you and I share that."

Callie squeezed her eyes shut, and when she opened them, Reverend Sadler was gone.

•   •   •

"Callie, what's wrong?" asked Toribio, as he stepped out into the garden area. He gazed at her with grave concern. "Who were you talking to?"

Callie's eyes were wide, and her mouth was open as if she might scream. She looked at her trembling hands, at the fishpond, and at Toribio as if seeing them for the first time. She reached out and patted his arm, making sure he was real.

Toribio produced a deck of cards from his pocket as he sat in the same chair Reverend Sadler had used moments earlier. He held them up in an offer to play.

"Maybe later," she whispered.

"I also brought some books." He pulled selections from a bookstore bag. "I didn't know what you'd feel like reading, so…"

"How kind of you."

"I know you like westerns. Brought one by Elmer Kelton…"

"Oh."

"And a murder mystery about…" He paused while looking at the cover. "…a guy with a hat."

"That's lovely."

"And a, um, Harlequin Romance—this fellow lost his shirt, I guess."

"You look dapper," Callie said. She reached out to touch the gray Crazy Lace stone centerpiece of his bolo tie.

"Shined my boots."

"Isn't this the most marvelous dress?" Callie asked while stroking a palm across the shoulder of her hospital gown. "You in that starched white shirt and bolo, me in my print. Aren't we glorious?"

Toribio opened his mouth but clamped it shut as Dr. Plumber peeked out.

"Everything okay out here?"

"Hate you," Callie responded in a sing-song tone. The doctor's head disappeared.

"I don't know what to do," said Callie.

Toribio sat staring at the koi.

"Should I try to ground her if she won't stop going to church? I've never done that before. Do you think it would work?"

"Oh, Callie, I—"

"You're right. This is a phase. It will pass."

A maintenance man in forest green coveralls came out to feed the fish. Callie and Toribio watched as he scattered pellets over the water surface. The Koi leaped, and the pellets were gone in seconds. Oily shimmers floated like rainbows where the food had bobbed before being slurped in by the fish.

"Little spilled rainbows," said Callie as she watched the colorful shimmers disperse. "Seems like that's all there is—rainbow spills at the amusement park, rainbows spilled in my heart."

She let out a primal scream and leaped into the pond. Toribio saw her exhale bubbles, and he was about to go in after her until her head popped up.

Hospital staff members burst through the glass door. Toribio glanced at Callie, then back at the advancing medical staff who looked like they were about to yank her out.

"Stop!" It was such a commanding tone the medical people skidded to a halt.

"She's fine now. Leave us a few minutes."

The staff retreated to watch from a window. An orange and white Koi burbled by Callie's hip. Toribio stepped into the pond beside Callie and stroked her soaking hair.

"Cocinero, I am so grateful for you," Callie whispered.

He pulled a lily pad from behind her ear and kissed the spot where it had been. "I've been meaning to tell you...my actual name is Toribio."

"Toribio? That's your name?"

He grinned and shrugged a yes.

Callie chuckled. "So, what is Cocinero? Like a nickname?"

"Alas...just like a nickname."

"Huh. Well...I'm glad to know."

Toribio squinted hard and let out a long sigh.

"Also...I'm in love with you."

Callie sobbed again and put her hands to her face.

"I'm such a mess. How could you love...this?"

He cupped water from the pond in both hands and let it cascade off her forehead. "We can put all the rainbow colors back, better than before."

"I've been so prideful."

"We can put the colors back."

CHAPTER TWENTY-THREE

Later that evening it was All-You-Can-Eat-Shrimp night at the Wagon Wheel. Errol and Cleft sat at the counter as Toribio served Errol plate after plate and Cleft picked at his first helping.

"I know what you're sayin'," said Errol, dipping his next bite into a swirl of cocktail and tartar sauce. "I could've lost my appetite over Callie going to the hospital, too. Here's the thing though: I can't imagine her worrying about us eating, but I sure can imagine her getting onto us about not eating. She'd want us to gourd ourselves with all them golden-y popcorn shrimps, and I for one am doing that in her honor. You gonna finish your baked potato?"

Cleft sipped his tea and checked his watch. "Go ahead. I'm going on patrol in ten minutes."

Commissioner Pastal walked in and took a seat at the counter. He smirked at Cleft before picking up a menu and pretending he was considering anything other than the unlimited shrimp.

"Sombitch," whispered Errol as he speared Cleft's potato. "Not sure Callie would welcome that rascal."

"Ignore him."

"But like I was saying before. Now that I'm not the sheriff, I need to be working on my raisin deeter."

"Your what?"

"Raisin deeter. It's European for my reason for being alive. I need me one."

"What direction were you considering?" asked Cleft, who was trying to take his own advice for ignoring Commissioner Pastal. The Commissioner wasn't having it.

"I'll have the shrimp," Commissioner Pastal called out to Toribio. Toribio paused as if considering throwing the man out, but he threw a fresh batch in to cook. Commissioner Pastal turned to face Cleft.

"What can I do for you, Commissioner?"

"What can you do for me? You can do your job, Sheriff. That's what you can do."

"You're referring to the eviction notices?"

"Of course I am! I'd like to know why not a single one has been served. Not a one."

"Sir, they're not legal. A federal magistrate who has no jurisdiction here signed them. Surely you don't want me, as the representative of Elixir Springs County, serving illegal eviction notices."

"It's all legal, I checked."

Cleft wiped his mouth with a napkin.

"Let me put it another way. I'm not going to do it."

"Why not?"

"Because it's wrong. What you and Sophie are doing is flat out wrong. You can fire me, I suppose, but you'll have to get a deciding vote from the county commissioners to do it."

"That's exactly what I'm going to do."

"You have a quorum problem, Commissioner. Mr. and Mrs. Henley are at their timeshare cabin in Branson. Commissioner Banders is among the folks you're trying to evict, so I doubt you'd have his support. The last commissioner besides you is Callie, and we both know where she is. Errol appointed me sheriff while he was still sheriff, so until you guys vote me out, I'm in."

"How could this be?"

"It's all legal—I checked."

Pastal left the counter for a booth. "I'll have your badge for this. Mark my word."

"Duly marked."

Errol shoved two jumbo shrimp in his mouth and talked around them.

"Got me one."

"What's that?" asked Cleft, who was still staring at the commissioner.

"My raisin deeter. Got me one just now."

"Oh?"

Errol crammed another shrimp and pointed to the back of Pastal's head.

"You're gonna be needin' a deputy."

• • •

Callie sat in a stuffed chair in the hospital common room, watching as other patients shuffled in. Some sat to play board games, some read, most stared at something far away no one else could see. She was relieved that no one tried to talk to her.

Callie thought about the experience of Gershom Sadler coming to visit her. She knew it had been a delusion, but it had seemed so real. What if Sophie was right? What if she was falling into an abyss of dementia? Toribio's visit had been her salvation, and it had broken her heart when the medical staff insisted morning visiting hours were over.

Callie thought about skipping lunch, but she'd not eaten since before Beefo's rampage the day before. Her stomach rumbled, so she stifled her anxiety about mingling with other patients and headed to the dining hall. It was with a mixture of joy and amazement when Callie trudged through the hall leading to the food line and spied Luz smiling up at her from a wheelchair.

"First day is always the toughest," Luz said.

They talked and laughed the rest of the morning between being interrupted by hospital staff for check-in procedures, a shower, a blood draw, and a physical exam. Hardly a minute went by when they didn't embrace, squeal or laugh out loud. The hospital staff mostly left them alone, though Dr. Plumber often stared and took notes.

Luz initiated a delightful game in which she called herself by a different name each time someone approached them. For the frumpy Dr. Plumber, Luz held out her hand in a genteel, southern fashion and informed the doctor she was in the presence of Scarlett O'Hara. At lunch she'd been Barbara Bush for the cafeteria staff, and at yoga class she was Carol Channing, complete with a delightful rendition of Hello Dolly. Little of what Luz said made sense in those first few days, but Callie didn't mind. She was amazed at her friend's vivacious and irreverent attitude, and she was thankful for her presence.

That night Callie sank to her knees in her room and rested her elbows on the bed.

"I don't think I could make it through this without Luz," she whispered into her clasped hands. "I was terrified, and somehow you sent Luz here to help me through. I thank you for that. I thank you."

It was her first prayer in thirty years.

· · ·

"It's time for us to leave," announced Luz after twenty-nine days in the hospital.

"I don't know how," replied Callie.

"I've heard you say that before, and you've always figured out a way."

Callie snorted, but she shook her head.

"I'm not sure it's time."

"For goodness' sakes, sweetie, how could it not be time?"

"For one thing, there's a security code on the door."

"That's the easy part, and you know it. Why do you think it's not time?"

"Do you think He's forgiven me?' asked Callie, and then, "Shush," as she saw her psychiatrist breeze into her hospital wing.

"It's time for your meds," announced Dr. Plumber.

"Don't need them."

"You've been here four weeks. You should know the routine by now."

"You take them."

"I've ordered them for you," said Dr. Plumber. "The same order as every other day."

"I wouldn't take them," piped in Luz.

"No thank you," said Callie, "but would you please bring me my slippers, and perhaps a fudgesicle."

"Please don't make this hard—again," sighed Dr. Plumber, as she motioned for a burly orderly to come help her.

Callie took the pills. "I'm only taking them so you'll get your frumpy butt out of here so I can talk to my friend."

"Thank you so much," said Dr. Plumber.

"You're welcome. Now be a good girl and go get yourself a case of gonorrhea."

Luz spread her arms as if to hug Dr. Plumber as she stomped away.

"Sweetie, there was never anything to forgive. What happened to you is called life. It wasn't God's curse or Gershom Sadler's game. It was just life, and if you'll get the hell out of here, it still could be. I promise, Callie. I promise, it's time."

Callie spit out the pills.

• • •

Callie's section of the hospital was a lockdown facility. Not that she or any of the other residents were assumed dangerous, but they were all considered to be suffering from some level of dementia or psychosis. It wouldn't do to have an Alzheimer's or brain-injured patient wander away.

Such a calamity had occurred on occasion before the hospital installed the security lock system. Elderly people who had forgotten their own names and the precious members of their families knew one thing for certain—escape meant freedom. Once outside they all acted as if they were wolves on the Alaskan tundra, bolting at the fastest pace their walkers and wheelchairs allowed in whatever direction happened to lie straight ahead.

Thus, a heavy door with a coded lock keypad stymied Callie. For days she hovered near the front door trying to sneak a peek as staff members went in and out. This required some acting on her part as she pretended to be catatonic anytime she wasn't in her own room or eating. Although she couldn't see all the numbers as they were punched in, she knew for certain it was a five-digit sequence. She was confident that given enough time she'd figure it out.

One day Luz approached with a special gleam in her eye. Callie was slumped in an overstuffed faux-leather chair, wearing a hospital gown, a pink shower cap she'd "borrowed" from one of the more delusional residents, and a pair of yellow galoshes one of the custodians had left inside the front doors upon arriving at work during a downpour. Callie had been on security door surveillance for nine days, so she paid little mind as Luz wheeled across the dayroom and bashed her wheelchair legs against Callie's chair.

"Let's play Yahtzee!"

"Not right now," said Callie.

Luz mumbled, "Dreadful attitude," as she opened the game box lid and flopped a score pad onto an end table by Callie's knee. She scrutinized the lead points of two pencils as if judging pickle entries at a county fair.

"You want the yellow pencil to keep score or the blue one? Blue one's sharper, but…teeth marks."

Callie didn't answer, being so focused on her mission, so Luz shrugged and rolled the blue one toward Callie's score card. Callie acknowledged her old friend's presence with a plastic smile as Luz shook the dice cup and crowed, "Come on, baby! Give momma a Yahtzee!" She rolled with all the drama of a Vegas craps table.

Three rolls earned Luz a score of six for the "two's" row, and she passed the dice to Callie. Callie obliged her with a halfhearted roll, but her eyes never left the mysterious keypad any time a hospital employee ventured close to the door. She and Luz played for twenty minutes in this manner, with Luz racking up points and Callie neglecting to jot down her score.

"You're not paying attention," said Luz.

"Hmm? Oh, sorry."

Luz handed her the dice cup. "This is for the world championship; in case I didn't mention it."

Callie spilled the dice on the plastic tabletop, but the cubes hadn't even finished tumbling before she turned back to watch the exit.

Luz, however, gazed transfixed at the rolled dice. An overhead address informed the dayroom that pudding was available on the veranda; an orderly bustled by with a bedpan and a stack of towels; an aged man on oxygen fiddled with missed buttons on his pajama top.

Luz whispered, "Callie. You rolled a Yahtzee."

It was the whisper that did it, and Callie twisted in the chair to face her friend. Something in Luz's expression was more focused, more targeted than anything Callie had seen in her during all the days they'd been confined. For days Luz had often held bizarre, delusional conversations about how hot it was picking the okra today or how silly Roy Mercer was for thinking she'd go to the dance with him if his parents wouldn't let him borrow the car; how excited she was to have made an A in history, or what the

Swan had done to her on the day she'd been Leda. Now Luz was contemplating Callie with eyes more alive than Callie had seen in so very long.

Callie looked down at the dice, and her lips pursed in confusion. A Yahtzee score required that all five dice roll to the same number, but those in front of her were all different. Further, they were not splayed across the table but placed in a tight row. Callie looked up at Luz, who was smiling mischievously.

Luz took her gaze from Callie to glance at the row of numbers on the dice, and then she raised her head to stare at the exit door with the intensity of a lap dog eyeing a treat. Luz looked back down at the dice, furrowing her brow as if trying to point at something before she turned once more to the security door and darted her head forward.

Callie brightened and hugged her before rising from her chair and creeping toward the door. She stifled a gleeful squeal when the numbers on the dice worked for the code, and she looked around for staff as a sly smile spread across her cheeks. Seeing no one, she grabbed Luz's wheelchair handles, snuck out the door, and broke into a sprint.

•   •   •

Mr. Smith and Ms. Jones with the Office of Internal Logistics stood outside the gates of Callie's amusement park. Both appeared on edge as they glanced about.

"I assure you, the bull is in a pen on the other side of the property," Commissioner Pastal said as he wiped his neck with a bandanna.

"So, when do you expect Ms. Wind?" asked Ms. Jones.

"Well, like I said, I expect Sophie to be here any second now."

"Did she forget about our appointment?" asked Mr. Smith.

"I imagine she's been caught up in traffic," replied Commissioner Pastal. He felt his tongue go dry when Mr. Smith and Ms. Jones looked over their shoulders at the complete absence of passing cars.

"And do you expect Ms. Wind to have the proper documentation so we can get started with the survey crews?" asked Ms. Jones.

"She has a court ordered power of attorney in hand," replied Commissioner Pastal, thankful he could provide at least a little concrete information.

"Because time is of the essence," said Mr. Smith.

"I expect her any second now."

.   .   .

Sophie was late for a meeting with the telescope project team. She was speeding and distracted. One moment she was pushing buttons on her car's radio trying to find KIK'N Country, and the next she was spinning. Her car rotated twice, ramped backwards over a guardrail, and plunged forty feet off Pastal Bridge to land in roiling river water, all because Sophie looked up from the console to see her mother pushing a wheelchair across the road.

Sophie's car sank with the trunk settling into the sediment and her car's grill facing back up toward the bridge. A battered and panicked Sophie craned her neck up to catch the last few inches of air pocket at the top of her car. She struggled to get her bent door open as she realized she was going to die.

Sheriff Cleft Hawley had just pulled off a dirt road in his patrol truck when he saw Sophie's Cadillac go airborne. He called out to Joyce on the radio what he'd witnessed, stripped off his gun belt and boots, and plunged headfirst into the vortex below.

The steering wheel in Sophie's car was bent, causing the horn to sound like an angry howl underwater. The headlights cast a yellowed halo through the silt.

Cleft frog-kicked down and yanked on the door handle. Sophie pounded on the window with her palms, screaming bubbles as

Cleft elbowed the glass again and again. He wished he'd not stripped off his belt so he would have his baton. Cleft groped the disturbed silt bed until he came up with a softball sized chunk of concrete. His lungs shrieked at him to retreat to the surface, and Sophie pleaded for him not to leave. The rock did its job, the window shattered, and Cleft yanked her out and up.

He held her as they floated downstream, both too tired to swim for shore yet. He was glad she didn't struggle as he aimed their feet downstream and helped keep her head above the water. She wept as he stroked her hair and told her everything would be okay as the water nudged them toward a bank.

"You okay?" Cleft asked once they'd gotten to shore and caught their breath.

She spoke in a low voice as she gazed out at the current. "Do you remember the scorpion you came over to kill that night?"

He chuckled and nodded at the memory.

"Thanks for coming again."

•   •   •

Callie and Luz headed for the fruit stand Callie had seen on her way to the hospital. An elderly Honduran couple who sold fruits and vegetables, fresh meats, polished quartz, and decorative purses operated the stand. The chubby little wife had wrinkles as deep as saddle etchings and a smile so sincere you'd think she'd just been given a kitten.

Callie had never met them, but she knew in her heart they'd help. So, she walked in that direction as Luz rolled along and sang "The Impossible Dream."

Half a mile from the stand Luz stopped rolling her wheels. She coasted a few more feet before the chair came to a stop.

"I think I'm done for today," she said as she placed her hands on her lap.

"You can't be done. We're not there yet."

"I'm done."

Callie rolled her eyes and pushed the wheelchair the rest of the way. Soon she was huffing and puffing too hard to speak, but Luz was doing enough talking for the both of them. Not that much of what she had to say made sense. If she wasn't acting out scenes from Broadway, she was quoting historical figures.

Callie was on her last leg when she and Luz came to rest in front of the little fruit stand. The wife saw Callie's exhaustion and brought her a large glass of *horchata* over ice. Her husband made Callie a sandwich.

"It's that woman who waved from the police car last month," said the husband in Spanish.

"Ah," replied his wife, her eyes growing wide. "I thought I recognized her. *Pobrecita.* She's exhausted."

Luz stood up from the wheelchair to wander around the stand and up the path leading to the couple's home.

"I like this place," she said to Callie.

"It's nice here," replied Callie, which brought appreciative smiles from the couple who'd been staring at her in friendly bewilderment.

"I think I'll stay a while," Luz announced. Callie nodded as if she'd known this would happen.

"I think this is a wonderful place for you," said Callie. The couple bowed their heads in humble pride.

"You'll be fine, now," said Luz, who had already turned toward the pretty little house. "It's time for you to go home, Callie, but I'll be around if you need me."

Callie's eyes filled.

"Thank you."

"You are most welcome," the happy couple replied, and the woman patted her arm.

Callie finished her snack and chatted with the couple for some time. She said her thanks and took her leave, hugging them both before re-embarking on her journey. The husband and wife watched until she was around a bend before turning to one another with confusion.

"Why is she pushing an empty wheelchair?" the woman whispered. He responded with a puzzled shrug.

. . .

A bedraggled Cleft and Sophie slipped and plodded up the muddy riverbank toward the rescuers searching for them upstream. Cleft wondered how many times he'd imagined rescuing Sophie over the years. The visions all had a similar theme: she was held by bank robbers and he arrived in the nick of time to vanquish them all and carry her to safety; she was being stalked by a sinister psychopath, and he traveled to Austin to keep her safe; she needed a kidney, and he was the only person in the world with a suitable tissue match.

In each scenario he'd played over the years, he left her in the end. She would say, "Cleft, I was wrong to abandon you on that vasectomy surgical table. You're my hero and the only man for me."

And like the proverbial Rhett Butler, he would say something pithy, better than "I don't give a damn," but similar. He would leave her there a trembling mass of desire and self-loathing, realizing all she'd given up.

She'd been gracious when she thanked him after he rescued her from the river. Hell, she even gave him a hug. It never occurred to him to say anything of a barbed nature, and she never declared what a fool she'd been. The first responders provided towels, checked them over to make sure they were relatively unscathed, and placed them in separate cars for the drive into town. That was it.

Truth be told, though, both relished one thankful, weary smile while staring out the windows of their respective rides and considering all the what-if's that might have been.

.   .   .

Callie thumbed a ride with a farmer driving a flatbed pickup. He'd
been confounded upon finding her pushing a wheelchair along the
otherwise deserted highway. The ride to Pioneer Days was
pleasant, and the truck driver enjoyed Callie's vivid stories of her
previous days hitching rides and waiting tables. She was home by
mid-day.

"Callie?" Toribio said as she approached his front porch.
"What are you doing out?"

"I took an early release."

He looked at her with a squint before breaking into a grin.

"You escaped?"

"I did."

Toribio guffawed and leaped over the four steps of his porch
to grab her up in a bear hug. She laughed as well as she looked
down into his eyes. Callie kissed him, holding his neck with both
hands so he couldn't pull away.

CHAPTER TWENTY-FOUR

Sophie roamed her mother's amusement park with damp hair and clothes after the rescue, feeling aimless for the first time in years. She wondered about her personal destiny, the desires of her heart versus her calling, and what the hell she was doing in a place she swore never to visit again.

The crowds were sparse, but the nightlights were on, and square dance music was playing. She had to admit it was nice in a way, and she found herself remembering pleasant little moments from her previous life.

Over by the Buck Skinner Thrill Swing was where she once found a missing child and was lauded a "little hero" when she was eleven. The bathroom by the petting zoo was where she'd had her first kiss, a boy on a family reunion, sixth grade, a surprising amount of tongue.

She'd served ice cream every day of her fourteenth summer, making enough to buy a real rabbit fur coat before winter; drawn a picture of a violet dragon for her mother by the Foaming Frontier Fountain; comforted an old man who fell off a step from the Trailblazer Twister and broke his hip one Saturday night when she and Cleft had been on a date.

She found herself at the midway, mesmerized by the teenagers, families and soldiers playing games of chance at colorful booths.

She meandered until she came to the flashing lights of the roulette wheel, but there she stopped in her tracks when she recognized the operator.

The woman whom Sophie first met fixing the clogged filter for her Wind Center waterfall was tending the game. She was buffing the wheel with a cloth, and Sophie saw she was wearing a name tag when she turned to greet her. This time Sophie caught a glance so she could address her old employee by name.

"Luz? What are you doing here?"

"Sophie! So nice to see you again."

Sophie shook her head in confusion. "I don't understand. The last time I saw you, you were standing in the pond at the cathedral in Austin. You work here now?"

Luz smiled and pointed to the roulette wheel.

"Would you like to play?"

• • •

Callie and Toribio were still embracing as Errol screeched up in his old pickup. His back tires fish-tailed to a stop, raising a dust cloud.

"Real happy for you two," Errol called out from the driver's seat, "but there's some shenabigans goin' on at the entry gate. Y'all had best get up there."

"What's going on?" asked Callie.

"It's the Commissioner and them two federal folks. They're doing some plotifyin'."

"What kind of plotting?" asked Toribio.

"The takin' your property kind!"

"Are you talking about that man and woman who were in the restaurant a few weeks back?"

"Yes'm."

"The trespassers," said Toribio.

"The ones who didn't appreciate the choices on our menu," said Callie. She smirked and developed a plan.

"Let's take care of this right now. Toribio, would you mind grabbing your grill and coming with me?"

Toribio jumped on the porch to grab his charcoal grill.

"Good," said Callie. "We have a few other things to gather, and then we can head over."

"What do you think she's plannin'?" Errol asked of Toribio.

"Something rash," Toribio said with a grin as he fell in behind the woman he would follow anywhere.

• • •

Mr. Smith felt mounting indignation about the white caliche dust on his black wingtips and the fact Sophie Wind was half an hour late. Ms. Jones regretted eating breakfast, as the heat shimmers were making her nauseous. Commissioner Pastal passed the time pacing between his car and Callie's chain link fence, trying repeatedly to get Sophie on her phone.

"Sophie, I need you to call me back right now," Commissioner Pastal seethed into his brand-new Nokia mobile telephone, while smiling over his shoulder at the two government employees. He snuck a swig of antacid and dialed again.

A strong smell wafted past. Ms. Jones gagged and waved her hand in front of her face.

"Sorry about that," said Commissioner Pastal. "They just spread some chicken—um—fertilizer a couple of fields over. Pretty potent when the wind blows right if you're not used to it."

Mr. Smith undid his tie as he retched as well.

Which was when Callie arrived, pushing Reverend Gershom Sadler in the wheelchair she'd borrowed from the hospital. The reverend's boots were braced on the feet portion of the chair. The small of his spine was supported by the back of the wheelchair and his head was up by Callie's shoulder, so that his stiff frame appeared like a teeter-totter board.

Commissioner Pastal dropped his new phone onto the gravel. Mr. Smith and Ms. Jones stood agape as Callie shuffled past them and through the entrance gate. Toribio walked beside her, wheeling his barbeque grill. Errol came behind holding a wire-mesh cage with two live chickens.

Callie positioned herself and Reverend Sadler inside her fence, staring at the little group as Toribio emptied an entire bottle of lighter fluid onto the charcoal. Standing well back, Toribio tossed a lit match onto the grill, setting off a fireball. Mr. Smith peed himself a little.

Pupils from all eyes dilated as they watched Toribio select one of the chickens from Errol's cage. Commissioner Pastal groaned, realizing what was about to happen. With no fanfare and no wavering of Callie's piercing gaze, Toribio wrung the bird's neck sharply enough that its head separated from its body.

The chicken body ran around in a blood-splattering circle for a few seconds before it bumped into Reverend Sadler's frosty leg and plopped to the ground. Toribio split the bird with his knife, peeled back enough skin that he could access flesh, and carved out a chunk of breast meat. This he tossed onto the flame.

Mr. Smith groaned and closed his eyes against the nightmare.

Ms. Jones moaned and looked away.

Commissioner Pastal put both hands over his face.

"Smells real good!" said Errol.

Toribio pulled the second bird from the cage. The animal squawked. A moan escaped from Ms. Jones' lips.

"Don't you do it," demanded Commissioner Pastal.

Beefo meandered up to the gate and stood as if watching a stage play. His presence added to the dread developing in Mr. Smith and Ms. Jones as evidenced by aghast looks from each. The old bull seemed content to stand and stare.

Toribio held the bird aloft as he and Callie had planned. For several seconds the only sounds were from the irritated bird and the crackle and hiss from the fire.

Mr. Smith and Ms. Jones had faced determined resistance before. In all their experience neither had ever felt more dread as Callie, Toribio and Reverend Sadler stared at them deadpan.

"Go...away," said Callie in a voice quiet and cold.

Mr. Smith turned and fast-walked back to their government-issued sedan. Ms. Jones backed away with her hands held up in a "wait, don't do it" fashion. Mr. Smith couldn't get the car door open. The poultry poop scent wafted past once more, and Ms. Jones upchucked on her shoes.

"Oh, for goodness' sake, Callie!" yelled Commissioner Pastal. He opened the car for Mr. Smith and Ms. Jones before running around to the driver's side.

Toribio smiled when Callie turned and kissed him on the cheek after everyone else had gone. Beefo tugged at a patch of grass. Errol flipped the chicken breast on the grill.

•   •   •

Sophie pulled three one-dollar-bills from her purse and handed them over to Luz. She smiled, remembering how good her mother was at getting people to sit in this same chair and pull dollars from wallets. Prizes on the wheel ranged from stuffed animals to free rides in the park, with the grand prize being a meal at the Wagon Wheel. Sophie desired none of the prizes, but waves of nostalgia buffeted her soul. She spun the wheel with enthusiasm.

"You won a sock monkey!" crowed Luz, who reached up on a shelf to collect the prize.

"Why don't you keep it," replied Sophie.

Luz held out a half-eaten cinnamon roll. "Want some?"

"No thank you." Sophie spun the wheel again and won a free snow cone. She and Luz clapped and laughed.

"On second thought, maybe a little," said Sophie as she pulled off a bit of Luz's pastry.

Bells and whistles went off from games all around them. Lights flashed, balloons popped, and people squealed.

Sophie reached back up to the roulette wheel and spun it again. She watched the wheel with more concentration than in all the hundreds of times she'd played before. It landed on a line between a Spin Again and Free Carousel Ride.

"You get to choose," said Luz, her voice so quiet Sophie barely heard. Luz was watching Sophie like an observer at a championship chess match.

"I think…I guess I'll take the carousel ride."

Luz handed a ride ticket to Sophie with the solemnity of a bailiff delivering a jury's verdict to a judge.

"Very well."

•　•　•

Commissioner Pastal was incensed that Callie had embarrassed him in front of the Office of Internal Logistics people. He went in search of her at the restaurant with the intention of giving her a piece of his mind, and he found her cutting ribs using an enormous cleaver. Callie and Toribio were whistling a tune as they worked side by side. Neither looked up at him, but it was clear they knew he was there.

It took Pastal a moment to realize the tune was *El Degüello*, a melody blared from Mexican Army trumpeters during Santa Anna's siege of the Alamo. It had been played to convey a message of "no quarter" if the fort's defenders would not surrender.

Callie chopped down into the beef cartilage with her huge knife.

Pastal cleared his throat and said, "I came to tell you something that isn't easy to tell. Has to be said, though. Opportunity has come to this county, and you're squandering it.

I won't abide it, Callie. I won't, but I didn't think it was right to do something behind your back."

She yanked two ribs apart like wishbones as she answered.

"You've already gone behind my back. I know you plotted with my daughter. What makes it so you have to come tell me now?"

"You may have scared those folks off forever. How could you?"

Callie laughed. "The look on your face when Toribio started that fire."

"Why won't you play ball? Life would be easier if you'd just cooperate."

She whacked down through rib tendon.

"What fun would an easy life be?"

"I want you to know you'll always have a home. You can stay with me, or—or I'll set you up in your own little cottage if you prefer."

"I would prefer to go back to the hospital than live with you." Toribio smirked.

"Maybe I should send you back to the hospital. How did you get out?"

"It was time for me to go."

"Who said?" demanded Pastal, his neck reddening.

"Commissioner?" said Toribio.

"What is it?" Pastal barked.

"I was wondering what happens to someone who participates in making false allegations against someone for the purpose of getting property from that person."

"What are you talking about?"

"I mean, look at her," Toribio continued. "She's not insane, but allegations were made."

Callie smiled and pointed her large knife at Toribio with a wink. Toribio chuckled in response.

Pastal was shaking, but he took a deep breath and straightened his spine.

"Fine. I'm glad you're doing better, Callie. But I'm going to see Reverend Sadler buried once and for all. It's not decent the way you've treated him."

"Not decent? I take him out for a horseback ride on a pretty day every year. He gets his wish to keep controlling me and everyone around him. He must be loving all this controversy and intrigue."

"It's not—"

"And besides, why is it so all-fired important to you the county gets my property? They're going to turn right around and sell it to a government agency that will dig holes so deep nothing you've built will remain."

Pastal looked away, and Callie understood.

"Ahh…but of course," she said, her face brightening with the revelation. "It's to get your name on the building or something like that?"

Pastal's face went crimson, and he could not meet her gaze. Callie smirked at him as she had at Reverend Sadler while holding a willow branch in her hand so many years ago.

"Your name on another building at the expense of…everything. You must be so proud."

"*La ironía*," whispered Toribio as Pastal stormed from the restaurant.

• • •

Sophie approached the carousel with her usual purposeful stride. The closer she came to the ride, however, the more she felt trepidation, like the first time she spoke in front of an audience.

The ride was filling with other visitors, and it surprised her to see Luz was now the ticket-taker. It startled her more when Luz turned in front of Sophie and bounded onto the carousel.

"Come on!" said Luz as if the two were adolescent best friends.

It was a ride figurine Sophie had never seen before. Luz sat in a two-seat carriage being pulled by two beautiful horses. Both animals were snow white with periwinkle manes and tails, gilded in gold with sparkling reins leading back to a carriage boasting jewels and wrought figures of petals and cherubs. It looked like something out of a royal procession, and Sophie caught her breath at the magnificence.

Sophie sat next to her new friend on a velvet cushion. The music changed to ragtime piano as the creaky ride lurched forward. Luz took Sophie's hand in her own, and the sensation felt so natural Sophie never gave it a second thought. The ride moved at a pleasant pace, and at first Sophie found she was enjoying herself.

The ride picked up speed, and Sophie worried the old carousel might not be able to withstand the force. She glanced at Luz and saw she looked worry free. Another rotation, more speed, and the pleasant carousel ride began to feel less like a mild distraction and more like an adrenaline-pumping thrill ride. Sophie grabbed the edges of the carriage, and it appeared as if the manes of the two horses were flowing in the wind.

A wand flipped down from the outer edge of the carousel, and there at its tip was the traditional brass ring. Sophie reached out for it, but she missed. It came back around in seconds, and she believed if she could just pull the ring, somehow the whole ride would stop.

The ring whirled past at a dizzying speed, and Sophie feared her arm would be pulled out of socket if she grabbed the thing. Other hands reached for it as well, those of exhausted parents with small children on their laps and guffawing pre-teens more intent on their corn dogs and popsicles. Sophie low-grunted like a badger defending territory and stretched once more.

Luz nudged her out of the carriage, holding her hand to allow her to lean far out. Sophie was afraid Luz would let go, but their grips held. On the seventh rotation she scored the ring and let out a victory shriek. Luz pulled her back in, and Sophie sat back on the cushion.

Luz pulled a loop of string from her pocket and began forming various Cat's Cradle shapes. "What are you going to do with it?"

Sophie felt silly about her imagination. She looked around and saw no evidence the others who had been on the ride had experienced it as she had. Families with small children chatted and laughed as they exited, announcing their plans for the next ride or to go have a picnic. She looked back down at the ring and turned it over in her hands.

"I don't know what to do with it."

"You could toss it in the clown's mouth and get another free ride," Luz offered. She pointed to the gaping-mouthed clown figure by the exit holding a sign inviting ring-holders to redeem the brass ring for another go. Luz grinned like a child when the string in her hand took the form of a Jacob's Ladder.

Sophie stared at the trinket ring as if she couldn't decide how to redeem it.

"I wonder if you'd keep it for me."

Luz smiled and held out her hands. Sophie dropped the ring onto Luz' lap through the gaps in the string, hugged her new friend, and drifted into the crowd.

She wandered and reminisced for another hour, less a participant than a spectator. Two boys bumped her on their way to the Wigwam, but even the jostle and their over-the-shoulder apology wasn't enough to bring her from a powerful sense that she was floating.

•   •   •

Tick Day always bustled. There was the dip tank to prepare, cows to be herded, and delousing journals to update. Richard Pastal hired twenty extra men from the amusement park for this semiannual event held on the southernmost end of his dusty acreage.

He'd arrived early to set up his grill and hang the traditional Tick Day banner reading: "Tick Day: Sponsored by Pastal's Jewelry and Pawn." He stood back to admire the sign, rubbing his hands in anticipation of the fun day in store.

The dip tank was a narrow twenty-foot pool sunk into the soil, filled to the edges with a solution of insecticide and muddy water. Pastal's herd plodded into the mixture after moseying through an S curve of tapering walls designed to funnel them toward the bath. When the cattle emerged from the other end their faces were swarming with fleas and ticks heading to higher ground to avoid the poison. The crawling parasites were attacked with men wielding rags dripping in the same milky chemical solution.

Errol was among those hired for the day. His job was to swab the ears and nostrils of each animal, drenching the fleeing ticks. From a distance the ground at the muddy exit looked as if someone had walked around with a giant pepper grinder. The air around the tank was plague–thick with flies.

One cow bolted, stepping on Errol's left foot. It didn't hurt much because of his steel-toed boots, but it gave him an opportunity to limp away from the line and take a break. Errol washed his hands with a hand-pump fountain and a palm-full of powdered laundry detergent before heading over to a little tent set a few yards away.

Commissioner Pastal had stopped participating in the actual dipping process many years ago. Some of the men wondered if he'd ever done it, but he was the boss and he paid well. Pastal helped, instead, by grilling steaks for the men throughout the day.

"Hello, Errol," said Commissioner Pastal. It was clear he wasn't thrilled to be speaking with Errol, but it was tradition that he offered Tick-Day employees a chunk of grilled meat. He handed Errol his share and turned back to the coals.

"Thank you, sir."

Pastal never purchased plastic ware or paper plates for these occasions, preferring to pinch pennies by handing a sizzling steak to his cowhands in a paper towel. Errol was used to this, and he bit into his steak like a sandwich.

"Golly, Commissioner. That's like—like—real pleasurable."

All eyes turned toward the east. There was Callie, leading Beefo on a rope with a clear intention of dipping her animal. Toribio walked beside the two, patting the animal on the haunches.

"You will stop, Callie!" screeched Commissioner Pastal. He advanced with his grill tongs raised to wave her off. "That animal is not welcome here, and neither are you."

"Don't be silly. He needs a bath."

"Well, he'll not get one here."

In an action Pastal would regret in the next few moments, he stepped toward Callie, which Beefo interpreted as aggression. Beefo was not familiar with the self-defense statutes in Texas, but he knew right from wrong. He decided this angry man was wrong, and he remembered the old days and what he most enjoyed doing with cowboys. Commissioner Pastal yelped as Beefo clamped jaws around his upper arm and dragged him backwards. Pastal's attempts to slap at the bull with the barbeque tongs only made the beast clamp down harder.

Errol and the other hands turned to stare at a whimpering Commissioner Pastal, but none of them moved to help him. They all knew once Beefo took you in his grip, there was little they could do to help and a lot they could do to make things worse. Commissioner Pastal dropped the grill tongs to show Beefo he surrendered.

"Anyone have any Vicks?" called out one man. No one answered.

"We may have to shoot him," someone suggested.

"Nobody is shooting," Callie clarified.

Bulls who survive one battle with a matador in the middle of an arena surrounded by thousands of cheering fans and a chorus of *Olé's* are able to grasp the concept of feint and subterfuge. So, the fact Beefo understood the powerful leverage of hostage-taking wasn't remarkable. He knew what he was doing as he dragged, yanked and tugged the offensive human like a sack of grain.

Beefo snorted and spewed. He lashed his tail like a stegosaurus fending off a raptor. He gouged to and fro with his horns, and he shoved a massive shoulder into Commissioner Pastal's large grill causing it to topple and ruin all the sizzling meat. He mule-kicked a dent the size of a suitcase in the driver's door of Pastal's Suburban, and he smashed the windshield with his horns. It was evident Beefo was enjoying himself.

Errol picked up a frayed broom from the tail bed of a truck and strode toward the bull with grim resolve.

"Don't hit me!" screamed Pastal.

"I'm not gonna hit you," said Errol. "I'll just bonk him a little, see if he'll let you go."

Beefo responded by jerking Pastal off the ground like a shield.

"Errol, you put that broom down!" demanded Callie.

"No bonking!" moaned Pastal. "Oh, Lord, he's killing me."

Errol backed away, and silence descended over the group. Beefo adopted a pose he'd always used right after a touchdown back in the glory days. He raised his horns and jutted out his chest, forcing Pastal to balance on his tiptoes to take some weight off his tortured arm.

Callie sighed and stepped into the round pen. No one could hear what Callie murmured to Beefo as she approached the beast. Beefo turned his attention toward Callie, and it seemed the bull was inclined to listen.

Toribio also stepped into the round pen. He began to sing in low tones as Callie approached the massive animal. Neither Beefo nor the men assembled understood the words of the song, though animal and man alike recognized it for something old and precious.

Toribio sang a lament heralding the anguish of a land which must someday fall back into the sea, a history of conquest and assimilation, of having to leave one's home and loved ones in search of a better life, and of love so star-crossed as to burst one's heart from desperate joy.

He sang so passionately, many of the men felt their throats grow thick. Commissioner Pastal stopped whimpering as if he knew his salvation had come. Callie continued her slow approach, and Beefo lowered his huge head as she came closer. Callie lowered her head as well until her forehead touched Beefo's. They stood there, their eyes closed, sharing their breath and a sense of peace.

Beefo finally snorted and released Pastal who dropped to the ground and scrambled away. The bull ambled into the chemical dip where he stood at shoulder depth while dead parasites bubbled to the surface.

Commissioner Pastal plopped on the tailgate of his truck and wondered what the hell had happened. He looked back and forth between Callie and the lolling bull in his tick tank.

His arm throbbed. Inexplicably this reminded him of the Olympic torch runner who'd inspired him so many years earlier. Commissioner Pastal imagined the arm of that runner had throbbed as well, and he felt ashamed his own pain had come as the result of less than heroic actions.

"Callie," he called out, trying to control a quaver in his voice. "I...I'm sorry."

Callie looked at him for the longest time before she squared her shoulders to address him.

"See? Now doesn't that feel better?"

Beefo turned his head as if listening to the conversation. No sooner had Commissioner Pastal issued his apology than the bull waded out of the tank and trotted toward the Tick Day banner. Beefo picked up speed, piercing the fabric with his mighty horns. He kicked up his back legs and flopped on his back to scratch his shoulders and rump in a patch of yellow daisies.

Beefo scrambled back to his feet and took off at a gallop across the field of waist-high alfalfa, the wildflowers tangled between his horns, the sun casting a glow over his neck hump, and the Tick Day banner streaming behind like angel wings.

"Kinda looks like he's flyin'," said Errol.

. . .

Sophie ended up at her mother's house at dusk, though she had no memory of walking there. She stared at her old porch and at the odd hubcap tree mobile, appreciating its soothing clangs as breezes caressed the branches.

Sophie perused once more the artifacts of her past life about the yard: the porch swing where she and her mother sang Beatles songs and painted their toes; the cement sculpture of a pig with green marbles for the eyes they'd made together in an art class; a terrarium perched on a tree stump near the barn.

Sophie wanted more than anything to lie down on her old bed and sleep. She considered knocking on her mother's door, but she knew that would involve dialogue and energy. No, she thought, it would be best to leave that discussion for later.

Sophie moved toward the shed, still walking without clear purpose. She noticed the barn door was open. Nothing was changed from that time so many years ago when she'd collected her mother for church. Halters and feed buckets hung on one wall, gardening tools on the opposite side, hay bales stacked in the middle. It was all familiar, and she took it all in as a hail from an old friend.

It seemed no power on Earth could have curbed her urge to lie down. With the softest of sighs, she pulled a horse blanket onto the hay as the final rays of sunset were hidden by her mother's house. Her last act before sleep was to pull the little Barbie doll dress from her pants pocket and clutch it to her chest.

. . .

Callie had stepped in a large urine puddle as she filled Beefo's grain bucket, so her right boot was caked and heavy as she walked toward the barn. It was intriguing to her how little surprise she felt finding her daughter asleep atop a stack of hay bales. Sophie never woke as her mother replaced the musty horse blanket with a clean sheet she fetched from the laundry.

Callie wasn't sleepy, and she had no desire to leave her daughter's side. She went in search of her Sears and Roebucks catalog. She'd last left it on top of Sadler's casket, and she shuddered at the chilling blast upon opening the freezer.

Callie squeezed in past his casket upon realizing the catalog had slipped off the lid onto the floor beyond. She spotted a cardboard box she'd placed there years earlier after taking possession of the property, a box she'd filled with items from Gershom Sadler's house before it was demolished to make room for the park rides.

She'd considered throwing the possessions out at the time, but somehow, she didn't have the heart. The man had been a miserable presence in her life, but he'd provided shelter and food. Throwing out personal items hadn't seemed right, but she deemed storing them in his frigid mausoleum appropriate.

She grabbed her catalog and hoisted the cardboard box onto the casket lid before scooching back out into the warmer air. She carried the box to her pickup bench seat and rummaged through the contents. She found little of interest: his minister's collar, an onyx tie pin, a bland letter from his mother wherein she used most of the page to describe a new bread recipe.

Callie remembered from those years before that she'd retained his bible and a pocket watch, both of which were placed with him inside the casket on the insistence of Commissioner Pastal. She'd also kept a Farmer's almanac from 1966, and a school yearbook.

She'd been too angry and hurt to look at the yearbook back then, but now she felt curious.

She found him on page 84 of the Trinity University 1923 annual filled with portraits of students by grade level and group pictures of athletic teams and clubs. Gershom Sadler was posed in front of the college's administration building with a group of six others. They all wore a white jersey with a large dark T, each man wielding a tennis racquet and glaring into the camera lens like steely-eyed warriors. It was the Trinity University Tigers Tennis Team, Waxahachie, Texas campus.

Callie's eyes shot to the Dunlop tennis racquet nailed to the joist above her head, and back down to the black-and-white photo. Gershom Sadler's hair had been slicked back even then, but Callie thought she saw a hint of sideburn. He appeared grim but not angry, passionate for life instead of passionately indignant. The racquet mystery was solved, but she could not stop looking into the eyes of this boy who'd grown into a man she so needed to stop loathing.

Callie placed the yearbook back in the box and looked over at Sophie who was snoring. She spent the next hours perusing the weathered Sears and Roebucks catalog and staring at her daughter in sage and hopeful ways.

• • •

Callie left the barn at dawn to shower and have breakfast. She'd created a list of things she wanted to accomplish that day, which meant she'd need to get started right away. She pulled a piece of straw from her sleeping daughter's hair before heading to the house.

Sophie awoke a few minutes later, somehow knowing the day would be significant. She brushed hay from her clothing and wiped a drool line from her cheek before venturing outside. She considered knocking on her mother's door, but she couldn't find the courage to step up on the porch.

I haven't even brushed my teeth.

She ventured off in the direction of the front gate. Her plan was to call Commissioner Pastal for a ride so she could get back to her hotel and get cleaned up.

Maybe I could call Cleft instead...

She slapped herself in the face for even thinking such a thing. "You will NOT call Cleft Hawley!"

It was a lovely morning, however, cool and bright, and the grazing fields beyond seemed to suggest a stroll.

Yes. A walk to clear my head first.

You will not call Cleft.

• • •

Toribio spent the day after Callie's return from the hospital driving about the county and considering the future. The fact that he loved Callie was not in question. What bothered him was that for the first time he held hope she might return his feelings. It was terrifying to imagine he was wrong.

He bought a sack of groceries from a pleasant couple running a roadside stand. He drove to a pasture where he hiked near the wood line to one of his favorite thinking spots beyond the amusement park sounds. He sat on a felled tree and started a little fire beneath the blade of an old plow he'd placed there years earlier.

Toribio grilled flank steak with peppers and onions on the flat portion of the heated plow. The aroma brought him out of his reverie. He sighed as he offered thanks for his meal, and he set to work writing a poem. The cooking, the tranquility of the setting, his acceptance that there were some things he could not fix or understand, and his renewed concentration on the love of his life allowed the tensions of the last few days to fall away.

Thus, he felt more curiosity than annoyance when he saw Sophie ambling toward him from across the pasture. Toribio patted a cornmeal dough into a thick tortilla before tossing it onto the sizzling plow.

"Hello," said Sophie. "Are you speaking to me?"

"Hello."

"May I sit?"

He motioned her to sit on the log. Neither spoke for a few minutes as the tortilla toasted, both entranced by the fire. Toribio cut some of the steak into strips, which he piled onto the tortilla and heaped on caramelized onions and peppers. He handed it to her with a napkin and fork in a most gracious manner.

"Thank you." Sophie realized she hadn't eaten since the day before. Her first bite was glorious, and she savored it as if she'd been eating the chef's special at the five-star Fonda San Miguel in Austin. "It's even better than I remember."

Toribio took a moment to stoke the fire.

"It's a hard thing, almost dying," he murmured.

Sophie jerked in surprise that he knew about the incident in the river, but of course he did. *Nothing happens around here that he doesn't know.*

She shuddered like a dog after a bath, as if trying to throw off the terror she'd felt.

"Kind of resets the bar on priorities, doesn't it?"

Toribio rapped his metal spatula on the hot plow, creating a pleasant gong sound as if to put a period on such terrible thoughts. Sophie reached forward with her fork and did the same.

"I hear Momma is out of the hospital," said Sophie.

Toribio flattened another ball of dough.

"How is she? I mean, does she look…"

Toribio's lips pursed in a look of frustration Sophie had never seen on him before.

"She's not loco, Sophie."

Sophie nodded acknowledgement.

"That's an amazing skill you have. Being able to chastise someone with just four words."

The darkness fell from Toribio's face, and he smiled.

Sophie reached over and pat him on the arm.

"I deserved it."

Toribio looked at her in a way no man ever had. She couldn't put her finger on it at first. His look conveyed wisdom and loyalty, as well as an unconditional love and a confidence she would do good things with her life.

He looks so...paternal!

Sophie pulled the remaining eviction notices from her purse, and she was unable to stifle a sob when she realized Toribio's notice was on top.

"What have I done?" It came out as a whisper, but the intensity of her anguish projected something more like a shriek.

Toribio glanced over her shoulder and grunted when he understood what she was holding.

Sophie bent as if she'd been socked in the gut.

"What I've done is...is unforgiva—"

Toribio held up his spatula to stop her.

"Do you remember the time I drove you to the movies after you and your mother had a fight?"

The eviction notices trembled in Sophie's hands.

"She'd torn up my stuff. I'd never seen her be cruel before."

Toribio scraped the plow and gave a nonchalant shrug.

"Sometimes we do life wrong for a bit." He paused to lay a hand on her shoulder and nudge her to sit up straight again.

Sophie cleared her throat and said, "You used to tell me I'd live in a castle someday. I sure did latch on to that dream. Maybe I don't know any other way."

He chuckled. "I was speaking to a child, and I wanted you to be happy."

"You're saying I can't be happy in a castle?"

"That's not what castles are made for. I'm saying you can't be happy doing your life wrong."

Sophie gaped at Toribio as if he'd spoken in Spanish and she was struggling to translate the words. She nodded, a resolute nod of the variety reserved for life-altering epiphanies, and she tossed the notices beneath the hot plow. The two of them held hands and watched as the pages caught flame and burned to ash.

She whispered again, but the tone of despair was gone.

"I'm really sorry I didn't miss you enough."

"*Princesa*," he chuckled, leaning to kiss the top of her head.

CHAPTER TWENTY-FIVE

Commissioner Pastal was heartbroken, but he forced his face to keep smiling while Mr. Smith and Ms. Jones from the Office of Internal Logistics broke the bad news. The three of them were standing around a hole in the ground just inside the fence line on a grazing field Pastal leased from Callie. The hole was a smidge wider than a beef carcass, and it had been covered for who knew how long by agave cactus and a red ant mound taller than Pastal's knees.

Beefo was nowhere to be seen, but Mr. Smith was wearing a hardhat and a baseball catcher's chest protector as he paced and wrung his hands behind his back. Ms. Jones' hands were on her hips, and one index finger kept tapping her pelvic bone in evident impatience.

"Obviously we can't move forward with the project in Elixir Springs County."

Commissioner Pastal raised his own finger as if about to make a point. "But what if we—"

"Let me be clear..." She glared at Mr. Smith, who was pacing while staring out across the field with both palms shading his eyes. "Focus," she hissed before turning her attention back to Pastal. "We simply can't recommend this site given the unruliness of the citizenry."

"But…"

"Not to mention a homicidal bull left unchecked and roaming the property."

Mr. Smith chimed in. "Who poses a threat to all stakeholders."

Pastal wiped his brow on his sleeve. "Beefo will never again—"

"Commissioner," said Ms. Jones in a tone conveying definitive punctuation at the end of a discussion. "At this time, we consider negotiations to have stalled in a manner unlikely to be mitigated."

The dirt around the hole shifted, and a bearded face emerged as if Earth was birthing a fully formed man.

"It's pristine!"

Ms. Smith stared down at the man.

"Of course, now there is this new wrinkle."

"What's pristine?" asked Pastal.

"The cavern!" said the man whom Pastal would later refer to as "Professor Something-or-Other."

"Fully formed stalactites and helictites, soda straws and columns with icy surfaces as far back as we could crawl."

Commissioner Pastal had never met the professor before this day, but he found the man's chirpy cheer irritating. Professor had forgotten to turn off his headlamp, and he kept pointing and beaming at the entrance as if showing off his first grandbaby.

The professor turned to Mr. Jones and Ms. Smith.

"I cannot thank you enough for forwarding your geological survey. You were correct. There is an intact cavern just below our feet!" He took a step forward to hug Ms. Smith. She put her hands out and took a step back.

The professor looked down at his mud-covered beard and coveralls.

"Of course, of course. I'm filthy."

"We'll leave you to it, then," said Ms. Jones who turned and tromped off. Mr. Smith followed at a bird-like gait as they left the field, ever watchful for charging beasts.

The professor called out, "Thanks again," to the backs of the retreating government workers. He looked back down at the hole and smiled as two people who'd been introduced as graduate students followed him out. Both wore overjoyed faces. One, a middle-aged woman with mud smeared in her teeth, nostrils and tie-dye skirt, blurted, "Professor, did you see? They're perfectly mummified!"

The professor did a little jump for joy. "I saw! I was just telling the commissioner. It's perfect!"

The academics spent the next few minutes giving an oral report to Commissioner Pastal, confident he would be as happy about their find as they were.

He was not.

"When you say 'mummified,' what exactly do you mean?" he asked.

"It's extraordinary," said the professor. "A team of Spaniards likely mining for silver, at least four-hundred years old!"

"Maybe five hundred!" said the tie-dye wearing woman. Pastal was distracted to see wildflowers woven around her spelunker's headlamp.

"They are so preserved by the chamber's frost and a thick layer of acidic mud that we could make out fingerprints on some," said the professor. "Everything is there: their clothing, tools, weapons."

"They all died at once?" asked Pastal.

"Evidently so," said the professor, the first somber tone hitting his voice. "It appears they'd been drinking."

"Clay flasks all over the place down there, all wine-stained," said the woman.

The other student, a twenties male sporting a pitiful beard-fuzz, piped up. "Dudes were partying in a cave!"

"Indeed," said the professor. "They may have succumbed to alcohol and fatigue and expired from hypothermia. Absolutely pristine."

"So, how long until you can get them out of there and to a museum or something?"

The three academicians fell silent for the first time since they'd burst into Pastal's office to drag him and the government duo out to the cavern. It was the first moment the professor or his students had realized this man might not be as excited as they felt, and the professor attempted a diplomatic response, broached in a manner reserved for politicians and benefactors.

"Your honor, this project is extraordinary in the annals of anthropology. I have never heard of such a find, nor do I imagine there has ever been one of this magnitude. To appropriately catalogue, photograph, preserve and, yes, share this find with the world will take years."

Pastal swallowed hard.

"Years?"

The tie-dye woman bounded over the entrance to the mine and followed with a gleeful little jig.

"We're gonna be here for ages!"

The professor added, "But don't worry, Commissioner. This is a boon for your county. Elixir Springs just landed on a very lucrative international map!"

Pastal stood a little straighter.

"We're on a map!?"

"We'll need access to this area of the property," said the professor. "That's why we contacted you. To see if you have any influence with the owner."

· · ·

Sophie was surprised to see her mother mopping the floor, and impressed with how much cleaner her mother's home was than it had been during her last visit. It was tidy and smelled good. Books were on shelves, and there was not an ashtray or cigarette butt to be seen. The bed had been moved from the living room to the actual bedroom, and the matador Elvis had been transferred to a place of honor above the bookshelf.

Neither spoke during an embrace befitting their years of separation. Callie smelled Sophie's hair and Sophie wrapped her arms tighter around her mother's neck.

"I made us a sandwich," said Callie, motioning Sophie onto the back porch where lemonade and sandwiches were waiting.

"Pimiento cheese?" said Sophie in delight.

"Cut in triangles—"

"—not rectangles!" they said together.

"What was happening before you went to sleep?" asked Callie once they sat.

"Nothing really. I wandered around the park, and I came here and fell asleep. I had a dream."

"Tell me about it."

"Tell you?"

"The dream—tell me."

"There was a kind woman who gave me a ride on the carousel. I grabbed a brass ring."

"The woman…was it Luz?"

"How did you…?"

"Luz is my friend. She's helped me in the times I've needed her the most."

"She helps you?"

"Most of my life now."

"But my dreams…how?"

"Oh, I have no idea how."

"There has to be an explanation."

"I've come to realize not knowing the answer to some mysteries is the best answer we could ever get."

"What does that even mean? I've made a living telling people how to answer life's mysteries, and now I have no idea how to do it myself."

"Sugar, life is just a long practice run. Hopefully we get better at it, but there's no way we ever get it perfect."

Sophie stared at the sandwich in her hands and responded in a voice that sounded like she was eight years old again.

"I knew perfectly well what to do when I came back here."

"And now?"

Sophie shrugged.

"I know I hurt you when I left. I just never realized how much until I came home."

Callie sighed. "It's occurred to me within the last few days you did what I asked of you."

Sophie's brows furrowed in clear confusion.

"Take care of you. That was my last rule, and that's what you did."

Callie raised her sandwich as if she were going to take a bite, but she paused.

"I wanted what was best for you, and I know I tried too hard sometimes. Your reasons for sending me away to the mental hospital were wrong, and we both know it, but..."

"I'm sorry about that, but in my defense, you did attack a frozen mummy, and you were talking to yourself."

"Lord, Sophie, Gershom Sadler needed a good swatting, and I wasn't talking to myself."

Sophie's face transformed into a grin.

"You went kind of nutso in that courtroom."

Callie rubbed the skin on the back of one hand as she answered.

"For a while there I felt like your Barbie doll bouncing on a slice of banana bread, but going to the hospital gave me time to reflect on where you and I went wrong."

Sophie took a sip of lemonade and wiped her lipstick smudge off the glass with a thumb.

"So, maybe that tantrum was a way for you to follow your own rule."

"I don't understand."

"Momma, maybe that was your way of taking care of you, getting away from everything hurting you so you could be strong when you came home."

Callie softened.

"Maybe you're right. All I know for now is that I don't care about the business or the property or what happens to it. It was all for you anyway, but somehow it ended up being a wedge that separated us."

They embraced again and chuckled at how snotty their noses had become and how Sophie's makeup had run, and about how happy they were to be talking again.

"So, what do we do now?" asked Sophie.

"How about we start by getting a snow cone?"

CHAPTER TWENTY-SIX

Cleft was packing a duffel bag when Sophie visited him at his trailer the next day. She'd expected guns to be lying around, clothes on the floor, a mound of dirty dishes. Instead, she was flabbergasted to see books on subjects including philosophy, biography, and a variety of sciences stacked in some places floor-to-ceiling. The screen of Cleft's television was covered with a horizontal stack on criminal court cases, and a shelf running the width of his living room held titles on literature, art, and music.

"What is all this?" Sophie said as she gazed about.

Cleft scratched under his hat brim and grimaced.

"I know, I oughtta trade some at a used bookstore, but I just never have the heart once I finish one."

"But, I mean…when?"

He chuckled. "Hobby I picked up on the road when I was doing long-hauls. Something to do in the sleeping cab after a long day." He glanced at the collection. "Guess it sort of took hold after a while."

She looked down at the duffel bag.

"You're leaving?"

"For a while," he replied as he tried to cram one more t-shirt into the bag.

"Where?"

"The police academy in Austin. Figured I'd best get trained back up right if I'm gonna be doing this lawman stuff."

"What about your job?"

"Errol is going to fill in for a few weeks. I've given him an order he's not to serve any eviction notices if that's what you're thinking."

Sophie responded with a tired smile.

"No, in fact, I've had a vision of sort. No evictions, no big project."

"What then?" he asked.

She shrugged. He stared at her, his eyes widening as he realized she really had no idea what would come next. She reached to brush a lock of his hair.

"Thank you again for coming to my rescue."

Cleft pulled a ball cap from a nail on the wall and stuffed it into his bag.

"Thought about saving you so many times over the years."

"Saving me?"

"Goofy daydreams about being a hero. Stupid stuff."

She moved another step within the trailer foyer.

"Not so stupid. Gallant is one of your best things."

She moved to kiss him, but at the last moment he pulled back.

"I've always hoped that would happen."

"But?"

"It's just…you don't deserve me."

She nodded, amazed she understood what he was saying.

He shouldered his duffel bag.

"And, truth is, I haven't done everything I should to earn you."

She placed her palm on his cheek.

"Do you think it's possible to end that thought with 'yet?'"

He closed his eyes at the softness of her touch and grinned like a kid who'd just opened a 1972 Chevy Vega door for the most beautiful gal in the world.

"How about we go cavort a bit when we get past 'yet.'"

CHAPTER TWENTY-SEVEN

The next morning Toribio loaded Gershom Sadler back into the hospital wheelchair and pushed him out from the barn. Callie was waiting outside wearing jeans, a western straw hat, and every piece of turquoise jewelry she'd ever bought. Toribio smiled at her and grasped the handles of the wheelchair to move on, but she put a hand on his chest to hold him in check.

"I need to do this one on my own."

Toribio bowed gallantly. She loved him for that; she loved him for many reasons, and she stood on tiptoes to kiss him.

"Fair to say I have a few regrets," she purred, "but waiting so long to do that is my biggest one."

Toribio grinned as she shoved the wheelchair forward and called, "I'll be back soon," over her shoulder.

Callie pushed Reverend Sadler through the park until they arrived at the carousel. Pioneer Days hadn't yet opened, and the two of them were alone. She parked him and climbed up onto the platform where she opened the door in the hub.

"Thought it would be nice for you to be able to see your cross while we talk." Her face appeared relaxed as she pulled his frozen shell up onto the platform and propped him against the haunch of one of the ride ponies. She mounted the next pony over and sat sidesaddle.

"All these years I spent wandering without ever leaving this place."

Wind ruffled the old man's hair, and the carousel creaked.

"I figured it out. I'm not a harlot, Gershom, but you are a false prophet."

Callie paused for a moment, choked up, unwilling to continue until she could control her own voice.

"What a perfect disguise you created. It fooled me for the longest time."

She slid off the pony and smoothed her jeans.

"Time for you to move on."

She paused again, tilting her head as if she were listening. She smiled in a kind way.

"You're afraid because you don't know, do you? A false prophet can't really know."

Sadler stared back at her, and Callie could swear his facial expression had changed from smug to concerned.

"You took me in when I was lost. That'll count for something."

Callie reached into the hub to flip the ON switch, flooding the ride in lights and music before springing off the platform. She watched Reverend Sadler round the bend one last time before pirouetting back toward life, humming with the calliope tune, and waltzing every step of the way.

The End

BOOK CLUB
DISCUSSION QUESTIONS

1. How does Callie's relationship with the reverend shape her views on religion and authority throughout the novel?

2. The reverend's will imposes a strange and controlling requirement on Callie. What do you think this demand represents, both literally and symbolically?

3. What role does Toribio play in Callie's journey toward healing and personal growth?

4. The theme of forgiveness is central to Callie's arc. What do you think it took for Callie to finally forgive her adoptive father?

5. Mental illness plays a role in Callie's later life. How is her mental health portrayed, and do you think the story offers a fair depiction of her struggle?

6. Sophie's quest for fame and power contrasts sharply with Callie's desire for simplicity and peace. Do you think the novel presents one lifestyle as superior, or is there a more nuanced message?

7. The supernatural elements, like Luz's angelic presence, add a layer of magical realism to the story. How do these elements affect the tone of the novel?

8. What is the significance of the title *Carousel Grift*?

9. What are your feelings regarding the relative power and
    control imbalance of Reverend Sadler and young Callie?

10. How do you interpret the novel's ending, particularly in
    terms of Callie's relationship with Sophie, Toribio, and
    herself?

ACKNOWLEDGEMENTS

This novel is over a dozen years in the making, often shelved when the demands of life and other projects held sway, but never forgotten. It has always been a labor of love and respect for all those out there who escaped a toxic home for the simple, obstinate objective to ultimately thrive. Over the course of my thirty-year career in public safety, I saw so many who'd been bullied and crushed by people in positions of relative power, only to later flourish and pass along the courage and wisdom they'd earned to others. This is their story. I don't merely acknowledge them here; I salute them.

No one was more surprised than I when told by an English teacher friend that I'd written something called "women's fiction." I had to look it up. Shortly thereafter I contacted Barbara Claypole White, a gifted writer and early leader of the Women's Fiction Writers Association who assured me that I had, in fact, penned something that fell within their genre. I'd say "flabbergasted" is the best word choice for how I felt, but I joined their group and received immediate welcome. That membership, now going on nine years, has gifted me with lifelong encouragement, friendship, and talent.

Ah, and let's not forget the beta readers, those angels who agreed to read various chapters and let me know where I'd gone off the road, crashed through barbed wire fencing, and slammed into a drainage ditch. Laura Gray, Laura Kaste Broullire, Karen Tkacik Cimms, Gretchen Anthony, Peggy Trieber, Jen Brockman, Bob Ford, Susan Colvin, Jayne Johnson, Molly Giles, Jules Taylor, Dianne Villegas, Kat Paulson, Ann Everett, Louise Shaper, Shawna Thorup, JoBeth Penberthy, Lourdes Maier, and Sharon Shaw-Eastin, I learned something from each of you, and I am forever grateful.

Many thanks as well to the professional editors who yanked out their polishing cloths to make this thing shine. Judith Newman, Paula Stokes, Kim Lindman, and Mary Ellen Bramwell, your expertise, clarity, and acumen are a credit to your profession. I'm also thankful for the leadership and staff at Black Rose. Their ability to share my vision, as well as their marketing and business savvy, have helped bring this story to the life it deserves.

And finally, eternal love and gratitude to my family. Your loyalty and patience are the foundation for all I am and will ever become. You're all quirky and brave and beautiful, and every one of you is here to make the world a better place. I am so proud to be a part of your life.

David Lane Williams and his best friend used two gallons of go-kart paint on themselves one Texas afternoon in 1970. He recalls the liberal use of acetone, a bristle brush, and expletives by their parents. D.L. recovered in time for a decorated thirty-year career in public safety with assignments including paramedicine, helicopter rescue, patrol, mental health liaison, and detective. He now teaches criminology at the University of Arkansas. He and his family have settled in the Ozarks where they offer a haven for rescued donkeys and horses. In his spare time, he enjoys baiting fish hooks for his grandkids, relocating possums from the chicken coop to the woods, and trying (so far unsuccessfully) to make friends with a family of river otters living nearby.

NOTE FROM DAVID LANE WILLIAMS

Word-of-mouth is crucial for any author to succeed. If you enjoyed *Carousel Grift*, please leave a review online—anywhere you are able. Even if it's just a sentence or two. It would make all the difference and would be very much appreciated.

Thanks!
David Lane Williams

We hope you enjoyed reading this title from:

www.blackrosewriting.com

Subscribe to our mailing list – *The Rosevine* – and receive **FREE** books, daily deals, and stay current with news about upcoming releases and our hottest authors.
Scan the QR code below to sign up.

Already a subscriber? Please accept a sincere thank you for being a fan of Black Rose Writing authors.

View other Black Rose Writing titles at
www.blackrosewriting.com/books and use promo code
PRINT to receive a **20% discount** when purchasing.